From the Dead

The Hippocampus Press Classics of Gothic Horror Series

Edited by S. T. Joshi

Johnson Looked Back: The Collected Weird Stories of Thomas Burke
The Harbor-Master: Best Weird Stories of Robert W. Chambers
Lost Ghosts: The Complete Weird Stories of Mary E. Wilkins Freeman
Back There in the Grass: The Horror Tales of
Irvin S. Cobb and Gouverneur Morris
The Mummy's Foot and Other Fantastic Tales, Théophile Gautier
Twin Spirits: The Complete Weird Stories of W. W. Jacobs
From the Dead: The Complete Weird Stories of E. Nesbit
Frankenstein and Others: The Complete Weird Fiction of Mary Shelley

FROM THE DEAD

THE COMPLETE WEIRD STORIES OF E. NESBIT

Edited by S. T. Joshi

Hippocampus Press

New York

Published by Hippocampus Press
P.O. Box 641, New York, NY 10156.
http://www.hippocampuspress.com

Cover art © 2018 by Aeron Alfrey
Cover design and "Classics of Gothic Horror" logo by Dan Sauer,
dansauerdesign.com
Hippocampus Press logo designed by Anastasia Damianakos.

First Edition
1 3 5 7 9 8 6 4 2

ISBN: 978-1-61498-214-2

CONTENTS

INTRODUCTION

To say that the life of E. Nesbit was eventful would be putting it mildly. Her life span covered some of the most traumatic years of English (and Western) history, from the end of the Victorian era through World War I and into the Roaring Twenties; and her tumultuous personal relationships—with her siblings, her husband, several lovers, numerous friends and colleagues, and her five children (three natural-born, two adopted)—created such turmoil at various stages of her life that one wonders how she managed to get as much writing done as she did. But she did produce an immense quantity of work—poems, stories, articles, sketches, and most of all an array of children's books that established her as one of the pioneering writers in that field. That she managed, along the way, to write a brace of splendid weird tales was in some ways a lucky accident.

Edith Nesbit was born on August 15, 1858, in Kennington, a district of South London. She was the fourth child of Sarah and John Collis Nesbit. John ran a small agricultural college, but he died unexpectedly in 1862. Sarah managed to take over the administration of the college and ran it successfully for several years. But Edith's older sister, Mary (called Minnie), contracted tuberculosis in 1866; as a means of alleviating her condition, her mother took the family to the coastal town of Brighton, where Edith (usually called Daisy as a child) attended a private school run by a Mrs Arthur; she later attended a boarding school in Stamford, in Lincolnshire. Both these brief educational stints were unhappy experiences for Edith, as she endured harsh discipline and suffered from homesickness. In 1867 her mother took the family to France for an extended trip, and Mary spent months learning French. The family later went on to Spain. After a brief return to England, the Nesbits settled in the town of Dinan, in Brittany, where Edith was enrolled for a short time in a school run by an Ursuline convent; still later, she was sent to study at a school run by Moravian sisters in Düsseldorf. (One thinks of Algernon Blackwood, who was enrolled for a year [1885-86] in a school run by the Moravian Brotherhood in Königsfeld.) But at the outbreak of the Franco-Prussian War in 1870, the Nesbits were obliged to return to England.

Edith's first literary work was a poem that she wrote at the age of eleven. She wrote poetry extensively in the years 1872-75, when the family was living in Halstead, Kent. These were among the happiest years of Edith's early life. The earliest known publication of her work was a poem that appeared in *Good Words* (the periodical formerly run by Charles Dickens) in December 1876.

Financial difficulties forced the family to move from Halstead to Islington. It was in 1877 that Edith met her future husband, Hubert Bland. At this time she was engaged to a bank clerk named Stuart Smith; but by 1878 she had freed herself from Smith and become engaged to Hubert. Bland was himself engaged to another woman, Maggie Doran, and in fact later had a child by her. He continued to see—and be intimate with—Maggie for years or decades after his marriage to Edith. Edith's mother did not approve of the association with Hubert, chiefly because his own job prospects seemed doubtful. He himself was for a time a bank clerk, but then put his modest resources into various businesses, none of which were notably successful. The sexual irregularities that dogged both Edith's and Hubert's adult life were on display at the time of their marriage on April 22, 1880: exactly two months later, on June 22, she gave birth to her first son, Paul.

For the entirety of their married life, the Blands lived in various rented quarters in various London suburbs; even at the height of Edith's literary success, in the first decade of the twentieth century, they never purchased a house. In the years following her marriage, Edith began writing stories prolifically for magazines; she also made extra income by making hand-painted greeting cards. A daughter, Mary Iris, was born on December 2, 1881. Hubert at first collaborated with Mary on her stories and other work, but later established himself as a distinguished journalist and reviewer. Both of them were founding members of the Fabian Society, the moderate socialist organisation that established itself in 1883-84 and advocated gradual conversion from capitalism to socialism. Edith, however, did not become entirely "advanced" in her thinking; she retained vestiges of her Anglican religious upbringing and also maintained a vestigial belief in traditional social and economic roles for women, even though she herself did not conform to those roles, frequently earning far more income than her husband. In her views on women, which included a vehement objection to woman suffrage, she was probably influenced in part by her strong-willed and dogmatic husband, who frequently spoke out on the subject.

A third child, Fabian, was born on January 8, 1885. Later that year, her first book—a novel written with Hubert, *The Prophet's Mantle*—appeared. This was a complex work in the Victorian manner, featuring a multitude of characters and incidents in the manner of Dickens. But it was through her socialist connections that Edith and Hubert became acquainted with some of the most notable literary figures of the day. She first met George Bernard Shaw in 1884 at a meeting of the Fabian Society. The most peculiar relation Edith ever established was with Alice Hoatson, an editor at *Sylvia's Home Journal,* where some of her early work appeared. Edith professed great fondness for Alice; but Alice quickly became Hubert's mistress and eventually bore him two children. The first of these, Rosamund, was born in 1886; at this time, Alice moved in with the Blands, and they raised Rosamund as if she were a child of theirs. In part this was done to shield Alice from the social ostracism she would have encountered as an unwed mother; but the arrangement also had the advantage of allowing Alice to be a kind of "wife" to both Edith and Hubert, tending to the children while both the others focused on their writing.

But the complex and emotionally wrenching situation must have been a strain for Edith, and matters were not helped when she gave birth to a stillborn child in early 1886. Edith had by this time developed an infatuation with Shaw, and at least initially he responded in kind. Whether they actually became intimate is a matter of doubt, but there is no denying that Edith suggested that she and Shaw run away together. Shaw, who himself was married at the time, began pulling away from Edith and later denied that he had ever had any kind of affair with her. Meanwhile, Edith was fully aware of Hubert's sexual relations with Alice; whether she knew that he was also continuing his relations with Maggie Doran is not clear, but there were any number of outbursts in the family, in part spurred by Edith's penchant for self-dramatization.

Edith herself developed relations (which may or may not have included a sexual element) with any number of younger men, the first of whom was a man named Noel Griffith, whom she met in 1887; later, she had a brief affair with the poet Richard Le Gallienne. Friendships of a more orthodox sort also developed with such writers as Oliver Schreiner (*The Story of an African Farm,* 1883), Laurence Housman (a widely published novelist and the brother of A. E. Housman), and others. The British literary scene of the time was a relatively small one, and leading writers quickly became acquainted with one another and maintained contact through numerous gatherings, soirées, and other events. Edith herself enjoyed being the hostess of many parties thrown for literary and other friends throughout her adult life.

Nesbit had published several books of poetry in the later 1880s, and for decades she considered herself chiefly a poet; she was disappointed that her poetry was not more highly regarded, but its chief deficiency is its fundamental unoriginality, as it is largely derived from her enthusiastic reading of the Brownings and other poets of the day. By the early 1890s, Nesbit gradually turned to prose; spurred on by an editor, Robert Ellice Mack, she took to writing children's stories. Much work during this period was cowritten with Oswald Barron, another younger man with whom Nesbit carried on a languid affair for years.

Two books that are of direct interest to us appeared in 1893: *Grim Tales* and *Something Wrong.* The former consists entirely of weird tales, originally published in such leading magazines as *Temple Bar, Argosy, Longman's,* and the like. The latter, although one reviewer referred to it as containing stories written "in the manner of Edgar Allan Poe,"[1] in fact contains only one weird specimen, "Hurst of Hurstcote." These books attracted little interest, but that could not be said for *The Story of the Treasure Seekers* (1899), the first of her books about the rambunctious Bastable family. It was an immediate success and remained so throughout Nesbit's lifetime, having been reprinted fifteen times through 1928. The significance of the book lies in the realism of its treatment of childhood pleasures and traumas; in these and other books about the Bastable family, Nesbit largely eschewed the benign fantasy that often made children's books seem insubstantial or remote from reality.

Nesbit did write a number of stories and novels for adults, including such a bold work as *The Secret of Kyriels* (1899), a novel frankly dealing with female sexuality. Her affair with Bernard Shaw was transmuted into the

---

1. Unsigned review, *Spectator* (18 November 1893): 37.

novel *Daphne in Fitzroy Street* (1909). But it was her children's books that won her fame and fortune, including *The Wouldbegoods* (1901), *Five Children and It* (1902), *The New Treasure Seekers* (1904), *The Phoenix and the Carpet* (1904), *The Railway Children* (1906), *The Enchanted Castle* (1907), and others. Some of these books address the grim social realities of the day, such as poverty, imprisonment, racial prejudice, and the like. Several of them also have a significant fantasy element: *The Five Children and It,* basically a work about her own children, also involves a curious creature called the psammead; *The Enchanted Castle* introduces us to horrible creatures called the Ugly-Wuglies and perhaps constitutes the closest Nesbit came to writing a horror tale for children. Many of these books first appeared as serials in the *Strand Magazine,* which paid the unprecedented amount of £30 per episode; for many years the *Strand* published a Nesbit story in every issue.

Nesbit's personal life continued to be traumatic even in the course of the celebrity she acquired in the first decade of the twentieth century. A second child, John, was born to Alice on October 6, 1899. Then, in 1900, her fifteen-year-old son Fabian died as a result of a botched operation to remove adenoids. In that year Hubert joined the Catholic Church, and a few years later Edith joined him. It is not clear what changes this conversion created in either their personal life or their literary work.

Then there was their involvement with H. G. Wells. The couple had first met Wells in 1902, as he was himself an ardent socialist. But around 1908 Wells developed an infatuation with Edith's adopted daughter Rosamund, who was twenty-two at the time; although Wells was married and twenty years her senior, the two tried to run away together, but were stopped at a train station in London. An enormous row ensued, and of course the Blands' association with Wells was permanently terminated. Wells gained his revenge by maliciously depicting a couple clearly based on the Blands in his novel *The New Machiavelli* (1911). Shaw had a field day writing satirical letters on the whole imbroglio.

Nesbit continued to develop acquaintances with notable writers, including E. M. Forster and the young Lord Dunsany. She not only admired Dunsany's stories of ethereal fantasy (she published some of them in a short-lived periodical, the *Neolith* [1907–08], an exquisite example of handset type and fine printing) but was captivated by a week-long stay with Lord and Lady Dunsany at Dunsany Castle in Ireland. But Edith's "great decade" of writing ended ominously when, in 1910, Hubert suffered a detached retina and became virtually blind; he began relying even more heavily on Alice to continue his literary work, and he seemed to be growing apart from his nominal wife. Edith's association with the *Strand* ended in 1913, and her last children's book was *Wet Magic* (1913); this led to money shortages for the family. The Blands had, since 1899, been staying in a large house called Well Hall, Eltham, in the borough of Greenwich; but although the spacious house and generous acreage were an ideal place for the Blands to write, it became increasingly expensive to maintain.

Hubert Bland died on April 14, 1914. Alice continued living with Edith, although relations were apparently quite strained. When the war broke out in August, Nesbit quickly edited a volume of *Battle Songs* (1914) as a patriotic gesture; her occasionally ferocious anti-German fulminations in letters alienated some of her literary associates. In 1915 she received a Civil List pension from the British government for her services to literature; but it amounted to only £60 a year (Arthur Machen, in 1931, received a Civil List pension of £100 a year) and was not enough to offset her financial difficulties. She was forced to take in paying guests (which she alternately referred to in letters as "P.G.'s" or, more unkindly, "pigs") and also sold produce from her garden; for a time she tried to raise chickens, but they all perished from disease.

It was, then, something of a blessing that, in 1916, she met Thomas Terry Tucker (nicknamed "the Skipper"), a marine engineer about two years the elder; he began to help Edith around the house and estate. He was immediately taken with her and proposed marriage; at first she declined, but then she acceded, marrying him on February 20, 1917. Although he was of equable temper and habitually deferential to his wife (as the domineering Hubert had never been), Tucker evoked opposition from Edith's children, chiefly because he was not a "gentleman": the social gulf between this rough-hewn working-class man and his elegant, refined, literarily accomplished wife bothered them, although Edith herself seemed unconcerned about the matter and was genuinely in love with him. Soon after the marriage Alice Hoatson was pointedly asked to leave the household: with the children grown up and the strange bond—Hubert—that had united them gone, her role in the family was at an end.

Through Thomas's influence, Edith decided at last to give up Well Hall; they purchased a small cottage near the town of St. Mary in the

Marsh, a village in Kent, where one of her neighbors was the young Noël Coward. By this time Edith herself was in poor health, thanks to a chronic smoking habit (at one period she smoked forty cigarettes a day). For the last two years of her life she suffered painfully from what was probably lung cancer, and she died on May 4, 1924. Her funeral was attended by, among others, Lord and Lady Dunsany.

E. Nesbit's work as a children's writer justifies the bold comment by her most recent biographer, Julia Briggs, that she "is the first modern writer for children."[2] Her weird tales were essentially a sideline, but she revealed a remarkable range in the eighteen tales that can be considered weird; indeed, these tales come close to exhibiting the full scope of themes, motifs, and approaches of the weird literature of the period.

Many of the most gripping elements in Nesbit's weird stories derive from her own terrors and phobias, many of them dating to her earliest years. She attested to both a fear of the dark and a fear of the dead, and these two conceptions figure largely in her weird work. She spoke of them at length in a serial, *My School-Days,* published in the *Girl's Own Paper* in 1896-97. Here is an account of the fears she experienced during her initial trip to France in 1867:

> I lay awake in the dark, the light from the oil lamp in the street came through the persiennes and fell in bright bars on the wall. As I grew drowsier I seemed to read there in letters of fire *"Débit de Tabac".*
>
> Then I fell asleep, and dreamed that my father's ghost came to me, and implored me to have the horrible French inscription erased from his tomb—"for I was an Englishman," he said.
>
> Then I woke, rigid with terror, and finally summoned courage to creep across the corridor to my mother's room and seek refuge in her arms. I am particular to mention this dream because it is the first remembrance I have of any terror of the dead, or of the supernatural. I do not at all know how it had its rise . . .[3]

---

2. Julia Briggs, *A Woman of Passion: The Life of E. Nesbit, 1858-1924* (London: Hutchinson, 1987), xi.

3. *My School-Days,* Part III; cited in Briggs, 12-13.

Another nightmare—this time about mummies that she saw in the catacombs of Bordeaux—also affected her:

> The mummies of Bordeaux were the crowning horror of my childish
> life; it is to them, I think, more than to any other thing, that I owe
> nights and nights of anguish and horror, long years of bitterest fear and
> dread. All the other fears could have been effaced, but the shock of
> that night branded in on my brain and I never forgot it. For many years
> I could not bring myself to go about any house in the dark, and long af-
> ter I was a grown woman I was tortured, in the dark watches, by imagi-
> nation and memory, who rose strong and united, overpowering my will
> and my reason as utterly as in my baby days.[4]

A passage like this makes one wonder why Nesbit wrote no tales explicitly
involving mummies. This passage appears in an entire chapter of *My
School-Days* devoted to the mummies of Bordeaux; this and an earlier
chapter, on her fear of the dark, are so striking that they are worth including as an appendix to this book.

As noted, Nesbit assembled an entire volume of weird tales early in her
career, *Grim Tales* (1893); she reprinted all but one of them ("The Mass
for the Dead"), along with "Hurst of Hurstcote" (from *Something Wrong,*
1893) and other, uncollected tales in the seminal volume *Fear* (1910). A
number of weird tales appeared subsequent to this book, but they were not
gathered in any volumes during her lifetime.

Several of Nesbit's earliest weird stories effect a union between weird-
ness and romance in an effective manner. These tales use the supernatural
as a metaphor for underscoring moral or social conceptions facing us in
our everyday lives. "John Charrington's Wedding" (1891), for example,
tells of a man who speaks of the virtues of persistence in affairs of the
heart—so it is not at all unexpected that he keeps the appointment for his
wedding, even after his death. "The Ebony Frame" (1891) poignantly tells
of a man's love for the ghost of a woman whom his ancestor knew in the
past—but this scenario is a transparent metaphor for his dissatisfaction with
the woman he is courting in real life. Somewhat similar, although less emotionally intense, is "Uncle Abraham's Romance" (1893), a brief tale of a

---

4. *My School-Days,* Part V; cited in Briggs, 13–14.

man who loves a female ghost. "The Mass for the Dead" (1892), although generally excluded from collections of Nesbit's weird work, does seem to have a subtle but clearly traceable supernatural element, especially when the two lovers at the center of the tale both hear an organ playing the mass for the dead when it later becomes evident that no organ was playing at the time. Here again a difficult emotional situation—the tortured love triangle where two men are vying for a woman's affections—is given a supernatural dimension. Much the same could be said for "From the Dark," a tragic tale of love and death with an ambiguously supernatural ending.

"The Mystery of the Semi-Detached" (1893) once again focuses on domestic issues, but is the somewhat predictable tale of a man who has a vision of his fiancée's throat being cut—a vision that turns out to be a glimpse of the future involving another person entirely. Perhaps the grimmest—and certainly the most celebrated—of Nesbit's weird tales is "Man-Size in Marble" (1893), where we are shewn nothing less than a full-fledged rape of a woman by a stone statue. Julia Briggs maintains that the tale was likely influenced by Prosper Mérimée's classic tale of a living statue, "La Vénus d'Ille" ("The Venus of Ille," 1837), and this is probable. We must admire the artistry whereby the confirmation of the supernatural element is withheld until the final line of the story.

Continuing the theme of domestic horror is "Hurst of Hurstcote" (1893), where a man conducts an experiment whereby he hypnotizes his wife so that her soul remains in her body even after her death. One might have thought that this story was influenced by Arthur Machen's "The Great God Pan" or "The Inmost Light," both of which record similar experiments by male scientists on women (the latter actually hints that a woman's soul has been transferred into a gem); but Machen's tales were published a year after Nesbit's.

Nesbit appears to have written—or, at any rate, published—no weird tales between the years 1893 and 1905. During much of this period, of course, she was focused on writing her ever more popular children's books and stories. When she returned to the weird tale, her focus had shifted somewhat. "The Power of Darkness" (1905) naturally emphasizes her own fear of the dark, and does so effectively in spite of the hackneyed premise (two men dare each other to spend a night in a spooky waxworks museum). The delineation of psychological terror is grimly powerful, and the dispelling of the supernatural is managed without a sense of deflation or trickery. The same cannot quite be said for "The Head" (1907), a predictable non-supernatural tale of revenge and sadism. "In the Dark" (1910), however, is another powerful depiction of the psychological effects of terror; the ending seems to explode the supernatural manifestation, but ambiguities remain. "Number 17" (1910) is unusual in Nesbit's work in being a comic weird tale—but again, an ending that seems to dispel the supernatural only ends up leaving the matter in doubt and uncertainty.

The variety of Nesbit's weird work is highlighted by "The New Samson" (1909), which perhaps can best be characterized as an action thriller with an underlying element of psychological (but not supernatural) terror. Here a couple strives with great effort to save thousands of innocent lives from death at the hands of a dead architect who contrived to cause a theatre to collapse after his death. A somewhat contrived final twist underscores the element of petty revenge inherent in the tale.

A kind of proto-science-fictional element enters into two tales about secret and mysterious drugs, "The Three Drugs" (1908) and "The Five Senses" (1910). The former is again an interesting mix of a suspense/thriller scenario and supernaturalism, where a scientist hopes to have found a combination of drugs that will turn a person into a superman. The latter story tells of a scientist who has invented a series of drugs that will acutely enhance all five senses at once—apparently even after death.

Nesbit's latest weird tales would seem to be mere rehashes of earlier works, but there are points of interest in them nonetheless. "The Haunted House" (1915) appears to rework the motif of "The Three Drugs" in its depiction of a scientist who claims to have found a formula (by mingling the blood of the four chief races of humanity) to achieve immortality. A pseudo-supernatural conclusion concludes the tale effectively. "The Pavilion" (1915) reprises the central theme of "The Power of Darkness": here a pavilion is thought to be haunted, and two men battling for the love of a woman dare each other to spend a night there. This time, however, a supernatural conclusion is most emphatically at play.

It can be seen that E. Nesbit's weird work spans a wide range of subgenres—the ghost story, the "explained supernatural" (where the supernatural is suggested but explained away by natural means), the supernatural or non-supernatural thriller, the tale of psychological horror, the tale of ambiguous supernaturalism, and even some quasi-science-fiction narratives. Many of these subgenres would be developed extensively by later writers in the field, but Nesbit's contributions can hold their own with any work by either her predecessors or her successors. She was able to transmute her early fears of death and the dark into powerful weird tales where the emotions of love, revenge, rivalry, and hatred are elaborated with telling psychological insight and elaborated with vivid supernatural effects. Weird writing never constituted a major element in Nesbit's extensive literary work, but the tales she did write in this genre are among the most distinguished of their time.

A Note on This Edition

Most of the stories in this book have been taken from the collection *Fear* (1910); "The Mass for the Dead" and "The Mystery of the Semi-Detached," and "John Charrington's Wedding" are taken from *Grim Tales* (1893), while the uncollected stories are taken from their magazine appearances or book publications as specified in the bibliography. It is of interest to note that the magazine appearances of some of the stories differ, sometimes substantially, from the book appearances; but since the latter presumably constitute Nesbit's preferred texts, they have been used in this edition. There have been several other collections of Nesbit's weird tales— *E. Nesbit's Tales of Terror,* edited by Hugh Lamb (Methuen, 1983), subsequently revised as *In the Dark: Tales of Terror* (Equation, 1988) and *In the Dark* (Ash-Tree Press, 2000)—and they include stories not included here; but in my judgment these tales are not genuinely weird. They include "The Haunted Inheritance" (included in the collection *Man and Maid* [1906]), "The Letter in Brown Ink" (*Windsor Magazine,* August 1899), "The House of Silence" (in *Man and Maid*), and "The Detective" (in *The Christmas Spirit,* 1920). Of these, "The Haunted Inheritance" is a romantic story in which the ghostly phenomenon is quickly dispelled as trickery; "The Letter in Brown Ink" is a clearly non-supernatural tale of adventure and romance; "The House of Silence" is a crime/romance narrative; and "The Detective" is a crime story. One of the stories in *Fear,* "The Followers," is a non-weird love story.

From the Dead

John Charrington's Wedding

No one ever thought that May Foster would marry John Charrington; but he thought differently, and things which John Charrington intended should happen had a way of happening. He asked her to marry him before he went up to Oxford. She laughed and refused him. He asked her again next time he came home. Again she laughed, tossed her blonde head, and again refused. A third time he asked her; she said it was becoming a confirmed habit, and laughed at him more than ever.

John was not the only man who wanted to marry her; she was the belle of our village, and we were all in love with her more or less; it was a sort of fashion, like heliotrope ties or Inverness capes. Therefore we were as much annoyed as surprised when John Charrington walked into our little local club—we held it in a loft over the saddler's, I remember—and invited us all to his wedding.

"Your wedding?"

"You don't mean it?"

"Who's the happy fair? When's it to be?"

John Charrington filled his pipe and lighted it before he replied. Then he said:

"I'm sorry to deprive you fellows of your only joke, but Miss Foster and I are to be married in September."

"You don't mean it?"

"He's got the mitten again, and it's turned his head."

"No," I said, rising, "I see it's true. Lend me a pistol, someone, or a first-class fare to the other end of Nowhere. Charrington has bewitched the only pretty girl in our twenty-mile radius. Was it mesmerism, or a love-potion, Jack?"

"Neither, sir, but a gift you'll never have—perseverance—and the best luck a man ever had in this world."

There was something in his voice that silenced me, and all chaff of the other fellows failed to draw him further.

The queer thing about it was that, when we congratulated Miss Foster, she blushed, and smiled, and dimpled, for all the world as though she were in love with him and had been in love with him all the time. Upon my word, I think she had. Women are strange creatures.

We were all asked to the wedding. In Brixham, every one who was anybody knew everybody else who was anyone. My sisters were, I truly believe, more interested in the trousseau than the bride herself, and I was to be best man. The coming marriage was much canvassed at afternoon tea-tables, and at our little club over the saddler's; and the question was always asked: "Does she care for him?"

I used to ask that question myself in the early days of their engagement, but after a certain evening in August I never asked it again. I was coming home from the club through the churchyard. Our church is on a thyme-grown hill, and the turf about it is so thick and soft that one's footsteps are noiseless.

I made no sound as I vaulted the low wall and threaded my way between the tombstones. It was at the same instant that I heard John Charrington's voice and saw her. May was sitting on a low, flat gravestone, her face turned towards the full splendour of the setting sun. Its expression ended, at once and for ever, any question of love for him; it was transfigured to a beauty I should not have believed possible, even to that beautiful little face.

John lay at her feet, and it was his voice that broke the stillness of the golden August evening.

"My dear, I believe I should come back to you from the dead, if you wanted me!"

I coughed at once to indicate my presence, and passed on into the shadow fully enlightened.

The wedding was to be early in September. Two days before, I had to run up to town on business. The train was late, of course, for we were on the South-Eastern, and as I stood grumbling with my watch in my hand, whom should I see but John Charrington and May Foster. They were walking up and down the unfrequented end of the platform, arm-in-arm, looking into each other's eyes, careless of the sympathetic interest of the porters.

Of course I knew better than to hesitate a moment before burying myself in the booking-office, and it was not till the train drew up at the platform that I obtrusively passed the pair with my Gladstone, and took the corner in a first-class smoking-carriage. I did this with as good an air of not seeing them as I could assume. I pride myself on my discretion, but if John were travelling alone, I wanted his company. I had it.

"Hullo, old man," came his cheery voice, as he swung his bag into my carriage, "here's luck. I was expecting a dull journey."

"Where are you off to?" I asked, discretion still bidding me turn my eyes away, though I saw, without looking, that hers were red-rimmed.

"To old Branbridge's," he answered, shutting the door, and leaning out for a last word with his sweetheart.

"Oh, I wish you wouldn't go, John," she was saying in a low, earnest voice. "I feel certain something will happen."

"Do you think I should let anything happen to keep me, and the day after to-morrow our wedding day?"

"Don't go," she answered, with a pleading intensity that would have sent my Gladstone on to the platform, and me after it. But she wasn't speaking to me. John Charrington was made differently—he rarely changed his opinions, never his resolutions.

He just touched the ungloved hands that lay on the carriage door.

"I must, May. The old boy has been awfully good to me, and now he's dying I must go and see him, but I shall come home in time—" The rest of the parting was lost in a whisper and in the rattling lurch of the starting train.

"You're sure to come?" she spoke, as the train moved.

"Nothing shall keep me," he answered, and we steamed out. After he had seen the last of the little figure on the platform, he leaned back in his corner and kept silence for a minute.

When he spoke it was to explain to me that his godfather, whose heir he was, lay dying at Peasemarsh Place, some fifty miles away, and he had sent for John, and John had felt bound to go.

"I shall be surely back to-morrow," he said, "or, if not, the day after, in heaps of time. Thank Heaven, one hasn't to get up in the middle of the night to get married nowadays."

"And suppose Mr Branbridge dies?"

"Alive or dead, I mean to be married on Thursday!" John answered, lighting a cigar and unfolding the *Times*.

At Peasemarsh station we said "good-bye," and he got out, and I saw him ride off. I went on to London, where I stayed the night.

When I got home the next afternoon, a very wet one, by the way, my sister greeted me with: "Where's Mr Charrington?"

"Goodness knows," I answered testily. Every man since Cain has resented that kind of question.

"I thought you might have heard from him," she went on, "as you're to give him away to-morrow."

"Isn't he back?" I asked, for I had confidently expected to find him at home.

"No, Geoffrey"—my sister always had a way of jumping to conclusions, especially such conclusions as were least favourable to her fellow creatures—"he has not returned, and, what is more, you may depend upon it, he won't. You mark my words, there'll be no wedding tomorrow."

My sister Fanny has a power of annoying me which no other human being possesses.

"You mark my words," I retorted with asperity, "you had better give up making such a thundering idiot of yourself. There'll be more wedding tomorrow than ever you'll take first part in."

But though I could snarl confidently to my sister, I did not feel so comfortable when, late that night, I, standing on the doorstep of John's house, heard that he had not returned. I went home gloomily through the rain. Next morning brought a brilliant blue sky, gold sun, and all such softness of air and beauty of cloud as go to make a perfect day. I woke with a vague feeling of having gone to bed anxious, and of being rather averse from facing that anxiety in the light of full wakefulness.

With my shaving-water came a letter from John which relieved my mind, and sent me up to the Fosters with a light heart.

May was in the garden. I saw her blue gown among the hollyhocks as the lodge gates swung to behind me. So I did not go up to the house, but turned aside down the turfed path.

"He's written to you too," she said, without preliminary greeting, when I reached her side.

"Yes, I'm to meet him at the station at three, and come straight on to the church."

Her face looked pale, but there was a brightness in the eyes and a softness about the mouth that spoke of renewed happiness.

"Mr Branbridge begged him so to stay another night that he had not the heart to refuse," she went on. "He is so kind, but . . . I wish he hadn't stayed."

I was at the station at half-past two. I felt rather annoyed with John. It seemed a sort of slight to the beautiful girl who loved him, that he should come, as it were out of breath, and with the dust of travel upon him, to take her hand, which some of us would have given the best years of our life to take.

But when the three o'clock train glided in and glided out again, having brought no passengers to our little station, I was more than annoyed. There was no other train for thirty-five minutes; I calculated that, with much hurry, we might just get to the church in time for the ceremony; but, oh, what a fool to miss that first train! What other man would have done it?

The thirty-five minutes seemed a year, as I wandered round the station reading the advertisements and the time-tables and the company's bye-laws, and getting more and more angry with John Charrington. This confidence in his own power of getting everything he wanted the minute he wanted it, was leading him too far.

I hate waiting. Everyone hates waiting, but I believe I hate it more than anyone else does. The three-thirty-five was late too, of course.

I ground my pipe between my teeth and stamped with impatience as I watched the signals. Click. The signal went down. Five minutes later I flung myself into the carriage that I had brought for John.

"Drive to the church!" I said, as some one shut the door. "Mr Charrington hasn't come by this train."

Anxiety now replaced anger. What had become of this man? Could he have been taken suddenly ill? I had never known him have a day's illness in his life. And even so he might have telegraphed. Some awful accident must have happened to him. The thought that he had played her false never, no, not for a moment, entered my head. Yes, something terrible had happened to him, and on me lay the task of telling his bride. I almost wished the carriage would upset and break my head, so that someone else might tell her.

It was five minutes to four as we drew up at the churchyard. A double row of eager onlookers lined the path from lych-gate to porch. I sprang from the carriage and passed up between them. Our gardener had a good front place near the door. I stopped.

"Are they still waiting, Byles?" I asked, simply to gain time, for of course I knew they were, by the waiting crowd's attentive attitude.

"Waiting, sir? No, no, sir; why it must be over by now."

"Over! Then Mr Charrington's come?"

"To the minute, sir; must have missed you somehow, and I say, sir," lowering his voice, "I never see Mr John the least bit so afore, but my opinion is he's 'ad more than a drop; I wouldn't be going too far if I said he's been drinking pretty free. His clothes was all dusty and his face like a sheet. I tell you I didn't like the looks of him at all, and the folks inside are saying all sorts of things. You'll see, something's gone very wrong with Mr John, and he's tried liquor. He looked like a ghost, and he went in with his eyes straight before him, with never a look or a word for none of us; him that was always such a gentleman."

I had never heard Byles make so long a speech. The crowd in the churchyard were talking in whispers, and getting ready rice and slippers to throw at the bride and bridegroom. The ringers were ready with their hands on the ropes, to ring out the merry peal as the bride and bridegroom should come out.

A murmur from the church announced them; out they came. Byles was right. John Charrington did not look himself. There was dust on his coat, his hair was disarranged. He seemed to have been in some row, for there was a black mark above his eyebrow. He was deathly pale. But his pallor was not greater than that of the bride, who might have been carved in ivory—dress, veil, orange-blossoms, face and all.

As they passed out, the ringers stooped—there were six of them—and then, on the ears expecting the gay wedding peal, came the slow tolling of the passing bell.

A thrill of horror at so foolish a jest from the ringers passed through us all. But the ringers themselves dropped the ropes and fled like rabbits out into the sunlight. The bride shuddered, and grey shadows came about her mouth, but the bridegroom led her on down the path where the people stood with the handfuls of rice; but the handfuls were never thrown, and the wedding bells never rang. In vain the ringers were urged to remedy their mistake; they protested, with many whispered expletives, that they had not rung that bell; that they would see themselves further before they'd ring anything more that day.

In a hush, like the hush in the chamber of death, the bridal pair passed into their carriage, and its door slammed behind them.

Then the tongues were loosed. A babel of anger, wonder, conjecture from the guests and the spectators.

"If I'd seen his condition, sir," said old Foster to me as we drove off, "I would have stretched him on the floor of the church, sir, by Heaven I would, before I'd have let him marry my daughter!"

Then he put his head out the window.

"Drive like hell," he cried to the coachman; "don't spare the horses."

We passed the bride's carriage. I forebore to look at it, and old Foster turned his head away and swore.

We stood in the hall doorway, in the blazing afternoon sun, and in about half a minute we heard wheels crunching the gravel. When the carriage stopped in front of the steps, old Forster and I ran down.

"Great Heaven, the carriage is empty! And yet—"

I had the door open in a minute, and this is what I saw—

No sign of John Charrington; and of May, his wife, only a huddled heap of white satin, lying half on the floor of the carriage and half on the seat.

"I drove straight here, sir," said the coachman, as the bride's father lifted her out, "and I'll swear no one got out of the carriage."

We carried her into the house in her bridal dress, and drew back her veil. I saw her face. Shall I ever forget it? White, white, and drawn with agony and horror, bearing such a look of terror as I have never seen since, except in dreams. And her hair, her radiant blonde hair, I tell you it was white like snow.

As we stood, her father and I, half mad with the horror and mystery of it, a boy came up the avenue—a telegraph boy. They brought the orange envelope to me. I tore it open.

"*John Charrington was thrown from the dogcart on his way to the station at half-past one. Killed on the spot.*—BRANBRIDGE, Peasemarsh Place."

And he was married to May Foster in our Parish Church at half-past three, in presence of half the parish!

"I shall be married on Thursday dead or alive!"

What had passed in that carriage on the homeward drive? No one knows—no one will ever know.

Before a week was over they laid her beside her husband in the churchyard where they had kept their love-trysts.

This is the true story of John Charrington's wedding.

The Ebony Frame

To be rich is a luxurious sensation, the more so when you have plumbed the depths of hard-upness as a Fleet Street hack, a picker-up of unconsidered pars, a reporter, an unappreciated journalist; all callings utterly inconsistent with one's family feeling and one's direct descent from the Dukes of Picardy.

When my Aunt Dorcas died and left me seven hundred a year and a furnished house in Chelsea, I felt that life had nothing left to offer except immediate possession of the legacy. Even Mildred Mayhew, whom I had hitherto regarded as my life's light, became less luminous. I was not engaged to Mildred, but I lodged with her mother, and I sang duets with Mildred and gave her gloves when it would run to it, which was seldom. She was a dear, good girl, and I meant to marry her some day. It is very nice to feel that a good little woman is thinking of you—it helps you in your work—and it is pleasant to know she will say "Yes," when you say, "Will you?"

But my legacy almost put Mildred out of my head, especially as she was staying with friends in the country.

Before the gloss was off my new mourning, I was seated in my aunt's armchair in front of the fire in the drawing-room of my own house. My own house! It was grand, but rather lonely. I did think of Mildred just then.

The room was comfortably furnished with rosewood and damask. On the walls hung a few fairly good oil paintings, but the space above the mantelpiece was disfigured by an exceedingly bad print, "The Trial of Lord William Russell," framed in a dark frame. I got up to look at it. I had visited my aunt with dutiful regularity, but I never remembered seeing this frame before. It was not intended for a print, but for an oil-painting. It was of fine ebony, beautifully and curiously carved.

I looked at it with growing interest, and when my aunt's housemaid—I had retained her modest staff of servants—came in with the lamp, I asked her how long the print had been there.

"Mistress only bought it two days before she was took ill," she said; "but the frame—she didn't want to buy a new one—so she got this out of the attic. There's lots of curious old things there, sir."

"Had my aunt had this frame long?"

"Oh, yes, sir! It must have come long before I did, and I've been here seven years come Christmas. There was a picture in it. That's upstairs too—but it's that black and ugly it might as well be a chimney-back."

I felt a desire to see this picture. What if it were some priceless old master, in which my aunt's eyes had only seen rubbish?

Directly after breakfast next morning, I paid a visit to the attic.

It was crammed with old furniture enough to stock a curiosity shop. All the house was furnished solidly in the Mid-Victorian style, and in this room everything not in keeping with the drawing-room-suite ideal was stowed away. Tables of papier-maché and mother-of-pearl, straight-backed chairs with twisted feet and faded needle-work cushions, fire-screens of gilded carving and beaded banners, oak bureaux with brass handles, a little work-table with its faded, moth-eaten, silk flutings hanging in disconsolate shreds; on these, and the dust that covered them, blazed the full daylight as I pulled up the blinds. I promised myself a good time in re-enshrining these household gods in my parlour, and promoting the Victorian suite to the attic. But at present my business was to find the picture as "black as the chimney back"; and presently, behind a heap of fenders and boxes, I found it.

Jane, the housemaid, identified it at once. I took it downstairs carefully, and examined it. Neither subject nor colour was distinguishable. There was a splodge of a darker tint in the middle, but whether it was figure, or tree, or house, no man could have told. It seemed to be painted on a very thick panel bound with leather. I decided to send it to one of those persons who pour on rotting family portraits the water of eternal youth; but even as I did so, I thought—why not try my own restorative hand at a corner of it.

My bath-sponge soap and nail-brush, vigorously applied for a few seconds, shewed me that there was no picture to clean. Bare oak presented itself to my persevering brush. I tried the other side, Jane watching me with indulgent interest. The same result. Then the truth dawned on me. Why was the panel so thick? I tore off the leather binding, and the panel divided and fell to the ground in a cloud of dust. There were two pictures—they had been nailed face to face. I leaned them against the wall, and the next moment I was leaning against it myself.

For one of the pictures was myself—a perfect portrait—no shade of expression or turn of feature wanting. Myself—in the dress men wore when James the First was King. When had this been done? And how, without my knowledge? Was this some whim of my aunt's?

"Lor', sir!" the shrill surprise of Jane at my elbow; "what a lovely photo it is! Was it a fancy ball, sir?"

"Yes," I stammered. "I—I don't think I want anything more now. You can go."

She went; and I turned, still with my heart beating violently, to the other picture. This was a beautiful woman's picture—very beautiful she was. I noted all her beauties—straight nose, low brows, full lips, thin hands, large, deep, luminous eyes. She wore a black velvet gown. It was a three-quarter-length portrait. Her arms rested on a table beside her, and her head on her hands; but her face was turned full forward, and her eyes met those of the spectator bewilderingly. On the table by her were compasses and shining instruments whose uses I did not know, books, a goblet, and a heap of papers and pens. I saw all this afterwards. I believe it was a quarter of an hour before I could turn my eyes from hers. I have never see any other eyes like hers; they appealed, as a child's or a dog's do; they commanded, as might those of an empress.

"Shall I sweep up the dust, sir?" Curiosity had brought Jane back. I acceded. I turned from her my portrait. I kept between her and the woman in the black velvet. When I was alone again I tore down "The Trial of Lord William Russell," and I put the picture of the woman in its strong ebony frame.

Then I wrote to a frame-maker for a frame for my portrait. It had so long lived face to face with this beautiful witch that I had not the heart to banish it from her presence; I suppose I am sentimental—if it be sentimental to think such things as that.

The new frame came home, and I hung it opposite the fireplace. An exhaustive search among my aunt's papers shewed no explanation of the portrait of myself, no history of the portrait of the woman with the wonderful eyes. I only learned that all the old furniture together had come to my aunt at the death of my great-uncle, the head of the family; and I should have concluded that the resemblance was only a family one, if everyone who came in had not exclaimed at the "speaking likeness." I adopted Jane's "fancy ball" explanation.

And there, one might suppose, the matter of the portraits ended. One might suppose it, that is, if there were not evidently a good deal more written here about it. However, to me then the matter seemed ended.

I went to see Mildred; I invited her and her mother to come and stay with me. I rather avoided glancing at the picture in the ebony frame. I could not forget, nor remember without singular emotion, the look in the eyes of that woman when mine first met them. I shrank from meeting that look again.

I reorganised the house somewhat, preparing for Mildred's visit. I brought down much of the old-fashioned furniture, and after a long day of arranging and re-arranging, I sat down before the fire, and lying back in a pleasant languor, I idly raised my eyes to the picture of the woman. I met her dark, deep, hazel eyes, and once more my gaze was held fixed as by strong magic—the kind of fascination that keeps one sometimes staring for whole minutes into one's own eyes in the glass. I gazed into her eyes, and felt my own dilate, pricked with a smart like the smart of tears.

"I wish," I said, "oh, how I wish you were a woman and not a picture! Come down! Ah, come down!"

I laughed at myself as I spoke; but even as I laughed, I held out my arms.

I was not sleepy; I was not drunk. I was as wide awake and as sober as ever was a man in the world. And yet, as I held out my arms, I saw the eyes of the picture dilate, her lips tremble—if I were to be hanged for saying it, it is true.

Her hands moved slightly; and a sort of flicker of a smile passed over her face.

I sprang to my feet. "This won't do," I said aloud. "Firelight does play strange tricks. I'll have the lamp."

I made for the bell. My hand was on it, when I heard a sound behind me, and turned—the bell still unrung. The fire had burned low and the corners of the room were deeply shadowed; but surely, there—behind the tall worked chair—was something darker than a shadow.

"I must face this out," I said, "or I shall never be able to face myself again." I left the bell, I seized the poker, and battered the dull coals, to a blaze. Then I stepped back resolutely, and looked at the picture. The ebony frame was empty! From the shadow of the worked chair came a soft rustle, and out of the shadow the woman of the picture was coming—coming towards me.

I hope I shall never again know a moment of terror as blank and absolute. I could not have moved or spoken to save my life. Either all the known laws of nature were nothing, or I was mad. I stood trembling, but, I am thankful to remember, I stood still, while the black velvet gown swept across the hearthrug towards me.

Next moment a hand touched me—a hand, soft, warm, and human—and a low voice said, "You called me. I am here."

At that touch and that voice, the world seemed to give a sort of bewildering half-turn. I hardly know how to express it, but at once it seemed not awful, not even unusual, for portraits to become flesh—only most natural, most right, most unspeakably fortunate.

I laid my hand on hers. I looked from her to my portrait. I could not see it in the firelight.

"We are not strangers," I said.

"Oh, no, not strangers." Those luminous eyes were looking up into mine, those red lips were near me. With a passionate cry, a sense of having recovered life's one great good, that had seemed wholly lost, I clasped her in my arms. She was no ghost, she was a woman, the only woman in the world.

"How long," I said, "how long is it since I lost you?"

She leaned back, hanging her full weight on the hands that were clasped behind my head.

"How can I tell how long? There is no time in hell," she answered.

It was not a dream. Ah! no—there are no such dreams. I wish to God there could be. When in dreams do I see her eyes, hear her voice, feel her lips against my cheek, hold her hands to my lips, as I did that night, the supreme night of my life! At first we hardly spoke. It seemed enough

> ". . . after long grief and pain,
> To feel the arms of my true love
> Round me once again."

It is very difficult to tell my story. There are no words to express the sense of glad reunion, the complete realisation of every hope and dream of a life, that came upon me as I sat with my hand in hers, and looked into her eyes.

How could it have been a dream, when I left her sitting in the straight-backed chair, and went down to the kitchen to tell the maids I should want nothing more—that I was busy, and did not wish to be disturbed; when I fetched wood for the fire with my own hands, and, bringing it in, found her still sitting there—saw the little brown head turn as I entered, saw the love in her dear eyes; when I threw myself at her feet and blessed the day I was born, since life had given me this.

Not a thought of Mildred; all other things in my life were a dream—this, its one splendid reality.

"I am wondering," she said, after a while, when we had made such cheer, each of the other, as true lovers may after long parting—"I am wondering how much you remember of our past?"

"I remember nothing but that I love you—that I have loved you all my life."

"You remember nothing—really nothing?"

"Only that I am truly yours; that we have both suffered; that—tell me, my mistress dear, all that you remember. Explain it all to me. Make me understand. And yet— No, I don't want to understand. It is enough that we are together."

If it was a dream, why have I never dreamed it again?

She leaned down towards me, her arm lay on my neck, and drew my head till it rested on her shoulder. "I am a ghost, I suppose," she said, laughing softly; and her laughter stirred memories which I just grasped at and just missed. "But you and I know better, don't we? I will tell you everything you have forgotten. We loved each other—ah! no, you have not forgotten that—and when you came back from the wars, we were to be married. Our pictures were painted before you went away. You know I was more learned than women of that day. Dear one, when you were gone, they said I was a witch. They tried me. They said I should be burned. Just because I had looked at the stars and gained more knowledge than other women, they must needs bind me to a stake and let me be eaten by the fire. And you far away!"

Her whole body trembled and shrank. Oh love, what dream would have told me that my kisses would soothe even that memory?

"The night before," she went on, "the devil did come to me. I was innocent before—you know it, don't you? And even then my sin was for you—for you—because of the exceeding love I bore you. The devil came, and I sold my soul to eternal flame. But I got a good price. I got the right to come back through my picture (if anyone, looking at it, wished for me), as long as my picture stayed in its ebony frame. That frame was not carved by man's hand. I got the right to come back to you, oh, my heart's heart. And another thing I won, which you shall hear anon. They burned me for a witch, they made me suffer hell on earth. Those faces, all crowding round, the crackling wood and the choking smell of the smoke—"

"Oh, love, no more, no more!"

"When my mother sat that night before my picture, she wept and cried, 'Come back, my poor, lost child!' And I went to her with glad leaps of heart. Dear, she shrank from me, she fled, she shrieked and moaned of ghosts. She had our pictures covered from sight, and put again in the ebony frame. She had promised me my picture should stay always there. Ah, through all these years your face was against mine."

She paused.

"But the man you loved?"

"You came home. My picture was gone. They lied to you, and you married another woman; but some day I knew you would walk the world again, and that I should find you."

"The other gain?" I asked.

"The other gain," she said slowly, "I gave my soul for. It is this. If you also will give up your hopes of heaven, I can remain a woman, I can remain in your world—I can be your wife. Oh my dear, after all these years, at last—at last!"

"If I sacrifice my soul," I said slowly, and the words did not seem an imbecility, "if I sacrifice my soul I win you? Why, love, it's a contradiction in terms. You *are* my soul."

Her eyes looked straight into mine. Whatever might happen, whatever did happen, whatever may happen, our two souls in that moment met and became one.

"Then you choose, you deliberately choose, to give up your hopes of heaven for me, as I gave up mine for you?"

"I will not," I said, "give up my hope of heaven on any terms. Tell me what I must do that you and I may make our heaven here, as now?"

"I will tell you to-morrow," she said. "Be alone here to-morrow night—twelve is ghost's time, isn't it?—and then I will come out of the picture, and never go back to it. I shall live with you, and die, and be buried, and there will be an end of me. But we shall live first, my heart's heart."

I laid my head on her knee. A strange drowsiness overcame me. Holding her hand against my cheek, I lost consciousness. When I awoke, the grey November dawn was glimmering, ghost-like, through the uncurtained window. My head was pillowed on my arm, and rested—I raised my head quickly—ah! not on my lady's knee, but on the needle-worked cushion of the straight-backed chair. I sprang to my feet. I was stiff with cold and dazed with dreams, but I turned my eyes on the picture. There she sat, my lady, my dear love. I held out my arms, but the passionate cry I would have uttered died on my lips. She had said twelve o'clock. Her lightest word was my law. So I only stood in front of the picture, and gazed into those grey-green eyes till tears of passionate happiness filled my own.

"Oh! my dear, my dear, how shall I pass the hours till I hold you again?"

No thought, then, of my whole life's completion and consummation being a dream.

I staggered up to my room, fell across my bed, and slept heavily and dreamlessly. When I awoke it was high noon. Mildred and her mother were coming to lunch.

I remembered, at one o'clock, Mildred coming and her existence.

Now, indeed the dream began.

With a penetrating sense of the futility of any action apart from her, I gave the necessary orders for the reception of my guests. When Mildred and her mother came I received them with cordiality; but my genial phrases all seemed to be someone else's. My voice sounded like an echo; my heart was not there.

Still, the situation was not intolerable, until the hour when afternoon tea was served in the drawing-room. Mildred and her mother kept the conversational pot boiling with a profusion of genteel commonplaces, and I bore it, as one in sight of heaven can bear mild purgatory. I looked up at my sweetheart in the ebony frame, and I felt that anything which might happen, any irresponsible imbecility, any bathos of boredom, was nothing, if, after all, *she* came to me again.

And yet, when Mildred, too, looked at the portrait and said: "Doesn't she think a lot of herself? Theatrical character, I suppose? One of your flames, Mr Devigne?" I had a sickening sense of impotent irritation which became absolute torture when Mildred—how could I ever have admired that chocolate-box barmaid style of prettiness—threw herself into the high-backed chair, covering the needlework with ridiculous flounces, and added, "Silence gives consent! Who is it, Mr Devigne? Tell us all about her: I am sure she has a story."

Poor little Mildred, sitting there smiling, serene in her confidence that her every word charmed me—sitting there with her rather pinched waist, her rather tight boots, her rather vulgar voice—sitting in the chair where my dear lady had sat when she told me her story! I could not bear it.

"Don't sit there," I said, "it's not comfortable!"

But the girl would not be warned. With a laugh that set every nerve in my body vibrating with annoyance, she said, "Oh, dear! mustn't I even sit in the same chair as your black-velvet woman?"

I looked at the chair in the picture. It was the same, and in her chair Mildred was sitting. Then a horrible sense of the reality of Mildred came upon me. Was all this a reality after all? But for fortunate chance, might Mildred have occupied, not only her chair, but her place in my life? I rose.

"I hope you won't think me very rude," I said, "but I am obliged to go out."

I forget what appointment I alleged. The lie came readily enough.

I faced Mildred's pouts with the hope that she and her mother would not wait dinner for me. I fled. In another minute I was safe, alone, under the chill, cloudy, autumn sky—free to think, think, think of my dear lady.

I walked for hours along streets and squares; I lived over and over again every look, word and hand-touch—every kiss; I was completely, unspeakably happy.

Mildred was utterly forgotten; my lady of the ebony frame filled my heart, and soul, and spirit.

As I heard eleven boom through the fog, I turned and went home.

When I got to my street, I found a crowd surging through it, a strong red, light filling the air.

A house was on fire. Mine!

I elbowed my way through the crowd.

The picture of my lady—that, at least, I could save.

As I sprang up the steps, I saw, as in a dream—yes, all this was *really* dreamlike—I saw Mildred leaning out of the first-floor window, wringing her hands.

"Come back, sir," cried a fireman; "we'll get the young lady out right enough."

But *my* lady? The stairs were crackling, smoking, and as hot as hell. I went up to the room where her picture was. Strange to say, I only felt that the picture was a thing we should like to look on through the long, glad, wedded life that was to be ours. I never thought of it as being one with her.

As I reached the first floor I felt arms about my neck. The smoke was too thick for me to distinguish features.

"Save me," a voice whispered. I clasped a figure in my arms and bore it with a strange dis-ease, down the shaking stairs and out into safety. It was Mildred. I knew that directly I clasped her.

"Stand back," cried the crowd.

"Everyone's safe," cried a fireman.

The flames leaped from every window. The sky grew redder and redder. I sprang from the hands that would have held me. I leaped up the steps. I crawled up the stairs. Suddenly the whole horror came to me. *"As long as my picture remains in the ebony frame."* What if picture and frame perished together?

I fought with the fire and with my own choking inability to fight with it. I pushed on. I must save my picture. I reached the drawing-room.

As I sprang in, I saw my lady, I swear it, through the smoke and the flames, hold out her arms to me—to me—who came too late to save her, and to save my own life's joy. I never saw her again.

Before I could reach her, or cry out to her, I felt the floor yield beneath my feet, and I fell into the flames below.

How did they save me? What does that matter? They saved me some-how—curse them. Every stick of my aunt's furniture was destroyed. My friends pointed out that, as the furniture was heavily insured, the careless-ness of a nightly-studious housemaid had done me no harm.

No harm!

That was how I won and lost my only love.

I deny, with all my soul in the denial, that it was a dream. There are no such dreams. Dreams of longing and pain there are in plenty; but dreams of complete, of unspeakable happiness—ah, no—it is the rest of life that is the dream.

But, if I think that, why have I married Mildred and grown stout, and dull, and prosperous?

I tell you, it is all *this* that is the dream; my dear lady only is the reality. And what does it matter what one does in a dream?

The Mass for the Dead

I was awake—widely, cruelly awake. I had been awake all night; what sleep could there be for me when the woman I loved was to be married next morning—married, and not to me?

I went to my room early; the family party in the drawing-room maddened me. Grouped about the round table with the stamped plush cover, each was busy with work, or book, or newspaper, but not too busy to stab my heart through and through with their talk of the wedding.

Her people were near neighbours of mine, so why should her marriage not be canvassed in my home circle?

They did not mean to be cruel; they did not know that I loved her; but she knew it. I told her, but she knew it before that. She knew it from the moment when I came back from three years of musical study in Germany—came back and met her in the wood where we used to go nutting when we were children.

I looked into her eyes, and my whole soul trembled with thankfulness that I was living in a world that held her also. I turned and walked by her side, through the tangled green wood, and we talked of the long-ago days, and it was, "Have you forgotten?" and "Do you remember?" till we reached her garden gate. Then I said—

"Good-bye; no, *auf wiedersehn*, and in a very little time, I hope."

And she answered—

"Good-bye. By the way, you haven't congratulated me yet."

"Congratulated you?"

"Yes, did I not tell you I am to marry Mr Benoliel next month?"

And she turned away, and went up the garden slowly.

I asked my people, and they said it was true. Kate, my dear playfellow, was to marry this Spaniard, rich, wilful, accustomed to win, polished in manners and base in life. Why was she to marry him?

41

"No one knows," said my father, "but her father is talked about in the city, and Benoliel, the Spaniard, is rich. Perhaps that's it."

That was it. She told me so when, after two weeks spent with her and near her, I implored her to break so vile a chain and to come to me, who loved her—whom she loved.

"You are quite right," she said calmly. We were sitting in the window-seat of the oak parlour in her father's desolate old house. "I do love you, and I shall marry Mr Benoliel."

"Why?"

"Look around you and ask me why, if you can."

I looked around—on the shabby, bare room, with its faded hangings of sage-green moreen, its threadbare carpet, its patched, washed-out chintz chair-covers. I looked out through the square, latticed window at the ragged, unkempt lawn, at her own gown—of poor material, though she wore it as queens might desire to wear ermine—and I understood.

Kate is obstinate; it is her one fault; I knew how vain would be my entreaties, yet I offered them; how unavailing my arguments, yet they were set forth; how useless my love and my sorrow, yet I shewed them to her.

"No," she answered, but she flung her arms round my neck as she spoke, and held me as one may hold one's best treasure. "No, no; you are poor, and he is rich. You wouldn't have me break my father's heart: he's so proud, and if he doesn't get some money next month, he will be ruined. I'm not deceiving any one. Mr Benoliel knows I don't care for him; and if I marry him, he is going to advance my father a large sum of money. Oh, I assure you that everything has been talked over and settled. There is no going from it."

"Child! child!" I cried, "how calmly you speak of it! Don't you see that you are selling your soul and throwing mine away?"

"Father Fabian says I am doing right," she answered, unclasping her hands, but holding mine in them, and looking at me with those clear, grey eyes of hers. "Are we to be unselfish in everything else, and in love to think only of our own happiness? I love you, and I shall marry him. Would you rather the positions were reversed?"

"Yes," I said, "for then I would make you love me."

"Perhaps *he* will," she said bitterly. Even in that moment her mouth trembled with the ghost of a smile. She always loved to tease. She goes through more moods in a day than most other women in a year. Drowning the smile came tears, but she controlled them, and she said—

"Good-bye; you see I am right, don't you? Oh, Jasper, I wish I hadn't told you I loved you. It will only make you more unhappy."

"It makes my one happiness," I answered; "nothing can take that from me. And that happiness he will never have. Say again that you love me!"

"I love you! I love you! I love you!"

With further folly of tears and mad loving words we parted, and I bore my heartache away, leaving her to bear hers into her new life.

And now she was to be married to-morrow, and I could not sleep.

When the darkness became unbearable I lighted a candle, and then lay staring vacantly at the roses on the wall-paper, or following with my eyes the lines and curves of the heavy mahogany furniture.

The solidity of my surroundings oppressed me. In the dull light the wardrobe loomed like a hearse, and my violin case looked like a child's coffin.

I reached a book and read till my eyes ached and the letters danced a pas fantastique up and down the page.

I got up and had ten minutes with the dumbbells. I sponged my face and hands with cold water and tried again to sleep—vainly. I lay there, miserably wide awake.

I tried to say poetry, the half-forgotten tasks of my school days even, but through everything ran the refrain—

"Kate is to be married to-morrow, and not to me, not to me!"

I tried counting up to a thousand. I tried to imagine sheep in a lane, and to count them as they jumped through a gap in an imaginary hedge—all the time-honoured spells with which sleep is wooed—vainly.

Then the Waits came, and a torture to the nerves was superadded to the torture of the heart. After fifteen minutes of carols every fibre of me seemed vibrating in an agony of physical misery.

To banish the echo of "The Mistletoe Bough," I hummed softly to myself a melody of Palestrina's, and felt more awake than ever.

Then the thing happened which nothing will ever explain. As I lay there I heard, breaking through and gradually overpowering the air I was suggesting, a harmony which I had never heard before, beautiful beyond description, and as distinct and definite as any song man's ears have ever listened to.

My first half-formed thought was, "more Waits," but the music was choral music, true and sweet; with it mingled an organ's notes, and with every note the music grew in volume. It is absurd to suggest that I dreamed it, for, still hearing the music, I leaped out of bed and opened the window. The music grew fainter. There was no one to be seen in the snowy garden below. Shivering, I shut the window. The music grew more distinct, and I became aware that I was listening to a mass—a funeral mass, and one which I had never heard before. I lay in my bed and followed the whole course of the office.

The music ceased.

I was sitting up in bed, my candle alight, and myself as wide awake as ever, and more than ever possessed by the thought of *her*.

But with a difference. Before, I had only mourned the loss of her: now, my thoughts of her were mingled with an indescribable dread. The sense of death and decay that had come to me with that strange, beautiful music, coloured all my thoughts. I was filled with fancies of hushed houses, black garments, rooms where white flowers and white linen lay in a deathly stillness. I heard echoes of tears, and of dim-voiced bells tolling monotonously. I shivered, as it were on the brink of irreparable woe, and in its contemplation I watched the dull dawn slowly overcome the pale flame of my candle, now burnt down into its socket.

I felt that I must see Kate once again before she gave herself away. Before ten o'clock I was in the oak parlour. She came to me. As she entered the room, her pallor, her swollen eyelids and the misery in her eyes wrung my heart as even that night of agony had not done. I literally could not speak. I held out my hands.

Would she reproach me for coming to her again, for forcing upon her a second time the anguish of parting?

She did not. She laid her hands in mine, and said—

"I am thankful you have come; do you know, I think I am going mad? Don't let me go mad, Jasper."

The look in her eyes underlined her words.

I stammered something and kissed her hands. I was with her again, and joy fought again with grief.

"I must tell some one. If I am mad, don't lock me up. Take care of me, won't you?"

Would I not?

"Understand," she went on, "it was not a dream. I was wide awake, thinking of you. The Waits had not long gone, and I—I was looking at your likeness. I was not asleep."

I shivered as I held her fast.

"As Heaven sees us, I did not dream it. I heard a mass sung, and, Jasper, it was a mass for the dead. I followed the office. You are not a Catholic, but I thought—I feared—oh, I don't know what I thought. I am thankful there is nothing wrong with you."

I felt a sudden certainty, and complete sense of power possess me. Now, in this her moment of weakness, while she was so completely under the influence of a strong emotion, I could and would save her from Benoliel, and myself from life-long pain.

"Kate," I said, "I believe it is a warning. You shall not marry this man. You shall marry me, and none other."

She leaned her head against my shoulder; she seemed to have forgotten her father and all the reasons for her marriage with Benoliel.

"You don't think I'm mad? No? Then take care of me; take me away; I feel safe with you."

Thus all obstacles vanished in less time than the length of a lover's kiss. I dared not stop to consider the coincidence of supernatural warning—nor what it might mean. Face to face with crowned hope, I am proud to remember that common sense held her own. The room in which we were had a French window. I fetched her garden hat and a shawl from the hall, and we went out through the still, white garden. We did not meet a soul. When we reached my father's garden I took her in by the back way, to the summer-house, and left her, though I was half afraid to leave her, while I went into the house. I snatched my violin and cheque book, took all my spare money, scrawled a line to my father and rejoined her.

Still no one had seen us.

We walked to a station five miles away; and by the time Benoliel would reach the church, I was leaving Doctors' Commons with a special licence in my pocket. Two hours later Kate was my wife, and we were quietly and prosaically eating our wedding-breakfast in the dining-room of the Grand Hotel.

"And where shall we go?" I said.

"I don't know," she answered, smiling; "you have not much money, have you?"

"Oh dear me, yes. I'm not rich, but I'm not absolutely a church mouse."

"Could we go to Devonshire?" she asked, twisting her new ring round and round.

"Devonshire! Why, that is where—"

"Yes, I know: Benoliel arranged to go there. Jasper, I am afraid of Benoliel."

"Then why—"

"Foolish person," she answered. "Do you think that Benoliel will be likely to go to Devonshire *now?*"

We went to Devonshire—I had had a small legacy a few months earlier, and I did not permit money cares to trouble my new and beautiful happiness. My only fear was that she would be saddened by thoughts of her father; but I am thankful to remember that in those first days she, too, was happy—so happy that there seemed to be hardly room in her mind for any thought but of me. And every hour of every day I said to my soul—

"But for that portent, whatever it boded, she might have been not my wife but his."

The first four or five days of our marriage are flowers that memory keeps always fresh. Kate's face had recovered its wild-rose bloom, and she laughed and sang and jested and enjoyed all our little daily adventures with the fullest, freest-hearted gaiety. Then I committed the supreme imbecility of my life—one of those acts of folly on which one looks back all one's life with a half stamp of the foot, and the unanswerable question, "How on earth could I have been such a fool?"

We were sitting in a little sitting-room, hideous in intention, but redeemed by blazing fire and the fact that two were there, sitting hand-in-hand, gazing into the fire and talking of their future and of their love. There was nothing to trouble us; no one had discovered our whereabouts, and my wife's fear of Benoliel's revenge seemed to have dissolved before the flame of our happiness.

And as we sat there, peaceful and untroubled, the Imp of the Perverse jogged my elbow, as, alas! he does so often, and I was moved to tell my wife that I, too, had heard that unearthly midnight music—that her hearing of it was not, as she had grown to think, a mere nightmare—a strange dream—but something more strange, more significant. I told her how I had heard the mass for the dead, and all the tale of that night. She listened silently, and I thought her strangely indifferent. When I had finished, she took her hand from mine and covered her face.

"I believe it was a warning to us to flee temptation. We ought never to have married. Oh, my poor father!"

Her tone was one that I had never heard before. Its hopeless misery appalled me. And justly. For no arguments, no entreaties, no caresses, could win my wife back to the mood of an hour before.

She tried to be cheerful, but her gaiety was forced, and her laughter stung my heart.

She spoke no more about the music, and when I tried to reason with her about it she smiled a gloomy little smile, and said—

"I cannot be happy. I will not be happy. It is wrong. I have been very selfish and wicked. You think me very idiotic, I know, but I believe there is a curse on us. We shall never be happy again."

"Don't you love me any more?" I asked like a fool.

"Love you?" She only repeated my words, but I was satisfied on that score. But those were miserable days. We loved each other passionately, yet our hours were spent like those of lovers on the eve of parting. Long, long silences took the place of foolish little jokes and childish talk which happy lovers know. And more than once, waking in the night, I heard my wife sobbing, and feigned sleep, with the bitter knowledge that I had no power to comfort her. I knew that the thought of her father was with her always, and that her anxiety about him grew, day by day. I wore myself out in trying to think of some way to divert her thoughts from him. I could not, indeed, pay his debts, but I could have him to live with us, a much greater sacrifice; and having a good connection, both as a musician and composer, I did not doubt that I could support her and him in comfort.

But Kate had made up her mind that the disgrace of bankruptcy would break her father's heart; and my Kate is not easy to convince or persuade.

At Torquay it occurred to me that perhaps it would be well for her to see a priest. True, Father Fabian had counselled her to marry Benoliel, but I could hardly believe that most priests would advise a girl to marry a bad man, whom she did not love, for the sake of any worldly gain whatsoever.

She received the suggestion with favour, but without enthusiasm, and we sought out a Catholic church to make inquiries. As we opened the outer door of the church we heard music, and as we stood in the entrance and I laid my hand on the heavy inner door, my other hand was caught by Kate.

"Jasper," she whispered, "it is the same!"

Some person opening the door behind us compelled us to move forward. In another moment we stood in the dusky church—stood hand-in-hand in dim daylight, listening to the same music that each had heard in the lonely night on the eve of our wedding.

I put my arm round my wife and drew her back.

"Come away, my darling," I whispered; "it is a funeral service."

She turned her eyes on me. "I must understand, I must see who it is. I shall go mad if you take me away now. I cannot bear any more."

We walked up the aisle, and placed ourselves as near as possible to the spot where the coffin lay, covered with flowers and with tapers burning about it. And we heard that music again, every note of it the same that each had heard before. And when the service was over I whispered to the sacristan—

"Whose music was that?"

"Our organist's," he answered; "it is the first time they've had it. Fine, wasn't it?"

"Who is the—who was—who is being buried?"

"A foreign gentleman, sir; they do say as his lady as was to be gave him the slip on his wedding day, and he'd given her father thousands they say, if the truth was known."

"But what was he doing here?"

"Well, that's the curious part, sir. To shew his independence, what does he do but go the same tour he'd planned for his wedding trip. And there was a railway accident, and him and every one in his carriage killed in a twinkling, so to speak. Lucky for the young lady she was off with somebody else."

The sacristan laughed softly to himself.

Kate's fingers gripped my arm.

"What was his name?" she asked.

I would not have asked: I did not wish to hear it.

"Benoliel," said the sacristan. "Curious name and curious tale. Every one's talking of it."

Every one had something else to talk of when it was found that Benoliel's pride, which had permitted him to buy a wife, had shrunk from reclaiming the purchase money when the purchase was lost to him. And to the man who had been willing to sell his daughter, the retention of her price seemed perfectly natural.

From the moment when she heard Benoliel's name on the sacristan's lips, all Kate's gaiety and happiness returned. She loved me, and she hated Benoliel. She was married to me, and he was dead; and his death was far more of a shock to me than to her. Women are curiously kind and curiously cruel. And she never could see why her father should not have kept the money. It is noteworthy that women, even the cleverest and the best of them, have no perception of what men mean by honour.

How do I account for the music? My good critic, my business is to tell my story—not to account for it.

And do I not pity Benoliel? Yes. I can afford, now, to pity most men, alive or dead.

From the Dead

ut true or not true, your brother is a scoundrel. No man—no decent man—tells such things."

"He did not tell me. How dare you suppose it? I found the letter in his desk; and since she was my friend and your sweetheart, I never thought there could be any harm in my reading anything she might write to my brother. Give me back the letter. I was a fool to tell you."

Ida Helmont held out her hand for the letter.

"Not yet," I said, and I went to the window. The dull red of a London sunset burned on the paper, as I read in the pretty handwriting I knew so well, and had kissed so often—

> "DEAR—I do—I do love you; but it's impossible. I must marry Arthur. My honour is engaged. If he would only set me free—but he never will. He loves me foolishly. But as for me—it is you I love—body, soul and spirit. There is no one in my heart but you. I think of you all day, and dream of you all night. And we must part. Goodbye—Yours, yours, yours,
>
> Elvira."

I had seen the handwriting, indeed, often enough. But the passion there was new to me. That I had not seen.

I turned from the window. My sitting-room looked strange to me. There were my books, my reading-lamp, my untasted dinner still on the table, as I had left it when I rose to dissemble my surprise at Ida Helmont's visit—Ida Helmont, who now sat looking at me quietly.

"Well—do you give me no thanks?"

"You put a knife in my heart, and then ask for thanks?"

"Pardon me," she said, throwing up her chin. "I have done nothing but shew you the truth. For that one should expect no gratitude—may I ask, out of pure curiosity, what you intend to do?"

"Your brother will tell you—"

She rose suddenly, very pale, and her eyes haggard.

"You will not tell my brother?"

She came towards me—her gold hair flaming in the sunset light.

"Why are you so angry with me?" she said. "Be reasonable. What else could I do?"

"I don't know."

"Would it have been right not to tell you?"

"I don't know. I only know that you've put the sun out, and I haven't got used to the dark yet."

"Believe me," she said, coming still nearer to me, and laying her hands in the lightest touch on my shoulders, "believe me, she never loved you."

There was a softness in her tone that irritated and stimulated me. I moved gently back, and her hands fell by her sides.

"I beg your pardon," I said. "I have behaved very badly. You were quite right to come, and I am not ungrateful. Will you post a letter for me?"

I sat down and wrote—

"I give you back your freedom. The only gift of mine that can please you now.—

Arthur."

I held the sheet out to Miss Helmont, but she would not look at it. I folded, sealed, stamped, and addressed it.

"Good-bye," I said then, and gave her the letter. As the door closed behind her, I sank into my chair, and cried like a child, or a fool, over my lost play-thing—the little, dark-haired woman who loved someone else with "body, soul, and spirit."

I did not hear the door, open or any foot on the floor, and therefore I started when a voice behind me said:

"Are you so very unhappy? Oh, Arthur, don't think I am not sorry for you!"

"I don't want anyone to be sorry for me, Miss Helmont," I said.

She was silent a moment. Then, with a quick, sudden, gentle movement she leaned down and kissed my forehead—and I heard the door softly close. Then I knew that the beautiful Miss Helmont loved me.

At first that thought only fleeted by—a light cloud against a grey sky—but the next day reason woke, and said:

"Was Miss Helmont speaking the truth? Was it possible that—"

I determined to see Elvira, to know from her own lips whether by happy fortune this blow came, not from her, but from a woman in whom love might have killed honesty.

I walked from Hampstead to Gower Street. As I trod its long length, I saw a figure in pink come out of one of the houses. It was Elvira. She walked in front of me to the corner of Store Street. There she met Oscar Helmont. They turned and met me face to face, and I saw all I needed to see. They loved each other. Ida Helmont had spoken the truth. I bowed and passed on. Before six months were gone, they were married, and before a year was over, I had married Ida Helmont.

What did it, I don't know. Whether it was remorse for having, even for half a day, dreamed that she could be so base as to forge a lie to gain a lover, or whether it was her beauty, or the sweet flattery of the preference of a woman who had half her acquaintance at her feet, I don't know; anyhow, my thoughts turned to her as to their natural home. My heart, too, took that road, and before very long I loved her as I never loved Elvira. Let no one doubt that I loved her —as I shall never love again—please God!

There never was anyone like her. She was brave and beautiful, witty and wise, and beyond all measure adorable. She was the only woman in the world. There was a frankness—a largeness of heart—about her that made all other women seem small and contemptible. She loved me and I worshipped her. I married her, I stayed with her for three golden weeks, and then I left her. Why?

Because she told me the truth. It was one night—late—we had sat all the evening in the verandah of our sea-side lodging, watching the moonlight on the water, and listening to the soft sound of the sea on the sand. I have never been so happy; I shall never be happy any more, I hope.

"My dear, my dear," she said, leaning her gold head against my shoulder, "how much do you love me?"

"How much?"

"Yes—how much? I want to know what place I hold in your heart. Am I more to you than anyone else?"

"My love!"

"More than yourself?"

"More than my life."

"I believe you," she said. Then she drew a long breath, and took my hands in hers. "It can make no difference. Nothing in heaven or earth can come between us now."

"Nothing," I said. "But, my dear one, what is it?"

For she was trembling, pale.

"I must tell you," she said; "I cannot hide anything now from you, because I am yours—body, soul and spirit."

The phrase was an echo that stung.

The moonlight shone on her gold hair, her soft, warm, gold hair, and on her pale face.

"Arthur," she said, "you remember my coming to Hampstead with that letter."

"Yes, my sweet, and I remember how you—"

"Arthur!" she spoke fast and low—"Arthur, that letter was a forgery. She never wrote it. I—"

She stopped, for I had risen and flung her hands from me, and stood looking at her. God help me! I thought it was anger at the lie I felt. I know now it was only wounded vanity that smarted in me. That I should have been tricked, that I should have been deceived, that I should have been led on to make a fool of myself. That I should have married the woman who had befooled me. At that moment she was no longer the wife I adored—she was only a woman who had forged a letter and tricked me into marrying her.

I spoke: I denounced her; I said I would never speak to her again. I felt it was rather creditable in me to be so angry. I said I would have no more to do with a liar and a forger.

I don't know whether I expected her to creep to my knees and implore forgiveness. I think I had some vague idea that I could by-and-by consent with dignity to forgive and forget. I did not mean what I said. No, oh no, no; I did not mean a word of it. While I was saying it, I was longing for her to weep and fall at my feet, that I might raise her and hold her in my arms again.

But she did not fall at my feet; she stood quietly looking at me.

"Arthur," she said, as I paused for breath, "let me explain—she—I—"

"There is nothing to explain," I said hotly, still with that foolish sense of there being something rather noble in my indignation, the kind of thing one feels when one calls one's self a miserable sinner. "You are a liar and a forger, that is enough for me. I will never speak to you again. You have wrecked my life—"

"Do you mean that?" she said, interrupting me, and leaning forward to look at me. Tears lay on her cheeks, but she was not crying now.

I hesitated. I longed to take her in my arms and say—"What does all that old tale matter now? Lay your head here, my darling, and cry here, and know how I love you."

But instead I said nothing.

"*Do* you mean it?" she persisted.

Then she put her hand on my arm. I longed to clasp it and draw her to me.

Instead, I shook it off, and said—

"Mean it? Yes—of course I mean it. Don't touch me, please. You have ruined my life."

She turned away without a word, went into our room, and shut the door.

I longed to follow her, to tell her that if there was anything to forgive, I forgave it.

Instead, I went out on the beach, and walked away under the cliffs.

The moonlight and the solitude, however, presently brought me to a better mind. Whatever she had done, had been done for love of me—I knew that. I would go home and tell her so—tell her that whatever she had done, she was my dear life, my heart's one treasure. True, my ideal of her was shattered, at least I felt I ought to think that it was shattered, but, even as she was, what was the whole world of women compared to her? And to be loved like that . . . was that not sweet food for vanity? To be loved more than faith and fair dealing, and all the traditions of honesty and honour? I hurried back, but in my resentment and evil temper I had walked far, and the way back was very long. I had been parted from her for three hours by the time I opened the door of the little house where we lodged. The house was dark and very still. I slipped off my shoes and crept up the narrow stairs, and opened the door of our room quite softly. Perhaps she would have cried herself to sleep, and I would lean over her and waken her with my kisses, and beg her to forgive me. Yes, it had come to that now.

I went into the room—I went towards the bed. She was not there. She was not in the room, as one glance shewed me. She was not in the house, as I knew in two minutes. When I had wasted a precious hour in searching the town for her, I found a note on my pillow—

"Good-bye! Make the best of what is left of your life. I will spoil it no more."

She was gone, utterly gone. I rushed to town by the earliest morning train, only to find that her people knew nothing of her. Advertisement failed. Only a tramp said he had seen a white lady on the cliff, and a fisherman brought me a handkerchief, marked with her name, which he had found on the beach.

I searched the country far and wide, but I had to go back to London at last, and the months went by. I won't say much about those months, because even the memory of that suffering turns me faint and sick at heart. The police and detectives and the Press failed me utterly. Her friends could not help me, and were, moreover, wildly indignant with me, especially her brother, now living very happily with my first love.

I don't know how I got through those long weeks and months. I tried to write; I tried to read; I tried to live the life of a reasonable human being. But it was impossible. I could not endure the companionship of my kind. Day and night I almost saw her face—almost heard her voice. I took long walks in the country, and her figure was always just round the next turn of the road—in the next glade of the wood. But I never quite saw her, never quite heard her. I believe I was not altogether sane at that time. At last, one morning, as I was setting out for one of those long walks that had no goal but weariness, I met a telegraph boy, and took the red envelope from his hand.

On the pink paper inside was written—

"Come to me at once I am dying you must come IDA
                    Apinshaw Farm Mellor Derbyshire"

There was a train at twelve to Marple, the nearest station. I took it. I tell you there are some things that cannot be written about. My life for those long months was one of them, that journey was another. What had her life been for those months? That question troubled me, as one is troubled in every nerve by the sight of a surgical operation, or a wound inflicted on a being clear to one. But the overmastering sensation was joy—intense, unspeakable joy. She was alive. I should see her again. I took out the telegram and looked at it: "I am dying." I simply did not believe it. She could not die till she had seen me. And if she had lived all these months without me, she could live now, when I was with her again, when she knew of the hell I had endured apart from her, and the heaven of our meeting. She must live; I could not let her die.

There was a long drive over bleak hills. Dark, jolting, infinitely wearisome. At last we stopped before a long, low building, where one or two lights gleamed faintly. I sprang out.

The door opened. A blaze of light made me blink and draw back. A woman was standing in the doorway.

"Art thee Arthur Marsh?" she said.

"Yes."

"Then th'art ower late. She's dead."

II.

I went into the house, walked to the fire, and held out my hands to it mechanically, for though the night was May, I was cold to the bone. There were some folks standing round the fire, and lights flickering. Then an old woman came forward, with the northern instinct of hospitality.

"Thou'rt tired," she said, "and mazed-like. Have a sup o' tea."

I burst out laughing. I had travelled two hundred miles to see *her*. And she was dead, and they offered me tea. They drew back from me as if I had been a wild beast, but I could not stop laughing. Then a hand was laid on my shoulder and someone led me into a dark room, lighted a lamp, set me in a chair, and sat down opposite me. It was a bare parlour, coldly furnished with rush chairs and much-polished tables and presses. I caught my breath, and grew suddenly grave, and looked at the woman who sat opposite me.

"I was Miss Ida's nurse," said she, "and she told me to send for you. Who are you?"

"Her husband—"

The woman looked at me with hard eyes, where intense surprise struggled with resentment.

"Then may God forgive you!" she said. "What you've done I don't know, but it'll be hard work forgivin' you, even for *Him!*"

"Tell me," I said, "my wife—"

"Tell you!" The bitter contempt in the woman's tone did not hurt me. What was it to the self-contempt that had gnawed my heart all these months. "Tell you! Yes, I'll tell you. Your wife was that ashamed of you, she never so much as told me she was married. She let me think anything I pleased sooner than that. She just come 'ere, an' she said, 'Nurse, take care of me, for I am in mortal trouble. And don't let them know where I am,' says she. An' me being well married to an honest man, and well-to-do here, I was able to do it, by the blessing."

"Why didn't you send for me before?" It was a cry of anguish wrung from me.

"I'd *never* 'a sent for you. It was *her* doin'. Oh, to think as God A'mighty's made men able to measure out such-like pecks o' trouble for us womenfolk! Young man, I don't know what you did to 'er to make 'er leave you; but it muster bin something cruel, for she loved the ground you walked on. She useter sit day after day a-lookin' at your picture, an' talkin' to it, an' kissin' of it, when she thought I wasn't takin' no notice, and cryin' till she made me cry too. She useter cry all night 'most. An' one day, when I tells 'er to pray to God to 'elp 'er through 'er trouble, she outs with *your* putty face on a card, she does, an', says she, with her poor little smile, 'That's my god, Nursey,' she says."

"Don't!" I said feebly, putting out my hands to keep off the torture; "not any more. Not now."

"Don't?" she repeated. She had risen, and was walking up and down the room with clasped hands. "Don't, indeed! No, I won't; but I shan't forget you! I tell you, I've had you in my prayers time and again, when I thought you'd made a light-o'-love of my darling. I shan't drop you outer them now, when I know she was your own wedded wife, as you chucked away when you tired of her, and left 'er to eat 'er 'art out with longin' for you. Oh! I pray to God above us to pay you scot and lot for all you done to 'er. You killed my pretty. The price will be required of you, young man, even to the uttermost farthing. Oh God in Heaven, make him suffer! Make him feel it!"

She stamped her foot as she passed me. I stood quite still. I bit my lip till I tasted the blood hot and salt on my tongue.

"She was nothing to you," cried the woman, walking faster up and down between the rush chairs and the table; "any fool can see that with half an eye. You didn't love her, so you don't feel nothin' now; but some day you'll care for someone, and then you shall know what she felt—if there's any justice in Heaven."

I, too, rose, walked across the room, and leaned against the wall. I heard her words without understanding them.

"Can't you feel *nothin'?* Are you made stone? Come an' look at 'er lyin' there so quiet. She don't fret arter the likes o' you no more now. She won't sit no more a-lookin' outer winder an' sayin' nothin'—only droppin' 'er tears one by one, slow, slow on her lap. Come an' see 'er; come an' see what you done to my pretty—an' then you can go. Nobody wants you 'ere. *She* don't want you now. But p'raps you'd like to see 'er safe under ground afore yer go? I'll be bound you'll put a big stone slab on 'er—to make sure she don't rise again."

I turned on her. Her thin face was white with grief and rage. Her claw-like hands were clenched.

"Woman," I said, "have mercy."

She paused and looked at me.

"Eh?" she said.

"Have mercy!" I said again.

"Mercy! You should 'a thought o' that before. You 'adn't no mercy on 'er. She loved you—she died loving you. An' if I wasn't a Christian woman, I'd kill you for it—like the rat you are! That I would, though I 'ad to swing for it arterwards."

I caught the woman's hands and held them fast, though she writhed and resisted.

"Don't you understand?" I said savagely. "We loved each other. She died loving me. I have to live loving her. And it's *her* you pity. I tell you it was all a mistake—a stupid, stupid mistake. Take me to her, and for pity's sake, let me be left alone with her."

She hesitated; then said, in a voice only a shade less hard: "Well, come along, then."

We moved towards the door. As she opened it, a faint, weak cry fell on my ear. My heart stood still.

"What's that?" I asked, stopping on the threshold.

"Your child," she said shortly.

That too! Oh, my love! oh, my poor love! All these long months!

"She allus said she'd send for you when she'd got over her trouble," the woman said, as we climbed the stairs. "'I'd like him to see his little baby, nurse,' she says; 'our little baby. It'll be all right when the baby's born,' she says. 'I know he'll come to me then. You'll see.' And I never said nothin', not thinkin' you'd come if she was your leavin's, and not dreamin' you could be 'er 'usband an' could stay away from 'er a hour—'er bein' as she was. Hush!"

She drew a key from her pocket and fitted it to a lock. She opened the door, and I followed her in. It was a large, dark room, full of old-fashioned furniture and a smell of lavender, camphor, and narcissus.

The big four-post bed was covered with white. "My lamb—my poor, pretty lamb!" said the woman, beginning to cry for the first time as she drew back the sheet. "Don't she look beautiful?"

I stood by the bedstead. I looked down on my wife's face. Just so I had seen it lie on the pillow beside me in the early morning, when the wind and the dawn came up from beyond the sea. She did not look like one dead. Her lips were still red, and it seemed to me that a tinge of colour lay on her cheek. It seemed to me, too, that if I kissed her she would awaken, and put her slight hand on my neck, and lay her cheek against mine—and that we should tell each other everything, and weep together, and understand, and be comforted.

So I stooped and laid my lips to hers as the old nurse stole from the room.

But the red lips were like marble, and she did not waken. She will not waken now ever any more.

I tell you again there are some things that cannot be written.

III.

I lay that night in a big room, filled with heavy dark furniture, in a great four-poster hung with heavy, dark curtains—a bed, the counterpart of that other bed from whose side they had dragged me at last.

They fed me, I believe, and the old nurse was kind to me. I think she saw now that it is not the dead who are to be pitied most.

I lay at last in the big, roomy bed, and heard the household noises grow fewer and die out, the little wail of my child sounding latest. They had brought the child to me, and I had held it in my arms, and bowed my head over its tiny face and frail fingers. I did not love it then. I told myself it has cost me her life. But my heart told me it was I who had done that. The tall clock at the stair-head sounded the hours—eleven, twelve, one, and still I could not sleep. The room was dark and very still.

I had not yet been able to look at my life quietly. I had been full of the intoxication of grief—a real drunkenness, more merciful than the sober calm that comes afterwards.

Now I lay still as the dead woman in the next room, and looked at what was left of my life. I lay still, and thought, and thought, and thought. And in those hours I tasted the bitterness of death. It must have been about three when I first became aware of a slight sound that was not the ticking of a clock. I say I first became aware, and yet I knew perfectly that I had heard that sound more than once before, and had yet determined not to hear it, *because it came from the next room*—the room where the corpse lay.

And I did not wish to hear that sound, because I knew it meant that I was nervous—miserably nervous—a coward, and a brute. It meant that I, having killed my wife as surely as though I had put a knife in her breast, had now sunk so low as to be afraid of her dead body—the dead body that lay in the next room to mine. The heads of the beds were placed against the same wall; and from that wall I had fancied that I heard slight, slight, almost inaudible sounds. So that when I say I became aware of them, I mean that I, at last, heard a sound so definite as to leave no room for doubt or question. It brought me to a sitting position in the bed, and the drops of sweat gathered heavily on my forehead and fell on my cold hands, as I held my breath and listened.

I don't know how long I sat there—there was no further sound—and at last my tense muscles relaxed, and I fell back on the pillow.

"You fool!" I said to myself; "dead or alive, is she not your darling, your heart's heart? Would you not go near to die of joy, if she came back to you? Pray God to let her spirit come back and tell you she forgives you!"

"I wish she would come," myself answered in words, while every fibre of my body and mind shrank and quivered in denial.

I struck a match, lighted a candle, and breathed more freely as I looked at the polished furniture—the common-place details of an ordinary room. Then I thought of her, lying alone so near me, so quiet under the white sheet. She was dead; she would not wake or move. But suppose she did move? Suppose she turned back the sheet and got up and walked across the floor, and turned the door-handle?

As I thought it, I heard—plainly, unmistakably heard—the door of the chamber of death open slowly. I heard slow steps in the passage, slow, heavy steps. I heard the touch of hands on my door outside, uncertain hands that felt for the latch.

Sick with terror, I lay clenching the sheet in my hands.

I knew well enough what would come in when that door opened—that door on which my eyes were fixed. I dreaded to look, yet dared not turn away my eyes. The door opened slowly, slowly, slowly, and the figure of my dead wife came in. It came straight towards the bed, and stood at the bed foot in its white grave-clothes, with the white bandage under its chin. There was a scent of lavender and camphor and white narcissus. Its eyes were wide open, and looked at me with love unspeakable.

I could have shrieked aloud.

My wife spoke. It was the same dear voice that I had loved so to hear, but it was very weak and faint now; and now I trembled as I listened.

"You aren't afraid of me, darling, are you, though I am dead? I heard all you said to me when you came, but I couldn't answer. But now I've come back from the dead to tell you. I wasn't really so bad as you thought me. Elvira had told me she loved Oscar. I only wrote the letter to make it easier for you. I was too proud to tell you when you were so angry, but I am not proud any more now. You'll love again now, won't you, now I am dead. One always forgives dead people."

The poor ghost's voice was hollow and faint. Abject terror paralysed me. I could answer nothing.

"Say you forgive me," the thin, monotonous voice went on; "say you love me again."

I had to speak. Coward as I was, I did manage to stammer—

"Yes; I love you. I have always loved you, God help me."

The sound of my own voice reassured me, and I ended more firmly than I began. The figure by the bed swayed a little, unsteadily.

"I suppose," she said wearily, "you would be afraid, now I am dead, if I came round to you and kissed you?"

She made a movement as though she would have come to me.

Then I did shriek aloud, again and again, and covered my face with the sheet and wound it round my head and body, and held it with all my force. There was a moment's silence. Then I heard my door close, and then a sound of feet and of voices, and I heard something heavy fall. I disentangled my head from the sheet. My room was empty. Then reason came back to me. I leaped from the bed.

"Ida, my darling, come back! I am not afraid! I love you. Come back! Come back!"

I sprang to my door and flung it open. Someone was bringing a light along the passage. On the floor, outside the door of the death chamber, was a huddled heap—the corpse, in its grave-clothes. Dead, dead, dead.

She is buried in Mellor churchyard, and there is no stone over her.

Now, whether it was catalepsy, as the doctor said, or whether my love came back, even from the dead, to me who loved her, I shall never know; but this I know, that if I had held out my arms to her as she stood at my bed-foot—if I had said, "Yes, even from the grave, my darling—from hell itself, come back, come back to me!"—if I had had room in my coward's heart for anything but the unreasoning terror that killed love in that hour, I should not now be here alone. I shrank from her—I feared her—I would not take her to my heart. And now she will not come to me anymore.

Why do I go on living?

You see, there is the child. It is four years old now, and it has never spoken and never smiled.

Uncle Abraham's Romance

N o, my dear," my Uncle Abraham answered me, "no—nothing romantic ever happened to me—unless—but no; that wasn't romantic either—"

I was. To me, I being eighteen, romance was the world. My Uncle Abraham was old and lame. I followed the gaze of his faded eyes, and my own rested on a miniature that hung at his elbow-chair's right hand, a portrait of a woman, whose loveliness even the miniature-painter's art had been powerless to disguise—a woman with large eyes that shone, and face of that alluring oval which one hardly sees nowadays.

I rose to look at it. I had looked at it a hundred times. Often enough in my baby days I had asked, "Who's that, uncle?" and always the answer was the same: "A lady who died long ago, my dear."

As I looked again at the picture, I asked, "Was she like this?"

"Who?"

"Your—your romance!"

Uncle Abraham looked hard at me. "Yes," he said at last. "Very—very like."

I sat down on the floor by him. "Won't you tell me about her?"

"There's nothing to tell," he said. "I think it was fancy mostly, and folly; but it's the realest thing in my life, my dear."

A long pause. I kept silent. You should always give people time, especially old people.

"I remember," he said in the dreamy tone always promising so well to the ear that loves a story—"I remember, when I was a young man, I was very lonely indeed. I never had a sweetheart. I was always lame, my dear, from quite a boy; and the girls used to laugh at me."

Silence again. Presently he went on—

"And so I got into the way of mooning off by myself in lonely places, and one of my favourite walks was up through our churchyard, which was set on a hill in the middle of the marsh country. I liked that because I never met anyone there. It's all over, years ago. I was a silly lad; but I couldn't bear of a summer evening to hear a rustle and a whisper from the other side of the hedge, or maybe a kiss, as I went by.

"Well, I used to go and sit all by myself in the churchyard, which was always sweet with the thyme and quite light (on account of its being so high) long after the marshes were dark. I used to watch the bats flitting about in the red light, and wonder why God didn't make everyone's legs straight and strong, and wicked follies like that. But by the time the light was gone I had always worked it off, so to speak, and could go home quietly, and say my prayers without bitterness.

"Well, one hot night in August, when I had watched the sunset fade and the crescent moon grow golden, I was just stepping over the low stone wall of the churchyard when I heard a rustle behind me. I turned round, expecting it to be a rabbit or a bird. It was a woman."

He looked at the portrait. So did I.

"Yes," he said, "that was her very face. I was a bit scared and said something—I don't know what—she laughed and said, did I think she was a ghost? and I answered back; and I stayed talking to her over the churchyard wall till 'twas quite dark, and the glow-worms were out in the wet grass all along the way home.

"Next night, I saw her again; and the next, and the next. Always at twilight time; and if I passed any lovers leaning on the stiles in the marshes it was nothing to me now."

Again my uncle paused. "It was very long ago," he said shyly, "and I'm an old man; but I know what youth means, and happiness, though I was always lame, and the girls used to laugh at me. I don't know how long it went on—you don't measure time in dreams—but at last your grandfather said I looked as if I had one foot in the grave, and he would be sending me to stay with our kin at Bath, and take the waters. I had to go. I could not tell my father why I would rather die than go."

"What was her name, Uncle?" I asked.

"She never would tell me her name, and why should she? I had names enough in my heart to call her by. Marriage? My dear, even then I knew marriage was not for me. But I met her night after night, always in our churchyard where the yew-trees were, and the old crooked gravestones so thick in the grass. It was there we always met and always parted. The last time was the night before I went away. She was very sad, and dearer than life itself. And she said—

"'If you come back before the new moon, I shall meet you here just as usual. But if the new moon shines on this grave and you are not here—you will never see me again any more.'"

"She laid her hand on the tomb against which we had been leaning. It was an old, lichened, weather-worn stone, and its inscription was just

'SUSANNAH KINGSNORTH
Ob. 1723.'

"'I shall be here,' I said.

"'I mean it,' she said, very seriously and slowly, 'it is no fancy. You will be here when the new moon shines?'

"I promised, and after a while we parted.

"I had been with my kinsfolk at Bath for nearly a month. I was to go home on the next day when, turning over a case in the parlour, I came up-on that miniature. I could not speak for a minute. At last I said, with dry tongue, and heart beating to the tune of heaven and hell:

"'Who is this?'

"'That?' said my aunt. 'Oh! she was betrothed to one of our family years ago, but she died before the wedding. They say she was a bit of a witch. A handsome one, wasn't she?'

"I looked again at the face, the lips, the eyes of my dear lovely love, whom I was to meet to-morrow night when the new moon shone on that tomb in our churchyard.

"'Did you say she was dead?' I asked, and I hardly knew my own voice.

"'Years and years ago! Her name's on the back, and the date—'

"I took the portrait out from its case—I remember just the colour of its faded, red-velvet bed, and read on the back—'Susannah Kingsnorth, *Ob. 1723.*'

"That was in 1823." My uncle stopped short.

"What happened?" I asked breathlessly.

"I believe I had a fit," my uncle answered slowly; "at any rate, I was very ill."

"And you missed the new moon on the grave?"

"I missed the new moon on the grave."

"And you never saw her again?"

"I never saw her again—"

"But, uncle, do you really believe? Can the dead—was she—did you—"

My uncle took out his pipe and filled it.

"It's a long time ago," he said, "a many, many years. Old man's tales, my dear Old man's tales. Don't you take any notice of them."

He lighted the pipe, and puffed silently a moment or two before he said: "But I know what youth means, and love and happiness, though I was always lame, and the girls used to laugh at me."

The Mystery of the Semi-Detached

He was waiting for her; he had been waiting an hour and a half in a dusty suburban lane, with a row of big elms on one side and some eligible building sites on the other—and far away to the south-west the twinkling yellow lights of the Crystal Palace. It was not quite like a country lane, for it had a pavement and lamp-posts, but it was not a bad place for a meeting all the same: and farther up, towards the cemetery, it was really quite rural, and almost pretty, especially in twilight. But twilight had long deepened into night, and still he waited. He loved her, and he was engaged to be married to her, with the complete disapproval of every reasonable person who had been consulted. And this half-clandestine meeting was tonight to take the place of the grudgingly sanctioned weekly interview—because a certain rich uncle was visiting at her house, and her mother was not the woman to acknowledge to a moneyed uncle, who might "go off" any day, a match so deeply ineligible as hers with him.

So he waited for her, and the chill of an unusually severe May evening entered into his bones.

The policeman passed him with but a surly response to his "Good night." The bicyclists went by him like grey ghosts with fog-horns; and it was nearly ten o'clock, and she had not come.

He shrugged his shoulders and turned towards his lodgings. His road led him by her house—desirable, commodious, semi-detached—and he walked slowly as he neared it. She might, even now, be coming out. But she was not. There was no sign of movement about the house, no sign of life, no lights even in the windows. And her people were not early people.

He paused by the gate, wondering.

Then he noticed that the front door was open—wide open—and the street lamp shone a little way into the dark hall. There was something

69

about all this that did not please him—that scared him a little, indeed. The house had a gloomy and deserted air. It was obviously impossible that it harboured a rich uncle. The old man must have left early. In which case—

He walked up the path of patent-glazed tiles, and listened. No sign of life. He passed into the hall. There was no light anywhere. Where was everybody, and why was the front door open? There was no one in the drawing-room, the dining-room and the study (nine feet by seven) were equally blank. Every one was out, evidently. But the unpleasant sense that he was, perhaps, not the first casual visitor to walk through that open door impelled him to look through the house before he went away and closed it after him. So he went upstairs, and at the door of the first bedroom he came to he struck a wax match, as he had done in the sitting-rooms. Even as he did so he felt that he was not alone. And he was prepared to see something; but for what he saw he was not prepared. For what he saw lay on the bed, in a white loose gown—and it was his sweetheart, and its throat was cut from ear to ear. He doesn't know what happened then, nor how he got downstairs and into the street; but he got out somehow, and the policeman found him in a fit, under the lamp-post at the corner of the street. He couldn't speak when they picked him up, and he passed the night in the police-cells, because the policeman had seen plenty of drunken men before, but never one in a fit.

The next morning he was better, though still very white and shaky. But the tale he told the magistrate was convincing, and they sent a couple of constables with him to her house.

There was no crowd about it as he had fancied there would be, and the blinds were not down.

As he stood, dazed, in front of the door, it opened, and she came out. He held on to the door-post for support.

"She's all right, you see," said the constable, who had found him under the lamp. "I told you you was drunk, but you would know best—"

When he was alone with her he told her—not all—for that would not bear telling—but how he had come into the commodious semi-detached, and how he had found the door open and the lights out, and that he had been into that long back room facing the stairs, and had seen something—in even trying to hint at which he turned sick and broke down and had to have brandy given him.

"But, my dearest," she said, "I dare say the house was dark, for we were all at the Crystal Palace with my uncle, and no doubt the door was open, for the maids will run out if they're left. But you could not have been in that room, because I locked it when I came away, and the key was in my pocket. I dressed in a hurry and I left all my odds and ends lying about."

"I know," he said; "I saw a green scarf on a chair, and some long brown gloves, and a lot of hairpins and ribbons, and a prayerbook, and a lace handkerchief on the dressing-table. Why, I even noticed the almanack on the mantelpiece—October 21. At least it couldn't be that, because this is May. And yet it was. Your almanack is at October 21, isn't it?"

"No, of course it isn't," she said, smiling rather anxiously; "but all the other things were just as you say. You must have had a dream, or a vision, or something."

He was a very ordinary, commonplace, City young man, and he didn't believe in visions, but he never rested day or night till he got his sweetheart and her mother away from that commodious semi-detached, and settled them in a quite distant suburb. In the course of the removal he incidentally married her, and the mother went on living with them.

His nerves must have been a good bit shaken, because he was very queer for a long time, and was always inquiring if any one had taken the desirable semi-detached; and when an old stockbroker with a family took it, he went the length of calling on the old gentleman and imploring him by all that he held dear, not to live in that fatal house.

"Why?" said the stockbroker, not unnaturally.

And then he got so vague and confused, between trying to tell why and trying not to tell why, that the stockbroker shewed him out, and thanked his God he was not such a fool as to allow a lunatic to stand in the way of his taking that really remarkably cheap and desirable semi-detached residence.

Now the curious and quite inexplicable part of this story is that when she came down to breakfast on the morning of the 22nd of October she found him looking like death, with the morning paper in his hand. He caught hers—he couldn't speak, and pointed to the paper. And there she read that on the night of the 21st a young lady, the stockbroker's daughter, had been found, with her throat cut from ear to ear, on the bed in the long back bedroom facing the stairs of that desirable semi-detached.

Man-Size in Marble

Although every word of this tale is true, I do not expect people to believe it. Nowadays a "rational explanation" is required before belief is possible. Let me, at once, offer the "rational explanation" which finds most favour among those who have heard the tale of my life's tragedy. It is held that we were "under a delusion," she and I, on that 31st of October; and that this supposition places the whole matter on a satisfactory and believable basis. The reader can judge, when he, too, has heard my story, how far this is an "explanation," and in what sense it is "rational." There were three who took part in this; Laura and I and another man. The other man lives still, and can speak to the truth of the least credible part of my story.

I never knew in my life what it was to have as much money as would supply the most ordinary needs of life—good colours, canvasses, brushes, books and cab-fares—and when we were married, we knew quite well that we should only be able to live at all by "strict punctuality and attention to business." I used to paint in those days, and Laura used to write, and we felt sure we could keep the pot at least simmering. Living in London was out of the question, so we went to look for a cottage in the country, which should be at once sanitary and picturesque. So rarely do these two qualities meet in one cottage that our search was for some time quite fruitless. We tried advertisements, but most of the desirable rural residences which we did look at proved to be lacking in both essentials, and when a cottage chanced to have drains, it always had stucco as well and was shaped like a tea-caddy. And if we found a vine or a rose-covered porch, corruption invariably lurked within. Our minds got so befogged by the eloquence of house-agents, and the rival disadvantages of the fever-traps and outrages to beauty which we had seen and scorned, that I very much doubt whether either of us, on our wedding morning, knew the difference between a house and a haystack. But when we got away from friends and house-agents on our honeymoon, our wits grew clear again, and we knew a pretty cottage when at last we saw one. It was at Brenzett—a little village set on a hill, over against the southern marshes. We had gone there from the little fishing village, where we were staying, to see the church, and two fields from the church we found this cottage. It stood quite by itself about two miles from Brenzett village. It was a low building with rooms sticking out in unexpected places. There was a bit of stonework—ivy-covered and moss-grown, just two old rooms, all that was left of a big house that once stood there—and round this stone-work the house had grown up. Stripped of its roses and jasmine, it would have been hideous. As it stood it was charming, and after a brief examination, enthusiasm usurped the place of discretion and we took it. It was absurdly cheap. The rest of our honeymoon we spent in grubbing about in second-hand shops in Ashford, picking up bits of old oak and Chippendale chairs for our furnishing. We wound up with a run up to town and a visit to Liberty's, and soon the low, oak-beamed, lattice-windowed rooms began to be home. There was a jolly old-fashioned garden, with grass paths and no end of hollyhocks, and sunflowers, and big lilies, and roses with thousands of small sweet flowers. From the window you could see the marsh-pastures, and beyond them the blue, thin line of the sea. We were as happy as the summer was glorious, and settled down into work sooner than we ourselves expected. I was never tired of sketching the view and the wonderful cloud effects from the open lattice, and Laura would sit at the table and write verses about them, in which I mostly played the part of foreground.

We got a tall, old, peasant woman to do for us. Her face and figure were good, though her cooking was of the homeliest; but she understood all about gardening, and told us all the old names of the coppices and corn-fields, and the stories of the smugglers and the highwaymen, and, better still, of the "things that walked," and of the "sights" which met one in lonely lanes of a starlight night. She was a great comfort to us, because Laura hated housekeeping as much as I loved folk-lore, and we soon came to leave all the domestic business to Mrs Dorman, and to use her legends in little magazine stories which brought in guineas.

We had three months of married happiness. We did not have a single quarrel. And then it happened. One October evening I had been down to smoke a pipe with the doctor—our only neighbour—a pleasant young Irishman. Laura had stayed at home to finish a comic sketch of a village episode for the *Monthly Marplot*. I left her laughing over her own jokes, and came in to see her a crumpled heap of pale muslin, weeping on the window seat.

"Good heavens, my darling, what's the matter?" I cried, taking her in my arms. She leaned her head against my shoulder, and went on crying. I had never seen her cry before—we had always been so happy, you see —and I felt sure some frightful misfortune had happened.

"What is the matter? Do speak!"

"It's Mrs Dorman," she sobbed.

"What has she done?" I inquired, immensely relieved.

"She says she must go before the end of the month, and she says her niece is ill; she's gone down to see her now, but I don't believe that's the reason, because her niece is always ill. I believe someone has been setting her against us. Her manner was so queer—"

"Never mind, Pussy," I said. "Whatever you do, don't cry, or I shall have to cry, too, to keep you in countenance, and then you'll never respect your man again."

She dried her eyes obediently on my handkerchief, and even smiled faintly.

"But, you see," she went on, "it is really serious, because these village people are so sheepy; and if one won't do a thing, you may be sure none of the others will. And I shall have to cook the dinners and wash up all the hateful, greasy plates; and you'll have to carry cans of water about, and clean the boots and knives—and we shall never have any time for work, or earn any money or anything. We shall have to work all day, and only be able to rest when we are waiting for the kettle to boil!"

I represented to her that, even if we had to perform these duties, the day would still present some margin for other toils and recreations. But she refused to see the matter in any but the greyest light. She was very unreasonable, and I told her so, but in my heart . . . well, who wants a woman to be reasonable?

"I'll speak to Mrs Dorman when she comes back, and see if I can't come to terms with her," I said. "Perhaps she wants a rise in her screw. It will be all right. Let's walk up to the church."

The church was a large and lonely one, and we loved to go there, especially upon bright nights. The path skirted a wood, cut through it once, and ran along the crest of the hill through two meadows and round the church-yard wall, over which the old yews loomed in black masses of shadow. This path, which was partly paved, was called the "bier-balk," for it had long been the way by which the corpses had been carried to burial. The church-yard was richly treed, and was shaded by great elms, which stood just outside and stretched their kind arms out over the dead. A large, low porch let one into the building by a Norman doorway and a heavy oak door studded with iron. Inside, the arches rose into darkness, and between them shone the reticulated windows, which stood out white in the moonlight. In the chancel, the windows were of rich glass, which shewed in faint light their noble colouring and made the black oak of the choir pews hardly more solid than the shadows. But on each side of the altar lay a grey marble figure of a knight in full armour, lying upon a low slab, with hands held up in everlasting prayer, and these figures, oddly enough, were always to be seen if there was any glimmer of light in the church. Their names were lost, but the peasants told of them that they had been fierce and wicked men, marauders by land and sea, who had been the scourge of their time, and had been guilty of deeds so foul that the house they had lived in—the big house, by the way, that had stood on the site of our cottage—had been stricken by lightning and the vengeance of Heaven. But for all that, the gold of their heirs had bought them a place in the church. Looking at the bad, hard faces reproduced in the marble, this story was easily believed.

The church looked at its best on that night, for the shadows of the yew trees fell through the windows upon the floor of the nave, and touched the pillars with tattered shadow. We sat down together without speaking, and watched the solemn beauty of the old church with some of that awe which inspired its early builders. We walked to the chancel and looked at the sleeping warriors. Then we rested on the stone seat in the porch, looking out over the stretch of quiet, moonlit meadows, feeling in every fibre of our being the peace of the night and of our happy love; and came away at last with a sense that even scrubbing and black-leading were, at their worst, but small troubles.

Mrs Dorman had come back from the village, and I at once invited her to a *tête-à-tête*.

"Now, Mrs Dorman," I said, when I had got her into my painting-room, "what's all this about your not staying with us?"

"I should be glad to get away, sir, before the end of the month," she answered, with her usual placid dignity.

"Have you any fault to find, Mrs Dorman?"

"None at all, sir; you and your lady have always been most kind, I'm sure—"

"Well, what is it? Are your wages not high enough?"

"No, sir, I gets quite enough."

"Then why not stay?"

"I'd rather not," with some hesitation. "My niece is ill."

"But your niece has been ill ever since we came."

No answer. There was a long and awkward silence. I broke it.

"Can't you stay for another month?" I asked.

"No, sir. I'm bound to go on Thursday."

And this was Monday.

"Well, I must say, I think you might have let us know before. There's no time now to get anyone else, and your mistress is not fit to do heavy housework. Can't you stay till next week?"

"I might be able to come back next week."

I was now convinced that all she wanted was a brief holiday, which we should have been willing enough to let her have, as soon as we could get a substitute.

"But why must you go this week?" I persisted. "Come, out with it."

Mrs Dorman drew the little shawl, which she always wore, tightly across her bosom, as though she were cold. Then she said, with a sort of effort:

"They say, sir, as this was a big house in Catholic times, and there was a many deeds done here."

The nature of the "deeds" might be vaguely inferred from the inflection of Mrs Dorman's voice, which was enough to make one's blood run cold. I was glad that Laura was not in the room. She was always nervous, as highly strung natures are, and I felt that these tales about our house, told by this old peasant woman with her impressive manner and contagious credulity, might have made our home less dear to my wife.

"Tell me all about it, Mrs Dorman," I said. "You needn't mind about telling me. I'm not like the young people, who make fun of such things."

Which was partly true.

"Well, sir," she sank her voice, "you may have seen in the church, beside the altar, two shapes—"

"You mean the effigies of the knights in armour?" I said cheerfully.

"I mean them two bodies drawed out man-size in marble," she returned; and I had to admit that her description was a thousand times more graphic than mine.

"They do say as on All Saints' Eve them two bodies sits up on their slabs and gets off of them, and then walks down the aisle *in their marble*"—(another good phrase, Mrs Dorman)—"and as the church clock strikes eleven, they walks out of the church door, and over the graves, and along the bier-balk, and if it's a wet night there's the marks of their feet in the morning."

"And where do they go?" I asked, rather fascinated.

"They comes back to their old home, sir, and if anyone meets them—"

"Well, what then?" I asked.

But no, not another word could I get from her, save that her niece was ill, and that she must go. After what I had heard I scorned to discuss the niece, and tried to get from Mrs Dorman more details of the legend. I could get nothing but warnings.

"Whatever you do, sir, lock the door early on All Saints' Eve, and make the blessed cross-sign over the doorstep and on the windows."

"But has anyone ever seen these things?" I persisted.

"That's not for me to say. I know what I know."

"Well, who was here last year?"

"No one, sir. The lady as owned the house only stayed here in the summer, and she always went to London a full month afore *the* night. And I'm sorry to inconvenience you and your lady, but my niece is ill, and I must go on Thursday."

I could have shaken her for her reiteration of that obvious fiction.

She was determined to go, nor could our united entreaties move her in the least.

I did not tell Laura the legend of the shapes that "walked in their marble," partly because a legend concerning our house might trouble my wife, and partly, I think, for some more occult reason. This was not quite the same to me as any other story, and I did not want to talk about it till the day was over. I had very soon almost ceased to think of the legend, however. I was painting a portrait of Laura, against the lattice window, and I could not think of much else. I had got a splendid background of yellow and grey sunset, and was working away with enthusiasm at her face. On Thursday Mrs Dorman went. She relented, at parting, so far as to say:

"Don't you put yourselves about too much, ma'am, and if there's any little thing I can do next week, I'm sure I shan't mind."

From which I inferred that she wished to come back to us after Hallowe'en. Up to the last she adhered to the fiction of the niece.

Thursday passed off pretty well. Laura shewed marked ability in the matter of steak and potatoes, and I confess that my knives, and the plates, which I insisted upon washing, were better done than I had dared to expect. It was all so good, so simple, so pleasant. As I write of it, I almost forget what came after. But now I must remember, and tell.

Friday came. It is about what happened on that Friday that this is written. I wonder if I should have believed it if anyone had told it to me. I will write the story of it as quickly and plainly as I can. Everything that happened on that day is burnt into my brain. I shall not forget anything, nor leave anything out.

I got up early, I remember, and lighted the kitchen fire, and had just achieved a smoky success, when my wife came running down, as sunny and sweet as the clear October morning itself. We prepared breakfast together, and found it very good fun. The housework was soon done, and when brushes and brooms and pails were quiet again, the house was still indeed. It is wonderful what a difference one makes in a house. We really missed Mrs Dorman, quite apart from considerations of pots and pans. We spent the day in dusting our books and putting them straight, and dined gaily on cold steak and coffee. Laura was, if possible, brighter and gayer and sweeter than usual, and I began to think that a little domestic toil was really good for her. We had never been so merry since we were married, and the walk we had that afternoon was, I think, the happiest time of all my life. When we had watched the deep scarlet clouds slowly pale into leaden grey against a pale-green sky, and saw the white mists curl up along the hedgerows in the distant marsh, we came back to the house, silently, hand in hand.

"You are sad, Pussy," I said half-jestingly, as we sat down together in our little parlour. I expected a disclaimer, for my own silence had been the silence of complete happiness. To my surprise, she said:

"Yes, I think I am sad, or rather I am uneasy. I hope I am not going to be ill. I have shivered three or four times since we came in, and it's not really cold, is it?"

"No," I said, and hoped it was not a chill caught from the treacherous marsh mists that roll up from the marshes in the dying light. No, she said, she did not think so. Then, after a silence, she spoke suddenly:

"Do you ever have presentiments of evil?"

"No," I said, smiling; "and I shouldn't believe in them if I had."

"I do," she went on; "the night my father died I knew it, though he was right away in the north of Scotland." I did not answer in words.

She sat looking at the fire in silence for some time, gently stroking my hand. At last she sprang up, came behind me, and drawing my head back, kissed me.

"There, it's over now," she said. "What a baby I am. Come, light the candles, and we'll have some of these new Rubinstein duets."

And we spent a happy hour or two at the piano.

At about half-past ten, I began to fill the good-night pipe, but Laura looked so white that I felt that it would be brutal of me to fill our sitting-room with the fumes of strong cavendish.

"I'll take my pipe outside," I said.

"Let me come too."

"No, sweetheart, not to-night; you're much too tired. I shan't be long. Get to bed, or I shall have an invalid to nurse to-morrow, as well as the boots to clean."

I kissed her and was turning to go, when she flung her arms round my neck and held me very closely. I stroked her hair.

"Come, Pussy, you're over-tired. The housework has been too much for you."

She loosened her clasp a little and drew a deep breath.

"No. We've been very happy to-day, Jack, haven't we? Don't stay out too long."

"I won't, Puss cat," I said.

I strolled out of the front door, leaving it unlatched. What a night it was! The jagged masses of heavy, dark cloud were rolling at intervals from horizon to horizon, and thin, white wreaths covered the stars. Through all the rush of the cloud river, the moon swam, breasting the waves and disappearing again in the darkness. When, now and again, her light reached the woodlands, they seemed to be slowly and noiselessly waving in time to the clouds above them. There was a strange, grey light over all the earth; the fields had that shadowy bloom over them which only comes from the marriage of dew and moonshine, or frost and starlight.

I walked up and down, drinking in the beauty of the quiet earth and changing sky. The night was absolutely silent. Nothing seemed to be abroad. There was no skurrying of rabbits, or twitter of half-asleep birds. And though the clouds went sailing across the sky, the wind that drove them never came low enough to rustle the dead leaves in the woodland paths. Across the meadow, I could see the church tower standing out black and grey against the sky. I walked there, thinking over our three months of happiness, and of my wife—her dear eyes, her pretty ways. Oh, my girl! my own little girl; what a vision came to me then of a long, glad life for you and me together!

I heard a bell-beat from the church. Eleven already! I turned to go in, but the night held me. I could not go back into our little warm rooms yet. I would go right on up to the church. I felt vaguely that it would be good to carry my love and thankfulness to the sanctuary, whither so many loads of sorrow and gladness had been borne by men and women dead long since.

I looked in at the low window as I went by. Laura was half lying on her chair in front of the fire. I could not see her face, only her head shewed dark against the pale blue wall. She was quite still. Asleep, no doubt. My heart reached out to her, as I went on. There must be a God, I thought, and a God that was good. How otherwise could anything so sweet and dear as she ever have been imagined?

I walked slowly along the edge of the wood. A sound broke the stillness of the night. I stopped and listened. The sound stopped too. I went on, and now distinctly I heard another step than mine answer mine like an echo. It was a poacher or a wood-stealer, most likely, for these were not unknown in our Arcadia. But, whoever it was, he was a fool not to step more lightly. I turned into the wood, and now the footstep seemed to come from the path I had just left. It must be an echo, I thought. The wood lay lovely in the moonlight. The large, dying ferns and the brushwood shewed where, through thinning foliage, the pale light came down. The tree trunks stood up like Gothic columns all around me. They reminded me of the church, and I turned into the bier-balk and passed through the corpse-gate between the graves to the low porch. I paused for a moment on the stone seat where Laura and I had last night watched the fading landscape. Then I noticed that the door of the church was open, and I blamed myself for having left it unlatched the other night. We were the only people who ever cared to come to the church except on Sundays, and I was vexed to think that through our carelessness the damp autumn airs had had a chance of getting in and injuring the old fabric. I went in. It will seem strange perhaps that I should have gone half-way up the aisle before I remembered—with a sudden chill, followed by as sudden a rush of self-contempt—that this was the very day and hour when, according to tradition, the "shapes drawed out man-size in marble," began to walk.

Having thus remembered the legend, and remembered it with a shiver of which I was ashamed, I could not do otherwise than walk up towards the altar, just to look at the figures—as I said to myself; really what I wanted was to assure myself, first, that I did not believe the legend, and, secondly, that it was not true. I was rather glad that I had come. I thought that now I could tell Mrs Dorman how vain her fancies were, and how peacefully the marble figures slept on through the ghostly hour. With my hands in my pockets, I passed up the aisle. In the grey, dim light, the eastern end of the church looked larger than usual, and the arches above the tombs looked larger too. The moon came out and shewed me the reason. I stopped short, my heart gave a great leap that nearly choked me, and then sank sickeningly.

The "bodies drawed out man-size" were gone, and their marble slabs lay wide and bare in the vague moonlight that slanted through the west window.

Were they really gone? or was I mad? Clenching my nerves, I stooped and passed my hand over the smooth slabs and felt their flat unbroken surface. Had someone taken the things away? Was it some vile practical joke? I would make sure, anyway. In an instant I had made a torch of a newspaper which happened to be in my pocket, and lighting it held it high above my head. Its yellow glare illumined the dark arches and those slabs. The figures *were* gone. And I was alone in the church; or was I alone?

And then a horror seized me, a horror indefinable and indescribable—an overwhelming certainty of supreme and accomplished calamity. I flung down the torch and tore along the aisle and out through the door, biting my lips as I ran to keep myself from shrieking aloud. Was I mad—or what was this that possessed me? I leaped the churchyard wall and took the straight cut across the fields, led by the light from our windows. Just as I got over the first stile, a dark figure seemed to spring out of the ground. Mad still with the certainty of misfortune, I made for the thing that stood in my path, shouting "Get out of the way, can't you?"

But my push met with a very vigorous resistance. My arms were caught just above the elbow and held as in a vice, and the raw-boned Irish doctor actually shook me.

"Would ye?" he cried in his own unmistakable accents—"would ye, then?"

"Let me go, you fool," I gasped. "The marble figures have gone from the church; I tell you they've gone."

He broke into a ringing laugh. "I'll have to give ye a draught to-morrow, I see. Ye've been smoking too much and listening to old wives' tales."

"I tell you I've seen the bare slabs."

"Well, come back with me. I'm going up to old Palmer's—his daughter's ill—it's only hysteria, but it's as bad as it can be; we'll look in at the church and let me see the bare slabs."

"You go if you like," I said, a little less frantic for his laughter, "I'm going home to my wife."

"Rubbish, man," said he; "d'ye think I'll permit of that? Are ye to go saying all yer life that ye've seen solid marble endowed with vitality, and me to go all my life saying ye were a coward? No, sir—ye shan't do ut!"

The quiet night—a human voice—and I think also the physical contact with this six feet of solid common sense, brought me back a little to my ordinary self, and the word "coward" was a shower-bath.

"Come on, then," I said sullenly, "perhaps you're right."

He still held my arm tightly. We got over the stile and back to the church. All was still as death. The place smelt very damp and earthy. We walked up the aisle. I am not ashamed to confess I shut my eyes; I knew the figures would not be there. I heard Kelly strike a match.

"Here they are, ye see, right enough; ye've been dreaming or drinking, asking yer pardon for the imputation."

I opened my eyes. By Kelly's expiring vesta I saw two shapes lying "in their marble" on their slabs. I drew a deep breath and caught his hand.

"I'm awfully indebted to you," I said. "It must have been some trick of light, or I have been working rather hard, perhaps that's it. Do you know, I was quite convinced they were gone."

"I'm aware of that," he answered rather grimly; "ye'll have to be careful of that brain of yours, my friend, I assure you."

He was leaning over and looking at the right-hand figure, whose stony face was the most villainous and deadly in expression. He struck another match.

"By Jove!" he said, "something has been going on here—this hand is broken."

And so it was. I was certain that it had been perfect the last time Laura and I had been there.

"Perhaps someone had *tried* to remove them," said the young doctor.

"That won't account for my impression," I objected.

"Too much painting and tobacco will account for what you call your impression," he said.

"Come along," I said, "or my wife will be getting anxious. You'll come in and have a drop of whisky, and drink confusion to ghosts and better sense to me."

"I ought to go up to Palmer's, but it's so late now, I'd best leave it till the morning," he replied. "I was kept late at the Union, and I've had to see a lot of people since. All right, I'll come back with ye."

I think he fancied I needed him more than did Palmer's girl, so, discussing how such an illusion could have been possible, and deducing from this experience large generalities concerning ghostly apparitions, we saw, as we walked up the garden path, that bright light streamed out of the front door, and presently saw that the parlour door was open too. Had she gone out?

"Come in," I said, and Dr Kelly followed me into the parlour. It was all ablaze with candles, not only the wax ones, but at least a dozen guttering, glaring, tallow dips, stuck in vases and ornaments in unlikely places. Light, I knew, was Laura's remedy for nervousness. Poor child! Why had I left her? Brute that I was.

We glanced round the room, and at first we did not see her. The window was open and the draught set all the candles flaring one way. Her chair was empty, and her handkerchief and book lay on the floor. I turned to the window. There, in the recess of the window, I saw her. Oh, my child, my love, had she gone to that window to watch for me? And what had come into the room behind her? To what had she turned with that look of frantic fear and horror? Had she thought that it was my step she heard and turned to meet—what?

She had fallen back against a table in the window, and her body lay half on it and half on the window-seat, and her head hung down over the table, the brown hair loosened and fallen to the carpet. Her lips were drawn back and her eyes wide, wide open. They saw nothing now. What had they last seen?

The doctor moved towards her. But I pushed him aside and sprang to her; caught her in my arms, and cried—

"It's all right, Laura! I've got you safe, dear!"

She fell into my arms in a heap. I clasped her and kissed her, and called her by all her pet names, but I think I knew all the time that she was dead. Her hands were tightly clenched. In one of them she held something fast. When I was quite sure that she was dead, and that nothing mattered at all any more, I let him open her hand to see what she held.

It was a grey marble finger.

Hurst of Hurstcote

We were at Eton together, and afterwards at Christchurch, and I always got on very well with him; but somehow he was a man about whom none of the other men cared very much. There was always something strange and secret about him; even at Eton he liked grubbing among books and trying chemical experiments, better than cricket or the boats. That sort of thing would make any boy unpopular. At Oxford it wasn't merely his studious ways and his love of science that went against him; it was a certain habit he had of gazing at us through narrowing lids, as though he were looking at us more from the outside than any one human being has a right to look at any other, and a bored air of belonging to another and higher race, whenever we talked the ordinary chatter about athletics and the Schools.

A wild paper on "Black Magic," which he read to the Essay Society, filled to overflowing the cup of his college's contempt for him. I suppose no man was ever, for so little cause, so much disliked.

When we went down I noticed—for I knew his people at home—that the sentiment of dislike which he excited in most men was curiously in contrast to the emotions which he inspired in women. They all liked him, listened to him with rapt attention, talked of him with enthusiasm undisguised. I watched their strange infatuation with calmness for several years, but the day came when he met Kate Danvers, and then I was not calm any more. She behaved like all the rest of the women, and to her, quite suddenly, Hurst threw the handkerchief. He was not Hurst of Hurstcote then, but his family was good, and his means not despicable, so he and she were conditionally engaged. People said it was a poor match for the beauty of the county; and her people, I knew, hoped she would think better of it. As for me—well, this is not the story of my life, but of his. I need only say that I thought him a lucky man.

I went to town to complete the studies that were to make me M.D.; Hurst went abroad to Paris, or Leipzig, or somewhere, to study hypnotism and prepare notes for his book on "Black Magic." This came out in the autumn, and had a strange and brilliant success. Hurst became famous, famous as men do become nowadays. His writings were asked for by all the big periodicals. His future seemed assured. In the spring they were married; I was not present at the wedding. The practice my father had bought for me in London claimed all my time, I said.

It was more than a year after their marriage that I had a letter from Hurst.

"Congratulate me, old man! Crowds of unknown uncles and cousins have died, and I am Hurst of Hurstcote, which, God wot, I never thought to be. The place is all to pieces, but we can't live anywhere else. If you can get away in September, come down and see us. We shall be installed. I have everything now that I ever longed for—cradle of our race and all that; the only woman in the world for my wife, and— But that's enough for any man, surely.

"JOHN HURST OF HURSTCOTE."

Of course I knew Hurstcote. Who does not? Hurstcote, which, seventy years ago, was one of the most perfect, as well as the finest, brick Tudor mansions in England. The Hurst who lived there seventy years ago noticed one day that his chimneys smoked, and called in a Hastings architect. "Your chimneys," said the local man, "are beyond me, but with the timbers and lead of your castle, and some nice new yellow bricks and stucco, I can build you a snug little house in the corner of your park, much more suitable for a residence than this old red brick building." So they gutted Hurstcote, and built the new house and faced it with stucco. All of which things you will find written in the Guide to Sussex. Hurstcote, when I had seen it, had been the merest shell. How would Hurst make it habitable? Even if he had inherited much money with the castle and intended to restore the building, that would be a work of years, not months. What would he do?

In September I went to see.

Hurst met me at Pevensey Station.

"Let's walk up," he said; "there's a cart to bring your traps. Eh, but it's good to see you again, Bernard."

It was good to see him again. And to see him so changed. And so changed for good, too. He was much stouter, and no longer wore the untidy, ill-fitting clothes of the old days. He was rather smartly dressed in grey stockings and knee-breeches, and wore a velvet shooting-coat. But the most noteworthy change was in his face; it bore no more the eager, inquiring, half-scornful, half-tolerant look, that had won him such ill-will at Oxford. His face now was the face of a man completely at peace with himself and the world.

"How well you look!" I said, as we walked along the level, winding road through the still marshes.

"How much better, you mean!" he laughed. "I know it. Bernard, you'll hardly believe it, but I'm on the way to be a popular man!"

He had not lost his old knack of reading one's thoughts.

"Don't trouble yourself to find the polite answer to that," he hastened to add. "No one knows so well as I how unpopular I was; and no one knows so well why," he added in a very low voice. "However," he went on gaily, "unpopularity is a thing of the past. The folk hereabout call on us, and condole with us on our hutch. A thing of the past, as I said—but what a past it was, eh? You're the only man who ever liked me. You don't know what that's been to me many a dark day and night. When the others were—you know—it was like a hand holding mine, to think of you. I've always thought I was sure of one soul in the world to stand by me."

"Yes," I said—"Yes."

He flung his arm over my shoulder with a frank, boyish gesture of affection, quite foreign to his nature as I had known it. Foreign as the bright frankness of his speech to his old scowling reticence.

"And I know why you didn't come to our wedding," he went on, "but that's all right now, isn't it?"

"Yes," I said again, for indeed it was. There are brown eyes in the world, after all, as well as blue.

"That's well," Hurst answered, and we walked on in satisfied silence, till we passed across the furze-crowned ridge, and went down the hill to Hurstcote. It lies in the hollow, ringed round by its moat, its dark red walls shewing the sky behind them. There was no welcoming sparkle of early litten candle, only the pale amber of the September evening shining through the gaunt unglazed windows.

Three planks and a rough handrail had replaced the old drawbridge. We passed across the moat, and Hurst pulled a knotted rope that hung beside the great iron-bound door. A bell clanged loudly inside. In the moment we spent there waiting, Hurst pushed back a briar that was trailing across the arch, and let it fall outside the handrail.

"Nature is too much with us here," he said, laughing. "The clematis spends its time tripping one up, or clawing at one's hair, and we are always expecting the ivy to force itself through the window and make an uninvited third at our dinner-table."

Then the great door of Hurstcote Castle swung back, and there stood Kate, a thousand times sweeter and more beautiful than ever. I looked at her with momentary terror and dazzlement. She was indeed much more beautiful than any woman with brown eyes could be. My heart almost stopped beating.

"With life or death in the balance: Right!"

To be beautiful is not the same thing as to be dear, thank God. I went forward, and took her hand with a free heart.

It was a pleasant fortnight I spent with them. They had had one tower completely repaired, and in its queer, eight-sided rooms we lived, when we were not out among the marshes, or by the blue sea at Pevensey.

Mrs Hurst had made the rooms pleasant with stuffs from Liberty's, and odds and ends of old oak and beechwood. The grassy space within the castle walls, with its underground passages, its crumbling heaps of masonry, overgrown with lush creepers, was better than any garden. There we met the fresh morning; there we lounged through lazy noons; there the grey evenings found us.

I have never seen any two married people so utterly, so undisguisedly in love as these were. I, the third, had no embarrassment in so being—for their love had in it a completeness, a childish abandonment, to which the presence of a third—a friend—was no burden. A happiness, reflected from theirs, shone on me. The days went by, dreamlike, and brought the eve of my return to London, and to the commonplaces of life.

We were sitting in the courtyard; Hurst had gone to the village to post some letters. A big moon was just shewing over the battlements when Mrs Hurst shivered.

"It's late," she said, "and cold; the summer is gone. Let us go in." So we went into the little warm room, where a wood fire flickered on a brick hearth, and a shaded lamp was already glowing softly. Here we sat on the cushioned seat in the open window, and looked out through the lozenge panes at the gold of the moon, and at the light of her making ghosts in the white mist that rose thick and heavy from the moat.

"I am so sorry that you are going," she said presently; "but you will come and skate on the moat with us at Christmas, won't you? We mean to have a mediaeval Christmas. You don't know what that is? Neither do I; but John does. He is very, very wise."

"Yes," I answered, "he used to know many things that most men don't even dream of as possible to know."

She was silent a minute and then shivered again. I picked up the shawl she had thrown down when we came in, and put it round her.

"Thank you! I think—don't you?—that there are some things that one is not meant to know, and some that one is meant *not* to know. You see the distinction?"

"I suppose so—yes."

"Did it never frighten you in the old days," she went on, "to see that John would never—was always—"

"But he has given all that up now."

"Oh yes, ever since our honeymoon. Do you know, he used to mesmerise me. It was horrible. And that book of his—"

"I didn't know you believed in Black Magic."

"Oh, I don't—not the least bit. I never was at all superstitious, you know. But those things always frighten me just as much as if I believed in them. And besides—I think they are wicked; but John— Ah! there he is! Let's go and meet him."

His dark figure was outlined against the sky behind the hill. She wrapped the soft shawl more closely around her, and we went out into the moonlight to meet her husband.

The next morning when I entered the parlour, I found that it lacked its chief ornament. The sparkling, white and silver breakfast accessories were there, but for my beautiful hostess I looked in vain. At ten minutes past nine Hurst came in looking horribly worried, and more like his old self than I had ever expected to see him.

"I say, old man," he said hurriedly, "are you really set on going back to town to-day—because Kate's ill—really ill I'm afraid. I can't think what's wrong. I want you to see her after breakfast."

I reflected a minute. "I can stay if I send a wire," I said.

"I wish you would, then," Hurst said, wringing my hand, and turning away; "she's been off her head most of the night, talking the most astounding nonsense. You must see her after breakfast. Will you pour out the coffee?"

"I'll see her first, please," I said, and he led me up the winding stair to the room at the top of the tower.

I found her quite sensible, but very feverish. I wrote a prescription, and rode Hurst's mare over to Eastbourne to get it made up. When I got back she was worse. It seemed to be a sort of aggravated marsh fever. I reproached myself with having let her sit by the open window the night before. But I remembered with some satisfaction that I had told Hurst that the place was not quite healthy. I only wish I had insisted on it more strongly.

For the first day or two, I thought it was merely a touch of marsh fever that would pass off with no more worse consequences than a little weakness; but on the third day, I perceived that she would die.

Hurst met me as I came from her bedside, stood back on the narrow landing for me to pass, and followed me down into the little sitting-room, which, deprived for three days of her presence, already bore the air of a room long deserted. He came in after me and shut the door.

"You're wrong," he said abruptly, reading my thoughts as usual; "she won't die—she can't die."

"She will," I bluntly answered, for I am no believer in that worst refinement of torture known as "breaking bad news gently." "Send for any other man you choose. I'll consult with the whole College of Physicians if you like. But nothing short of a miracle can save her."

"And you don't believe in miracles," he answered quietly. "I do, you see."

"My dear old fellow, don't buoy yourself up with false hopes. I know my trade; I wish I could believe I didn't. Go back to her now; you have not very long to be together."

I wrung his hand; he returned the pressure, but said almost cheerfully:

"You know your trade, old man, but there are some things you don't know. Mine, for instance—I mean my wife's constitution. Now, I know that thoroughly. And you mark my words—she won't die. You might as well say *I* was not long for this world."

"*You,*" I said, with a touch of annoyance, "you're good for another thirty or forty years."

"Exactly so," he rejoined quickly, "and so is she. Her life's as good as mine; you'll see—she won't die."

At dusk on the next day she died. He was with her; he had not left her since he had told me that she would not die. He was sitting by her, holding her hand. She had been unconscious for some time, when suddenly she dragged her hand from his, raised herself in bed, and cried out in a tone of acutest anguish:

"John! John! Let me go! For Heaven's sake, let me go!"

Then she fell back dead.

He would not understand—would not believe; he still sat by her, holding her hand, and calling on her by every name that love could teach him. I began to fear for his brain. He would not leave her, so by-and-by I brought him a cup of coffee in which I had mixed an opiate. In about an hour I went back and found him fast asleep, with his face on the pillow close by the face of his dead wife. The gardener and I carried him down to my bedroom, and I sent for a woman from the village. He slept for twelve hours. When he awoke his first words were:

"She is not dead! I must go to her!"

I hoped that the sight of her—pale and beautiful and still—with the white asters about her, and her cold hands crossed on her breast, would convince him; but no. He looked at her and said:

"Bernard, you're no fool; you know as well as I do that this is not death. Why treat it so? It is some form of catalepsy. If she should awake and find herself like this, the shock might destroy her reason."

And to the horror of the woman from the village, he flung the asters on to the floor, covered the body with blankets, and sent for hot-water bottles.

I was now quite convinced that his brain was affected, and I saw plainly enough that he would never consent to take the necessary steps for the funeral.

I began to wonder whether I had not better send for another doctor, for I felt that I did not care to try the opiate again on my own responsibility, and something must be done about the funeral.

I spent a day in considering the matter—a day passed by John Hurst beside his wife's body. Then I made up my mind to try all my powers to bring him to reason, and to this end I went once more into the chamber of death. I found Hurst talking wildly in low whispers. He seemed to be talking to some one who was not there. He did not know me, and suffered himself to be led away. He was in a high fever. He had broken down completely, the kind of break-down which in old novels used to be called brain fever. I actually blessed his illness, because it opened a way out of the dilemma in which I found myself. I wired for a trained nurse from town, and for the local under-taker. In a week she was buried, and John Hurst still lay unconscious and unheeding; but I did not look forward to his first renewal of consciousness.

Yet his first conscious words were not the inquiry I dreaded. He only asked whether he had been ill long, and what had been the matter. When I told him, he just nodded and went off to sleep again.

A few evenings later, I found him excited and feverish, but quite himself mentally. I said as much to him in answer to a question which he put to me:

"There's no brain disturbance now? I'm not mad or anything?"

"No, no, my dear fellow. Everything is as it should be."

"Then," he answered slowly, "I must get up and go to her."

My worst fears were realised.

In moments of intense mental strain the truth sometimes overpowers all one's better resolves. It sounds brutal, horrible. I don't know what I meant to say; what I said was:

"You can't; she's buried."

He sprang up in bed, and I caught him by the shoulders.

"Then it's true," he cried, "and I'm not mad. Oh, great God in Heaven, let me go to her; let me go! It's true! It's true!"

I held him fast, and spoke.

"I am strong—you know that. You are weak and ill; you are quite in my power—we're old friends, and there's nothing I wouldn't do to serve you. Tell me what you mean; I will do anything you wish." This I said to soothe him.

"Let me go to her," he said again.

"Tell me all about it," I repeated. "You are too ill to go to her. I will go, if you can collect yourself and tell me why. You could not walk five yards."

He looked at me doubtfully.

"You'll help me? You won't say I'm mad, and have me shut up? You'll help me?"

"Yes, yes—I swear it." All the time I was wondering what I should do to keep him where he was.

He lay back on his pillows, white and ghastly; his thin features and sunken eyes shewed hawklike above the rough growth of his four weeks' beard. I took his hand. His pulse was rapid, and his lean fingers clenched themselves round mine.

"Look here," he said, "I don't know— There aren't any words to tell you how true it is. I am not mad, I am not wandering. I am as sane as you are. Now listen, and if you have a human heart in you, you'll help me. When I married her, I gave up hypnotism and all the old studies; she hated the whole business. But before I gave it up, I hypnotised her, and when she was completely under my control I forbade her soul to leave her body till my time came to die."

I breathed more freely. Now I understood why he had said: "She *cannot* die."

"My dear old man," I said gently, "dismiss these fancies, and face your grief bravely. You can't control the great facts of life and death by hypnotism. She is dead; she is dead, and the body lies in its place. But her soul is with God who gave it."

"No!" he cried, with such strength as the fever had left in him. "No! no! Ever since I have been ill I have seen her, every day, every night, and always wringing her hands and moaning, 'Let me go, John—let me go.'"

"Those were her last words indeed," I said; "it is natural that they should haunt you. See, you bade her soul not leave her body. It has left it, for she is dead."

His answer came almost in a whisper, borne on the wings of a long, breathless pause.

"She is dead, but her soul has not left her body."

I held his hand more closely, still debating what I should do.

"She comes to me," he went on; "she comes to me continually. She does not reproach, but she implores: 'Let me go, John—let me go.' And I have no more power now; I cannot let her go, I cannot reach her. I can do nothing, nothing. Ah!" he cried, with a sudden, sharp change of voice that thrilled through me to the ends of my fingers and feet. "Ah, Kate, my life, I will come to you! No, no, you shan't be left alone among the dead. I am coming, dear."

He reached his arms out towards the door with a look of longing and love, so really, so patently addressed to a sentient presence, that I turned sharply to see if, in truth, perhaps— Nothing, of course, nothing.

"She is dead," I repeated stupidly. "I was obliged to bury her."

A shudder ran through him.

"I must go and see for myself," he said.

Then I knew—all in a minute—what to do.

"I will go," I said. "I will open her coffin, and if she is not—is not as other dead folk, I will bring her body back to this house."

"Will you go now?" he asked, with set lips.

It was nigh on midnight. I looked into his eyes.

"Yes, now," I said; "but you must swear to lie still till I return."

"I swear it." I saw that I could trust him, and I went to wake the nurse. He called weakly after me, "There's a lanthorn in the tool-shed—and, Bernard—"

"Yes, my poor old chap?"

"There's a screw-driver in the sideboard drawer."

I think until he said that, I really meant to go. I am not accustomed to lie, even to mad people, and I think I meant it till then.

He leaned on his elbow, and looked at me with wide open eyes.

"Think," he said, "what she must feel. Out of the body and yet tied to it, all alone among the dead. Oh, make haste, make haste, for if I am not mad, and I have really fettered her soul, there is but one way."

"And that is?"

"I must die too. Her soul can leave her body when I die."

I called the nurse and left him. I went out, and across the wold to the church, but I did not go in. I carried the screw-driver and the lanthorn, lest he should send the nurse to see if I had taken them. I leaned on the churchyard wall and thought of her. I had loved the woman, and I remembered it in that hour.

As soon as I dared, I went back to him—remember I believed him mad—and told the lie that I thought would give him most ease.

"Well?" he said eagerly, as I entered.

I signed to the nurse to leave us.

"There is no hope," I said, "you will not see your wife again, till you meet her in heaven."

I laid down the screw-driver and the lanthorn, and sat down by him.

"You have seen her?"

"Yes."

"And there's no doubt?"

"There is no doubt."

"Then I *am* mad; but you're a good fellow, Bernard, and I'll never forget it, in this world or the next."

He seemed calmer, and fell asleep with my hand in his. His last word was a "thank-you" that cut me like a knife.

When I went into his room next morning, he was gone. But on his pillow a letter lay, painfully scrawled in pencil, and addressed to me.

"You lied. Perhaps you meant kindly. You don't understand. She is not dead. She has been with me again. Though her soul may not leave her body, thank God it can still speak to mine. That vault—it is worse than a mere churchyard grave. Good-bye!"

I ran all the way to the church, and entered by the open door. The air was chill and dank after the crisp October sunlight. The stone that closed the vault of the Hursts of Hurstcote had been raised and was lying beside the dark, gaping hole in the chancel floor. The nurse, who had followed me, came in before I could shake off the horror that held me moveless. We both went down into the vault. Weak, exhausted by illness and sorrow, John Hurst had yet found strength to follow his love to the grave. I tell you he had crossed that wold alone, in the grey of the cold dawn; alone he had raised the stone and gone down to her. He had opened his wife's coffin, and he lay on the floor of the vault with his wife's body in his arms.

He had been dead some hours.

When I told my wife this story, her brown eyes filled with tears.

"You were quite right, he was mad," she said. "Poor things—poor lovers!"

But sometimes when I wake in the grey morning, and, between waking and sleeping, think of all those things that I must shut out from my sleeping and waking thoughts, I wonder was I right, or was he? Was he mad, or was I idiotically incredulous? For—and it is this thing that haunts me—when I found them dead together in the vault, she had been buried five weeks. But the body that lay in John Hurst's arms, among the mouldering coffins of the Hursts of Hurstcote, was perfect and beautiful as it had been when first he clasped her in his arms, a bride.

The Power of Darkness

It was an enthusiastic send-off. Half the students from her atelier were there, and twice as many more from other studios. She had been the belle of the Artists' Quarter in Montparnasse for three golden months. Now she was off to the Riviera to meet her people, and everyone she knew was at the Gare de Lyon to catch the last glimpse of her. And, as had been more than once said late of an evening, "to see her was to love her." She was one of those agitating blondes, with the naturally rippled hair, the rounded rose-leaf cheeks, the large violet-blue eyes, that looked all things and meant Heaven alone knew how little. She held her court like a queen, leaning out of the carriage window and receiving bouquets, books, journals, long last words, and last longing looks. All eyes were on her, and her eyes were for all—and her smile. For all but one, that is. Not a single glance went Edward's way, and Edward—tall, lean, gaunt, with big eyes, straight nose, and the mouth somewhat too small, too beautiful—seemed to grow thinner and paler before one's eyes. One pair of eyes at least saw the miracle worked, the paling of what had seemed absolute pallor, the revelation of the bones of a face that seemed already covered but by the thinnest possible veil of flesh.

And the man whose eyes saw this rejoiced, for he loved her, like the rest, or not like the rest, and he had had Edward's face before him for the last month, in that secret shrine where we set the loved and the hated, the shrine that is lighted by a million lamps kindled at the soul's flame, the shrine that leaps into dazzling glow when the candles are out and one lies alone on hot pillows to outface the night and the light as best one may.

"Oh, good-bye; good-bye, all of you," said Rose. "I shall miss you. Oh, you don't know how I shall miss you all!"

She gathered the eyes of her friends and her worshippers in a glance, as one gathers jewels on a silken string. The eyes of Edward alone seemed to escape her.

"*En voiture, messieurs et dames!*"

Folk drew back from the train. There was a whistle.

And then at the very last little moment of all, as the train pulled itself together for the start, her eyes met Edward's eyes. And the other man saw the meeting, and he knew—which was more than Edward did.

So when, the light of life having been borne away in the retreating train, the broken-hearted group dispersed, the other man—whose name, by the way, was Vincent—linked his arm in Edward's and asked cheerily:—

"Whither away, sweet nymph?"

"I'm off home," said Edward. "The seven-twenty to Calais."

"Sick of Paris?"

"One has to see one's people sometimes, don't you know, hang it all!" was Edward's way of expressing the longing that tore him for the old house among the brown woods of Kent.

"No attraction here now, eh?"

"The chief attraction has gone, certainly," Edward made himself say.

"But there are as good fish in the sea—"

"Fishing isn't my trade," said Edward.

"The beautiful Rose!" said Vincent.

Edward raised hurriedly the only shield he could find. It happened to be the truth as he saw it.

"Oh," he said, "of course, we're all in love with her—and all hopelessly."

Vincent perceived that this was truth, as Edward saw it.

"What are you going to do till your train goes?" he asked.

"I don't know. Café, I suppose, and a vilely early dinner."

"Let's look in at the Musée Grévin," said Vincent.

The two were friends. They had been school-fellows, and this is a link that survives many a strain too strong to be resisted by more intimate and vital bonds. And they were fellow-students, though that counts for little or much—as you take it. Besides, Vincent knew something about Edward that no one else of their age and standing even guessed. He knew that Edward was afraid of the dark, and why. He had found it out that Christmas which the two had spent at an English country house. The house was full; there was a dance. There were to be theatricals. Early in the new year the hostess meant to "move house" to an old convent, built in Tudor times, a beautiful palace with terraces and clipped yew trees, castellated battlements, a moat, swans, and a ghost story.

"You boys," she said, "must put up with a shake-down in the new house. I hope the ghost won't worry you. She's an old lady in a figured satin dress. Comes and breathes softly on the back of your neck when you're shaving. Then you see her in the glass, and as often as not you cut your throat." She laughed. So did Edward and Vincent and the other young men. There were seven or eight of them.

But that night, when sparse candles had lighted "the boys" to their rooms, when the last pipe had been smoked, the last "Good night" said, there came a fumbling with the handle of Vincent's door. Edward came in, an unwieldy figure, clasping pillows, trailing blankets.

"What the deuce?" queried Vincent, in natural amazement.

"I'll turn in here on the floor if you don't mind," said Edward. "I know it's beastly rot, but I can't stand it. The room they've put me into, it's an attic as big as a barn—and there's a great door at the end, eight feet high, and it leads into a sort of horror hole—bare beams and rafters, and black as night. I know I'm an abject duffer, but there it is—I can't face it."

Vincent was sympathetic; though he had never known a night terror that could not be exorcised by pipe, book, and candle.

"I know, old chap. There's no reasoning about these things," said he, and so on.

"You can't despise me more than I despise myself," Edward said. "I feel a crawling hound. But it is so. I had a scare when I was a kid, and it seems to have left a sort of brand on me. I'm branded 'coward,' old man, and the feel of it's not nice."

Again Vincent was sympathetic, and the poor little tale came out. How Edward, eight years old, and greedy as became his little years, had sneaked down, night-clad, to pick among the outcomings of a dinner party, and how, in the hall, dark with the light of an "artistic" coloured glass lantern, a white figure had suddenly faced him—leaned towards him, it seemed, pointed lead-white hands at his heart. That next day, finding him weak from his fainting fit, had shewn the horror to be but a statue, a new purchase of his father's, had mattered not one whit.

Edward shared Vincent's room, and Vincent, alone of all men, shared Edward's secret.

And now, in Paris, Rose speeding away towards Cannes, Vincent said:—
"Let's look in at the Musée Grévin."

The Musée Grévin is a waxwork show. Your mind, at the word, flies instantly to the excellent exhibition founded by the worthy Mme. Tussaud. And you think you know what waxworks mean. But you are wrong. The Musée Grévin contains the work of artists for a nation of artists. Wax—modelled and retouched till it seems as near life as death is: this is what one sees at the Musée Grévin.

"Let's look in at the Musée Grévin," said Vincent. He remembered the pleasant thrill the Musée had given him, and wondered what sort of a thrill it would give his friend.

"I hate museums," said Edward.

"This isn't a museum," Vincent said, and truly; "it's just waxworks."

"All right," said Edward, indifferently. And they went.

They reached the doors of the Musée in the grey-brown dusk of a February evening.

One walks along a bare, narrow corridor, much like the entrance to the stalls of the Standard Theatre, and such daylight as there may be fades away behind one, and one finds oneself in a square hall, heavily decorated, and displaying with its electric lights Loie Fuller in her accordion-pleated skirts, and one or two other figures not designed to quicken the pulse.

"It's very like Mme. Tussaud's," said Edward.

"Yes," Vincent said; "isn't it?"

Then they passed through an arch, and beheld a long room with waxen groups life-like behind glass—the *coulisses* of the Opéra, Kitchener at Fashoda—this last with a desert background lit by something convincingly like desert sunlight.

"By Jove!" said Edward. "That's jolly good."

"Yes," said Vincent again; "isn't it?"

Edward's interest grew.

The things were so convincing, so very nearly alive. Given the right angle, their glass eyes met one's own, and seemed to exchange with one meaning glances.

Vincent led the way to an arched door labelled "Galerie de la Révolution."

There one saw—almost in the living, suffering body—poor Marie Antoinette in prison in the Temple, her little son on his couch of rags, the rats eating from his platter, the brutal Simon calling to him from the grated window. One almost heard the words: "Holà, little Capet!—are you asleep?"

One saw Marat bleeding in his bath, the brave Charlotte eyeing him; the very tiles of the bath-room, the glass of the windows, with, outside, the very sunlight, as it seemed, of 1793, on that "yellow July evening, the thirteenth of the month."

The spectators did not move in a public place among waxwork figures. They peeped through open doors into rooms where history seemed to be re-lived. The rooms were lighted each by its own sun or lamp or candle. The spectators walked among shadows that might have oppressed a nervous person.

"Fine, eh?" said Vincent.

"Yes," said Edward; "it's wonderful."

A turn of a corner brought them to a room. Marie Antoinette fainting, supported by her ladies; poor, fat Louis by the window looking literally sick.

"What's the matter with them all?" said Edward.

"Look at the window," said Vincent.

There was a window to the room. Outside was sunshine—the sunshine of 1792—and gleaming in it, blonde hair flowing, red mouth half open, what seemed the just-severed head of a beautiful woman. It was raised on a pike, so that it seemed to be looking in at the window.

"I say," said Edward, and the head on the pike seemed to sway before his eyes.

"Mme. de Lamballe. Good thing, isn't it?" said Vincent.

"It's altogether too much of a good thing," said Edward. "Look here—I've had enough of this."

"Oh, you must see the Catacombs," said Vincent; "nothing gruesome, you know. Only early Christians being married and baptized, and all that."

He led the way down some clumsy steps to the cellars which the genius of a great artist has transformed into the exact semblance of the old Catacombs at Rome. The same rough hewing of rock, the same sacred tokens engraved strongly and simply; and among the arches of these subterranean burrowings the life of the early Christians, their sacraments, their joys, their sorrows—all expressed in groups of waxwork as like life as death is.

"But this is very fine, you know," said Edward, getting his breath again after Mme. de Lamballe, and his imagination loved the thought of the noble sufferings and refrainings of these first lovers of the crucified Christ.

"Yes," said Vincent, for the third time; "isn't it?"

They passed the baptism and the burying and the marriage. The tableaux were sufficiently lighted, but little light strayed to the narrow passage where the two men walked, and the darkness seemed to press, tangible as a bodily presence, against Edward's shoulder. He glanced backward.

"Come," he said; "I've had enough."

"Come on, then," said Vincent.

They turned the corner, and a blaze of Italian sunlight struck at their eyes with positive dazzlement. There lay the Coliseum—tier on tier of eager faces under the blue sky of Italy. They were level with the arena. In the arena were crosses; from them drooped bleeding figures. On the sand beasts prowled, bodies lay. They saw it all through bars. They seemed to be in the place where the chosen victims waited their turn, waited for the lions and the crosses, the palm and the crown. Close by Edward was a group—an old man, a woman, and children. He could have touched them with his hand. The woman and the man stared in an agony of terror straight in the eyes of a snarling tiger, ten feet long, that stood up on its hind feet and clawed through the bars at them. The youngest child only, unconscious of the horror, laughed in the very face of it. Roman soldiers, unmoved in military vigilance, guarded the group of martyrs. In a low cage to the left more wild beasts cringed and seemed to growl, unfed. Within the grating, on the wide circle of yellow sand, lions and tigers drank the blood of Christians. Close against the bars a great lion sucked the chest of a corpse, on whose bloodstained face the horror of the death-agony was printed plain.

"Good heavens!" said Edward. Vincent took his arm suddenly, and he started with what was almost a shriek.

"What a nervous chap you are!" said Vincent, complacently, as they regained the street where the lights were, and the sound of voices and the movement of live human beings—all that warms and awakens nerves almost paralyzed by the life in death of waxen immobility.

"I don't know," said Edward. "Let's have a vermouth, shall we? There's something uncanny about those wax things. They're like life—but they're much more like death. Suppose they moved? I don't feel at all sure that they don't move, when the lights are all out and there's no one there."

He laughed.

"I suppose you were never frightened, Vincent?"

"Yes, I was once," said Vincent, sipping his absinthe. "Three other men and I were taking turns by twos to watch by a dead man. It was a fancy of his mother's. Our time was up, and the other watch hadn't come. So my chap—the one who was watching with me, I mean—went to fetch them. I didn't think I should mind. But it was just like you say."

"How?"

"Why, I kept thinking, 'Suppose it should move.' It was so like life. And if it did move, of course it would have been because it *was* alive, and I ought to have been glad, because the man was my friend. But all the same, if he had moved I should have gone mad."

"Yes," said Edward, "that's just exactly it."

Vincent called for a second absinthe.

"But a dead body's different to waxworks," he said. "I can't understand anyone being frightened of *them*."

"Oh, can't you?" The contempt in the other's tone stung him. "I bet you wouldn't spend a night alone in that place."

"I bet you five pounds I do!"

"Done," said Edward, briskly. "At least, I would if you'd got five pounds."

"But I have. I'm simply rolling. I've sold my Dejanira; didn't you know? I shall win your money though, anyway. But you couldn't do it, old man. I suppose you'll never outgrow that childish scare."

"You might shut up about that," said Edward, shortly.

"Oh, it's nothing to be ashamed of; some women are afraid of mice or spiders. I say, does Rose know you're a coward?"

"Vincent!"

"No offence, old boy. One may as well call a spade a spade. Of course, you've got tons of moral courage and all that. But you *are* afraid of the dark—and waxworks!"

"Are you trying to quarrel with me?"

"Heaven in its mercy forbid. But I bet *you* wouldn't spend a night in the Musée Grévin and keep your senses."

"What's the stake?"

"Anything you like."

"Make it that if I do you'll never speak to Rose again, and, what's more, that you'll never speak to me," said Edward, white-hot, knocking down a chair as he rose.

"Done," said Vincent. "But you'll never do it. Keep your hair on. Besides, you're off home."

"I shall be back in ten days. I'll do it then," said Edward, and was off before the other could answer.

Then Vincent, left alone, sat still, and over his third absinthe remembered how, before she had known Edward, Rose had smiled on him more than the others, he thought. He thought of her wide, lovely eyes, her wild-rose cheeks, the scented curves of her hair, and then and there the devil entered into him.

In ten days Edward would undoubtedly try to win his wager. He would try to spend the night in the Musée Grévin. Perhaps something could be arranged before that. If one knew the place thoroughly! A little scare would serve Edward right for being the man to whom that last glance of Rose's had been given.

Vincent dined lightly, but with conscientious care—and as he dined he thought. Something might be done by tying a string to one of the figures and making it move when Edward was going through that impossible night among the effigies that are so like life—so like death. Something that was not the devil said:—

"You may frighten him out of his wits."

And the devil answered: "Nonsense; do him good. He oughtn't to be such a schoolgirl."

Anyway, the five pounds might as well be won to-night as any other night. He would take a great-coat, sleep sound in the place of horrors, and the people who opened it in the morning to sweep and dust would bear witness that he had passed the night there. He thought he might trust to the French love of a sporting wager to keep him from any bother with the authorities.

So he went in among the crowd, and looked about among the waxworks for a place to hide in. He was not in the least afraid of these lifeless images. He had always been able to control his nervous tremors in his time. He was not even afraid of being frightened, which, by the way, is the worst fear of all. As one looks at the room of the poor little Dauphin one sees a door to the left. It opens out of the room on to blackness. There were few people in the gallery. Vincent watched, and, in a moment when he was alone, stepped over the barrier and through this door. A narrow passage ran round behind the wall of the room. Here he hid, and when the gallery was deserted he looked out across the body of little Capet to the gaolers at the window. There was a soldier at the window too. Vincent amused himself with the fancy that this soldier might walk round the passage at the back of the room and tap him on the shoulder in the darkness. Only the head and shoulders of the soldier and the gaoler shewed, so, of course, they could not walk, even if they were something that was not waxwork.

Presently he himself went along the passage and round to the window where they were. He found that they had legs. They were full-sized figures, dressed completely in the costume of the period.

"Thorough the beggars are, even the parts that don't shew—artists, upon my word," said Vincent, and went back to his doorway, thinking of the hidden carving behind the capitals of Gothic cathedrals.

But the idea of the soldier who might come behind him in the dark stuck in his mind. Though still a few visitors strolled through the gallery, the closing hour was near. He supposed it would be quite dark. Then—and now he had allowed himself to be amused by the thought of something that should creep up behind him in the dark—he might possibly be nervous in that passage round which, if waxworks could move, the soldier might have come.

"By Jove!" he said; "one might easily frighten oneself by just fancying things. Suppose there were a back way from Marat's bath-room, and instead of the soldier Marat came out of his bath with his wet towels stained with blood and dabbed them against your neck!"

When next the gallery was deserted he crept out. Not because he was nervous, he told himself, but because one might be, and because the passage was draughty, and he meant to sleep.

He went down the steps into the Catacombs, and here he spoke the truth to himself.

"Hang it all," he said, "I *was* nervous. That fool Edward must have infected me. Mesmeric influences or something."

"Chuck it and go home," said common sense.

"I'm hanged if I do," said Vincent.

There were a good many people in the Catacombs at the moment. Live people. He sucked confidence from their nearness, and went up and down looking for a hiding-place.

Through rock-hewn arches he saw a burial scene—a corpse on a bier surrounded by mourners; a great pillar cut off half the still lying figure. It was all still and unemotional as a Sunday-school oleograph. He waited till no one was near, then slipped quickly through the mourning group and hid behind the pillar. Surprising—heartening, too, to find a plain rush-chair there, doubtless set for the resting of tired officials. He sat down in it, comforted his hand with the commonplace lines of its rungs and back. A shrouded waxen figure just behind him to the left of his pillar worried him a little, but the corpse left him unmoved as itself. A far better place, this, than that draughty passage where the soldier with legs kept intruding on the darkness that is always behind one.

Custodians went along the passages issuing orders. A stillness fell. Then, suddenly, all the lights went out.

"That's all right," said Vincent, and composed himself to sleep.

But he seemed to have forgotten what sleep was like. He firmly fixed his thoughts on pleasant things—the sale of his picture, dances with Rose, merry evenings with Edward and the others. But the thoughts rushed by him like motes in sunbeams—he could not hold a single one of them, and presently it seemed that he had thought of every pleasant thing that had ever happened to him, and that now, if he thought at all, he must think of the things one wants most to forget. And there would be time in the long night to think much of many things. But now he found that he could no longer think.

The draped effigy just behind him worried him again. He had been trying, at the back of his mind, behind the other thoughts, to strangle the thought of it. But it was there, very close to him. Suppose it put out its hand, its wax hand, and touched him? But it was of wax. It could not move. No, of course not. But suppose it *did?*

He laughed aloud, a short, dry laugh, that echoed through the vaults. The cheering effect of laughter has been over-estimated perhaps. Anyhow, he did not laugh again.

The silence was intense, but it was a silence thick with rustlings and breathings, and movements that his ear, strained to the uttermost, could just not hear. Suppose, as Edward had said, when all the lights were out these things did move. A corpse was a thing that had moved, given a certain condition—life. What if there were a condition, given which these things could move? What if such conditions were present now? What if all of them—Napoleon, yellow-white from his death sleep; the beasts from the amphitheatre, gore dribbling from their jaws; that soldier with the legs—all were drawing near to him in this full silence? Those death masks of Robespierre and Mirabeau—they might float down through the darkness till they touched his face. That head of Mme. de Lamballe on the pike might be thrust at him from behind the pillar. The silence throbbed with sounds that could not quite be heard.

"You fool," he said to himself; "your dinner has disagreed with you with a vengeance. Don't be an ass. The whole lot are only a set of big dolls."

He felt for his matches and lighted a cigarette. The gleam of the match fell on the face of the corpse in front of him. The light was brief, and it seemed, somehow, impossible to look by its light in every corner where one would have wished to look. The match burnt his fingers as it went out. And there were only three more matches in the box.

It was dark again, and the image left on the darkness was that of the corpse in front of him. He thought of his dead friend. When the cigarette was smoked out he thought of him more and more, till it seemed that what lay on the bier was not wax. His hand reached forward and drew back more than once. But at last he made it touch the bier and through the blackness travel up along a lean, rigid arm to the wax face that lay there so still. The touch was not reassuring. Just so, and not otherwise, had his dead friend's face felt, to the last touch of his lips. Cold, firm, waxen. People always said the dead were "waxen." How true that was! He had never thought of it before. He thought of it now.

He sat still—so still that every muscle ached; because if you wish to hear the sounds that infest silence you must be very still indeed. He thought of Edward, and of the string he had meant to tie to one of the figures.

"That wouldn't be needed," he told himself. And his ears ached with listening, listening for the sound that, it seemed, *must* break at last from that crowded silence.

He never knew how long he sat there. To move, to go up, to batter at the door and clamour to be let out—that one could have done if one had had a lantern or even a full match-box. But in the dark, not knowing the turnings, to feel one's way among these things that were so like life and yet were not alive—to touch, perhaps, these faces that were not dead and yet felt like death! His heart beat heavily in his throat at the thought.

No; he must sit still till morning. He had been hypnotized into this state, he told himself, by Edward, no doubt; it was not natural to him.

Then, suddenly, the silence was shattered. In the dark something moved, and, after those sounds that the silence teemed with, the noise seemed to him thunder-loud. Yet it was only a very, very little sound, just the rustling of drapery, as though something had turned in its sleep. And there was a sigh—not far off.

Vincent's muscles and tendons tightened like fine-drawn wire. He listened. There was nothing more. Only the silence, the thick silence.

The sound had seemed to come from a part of the vault where long ago, when there was light, he had seen a grave being dug for the body of a young girl martyr.

"I will get up and go out," said Vincent. "I have three matches. I am off my head. I shall really be nervous presently if I don't look out."

He got up and struck a match, refused his eyes the sight of the corpse whose waxen face he had felt in the blackness, and made his way through the crowd of figures. By the match's flicker they seemed to make way for him, to turn their heads to look after him. The match lasted till he got to a turn of the rock-hewn passage. His next match shewed him the burial scene. The little, thin body of the martyr, palm in hand, lying on the rock-floor in patient waiting, the grave-digger, the mourners. Some standing, some kneeling, one crouched on the ground.

This was where that sound had come from, that rustle, that sigh. He had thought he was going away from it. Instead he had come straight to the spot where, if anywhere, his nerves might be expected to play him false.

"Bah!" he said, and he said it aloud. "The silly things are only wax. Who's afraid?"

His voice sounded loud in the silence that lives with the wax people.

"They're only wax," he said again, and touched with his foot contemptuously the crouching figure in the mantle.

And, as he touched it, it raised its head and looked vacantly at him, and its eyes were bright and alive. He staggered back against another figure and dropped the match. In the new darkness he heard the crouching figure move towards him. Then the darkness fitted in round him very closely.

"What was it exactly that sent poor Vincent mad—you've never told me?" Rose asked the question. She and Edward were looking out over the pines and tamarisks across the blue Mediterranean. They were very happy, because it was their honeymoon.

He told her about the Musée Grévin and the wager, but he did not state the terms of it.

"But why did he think you would be afraid?"

He told her why.

"And then what happened?"

"Why, I suppose he thought there was no time like the present—for his five pounds, you know—and he hid among the waxworks. And I missed my train, and, *I* thought, there was no time like the present. In fact, dear, I thought if I waited I should have time to make certain of funking it. So I hid there, too. And I put on my big black capuchon, and sat down right in one of the waxwork groups—they couldn't see me from the gallery where you walk. And after they put the lights out I simply went to sleep. And I woke up—and there was a light, and I heard someone say:—

"'They're only wax,' and it was Vincent. He thought I was one of the wax people till I looked at him; and I expect he thought I was one of them even then, poor chap. And his match went out, and while I was trying to find my railway reading lamp that I'd got near me he began to scream. And the night-watchman came running. And now he thinks everyone in the asylum is made of wax, and he screams if they come near him. They have to put his food near him while he's asleep. It's horrible. I can't help feeling as if it were my fault somehow."

"Of course it's not," said Rose. "Poor Vincent! Do you know, I never *really* liked him."

There was a pause. Then she said:—

"But how was it *you* weren't frightened?"

"I was," he said, "horribly frightened. It—it—sounds idiotic, but I was really. And yet I *had* to go through with it. And then I got among the figures of the people in the Catacombs, the people who died for—for things, don't you know, died in such horrible ways. And there they were, so calm—

and believing it was all right. So I thought about what they'd gone through. It sounds awful rot, I know, dear, but I expect I was sleepy. Those wax people, they sort of seemed as if they were alive, and were telling me there wasn't anything to be frightened about. I felt as if I was one of them—and they were all my friends, and they'd wake me if anything went wrong. So I just went to sleep."

"I think I understand," she said. But she didn't.

"And the odd thing is," he went on, "I've never been afraid of the dark since. Perhaps his calling me a coward had something to do with it."

"I don't think so," said she. And she was right. But she would never have understood how, nor why.

The Shadow

This is not an artistically rounded off ghost story, and nothing is explained in it, and there seems to be no reason why any of it should have happened. But that is no reason why it should not be told. You must have noticed that all the real ghost stories you have ever come close to, are like this in these respects—no explanation, no logical coherence. Here is the story.

There were three of us and another, but she had fainted suddenly at the second extra of the Christmas dance, and had been put to bed in the dressing-room next to the room which we three shared. It had been one of those jolly, old-fashioned dances where nearly everybody stays the night, and the big country house is stretched to its utmost containing—guests harbouring on sofas, couches, settles, and even mattresses on floors. Some of the young men actually, I believe, slept on the great dining-table. We had talked of our partners, as girls will, and then the stillness of the manor house, broken only by the whisper of the wind in the cedar branches, and the scraping of their harsh fingers against our window panes, had pricked us to such a luxurious confidence in our surroundings of bright chintz and candle-flame and fire-light, that we had dared to talk of ghosts—in which, we all said, we did not believe one bit. We had told the story of the phantom coach, and the horribly strange bed, and the lady in the sacque, and the house in Berkeley Square.

We none of us believed in ghosts, but my heart, at least, seemed to leap to my throat and choke me there, when a tap came to our door—a tap faint, not to be mistaken.

"Who's there?" said the youngest of us, craning a lean neck towards the door. It opened slowly, and I give you my word the instant of suspense

113

that followed is still reckoned among my life's least confident moments. Almost at once the door opened fully, and Miss Eastwich, my aunt's housekeeper, companion and general stand-by, looked in on us.

We all said "Come in," but she stood there. She was, at all normal hours, the most silent woman I have ever known. She stood and looked at us, and shivered a little. So did we—for in those days corridors were not warmed by hot-water pipes, and the air from the door was keen.

"I saw your light," she said at last, "and I thought it was late for you to be up—after all this gaiety. I thought perhaps—" Her glance turned towards the door of the dressing-room.

"No," I said, "she's fast asleep." I should have added a good-night, but the youngest of us forestalled my speech. She did not know Miss Eastwich as we others did; did not know how her persistent silence had built a wall round her—a wall that no one dared to break down with the commonplaces of talk, or the littlenesses of mere human relationship. Miss Eastwich's silence had taught us to treat her as a machine; and as other than a machine we never dreamed of treating her. But the youngest of us had seen Miss Eastwich for the first time that day. She was young, crude, ill-balanced, subject to blind, calf-like impulses. She was also the heiress of a rich tallow-chandler, but that has nothing to do with this part of the story. She jumped up from the hearth-rug, her unsuitably rich silk lace-trimmed dressing-gown falling back from her thin collar-bones, and ran to the door and put an arm round Miss Eastwich's prim, lisse-encircled neck. I gasped. I should as soon have dared to embrace Cleopatra's Needle. "Come in," said the youngest of us—"come in and get warm. There's lots of cocoa left." She drew Miss Eastwich in and shut the door.

The vivid light of pleasure in the housekeeper's pale eyes went through my heart like a knife. It would have been so easy to put an arm round her neck, if one had only thought she wanted an arm there. But it was not I who had thought that—and indeed, my arm might not have brought the light evoked by the thin arm of the youngest of us.

"Now," the youngest went on eagerly, "you shall have the very biggest, nicest chair, and the cocoa-pot's here on the hob as hot as hot—and we've all been telling ghost stories, only we don't believe in them a bit; and when you get warm you ought to tell one too."

Miss Eastwich—that model of decorum and decently done duties, tell a ghost story!

"You're sure I'm not in your way," Miss Eastwich said, stretching her hands to the blaze. I wondered whether housekeepers have fires in their rooms even at Christmas time. "Not a bit"—I said it, and I hope I said it as warmly as I felt it. "I—Miss Eastwich—I'd have asked you to come in other times—only I didn't think you'd care for girls' chatter."

The third girl, who was really of no account, and that's why I have not said anything about her before, poured cocoa for our guest. I put my fleecy Madeira shawl round her shoulders. I could not think of anything else to do for her, and I found myself wishing desperately to do something. The smiles she gave us were quite pretty. People can smile prettily at forty or fifty, or even later, though girls don't realise this. It occurred to me, and this was another knife-thrust, that I had never seen Miss Eastwich smile—a real smile—before. The pale smiles of dutiful acquiescence were not of the same blood as this dimpling, happy, transfiguring look.

"This is very pleasant," she said, and it seemed to me that I had never before heard her real voice. It did not please me to think that at the cost of cocoa, a fire, and my arm round her neck, I might have heard this new voice any time these six years.

"We've been telling ghost stories," I said. "The worst of it is, we don't believe in ghosts. No one one knows has ever seen one."

"It's always what somebody told somebody, who told somebody you know," said the youngest of us, "and you can't believe that, can you?"

"What the soldier said, is not evidence," said Miss Eastwich. Will it be believed that the little Dickens quotation pierced one more keenly than the new smile or the new voice?

"And all the ghost stories are so beautifully rounded off—a murder committed on the spot—or a hidden treasure, or a warning . . . I think that makes them harder to believe. The most horrid ghost-story I ever heard was one that was quite silly."

"Tell it."

"I can't—it doesn't sound anything to tell. Miss Eastwich ought to tell one."

"Oh do," said the youngest of us, and her salt cellars loomed dark, as she stretched her neck eagerly and laid an entreating arm on our guest's knee.

"The only thing that I ever knew of was—was hearsay," she said slowly, "till just the end."

I knew she would tell her story, and I knew she had never before told it, and I knew she was only telling it now because she was proud, and this seemed the only way to pay for the fire and the cocoa, and the laying of that arm round her neck.

"Don't tell it," I said suddenly. "I know you'd rather not."

"I daresay it would bore you," she said meekly, and the youngest of us, who, after all, did not understand everything, glared resentfully at me.

"We should just *love* it," she said. "*Do* tell us. Never mind if it isn't a real, proper, fixed up story. I'm certain anything *you* think ghostly would be quite too beautifully horrid for anything."

Miss Eastwich finished her cocoa and reached up to set the cup on the mantelpiece.

"It can't do any harm," she said half to herself, "they don't believe in ghosts, and it wasn't exactly a ghost either. And they're all over twenty—they're not babies."

There was a breathing time of hush and expectancy. The fire crackled and the gas suddenly glared higher because the billiard lights had been put out. We heard the steps and voices of the men going along the corridors.

"It is really hardly worth telling," Miss Eastwich said doubtfully, shading her faded face from the fire with her thin hand.

We all said "Go on—oh, go on—do!"

"Well," she said, "twenty years ago—and more than that—I had two friends, and I loved them more than anything in the world. And they married each other—"

She paused, and I knew just in what way she had loved each of them. The youngest of us said—

"How awfully nice for you. Do go on."

She patted the youngest's shoulder, and I was glad that I had understood, and that the youngest of all hadn't. She went on.

"Well, after they were married, I did not see much of them for a year or two; and then he wrote and asked me to come and stay, because his wife was ill, and I should cheer her up, and cheer him up as well; for it was a gloomy house, and he himself was growing gloomy too."

I knew, as she spoke, that she had every line of that letter by heart.

"Well, I went. The address was in Lee, near London; in those days there were streets and streets of new villa-houses growing up round old brick mansions standing in their own grounds, with red walls round, you know, and a sort of flavour of coaching days, and post chaises, and Blackheath highwaymen about them. He had said the house was gloomy, and it was called 'The Firs,' and I imagined my cab going through a dark, winding shrubbery, and drawing up in front of one of these sedate, old, square houses. Instead, we drew up in front of a large, smart villa, with iron railings, gay encaustic tiles leading from the iron gate to the stained-glass-panelled door, and for shrubbery only a few stunted cypresses and aucubas in the tiny front garden. But inside it was all warm and welcoming. He met me at the door."

She was gazing into the fire, and I knew she had forgotten us. But the youngest girl of all still thought it was to us she was telling her story.

"He met me at the door," she said again, "and thanked me for coming, and asked me to forgive the past."

"What past?" said that high priestess of the *inàpropos,* the youngest of all.

"Oh—I suppose he meant because they hadn't invited me before, or something," said Miss Eastwich worriedly, "but it's a very dull story, I find, after all, and—"

"Do go on," I said—then I kicked the youngest of us, and got up to re-arrange Miss Eastwich's shawl, and said in blatant dumb show, over the shawled shoulder: "Shut up, you little idiot—"

After another silence, the housekeeper's new voice went on.

"They were very glad to see me, and I was very glad to be there. You girls, now, have such troops of friends, but these two were all I had—all I had ever had. Mabel wasn't exactly ill, only weak and excitable. I thought he seemed more ill than she did. She went to bed early and before she went, she asked me to keep him company through his last pipe, so we went into the dining-room and sat in the two arm chairs on each side of the fireplace. They were covered with green leather I remember. There were bronze groups of horses and a black marble clock on the mantelpiece—all wedding-presents. He poured out some whisky for himself, but he hardly touched it. He sat looking into the fire. At last I said:—

"'What's wrong? Mabel looks as well as you could expect.'

"He said, 'Yes—but I don't know from one day to another that she won't begin to notice something wrong. That's why I wanted you to come.

You were always so sensible and strong-minded, and Mabel's like a little bird or a flower.'

"I said yes, of course, and waited for him to go on. I thought he must be in debt, or in trouble of some sort. So I just waited. Presently he said:

"'Margaret, this is a very peculiar house—' He always called me Margaret. You see we'd been such old friends. I told him I thought the house was very pretty, and fresh, and homelike—only a little too new—but that fault would mend with time. He said:—

"'It is new: that's just it. We're the first people who've ever lived in it. If it were an old house, Margaret, I should think it was haunted.'

"I asked if he had seen anything. 'No,' he said, 'not yet.'

"'Heard then?' said I.

"'No—not heard either,' he said, 'but there's a sort of feeling: I can't describe it—I've seen nothing and I've heard nothing, but I've been so near to seeing and hearing, just near, that's all. And something follows me about—only when I turn round, there's never anything, only my shadow. And I always feel that I *shall* see the thing next minute—but I never do—not quite—it's always just not visible.'

"I thought he'd been working rather hard—and tried to cheer him up by making light of all this. It was just nerves, I said. Then he said he had thought I could help him, and did I think anyone he had wronged could have laid a curse on him, and did I believe in curses. I said I didn't—and the only person anyone could have said he had wronged forgave him freely, I knew, if there was anything to forgive. So I told him this too."

It was I, not the youngest of us, who knew the name of that person, wronged and forgiving.

"So then I said he ought to take Mabel away from the house and have a complete change. But he said No; Mabel had got everything in order, and he could never manage to get her away just now without explaining everything—'and, above all,' he said, 'she mustn't guess there's anything wrong. I daresay I shan't feel quite such a lunatic now you're here.'

"So we said good-night."

"Is that all the story!" said the third girl, striving to convey that even as it stood it was a good story.

"That's only the beginning," said Miss Eastwich. "Whenever I was alone with him he used to tell me the same thing over and over again, and at first when I began to notice things, I tried to think that it was his talk that had upset my nerves. The odd thing was that it wasn't only at night—but in broad daylight—and particularly on the stairs and passages. On the staircase the feeling used to be so awful that I have had to bite my lips till they bled to keep myself from running upstairs at full speed. Only I knew if I did I should go mad at the top. There was always something behind me—exactly as he had said—something that one could just not see. And a sound that one could just not hear. There was a long corridor at the top of the house. I have sometimes almost seen something—you know how one sees things without looking—but if I turned round, it seemed as if the thing drooped and melted into my shadow. There was a little window at the end of the corridor.

"Downstairs there was another corridor, something like it, with a cupboard at one end and the kitchen at the other. One night I went down into the kitchen to heat some milk for Mabel. The servants had gone to bed. As I stood by the fire, waiting for the milk to boil, I glanced through the open door and along the passage. I never could keep my eyes on what I was doing in that house. The cupboard door was partly open; they used to keep empty boxes and things in it. And, as I looked, I knew that now it was not going to be 'almost' any more. Yet I said, 'Mabel?' not because I thought it could be Mabel who was crouching down there, half in and half out of the cupboard. The thing was grey at first, and then it was black. And when I whispered, 'Mabel,' it seemed to sink down till it lay like a pool of ink on the floor, and then its edges drew in, and it seemed to flow, like ink when you tilt up the paper you have spilt it on; and it flowed into the cupboard till it was all gathered into the shadow there. I saw it go quite plainly. The gas was full on in the kitchen. I screamed aloud, but even then, I'm thankful to say, I had enough sense to upset the boiling milk, so that when he came downstairs three steps at a time, I had the excuse for my scream of a scalded hand. The explanation satisfied Mabel, but next night he said:—

"'Why didn't you tell me? It was that cupboard. All the horror of the house comes out of that. Tell me—have you seen anything yet? Or is it only the nearly seeing and nearly hearing still?'

"I said, 'You must tell me first what you've seen.' He told me, and his eyes wandered, as he spoke, to the shadows by the curtains, and I turned up all three gas lights, and lit the candles on the mantelpiece. Then we looked at each other and said we were both mad, and thanked God that Mabel at least was sane. For what he had seen was what I had seen.

"After that I hated to be alone with a shadow, because at any moment I might see something that would crouch, and sink, and lie like a black pool, and then slowly draw itself into the shadow that was nearest. Often that shadow was my own. The thing came first at night, but afterwards there was no hour safe from it. I saw it at dawn and at noon, in the dusk and in the firelight, and always it crouched and sank, and was a pool that flowed into some shadow and became part of it. And always I saw it with a straining of the eyes—a pricking and aching. It seemed as though I could only just see it, as if my sight, to see it, had to be strained to the uttermost. And still the sound was in the house—the sound that I could just not hear. At last, one morning early, I did hear it. It was close behind me, and it was only a sigh. It was worse than the thing that crept into the shadows.

"I don't know how I bore it. I couldn't have borne it, if I hadn't been so fond of them both. But I knew in my heart that, if he had no one to whom he could speak openly, he would go mad, or tell Mabel. His was not a very strong character; very sweet, and kind, and gentle, but not strong. He was always easily led. So I stayed on and bore up, and we were very cheerful, and made little jokes, and tried to be amusing when Mabel was with us. But when we were alone, we did not try to be amusing. And sometimes a day or two would go by without our seeing or hearing anything, and we should perhaps have fancied that we had fancied what we had seen and heard—only there was always the feeling of there being something about the house, that one could just not hear and not see. Sometimes we used to try not to talk about it, but generally we talked of nothing else at all. And the weeks went by, and Mabel's baby was born. The nurse and the doctor said that both mother and child were doing well. He and I sat late in the dining-room that night. We had neither of us seen or heard anything for three days; our anxiety about Mabel was lessened. We talked of the future—it seemed then so much brighter than the past. We arranged that, the moment she was fit to be moved, he should take her away to the sea, and I should superintend the moving of their furniture into the new house he had already chosen. He was gayer than I had seen him since his marriage—almost like his old self. When I said good-night to him, he said a lot of things about my having been a comfort to them both. I hadn't done anything much, of course, but still I am glad he said them.

"Then I went upstairs, almost for the first time without that feeling of something following me. I listened at Mabel's door. Everything was quiet. I went on towards my own room, and in an instant I felt that there was something behind me. I turned. It was crouching there; it sank, and the black fluidness of it seemed to be sucked under the door of Mabel's room.

"I went back. I opened the door a listening inch. All was still. And then I heard a sigh close behind me. I opened the door and went in. The nurse and the baby were asleep. Mabel was asleep too—she looked so pretty—like a tired child—the baby was cuddled up into one of her arms with its tiny head against her side. I prayed then that Mabel might never know the terrors that he and I had known. That those little ears might never hear any but pretty sounds, those clear eyes never see any but pretty sights. I did not dare to pray for a long time after that. Because my prayer was answered. She never saw, never heard anything more in this world. And now I could do nothing more for him or for her.

"When they had put her in her coffin, I lighted wax candles round her, and laid the horrible white flowers that people will send near her, and then I saw he had followed me. I took his hand to lead him away.

"At the door we both turned. It seemed to us that we heard a sigh. He would have sprung to her side, in I don't know what mad, glad hope. But at that instant we both saw it. Between us and the coffin, first grey, then black, it crouched an instant, then sank and liquefied—and was gathered together and drawn till it ran into the nearest shadow. And the nearest shadow was the shadow of Mabel's coffin. I left the next day. His mother came. She had never liked me."

Miss Eastwich paused. I think she had quite forgotten us.

"Didn't you see him again?" asked the youngest of us all.

"Only once," Miss Eastwich answered, "and something black crouched then between him and me. But it was only his second wife, crying beside his coffin. It's not a cheerful story, is it? And it doesn't lead anywhere. I've never told anyone else. I think it was seeing his daughter that brought it all back."

She looked towards the dressing-room door.

"Mabel's baby?"

"Yes—and exactly like Mabel, only with his eyes."

The youngest of all had Miss Eastwich's hands, and was petting them.

Suddenly the woman wrenched her hands away, and stood at her gaunt height, her hands clenched, eyes straining. She was looking at something that we could not see, and I know what the man in the Bible meant when he said: "The hair of my flesh stood up."

What she saw seemed not quite to reach the height of the dressing-room door handle. Her eyes followed it down, down—widening and widening. Mine followed them—all the nerves of them seemed strained to the uttermost—and I almost saw—or did I quite see? I can't be certain. But we all heard the long-drawn, quivering sigh. And to each of us it seemed to be breathed just behind us.

It was I who caught up the candle—it dripped all over my trembling hand—and was dragged by Miss Eastwich to the girl who had fainted during the second extra. But it was the youngest of all whose lean arms were round the housekeeper when we turned away, and that have been round her many a time since, in the new home where she keeps house for the youngest of us.

The doctor who came in the morning said that Mabel's daughter had died of heart disease—which she had inherited from her mother. It was that that had made her faint during the second extra. But I have sometimes wondered whether she may not have inherited something from her father. I have never been able to forget the look on her dead face.

The Head

I.

When your personal appearance is best described by the enumeration of your clothes, your character by the trade mark on the gilt waistband of your cigar, and your profession "just anything that comes along, don't you know," you are not exactly the right man in the right place, when you find yourself up to your knees in mud, your carriage with a wheel off lying prone in a ditch several fields off, and your chance of getting to the house, where a music hall star has given you an inconvenient rendezvous, less than the least crumb of the biscuit you wish you had put in your pocket before starting.

Morris Diehl cursed his luck in the grey of a winter's dusk. His driver had left the carriage and gone back with the horses to the inn where he had lunched. His boots were full of water, his high hat seamed and scratched by the skeleton-fingered trees that leaned here and there over the stone walls. His cigar, long since cold, its end wet and flattened and gnawed, lay foul between his lips. He threw it away. He was lost, beyond a doubt lost, on these confounded Derbyshire hills, where every field is just the same as every other field, and the stone walls have no more of individual distinction than the faint blue-grey lines of a copy book.

If he had only had the sense to stay where the coachman had left him or, better still, at the Inn, the Inn down in the valley, where the Station was—where there were lights, and voices and things to drink. Tottie de Vere, the star on whom hung all the hopes of his newest venture—a Company for promoting Cafés Chantants in Manchester, Liverpool, and Bolton—Tottie de Vere had declined to give him any appointment save this: he might call on her between six and seven at Sir Alexander Brisbane's, the grey house with acres of glass, ten miles from anywhere. And he had tried to keep the appointment, tried with unreasonable determination, and there he was.

Lights and voices—and things to drink. To eat, also. For Mr Diehl was not only thirsty. He was hungry as well, and cold and lonely. He thought of the Strand and the lights of the Strand, lights from restaurants and theatres, where one smelt French cooking, and the patchouli, and the Regalias. These were to him what, to some of us, the home pastures and the scent of stocks and woodsmoke are. He had waited by the carriage till he had grown certain that all men were alike and that his driver would, warmed and comforted in the ale-house, not be such a fool as to keep his promise and come back "with a trap." He had walked up and down the road for a while, the bleak wind nuzzling in between his neck and the fur collar of his big coat; and then he had started to reach Sir Alexander's on foot, seen a light, and been beguiled by it to what he esteemed a short-cut. Even if it were not Sir Alexander's light yet any light meant a possible fire—shelter, at any rate, from that too intimate North-Easter.

He was going now, difficultly towards the light. Across fields and over the eternal sameness of grey walls—black, they seemed, in that sombre twilight of cold stars. Beyond the last wall was a little hill brook. He was in it almost knee-deep before he guessed at anything worse than the cold muddy pastures. The next wall had a gate; he saw the blacker blank and made for it. His fur-lined coat caught on its hasp and ripped, loudly. And his hat was struck by some silly arch or other above the gate, and fell, rolling hollowly on the flags.

"Damn," said Mr Diehl. "Oh, damn and blast." He groped for the hat in the dark dampness, found it; and then he was at the door of the cottage whose windows, all alight, had beckoned him from afar.

"There must be a wedding or a wake," said he. "Copy, either way." He was, casually, a journalist when financial enterprises were cold to him.

He knocked. He had not been conscious of any movement in the house, but now he was conscious of a cessation of movement, and of a silence, as though something inside the house were holding its breath.

"Who's there?" The voice came from behind the door—low down, as though the speaker had been trying to look out into the dark through the keyhole.

"I've lost my way," said Mr Diehl.

"You'll find it—some way or other," said the voice.

"I'm very wet—and tired. I should be very grateful for a night's lodging, Sir."

He added the Sir because the note of the voice was distinctly feminine, and he saw that the door would open more readily to one whose honesty of purpose was so clear and fine, that it could persist even in the face of the conviction that there was "a man in the house." Mr Diehl's mind—it was not the mind of a fool—pictured a faded woman, her terror at this late visit soothed and charmed by the solid compliments it was part of his trade to sow broadcast, with both hands, on any soil. The harvest, he knew, rarely failed.

"Ah, have pity," he said, all the pathos of a hundred melodramas reinforcing the earnest pleading of gross physical discomfort. "I am lost on these wild moors—I shall die if you do not assist me. Have pity on me and God will reward you."

"You can go back the way you came," said the voice.

"I shall die," he said, piteously, but very distinctly, as his elocution master had taught him in the days when he meant to be an actor. "I shall die if you turn me away. My death will be at your door— Ah, save me, for the love of God."

"For the love of God?" the voice repeated slowly. "For the love . . ."

The rest was lost in the rusty withdrawal of bolts. The door creaked open a brilliant inch.

"No one's crossed this door this ten years past," said the voice—"but I can't let a human creature perish by fire or by cold. For the love of God, come in." The door was flung back. Within was a little square hall or lobby—narrow stairs led up in front of Mr Diehl. To the right, a closed door; to the left, the outer door held open.

"Go and stand on the stairs," said the thin treble voice, "till I get the door shut."

From the stairs Morris watched to see the door closed by that spare, fluttering woman's form. But it was a man who shut the door and barred it, and then turned to the visitor the cold, calm face of one wholly self-possessed.

"Come in," he said. "Since you *are* here, I'll do what I can for you. Get off your wet things. I'll go and fetch you a change."

Diehl, alone in a fire-lit kitchen, threw off the wet fur coat across a brown wood settle, loosened his squelching patent leather boots, and heard above him the muffled sound of footsteps on old worm-eaten boards, the creak of old beams, the opening and shutting of drawers and presses.

He had got to bare feet and a costume like that of a Corsican brother in reduced and muddy circumstances when his host returned, an armful of clothing over his arm.

"Here," he said in his thin treble, "get into these. It'll be easy. I was a bigger man than ever you'll be."

He was, now, a smaller man—smaller by the stooping shoulders, the narrow chest, the yellow leanness of wrists and neck, by, in a word, age. He was an old man, white-haired and pale. Nothing was young in face and figure, save only the eyes—and they would not have shone amiss in the face of an adventurer of twenty.

Hot gin and water, the generous half of a plate-pie, one's feet in borrowed large shoes among the grey ashes, to whose centre fire had been forced to life by big bellows . . .

Morris Diehl expanded—and, when expanded, he looked better than in his fur coat. He was resolved to stay the night. He pledged his host again and again in the hot sugary drink, adding strength to the other's glass from the brown demijohn, whenever the old man left the fire for more wood, or to fill the kettle, or to bring out his tobacco jar from the disused oven where he stored it—"to keep moist," he said. He grew more cordial, and Diehl, who was by nature an actor anywhere but on the boards, which paralysed him, set so gay a tune of good fellowship that the other's mind soon danced to it.

"I'm glad I let you in. Yes, by God, I'm glad I broke my vow. You're a good fellow, sir, pardoning the liberty, and this night's the whitest I've known for ten years. How old would you take me to be, now?"

The question was awkward. As a woman of thirty is said to subtract passionately to make a total of twenty-seven, so men who are far gone in their seventies will add to their years, and claim your amazed admiration as gaffers of eighty-six.

Diehl looked hard at the old man. He would have liked to rest his decision on the spinning of a coin.

"Not much past sixty," struck him as a tactful compromise.

The old man laughed, well pleased, as it seemed.

"I'm forty-three, come Lady Day, and seven days beyond," he said. "I was born on All Fools' Day, three-and-forty years ago, and christened April by the same token, like the fool I am. April Vane's my name. 'Vane by name and vain by nature,' they used to say when I was a young man—though you wouldn't think it to look at me now."

"I beg your pardon." Diehl had no other counter ready.

"Not at all, sir, not at all," the old man rejoined. "It 'ud be a wonder if you could guess my age. Why, my hair went white like you see it—in three days."

"You had some shock, I suppose," said Morris, and he sipped the hot gin; "it's a sad world, God help us."

"I don't tell my story to strangers," said the other, with shrill, sudden dignity.

"I trust," said Diehl in his best manner, "that I can sympathise with another man's sorrows without seeking to thrust myself into his confidence."

Even as he spoke, he saw how well the old man, the remote house, the air of mystery, would serve him in an article for the *Daily Bellower*—could he but learn the secret of this hermit's grief. He saw the headlines:

AN ENGLISH HERMIT
TRAGIC STORY
A BROKEN LIFE.

"No," said the other; "no—of course not. You're a gentleman. Anyone could see that. Let alone your fur coat."

"I've known trouble myself," said the guest, and told a tale. A long tale full of pathetic incidents, a tale whose dénouement may have been suggested by the prostrate stump of his cigar against the leg of the table—by that, or by something more subtle.

"I saw my angel girl," he ended, "at the window of that burning house. How could I save her? I rushed forward. 'Darling,' I cried, 'I am coming to rescue you!' I plunged among the burning *débris,* and knew no more, till I woke in hospital with a broken heart—and this."

He pulled up his sleeve and shewed a scar, got in a drunken fight with a Jew in Johannesburg—the weapons, whisky bottles.

"They cured my face burns," he added, smoothing his heavy moustache, "these hardly shew, even by daylight, but that scar I shall carry to my grave."

There was a silence. Then,

"Why did you go on living?" asked the other man, his voice tense as the string of a violin.

"I . . . oh . . . my poor old mother," said Diehl, whose mother had died in giving birth to him, her only child; "for her sake, don't you know, and my little sister."

"*I* went on living," said the other man, and now his voice was no longer like stretched wire, but like the sharp, unyielding blade of a steel poignard. "I went on living because . . ."

There was a silence. Diehl could almost hear his heart beat, so sure he was that there was here material for headlines—so keen was he to secure it.

He sighed elaborately. "Ah," he said, "it is a relief to tell your troubles to some one who understands."

He was quite right to say it. He really sometimes had a wonderful flair for the things to be said and not to say.

"Does it *really?*" asked the man with the young eyes—"relief, I mean? I've lived here ten years, and never a word except when I bought the things I needed. *Does* talking help? Are you sure? Doesn't it open the old wounds wide till the blood squirts out of them? Don't you wish afterwards that you'd held your silly tongue? Aren't you ashamed, and afraid, and sick with yourself for every word that's passed your lips about *her?*"

"No," said Diehl slowly, stretching his feet towards the ashes' red centre, "no; but then I've never told my story before to anyone but you. There's something about you—I don't know what it is—that makes me feel I can trust you. So I'm glad I've told you my story. If it's not bored you?"

The last five words were a false lead, but the other man did not notice it.

"I don't know," he said, "you may be right; and perhaps if I told some one I could trust, my brain and heart would leave off feeling as though they were going to burst, and make my clean floor all in a mess. You don't think I'm mad, do you?"

It was just what he was thinking, so, suddenly very anxious to be alone, with a locked door between him and his host, he said hastily:

"Not at all. But I see I've awakened painful memories with my talk.

Will you let me sleep here—on the settle—on the floor—anywhere—I don't want a bed. I won't give an ounce of trouble. May I?"

"May you what?"

"Spend the night," said Diehl and, laboriously explaining, added, "Sleep here, you know."

"In this house?"

"Of course."

"Yes." The answer was very strong, very definite. "You shall sleep here in this house—if you can. But first I should like to shew you the reason why I never sleep in this house. I sleep in the croft when it's warm, and, when it's winter, in the barn. But I keep the lights burning all night in every room."

"I don't half like this," Morris Diehl told himself, and perceived that attractive headlines may be bought too dearly. Aloud he said: "I'm so tired, I could sleep anywhere. I believe I'm almost asleep now. Won't you shew me whatever it is to-morrow?"

"To-morrow may never come," said the host cheerfully. "I'll go first—just to turn the lights full up and that. Then you shall see."

He went out, quite quietly and soberly, and Mr Diehl shivered. Now that he was warm and gin-filled, the bleak, windy hill-side, in the chessboard of those confounded stone walls, seemed a safety lightly thrown away.

"Alone with a lunatic," he mused, "in a house a hundred miles from anywhere." He fingered a short broad knife, whose sheath fitted closely against his hip.

"If the worst comes to the worst—in self-defence," he assured himself. "But all the same, I jolly well wish I was jolly well out of it. Silly lunatic!"

"Come, *now!*" said the voice of the silly lunatic, and said it so trustfully, yet so compellingly, that Mr Diehl rose and followed it, half reassured, half curious, and wholly overmastered.

"It's in the cellar," said the voice; "people do pry so."

Mr Diehl drew back; he could not help it.

"You're not afraid of a *cellar*," said the voice; "besides, it's what we call a basement in London."

Morris Diehl felt his knife's comforting weight and followed the voice. The stairs were of stone, broad and shallow—there were many of them.

The wavering, yellow light of the lamp the other man carried shewed the stairs neatly yellowed, as the Mid Country lovingly yellows the stones which make the floors to its homes.

The stairs ended in a flagged passage, with doors. Outside the right-hand door the lamp-bearer paused.

"You told me your story with words," said he. "I never heard so many words all different in all my born days. I haven't got no power of jaw like that there. You told me your story; and it's the same as my story. That's why I'm a-going to shew you my story. 'Cause I can't use my tongue worth tuppence—but my hands I can. Now, don't you be frightened; it ain't real."

Mr Diehl reassured himself with a laugh.

"I'm not so easily frightened," he said.

"Nor don't you laugh neither," said the old man, with sudden, breathless intensity. "I couldn't answer for myself what I should do, if you was to laugh in there. It's the work of my hands. And I love the work of my hands, same as Almighty God did. Don't you go to laugh in there, sir, or it'll be the worse for both of us. But you wouldn't," his voice grew suddenly tender, "ain't you shewed me your 'art—put it into my 'and to look at? Don't I know you?"

The dramatic instinct told Mr Diehl to hold out his hand, in the dim lamplight, and press the other man's, with a fine show of manly emotion.

"I was a stone-mason by trade," said the host, "apprenticed in the King's Road, Chelsea, I was; that's how I got the hang of it."

Mr Diehl had a sudden, swift vision of an elaborate monument erected in the cellar, over the body of the victim of homicidal mania.

"Now," said the other, and flung open the door.

Mr Diehl was prepared for a shock of some sort, but he was not prepared for the shock he got.

The opened door disclosed a village street, lit warm and red, a village street at night. It was the village where the inn was that he wished he had stayed at—where the lights were, and the voices, and the drinks. There, by the same token, was the Inn, its sign emblazoned with the arms of the local land-owner, lit redly by the flames of conflagration. There was the square church tower, flushed against a dark sky, the tombstones in the raised churchyard, gleaming rosy beneath the yew shadows. There was a crowd in the street—men with pails and cans of water. This side of the Inn, half the street was in flames; from the window of a burning house a girl leaned out; below, a man, holding a ladder, was in act to plant it against the window. At his feet lay a body—a dead man, as it seemed, but not dead by burning. Blood shewed at mouth and nose. The whole thing was worked out, with wax and wood and paint and paper, and a dozen odd, yet adequate, materials, at much less than half life-size, but so perfect were the perspective and the proportion, that that scene would have appeared to a spectator half-way up the village street just as, and not otherwise than, it now appeared to the spectator at the cellar door. The peculiar and desperate terror—the mad, splendid heroism that fire engenders—these were here, visible to the onlooker.

"Splendid. Ripping. A1." The words sprang to Mr Diehl's lips . . . and stayed there. The other man was speaking, and in a low, thin, untroubled voice.

"That's me," he said, "with the ladder. And that Dog in the gutter—that's him she threw me over for. She was Mrs Dog, her that was to have been Mrs April Vane. But I loved her. That's her leanin' out of their bedroom window. And when the fire broke out, where was he? In heaven, where he'd got the right to be by the marriage lines? Not him! He was in the public silly drunk. When I come along, he was crying—crying there in front of the house where she was a-burning, crying, and shivering, and saying, 'Oh, I shall be burnt, I know I shall.' And she was screaming, 'For God's sake save the child!'"

"What did you do?" Mr Diehl's voice was tactfully attuned.

"Knocked him down, of course. Thought I'd killed him. Wish I had. Then, when I'd got the ladder, and set it up against the window, I was three-quarters up it, when the window-frame went—burnt from underneath. I never see'd him again. He went to London, I've heard say. But I've made his face. You go in an' look, and you'll see the man I wish I'd swung for. If he'd been where he ought to a bin . . . but he left her all alone, along of the kid that wasn't three days old."

Again Morris wrung his hand. The vision of attractive headlines had faded, grown dim, vanished in the red glow of the burning village.

He walked gingerly into the picture, and looked closely at the wax puppets. Perfect in every detail, each little effigy was in itself a finer work of art even than the tableau which included them all.

"It's . . . it's beautiful," said Morris Diehl. "I never saw anything like it."

"It's taken me my life to make," said its maker.

"But why did you make it so small—why not life-size ? There'd have been room—for part of it, anyway."

"Money," came sharply the reply. "I've only got the house and the croft, and thirty pound a year that come to me from an uncle—too late for me to marry her."

"The whole thing's a marvel. You ought to have been a sculptor, with a proper studio and all that," said the guest.

"I ought to have been a married man with kids of my own," said the host.

"Wouldn't you like to make all this shoe life-size?" Morris Diehl asked gently.

"I'm putting by every week for that very thing."

"I could advance you the money," said the man who took his living where he found it.

"No, I won't be beholden to nobody." The tone was decisive.

"You needn't be beholden. Come to London. I'll find you a fine big room, twice the size of this; you shall make the things life-size—the best materials money can buy. We'll charge a shilling a head to come in and see it. You'll pay me back in no time, and make your fortune besides."

"I don't want to make my fortune," said the old man, staring with his young eyes at the blazing village street. "I want to get alongside of *him*."

"Well," said Mr Diehl, "you're much more likely to do that in London than here, you know. Suppose he saw the outside of our show, having been in a fire himself, it's a million to one he'd turn in to have a look—and then you could tell him what you thought of him."

"Do you think he *would?* Do you?"

"Certain of it," said Mr Diehl, who thought nothing less likely.

"Then I'll do it. All life-size—life-size."

"You could have men to help you."

"Not with the faces. The houses and that, I don't say. Not the faces."

"Of course not the faces," Mr Diehl assented cordially. "Let's come back to the fire, and talk it over. And to-morrow we'll get the agreement signed—and Tottie de Vere can go to the deuce. This is a big thing we're in now."

"Eh?" the other party to the agreement queried. He had not heard. All his senses were deep plunged in the joy of his masterpiece. He sighed at last, and spoke.

"There ought to be *noise*," he said—"that's the worst thing about a fire; when it's taking hold, it's as quiet as a mouse. When it's got hold, it roars like a lion, and screams—like a woman."

"We'll make it scream and roar. This thing's got to go. And it will go," said Morris Diehl.

II.

It did go. The whole picture—graduated houses, the little figures of wood, and wax, and paper, the ingenious lanterns that lighted, the tinsel flames that gleamed—all was taken to London, and set up in a big attic in Fitzroy Street. Mr Diehl brought men to see it. Men with shiny hats and fur coats, and cigars like his own. And when they had seen, they went away and drank brandy and soda at marble-topped tables, while Morris Diehl talked. And they "came into it" with him, as he had known they would. April Vane was shy and moody at first; would have no help; but when he saw the life-sized body, produced by a trained workman from one of his own little models, he drew a long breath. "You may go ahead," he said. "I'll have more time for the faces."

It cost the enterprising Mr Diehl a great deal of patience, and his enterprising friends a great deal of money. The big fight was over the subject of the tableau. Vane wanted to reproduce the village scene, exactly as it had been burnt on his mind. Diehl wanted the Great Fire of London, with old London Bridge, and the heads of the traitors above the gate. But though Vane had been the other man's slave, since the night he had thought he had seen the other man's heart, he was obstinate till Diehl said: "More people will come to the Great Fire of London than just to a village fire; you've got more chance of seeing *him*."

Then Vane yielded.

No expense was spared. The best scene-painters and carpenters that the Syndicate could buy for money were bought. An eminent archaeologist was fee'd to advise; an expert in acoustics solved the problem of the roar of fire triumphant. The thing was boomed a month in advance by all the venal press. A big place in the West End, that had failed as an Art Gallery, was hired for this that should not fail. Vane was often wearied, often disheartened.

"I like the other best," he said; "that was mine. This will be every-body's."

"Wait till you see the real thing all put together," Diehl urged continu-ally. He was very gentle and patient. It was important to him to keep the old man's adoration alive. "*That* will be yours, and you'll never be able to leave it. You mark my words."

The old man marked them, and they came true.

The thing caught on. "Have you seen the Great Fire of London?" people asked each other between dances and during dinners, in the train and on the tops of omnibuses. "Like Madame Tussaud's? Oh *no,* not in the least. It's absolutely thrilling. Just for the first moment, you can hardly believe it's not real. You *must* go!"

And everybody went. And it was not like Madame Tussaud's, nor like any waxwork show that ever was before. To the making of Madame Tus-saud's goes, perhaps, talent. To the making of the Musée Grévin, certainly, genius. But to the making of this went the heart and soul of a man.

And from the first moment, when he saw the completed picture per-fect, from the life-size figures in the foreground to the little paper figures in the far distance, he gave himself up to it, as to his real life. The interludes, when he shewed it to visitors mechanically warned not to pass its low barri-er, explained it in a monologue learned by heart—these were dull dreams. The real moments were those when he was alone—could overstep the bar-riers, clap the hurrying soldier on the back, whisper encouragement to the old woman hastening away on her son's strong arm, calling shrilly by name these images of dead citizens, who had been alive and furious in flight un-der the horror of that great blaze. For to him they were not strangers out of the time of the Second Charles. Each wore the face of some man or wom-an in the Derbyshire village. But to his own effigy he never spoke—nor to the woman whose face looked out of the burning window, nor to the corpse that lay at the feet of the ladder-bearer. For now there was no room for doubt that it was the figure of a corpse. That change he had made with-out consulting Mr Diehl and the Syndicate. Its mouth was bloody, as had been the mouth of the little effigy in the Derbyshire cellar, and the mouth of the man whom he had struck down long ago under the eyes of the de-serted wife. Only now the throat too was bloody.

"Oh, let him alone," said Mr Diehl, when one of the Syndicate remarked that by Jove it was just a bit too ghastly; "it pleases him, and you can't lay the horror on too thick for the B.P."

April Vane slept at his lodgings, but he did nothing else there, and not that every night. Sometimes he slept in the gallery on one of the red velvet seats, and always he ate and drank there, talking to the figures whenever he was alone with them. "They're company for me," he said, when Diehl tried remonstrance. And Diehl noted curiously that the life-sized figures did not hold for their maker the horror that, in the first little figures, had driven him to sleep in barn or croft—anywhere but in the house that held them.

It was in August, when the crowd had worn thin, that Vane stayed away for one day. "I've seen *him*," he told Diehl, standing by his bedside very early, for he had told the hotel people that it was a matter of life and death. "I must have a day off; I must try to find him."

"But who's to run the show?" asked Diehl, in his blue silk pyjamas and blue jowl.

"I must have my day off," said Vane. "I don't want to worry you, but I must have one day off. Shut the show up, or run it yourself."

The show was, that day, run by Mr Diehl. The takings were two bags of silver only that day—and that day the head was stolen. It was the head of the corpse, broken off sharp at the neck, where the blood began. It was stolen, and the careless, silk-hatted custodian knew no more than you or I who had done it.

Vane had not found the man he sought—but when he found out that theft he forgot the fruitless search. His grief was like that of a mother who loses her child, a woman who loses her lover.

"But it's all right," Diehl told him again and again. "Throw the corner of the mantle up—so—and it'll never shew. Or leave it as it is—it's pretty average ghastly like that."

It was. But—

"I want his face," Vane said, again and again.

"Well, then, for God's sake *make* his face"—Diehl was losing patience a little at last. "Make his face again, and have done with it!" he said, and lit one of his eternal cigars; "you can do it at home in the evenings."

"I can't do it," said Vane, very low. "I've been trying—I can't see his face."

"You sleep on it," said Mr Diehl cheerfully; "it'll come back to you all right in the morning. Besides, you've got the little one."

"I cut the face off that," said Vane gently; "I cut it off a little bit at a time, to see if it would bleed. I can't remember his face."

"That head must have been stolen for a lark," said Diehl. "Look here! I'll advertise for it, and we'll get it back all right."

"Yes—" said Vane, with trembling eagerness. "Get it back. I must see his face."

He saw it next day, on the shoulders of a living man—a tall, thick-set man, with dirty hands and a ready-made suit, who knocked at the gallery door, just as it was being closed. The same face, but not the same expression.

"You were advertising for a head," said the man.

"Yes," said Vane. "Come in," and he shut the door on the two of them.

"Well, I ain't a-goin' to name no names, but a pal of mine come in here day before yesterday, and one of your blasted dolls had got my pal's face—so he pinched it."

"Why?" Vane softly asked.

"Well, if a man ain't got a right to his own chump, what has he got a right to? But he'll let you have it back, but not for the fiver you offers. I take it if you offers five, you'll give twenty. Say the word, and put it down in writing to prevent mistakes, and I guarantee you shall have the head."

"Yes," said Vane. "I shall have the head."

He advanced on the other man, and now, for the first time, his own face shewed plainly.

"Great God,"—the man retreated, his hands held out as if to keep off something; and now he looked like the head that he had stolen. "My great God, it's April Vane."

"Yes, you'd better call on your God. It's April Vane," April Vane said, and came at him.

It must have been a couple of days later that Diehl strolled in at closing time with that member of the Syndicate who had felt so squeamish about the cut throat. The lights were low. There was no blaze to light up the picture, and the machine was silent that, in the day, roared and screamed in the very voice of fire.

"So you've got the head all right; you remember I told you you would," said Mr Diehl, glancing at the corpse.

"Yes," said April. "I've got the head—I remembered."

Mr Diehl went into the enclosure, and the cinders crunched under his boots.

"By Jove," he said, "you're an artist, Vane. I say, Montague, look at the corpse, the thing you didn't like—why, it's the best of the lot. You've improved it, Vane, old chap. It's just the old expression, but by George it's more lifelike than ever. What is it? something in the lie of the body, I suppose. It's just like life, isn't it now, Monty?"

"It is more like death," said Montague. "I don't like it, and it's stuffy in here and the place is as quiet as a churchyard. Come along out."

"You're a schoolgirl, Montague, a silly schoolgirl! I believe you're frightened of the thing." Mr Diehl kicked it contemptuously and without violence. "Good night, Vane. Why don't you go to one of the Halls and have a gay evening. I'll stand treat."

"You're always kind," said Vane gratefully, "but all the evenings will be gay now. I have got the head. I have remembered."

The two members of the Great Fire Syndicate went out into the light of Regent Street.

"Ugh," said Montague, "that place gives me the horrors."

"It's jolly well meant to," said Diehl, taking out his cigar-case. "That corpse . . ."

"It's not canny," said Montague and he laughed, not quite easily. "Why, it makes me fancy . . . I say, what's that on your boot? Good God, man, it's blood, as the chap says in the story."

"Don't talk rot," said Diehl. He did not see that his right foot had stained the pavement. Montague stopped.

"But—it *is* blood," he said.

The Three Drugs

I.

Roger Wroxham looked round his studio before he blew out the candle, and wondered whether, perhaps, he looked for the last time. It was large and empty, yet his trouble had filled it, and, pressing against him in the prison of those four walls, forced him out into the world, where lights and voices and the presence of other men should give him room to draw back, to set a space between it and him, to decide whether he would ever face it again—he and it alone together. The nature of his trouble is not germane to this story. There was a woman in it, of course, and money, and a friend, and regrets and embarrassments—and all of these reached out tendrils that wove and interwove till they made a puzzle-problem of which heart and brain were now weary. It was as though his life depended on his deciphering the straggling characters traced by some spider who, having fallen into the ink-well, had dragged clogged legs in a black zig-zag across his map of the world.

He blew out the candle and went quietly downstairs. It was nine at night, a soft night of May in Paris. Where should he go? He thought of the Seine, and took—an omnibus. The chestnut trees of the Boulevards brushed against the sides of the one that he boarded blindly in the first light street. He did not know where the omnibus was going. It did not matter. When at last it stopped he got off, and so strange was the place to him that for an instant it almost seemed as though the trouble itself had been left behind. He did not feel it in the length of three or four streets that he traversed slowly. But in the open space, very light and lively, where he recognised the Taverne de Paris and knew himself in Montmartre, the trouble set its teeth in his heart again, and he broke away from the lamps and the talk to struggle with it in the dark quiet streets beyond.

139

A man braced for such a fight has little thought to spare for the detail of his surroundings. The next thing that Wroxham knew of the outside world was the fact that he had known for some time that he was not alone in the street. There was someone on the other side of the road keeping pace with him—yes, certainly keeping pace, for, as he slackened his own, the feet on the other pavement also went more slowly. And now they were four feet, not two. Where had the other man sprung from? He had not been there a moment ago. And now, from an archway a little ahead of him, a third man came.

Wroxham stopped. Then three men converged upon him, and, like a sudden magic-lantern picture on a sheet prepared, there came to him all that he had heard and read of Montmartre—dark archways, knives, Apaches, and men who went away from homes where they were beloved and never again returned. He, too—well, if he never returned again, it would be quicker than the Seine, and, in the event of ultramundane possibilities, safer.

He stood still and laughed in the face of the man who first reached him.

"Well, my friend?" said he, and at that the other two drew close.

"Monsieur walks late," said the first, a little confused, as it seemed, by that laugh.

"And will walk still later, if it pleases him," said Roger. "Good-night, my friends."

"Ah!" said the second, "friends do not say adieu so quickly. Monsieur will tell us the hour."

"I have not a watch," said Roger, quite truthfully.

"I will assist you to search for it," said the third man, and laid a hand on his arm.

Roger threw it off. That was instinctive. One may be resigned to a man's knife between one's ribs, but not to his hands pawing one's shoulders. The man with the hand staggered back.

"The knife searches more surely," said the second.

"No, no," said the third quickly, "he is too heavy. I for one will not carry him afterwards."

They closed round him, hustling him between them. Their pale, degenerate faces spun and swung round him in the struggle. For there was a struggle. He had not meant that there should be a struggle. Someone would hear—someone would come.

But if any heard, none came. The street retained its empty silence, the houses, masked in close shutters, kept their reserve. The four were wrestling, all pressed close together in a writhing bunch, drawing breath hardly through set teeth, their feet slipping, and not slipping, on the rounded cobble-stones.

The contact with these creatures, the smell of them, the warm, greasy texture of their flesh as, in the conflict, his face or neck met neck or face of theirs—Roger felt a cold rage possess him. He wrung two clammy hands apart and threw something off—something that staggered back clattering, fell in the gutter, and lay there.

It was then that Roger felt the knife. Its point glanced off the cigarette-case in his breast pocket and bit sharply at his inner arm. And at the sting of it Roger knew that he did not desire to die. He feigned a reeling weakness, relaxed his grip, swayed sideways, and then suddenly caught the other two in a new grip, crushed their faces together, flung them off, and ran. It was but for an instant that his feet were the only ones that echoed in the street. Then he knew that the others too were running.

It was like one of those nightmares wherein one runs for ever, leaden-footed, through a city of the dead. Roger turned sharply to the right. The sound of the other footsteps told that the pursuers also had turned that corner. Here was another street—a steep ascent. He ran more swiftly—he was running now for his life—the life that he held so cheap three minutes before. And all the streets were empty—empty like dream-streets, with all their windows dark and unhelpful, their doors fast closed against his need.

Far away down the street and across steep roofs lay Paris, poured out like a pool of light in the mist of the valley. But Roger was running with his head down—he saw nothing but the round heads of the cobble stones. Only now and again he glanced to right or left, if perchance some window might shew light to justify a cry for help, some door advance the welcome of an open inch.

There was at last such a door. He did not see it till it was almost behind him. Then there was the drag of the sudden stop—the eternal instant of indecision. Was there time? There must be. He dashed his fingers through the inch-crack, grazing the backs of them, leapt within, drew the door after him, felt madly for a lock or bolt, found a key, and, hanging his whole weight on it, strove to get the door home. The key turned. His left hand, by which he braced himself against the door-jamb, found a hook and pulled on it. Door and door-post met—the latch clicked—with a spring as it seemed. He turned the key, leaning against the door, which shook to the deep sobbing breaths that shook him, and to the panting bodies that pressed a moment without. Then someone cursed breathlessly outside; there was the sound of feet that went away.

Roger was alone in the strange darkness of an arched carriage-way, through the far end of which shewed the fainter darkness of a courtyard, with black shapes of little formal tubbed orange trees. There was no sound at all there but the sound of his own desperate breathing; and, as he stood, the slow, warm blood crept down his wrist, to make a little pool in the hollow of his hanging, half-clenched hand. Suddenly he felt sick.

This house, of which he knew nothing, held for him no terrors. To him at that moment there were but three murderers in all the world, and where they were not, there safety was. But the spacious silence that soothed at first, presently clawed at the set, vibrating nerves already overstrained. He found himself listening, listening, and there was nothing to hear but the silence, and once, before he thought to twist his handkerchief round it, the drip of blood from his hand.

By and by, he knew that he was not alone in this house, for from far away there came the faint sound of a footstep, and, quite near, the faint answering echo of it. And at a window, high up on the other side of the courtyard, a light shewed. Light and sound and echo intensified, the light passing window after window, till at last it moved across the courtyard, and the little trees threw back shifting shadows as it came towards him—a lamp in the hand of a man.

It was a short, bald man, with pointed beard and bright, friendly eyes. He held the lamp high as he came, and when he saw Roger, he drew his breath in an inspiration that spoke of surprise, sympathy, and pity.

"Hold! hold!" he said, in a singularly pleasant voice, "there has been a misfortune? You are wounded, monsieur?"

"Apaches," said Roger, and was surprised at the weakness of his own voice.

"Your hand?"

"My arm," said Roger.

"Fortunately," said the other, "I am a surgeon. Allow me."

He set the lamp on the step of a closed door, took off Roger's coat, and quickly tied his own handkerchief round the wounded arm.

"Now," he said, "courage! I am alone in the house. No one comes here but me. If you can walk up to my rooms, you will save us both much trouble. If you cannot, sit here and I will fetch you a cordial. But I advise you to try and walk. That *porte cochère* is, unfortunately, not very strong, and the lock is a common spring lock, and your friends may return with *their* friends; whereas the door across the courtyard is heavy and the bolts are new."

Roger moved towards the heavy door whose bolts were new. The stairs seemed to go on for ever. The doctor lent his arm, but the carved bannisters and their lively shadows whirled before Roger's eyes. Also, he seemed to be shod with lead, and to have in his legs bones that were red-hot. Then the stairs ceased, and there was light, and a cessation of the dragging of those leaden feet. He was on a couch, and his eyes might close. There was no need to move any more, nor to look, nor to listen.

When next he saw and heard, he was lying at ease, the close intimacy of a bandage clasping his arm, and in his mouth the vivid taste of some cordial.

The doctor was sitting in an armchair near a table, looking benevolent through gold-rimmed pince-nez.

"Better?" he said. "No, lie still, you'll be a new man soon."

"I am desolated," said Roger, "to have occasioned you all this trouble."

"Not at all," said the doctor. "We live to heal, and it is a nasty cut, that in your arm. If you are wise, you will rest at present. I shall be honoured if you will be my guest for the night."

Roger again murmured something about trouble.

"In a big house like this," said the doctor, as it seemed a little sadly, "there are many empty rooms, and some rooms which are not empty. There is a bed altogether at your service, monsieur, and I counsel you not to delay in seeking it. You can walk?"

Wroxham stood up. "Why, yes," he said, stretching himself. "I feel, as you say, a new man."

A narrow bed and rush-bottomed chair shewed like doll's-house furniture in the large, high, gaunt room to which the doctor led him.

"You are too tired to undress yourself," said the doctor, "rest—only rest," and covered him with a rug, roundly tucked him up, and left him.

"I leave the door open," he said, "in case you have any fever. Good night. Do not torment yourself. All goes well."

Then he took away the lamp, and Wroxham lay on his back and saw the shadows of the window-frames cast on the wall by the moon now risen. His eyes, growing accustomed to the darkness, perceived the carving of the white panelled walls and mantelpiece. There was a door in the room, another door from the one which the doctor had left open. Roger did not like open doors. The other door, however, was closed. He wondered where it led, and whether it were locked. Presently he got up to see. It was locked. He lay down again.

His arm gave him no pain, and the night's adventure did not seem to have overset his nerves. He felt, on the contrary, calm, confident, extraordinarily at ease, and master of himself. The trouble—how could that ever have seemed important? This calmness—it felt like the calmness that precedes sleep. Yet sleep was far from him. What was it that kept sleep away? The bed was comfortable—the pillows soft. What was it? It came to him presently that it was the scent which distracted him, worrying him with a memory that he could not define. A faint scent of—what was it? Perfumery? Yes—and camphor—and something else—something vaguely disquieting. He had not noticed it before he had risen and tried the handle of that other door. But now— He covered his face with the sheet, but through the sheet he smelt it still. He rose and threw back one of the long French windows. It opened with a click and a jar, and he looked across the dark well of the courtyard. He leaned out, breathing the chill, pure air of the May night, but when he withdrew his head, the scent was there again. Camphor—perfume—and something else. What was it that it reminded him of? He had his knee on the bed-edge when the answer came to that question. It was the scent that had struck at him from a darkened room when, a child, clutching at a grown-up hand, he had been led to the bed where, amid flowers, something white lay under a sheet—his mother, they had told him. It was the scent of death, disguised with drugs and perfumes.

He stood up and went, with carefully controlled swiftness, towards the open door. He wanted light and a human voice. The doctor was in the room upstairs; he—

The doctor was face to face with him on the landing, not a yard away, moving towards him quietly in shoeless feet.

"I can't sleep," said Wroxham, a little wildly, "it's too dark—"

"Come upstairs," said the doctor, and Wroxham went.

There was comfort in the large, lighted room, with its shelves and shelves full of well-bound books, its tables heaped with papers and pamphlets—its air of natural everyday work. There was a warmth of red curtain at the windows. On the window ledge a plant in a pot, its leaves like red misshapen hearts. A green-shaded lamp stood on the table. A peaceful, pleasant interior.

"What's behind that door," said Wroxham, abruptly—"that door downstairs?"

"Specimens," the doctor answered, "preserved specimens. My line is physiological research. You understand?"

So that was it.

"I feel quite well, you know," said Wroxham, laboriously explaining—"fit as any man—only I can't sleep."

"I see," said the doctor.

"It's the scent from your specimens, I think," Wroxham went on; "there's something about that scent—"

"Yes," said the doctor.

"It's very odd." Wroxham was leaning his elbow on his knee and his chin on his hand. "I feel so frightfully well—and yet—there's a strange feeling—"

"Yes," said the doctor. "Yes, tell me exactly what you feel."

"I feel," said Wroxham, slowly, "like a man on the crest of a wave."

The doctor stood up.

"You feel well, happy, full of life and energy—as though you could walk to the world's end, and yet—"

"And yet," said Roger, "as though my next step might be my last—as though I might step into my grave."

He shuddered.

"Do you," asked the doctor, anxiously—"do you feel thrills of pleasure—something like the first waves of chloroform—thrills running from your hair to your feet?"

"I felt all that," said Roger, slowly, "downstairs before I opened the window."

The doctor looked at his watch, frowned and got up quickly. "There is very little time," he said.

Suddenly Roger felt an unexplained opposition stiffen his mind.

The doctor went to a long laboratory bench with bottle-filled shelves above it, and on it crucibles and retorts, test tubes, beakers—all a chemist's apparatus—reached a bottle from a shelf, and measured out certain drops into a graduated glass, added water, and stirred it with a glass rod.

"Drink that," he said.

"No," said Roger, and as he spoke a thrill like the first thrill of the first chloroform wave swept through him, and it was a thrill, not of pleasure, but of pain. "No," he said, and "Ah!" for the pain was sharp.

"If you don't drink," said the doctor, carefully, "you are a dead man."

"You may be giving me poison," Roger gasped, his hands at his heart.

"I may," said the doctor. "What do you suppose poison makes you feel like? What do you feel like now?"

"I feel," said Roger, "like death."

Every nerve, every muscle thrilled to a pain not too intense to be underlined by a shuddering nausea.

"Then drink," cried the doctor, in tones of such cordial entreaty, such evident anxiety, that Wroxham half held his hand out for the glass. "Drink! Believe me, it is your only chance."

Again the pain swept through him like an electric current. The beads of sweat sprang out on his forehead.

"That wound," the doctor pleaded, standing over him with the glass held out. "For God's sake, drink! Don't you understand, man? You *are* poisoned. Your wound—"

"The knife?" Wroxham murmured, and as he spoke, his eyes seemed to swell in his head, and his head itself to grow enormous. "Do you know the poison—and its antidote?"

"I know all." The doctor soothed him. "Drink, then, my friend."

As the pain caught him again in a clasp more close than any lover's he clutched at the glass and drank. The drug met the pain and mastered it. Roger, in the ecstasy of pain's cessation, saw the world fade and go out in a haze of vivid violet.

II.

Faint films of lassitude, shot with contentment, wrapped him round. He lay passive, as a man lies in the convalescence that follows a long fight with Death. Fold on fold of white peace lay all about him.

"I'm better now," he said, in a voice that was a whisper—tried to raise his hand from where it lay helpless in his sight, failed, and lay looking at it in confident repose—"much better."

"Yes," said the doctor, and his pleasant, soft voice had grown softer, pleasanter. "You are now in the second stage. An interval is necessary before you can pass to the third. I will enliven the interval by conversation. Is there anything you would like to know?"

"Nothing," said Roger; "I am quite contented."

"This is very interesting," said the doctor. "Tell me exactly how you feel."

Roger faintly and slowly told him.

"Ah!" the doctor said, "I have not before heard this. You are the only one of them all who ever passed the first stage. The others—"

"The others?" said Roger, but he did not care much about the others.

"The others," said the doctor frowning, "were unsound. Decadent students, degenerate Apaches. You are highly trained—in fine physical condition. And your brain! God be good to the Apaches, who so delicately excited it to just the degree of activity needed for my purpose."

"The others?" Wroxham insisted.

"The others? They are in the room whose door was locked. Look—you should be able to see them. The second drug should lay your consciousness before me, like a sheet of white paper on which I can write what I choose. If I choose that you should see my specimens—*Allons donc.* I have no secrets from you now. Look—look—strain your eyes. In theory, I know all that you can do and feel and see in this second stage. But practically—enlighten me—look—shut your eyes and look!"

Roger closed his eyes and looked. He saw the gaunt, uncarpeted staircase, the open doors of the big rooms, passed to the locked door, and it opened at his touch. The room inside was like the others, spacious and panelled. A lighted lamp with a blue shade hung from the ceiling, and below it an effect of spread whiteness. Roger looked. There *were* things to be seen.

With a shudder he opened his eyes on the doctor's delightful room, the doctor's intent face.

"What did you see?" the doctor asked. "Tell me!"

"Did you kill them all?" Roger asked back.

"They died—of their own inherent weakness," the doctor said. "And you saw them?"

"I saw," said Roger, "the quiet people lying all along the floor in their death clothes—the people who have come in at that door of yours that is a trap—for robbery, or curiosity, or shelter, and never gone out any more."

"Right," said the doctor. "Right. My theory is proved at every point. You can see what I choose you to see. Yes, decadents all. It was in embalming that I was a specialist before I began these other investigations."

"What," Roger whispered—"what is it all for?"

"To make the superman," said the doctor. "I will tell you."

He told. It was a long story—the story of a man's life, a man's work, a man's dreams, hopes, ambitions.

"The secret of life," the doctor ended. "That is what all the alchemists sought. They sought it where Fate pleased. I sought it where I have found it—in death."

Roger thought of the room behind the locked door.

"And the secret is?" he asked.

"I have told you," said the doctor impatiently; "it is in the third drug that life—splendid, superhuman life—is found. I have tried it on animals. Always they became perfect, all that an animal should be. And more, too—much more. They were too perfect, too near humanity. They looked at me with human eyes. I could not let them live. Such animals it is not necessary to embalm. I had a laboratory in those days—and assistants. They called me the Prince of Vivisectors."

The man on the sofa shuddered.

"I am naturally," the doctor went on, "a tender-hearted man. You see it in my face; my voice proclaims it. Think what I have suffered in the sufferings of these poor beasts who never injured me. My God! Bear witness that I have not buried my talent. I have been faithful. I have laid down all—love, and joy, and pity, and the little beautiful things of life—all, all, on the altar of science, and seen them consume away. I deserve my heaven, if ever man did. And now by all the saints in heaven I am near it!"

"What is the third drug?" Roger asked, lying limp and flat on his couch.

"It is the Elixir of Life," said the doctor. "I am not its discoverer; the old alchemists knew it well, but they failed because they sought to apply the elixir to a normal—that is, a diseased and faulty—body. I knew better. One must have first a body abnormally healthy, abnormally strong. Then, not the elixir, but the two drugs that prepare. The first excites prematurely the natural conflict between the principles of life and death, and then, just at the point where Death is about to win his victory, the second drug intensifies life so that it conquers—intensifies, and yet chastens. Then the whole life of the subject, risen to an ecstasy, falls prone in an almost voluntary submission to the coming super-life. Submission—submission! The garrison must surrender before the splendid conqueror can enter and make the citadel his own. Do you understand? Do you submit?"

"I submit," said Roger, for, indeed, he did. "But—soon—quite soon—I will not submit."

He was too weak to be wise, or those words had remained unspoken.

The doctor sprang to his feet.

"It works too quickly!" he cried. "Everything works too quickly with you. Your condition is too perfect. So now I bind you."

From a drawer beneath the bench where the bottles gleamed, the doctor drew rolls of bandages—violet, like the haze that had drowned, at the urgence of the second drug, the consciousness of Roger. He moved, faintly resistant, on his couch. The doctor's hands, most gently, most irresistibly, controlled his movement.

"Lie still," said the gentle, charming voice. "Lie still; all is well." The clever, soft hands were unrolling the bandages—passing them round arms and throat—under and over the soft narrow couch. "I cannot risk your life, my poor boy. The least movement of yours might ruin everything. The third drug, like the first, must be offered directly to the blood which absorbs it. I bound the first drug as an unguent upon your knife-wound."

The swift hands, the soft bandages, passed back and forth, over and under—flashes of violet passed to and fro in the air, like the shuttle of a weaver through his warp. As the bandage clasped his knees, Roger moved.

"For God's sake, no!" the doctor cried; "the time is so near. If you cease to submit it is death."

With an incredible, accelerated swiftness he swept the bandages round and round knees and ankles, drew a deep breath—stood upright.

"I must make an incision," he said—"in the head this time. It will not hurt. See! I spray it with the Constantia Nepenthe; that also I discovered. My boy, in a moment you know all things—you are as God. For God's sake, be patient. Preserve your submission."

And Roger, with life and will resurgent hammering at his heart, preserved it.

He did not feel the knife that made the cross-cut on his temple, but he felt the hot spurt of blood that followed the cut; he felt the cool flap of a plaster, spread with some sweet, clean-smelling unguent that met the blood and stanched it. There was a moment—or was it hours?—of nothingness. Then from that cut on his forehead there seemed to radiate threads of infinite length, and of a strength that one could trust to—threads that linked one to all knowledge past and present. He felt that he controlled all wisdom, as a driver controls his four-in-hand. Knowledge, he perceived, belonged to him, as the air belongs to the eagle. He swam in it, as a great fish in a limitless ocean.

He opened his eyes and met those of the doctor, who sighed as one to whom breath has grown difficult.

"Ah, all goes well. Oh, my boy, was it not worth it? What do you feel?"

"I. Know. Everything," said Roger, with full stops between the words.

"Everything? The future?"

"No. I know all that man has ever known."

"Look back—into the past. See someone. See Pharaoh. You see him—on his throne?"

"Not on his throne. He is whispering in a corner of his great gardens to a girl, who is the daughter of a water-carrier."

"Bah! Any poet of my dozen decadents who lie so still could have told me that. Tell me secrets—the *Masque de Fer.*"

The other told a tale, wild and incredible, but it satisfied the teller.

"That too—it might be imagination. Tell me the name of the woman I loved and—"

The echo of the name of the anesthetic came to Roger; "Constantia," said he, in an even voice.

"Ah," the doctor cried, "now I see you know all things. It was not murder. I hoped to dower her with all the splendours of the superlife."

"Her bones lie under the lilacs, where you used to kiss her in the spring," said Roger, quite without knowing what it was that he was going to say.

"It is enough," the doctor cried. He sprang up, ranged certain bottles and glasses on a table convenient to his chair. "You know all things. It was not a dream, this, the dream of my life. It is true. It is a fact accomplished. Now I, too, will know all things. I will be as the gods."

He sought among leather cases on a far table, and came back swiftly into the circle of light that lay below the green-shaded lamp.

Roger, floating contentedly on the new sea of knowledge that seemed to support him, turned eyes on the trouble that had driven him out of that large, empty studio so long ago, so far away. His new-found wisdom laughed at that problem, laughed and solved it. "To end that trouble I must do so-and-so, say such-and-such," Roger told himself again and again.

And now the doctor, standing by the table, laid on it his pale, plump hand outspread. He drew a knife from a case—a long, shiny knife—and scored his hand across and across its back, as a cook scores pork for cooking. The slow blood followed the cuts in beads and lines.

Into the cuts he dropped a green liquid from a little bottle, replaced its stopper, bound up his hand and sat down.

"The beginning of the first stage," he said; "almost at once I shall begin to be a new man. It will work quickly. My body, like yours, is sane and healthy."

There was a long silence.

"Oh, but this is good," the doctor broke it to say. "I feel the hand of Life sweeping my nerves like harp-strings."

Roger had been thinking, the old common sense that guides an ordinary man breaking through this consciousness of illimitable wisdom. "You had better," he said, "unbind me; when the hand of Death sweeps your nerves, you may need help."

"No," the doctor said, "and no, and no, and no many times. I am afraid of you. You know all things, and even in your body you are stronger than I. When I, too, am a god, and filled with the wine of knowledge, I will loose you, and together we will drink of the fourth drug—the mordant that shall fix the others and set us eternally on a level with the immortals."

"Just as you like, of course," said Roger, with a conscious effort after commonplace. Then suddenly, not commonplace any more—

"Loose me!" he cried; "loose me, I tell you! I am wiser than you."

"You are also stronger," said the doctor, and then suddenly and irresistibly the pain caught him. Roger saw his face contorted with agony, his hands clench on the arm of his chair; and it seemed that, either this man was less able to bear pain than he, or that the pain was much more violent than had been his own. Between the grippings of the anguish the doctor dragged on his watch-chain; the watch leapt from his pocket, and rattled as his trembling hand laid it on the table.

"Not yet," he said, when he had looked at its face, "not yet, not yet, not yet." It seemed to Roger, lying there bound, that the other man repeated those words for long days and weeks. And the plump, pale hand, writhing and distorted by anguish, again and again drew near to take the glass that stood ready on the table, and with convulsive self-restraint again and again drew back without it.

The short May night was waning—the shiver of dawn rustled the leaves of the plant whose leaves were like red misshaped hearts.

"Now!" The doctor screamed the word, grasped the glass, drained it and sank back in his chair. His hand struck the table beside him. Looking at his limp body and head thrown back, one could almost see the cessation of pain, the coming of kind oblivion.

III.

The dawn had grown to daylight, a poor, grey, rain-stained daylight, not strong enough to pierce the curtains and persiennes, and yet not so weak but that it could mock the lamp, now burnt low and smelling vilely.

Roger lay very still on his couch, a man wounded, anxious, and extravagantly tired. In those hours of long, slow dawning, face to face with the unconscious figure in the chair, he had felt, slowly and little by little, the recession of that sea of knowledge in which he had felt himself float in such content. The sea had withdrawn itself, leaving him high and dry on the shore of the normal. The only relic that he had clung to and that he still grasped was the answer to the problem of the trouble—the only wisdom that he had put into words. These words remained to him, and he knew that they held wisdom—very simple wisdom, too.

"To end the trouble, I must do so-and-so and say such-and-such."

But of all that had seemed to set him on a pinnacle, had evened him with the immortals, nothing else was left. He was just Roger Wroxham—wounded, and bound, in a locked house, one of whose rooms was full of very quiet people, and in another room himself and a dead man. For now it was so long since the doctor had moved that it seemed he must be dead. He had got to know every line of that room, every fold of drapery, every flower on the wall-paper, the number of the books, the shapes and sizes of things. Now he could no longer look at these. He looked at the other man.

Slowly a dampness spread itself over Wroxham's forehead and tingled among the roots of his hair. He writhed in his bonds. They held fast. He could not move hand or foot. Only his head could turn a little, so that he could at will see the doctor or not see him. A shaft of desolate light pierced the persienne at its hinge and rested on the table, where an overturned glass lay.

Wroxham thrilled from head to foot. The body in the chair stirred—hardly stirred—shivered rather—and a very faint, far-away voice said:—

"Now the third—give me the third."

"What?" said Roger, stupidly; and he had to clear his throat twice before he could say even that.

"The moment is now," said the doctor. "I remember all. I made you a god. Give me the third drug."

"Where is it?" Roger asked.

"It is at my elbow," the doctor murmured. "I submit—I submit. Give me the third drug, and let me be as you are."

"As *I* am?" said Roger. "You forget. *I* am bound."

"Break your bonds," the doctor urged, in a quick, small voice. "I trust you now. You are stronger than all men, as you are wiser. Stretch your muscles, and the bandages will fall asunder like snow-wreaths."

"It is too late," Wroxham said, and laughed; "all that is over. I am not wise any more, and I have only the strength of a man. I am tired and wounded. I cannot break your bonds—I cannot help you!"

"But if you cannot help me—it is death," said the doctor.

"It is death," said Roger. "Do you feel it coming on you?"

"I feel life returning," said the doctor; "it is now the moment—the one possible moment. And I cannot reach it. Oh, give it me—give it me!"

Then Roger cried out suddenly, in a loud voice: "Now, by God in heaven, you damned decadent, I am *glad* that I cannot give it. Yes, if it costs me my life, it's worth it, you madman, so that your life ends too. Now be silent, and die like a man, if you have it in you."

Only one word seemed to reach the man in the chair.

"A decadent!" he repeated. "I? But no, I am like you—I see what I will. I close my eyes, and I see—no—not that—ah!—not that!" He writhed faintly in his chair, and to Roger it seemed that for that writhing figure there would be no return of power and life and will.

"Not that," he moaned. "Not that," and writhed in a gasping anguish that bore no more words.

Roger lay and watched him, and presently he writhed from the chair to the floor, tearing feebly at it with his fingers, moaned, shuddered, and lay very still.

Of all that befell Roger in that house, the worst was now. For now he knew that he was alone with the dead, and between him and death stretched certain hours and days. For the *porte cochère* was locked; the doors of the house itself were locked—heavy doors and the locks new.

"I am alone in the house," the doctor had said. "No one comes here but me."

No one would come. He would die there—he, Roger Wroxham—"poor old Roger Wroxham, who was no one's enemy but his own." Tears pricked his eyes. He shook his head impatiently and they fell from his lashes.

"You fool," he said, "can't you die like a man either?"

Then he set his teeth and made himself lie still. It seemed to him that now Despair laid her hand on his heart. But, to speak truth, it was Hope whose hand lay there. This was so much more than a man should be called on to bear—it could not be true. It was an evil dream. He would wake presently. Or if it were, indeed, real—then someone would come, someone must come. God could not let nobody come to save him.

And late at night, when heart and brain had been stretched to the point where both break and let in the sea of madness, someone came.

The interminable day had worn itself out. Roger had screamed, yelled, shouted till his throat was dried up, his lips baked and cracked. No one heard. How should they? The twilight had thickened and thickened, till at last it made a shroud for the dead man on the floor by the chair. And there were other dead men in that house; and as Roger ceased to see the one he saw the others the quiet, awful faces, the lean hands, the straight, stiff limbs laid out one beyond another in the room of death. They at least were not bound. If they should rise in their white wrappings and, crossing that empty sleeping chamber very softly, come slowly up the stairs—

A stair creaked.

His ears, strained with hours of listening, thought themselves befooled. But his cowering heart knew better.

Again a stair creaked. There was a hand on the door.

"Then it is all over," said Roger in the darkness, "and I *am* mad."

The door opened very slowly, very cautiously. There was no light. Only the sound of soft feet and draperies that rustled.

Then suddenly a match spurted—light struck at his eyes; a flicker of lit candle-wick steadying to flame. And the things that had come were not those quiet people creeping up to match their death with his death in life, but human creatures, alive, breathing, with eyes that moved and glittered, lips that breathed and spoke.

"He must be here," one said. "Lisette watched all day; he never came out. He must be here—there is nowhere else."

Then they set up the candle-end on the table, and he saw their faces. They were the Apaches who had set on him in that lonely street, and who had sought him here—to set on him again.

He sucked his dry tongue, licked his dry lips, and cried aloud:—

"Here I am! Oh, kill me! For the love of God, brothers, kill me *now!*"

And even before he spoke, they had seen him, and seen what lay on the floor.

"He died this morning. I am bound. Kill me, brothers; I cannot die slowly here alone. Oh, kill me, for Christ's sake!"

But already the three were pressing on each other at a doorway suddenly grown too narrow. They could kill a living man, but they could not face death, quiet, enthroned.

"For the love of Christ," Roger screamed, "have pity! Kill me outright! Come back—come back!"

And then, since even Apaches are human, one of them did come back. It was the one he had flung into the gutter. The feet of the others sounded on the stairs as he caught up the candle and bent over Roger, knife in hand.

"Make sure," said Roger, through set teeth.

"Nom d'un nom," said the Apache, with worse words, and cut the bandages here, and here, and here again, and there, and lower, to the very feet.

Then this good Samaritan helped Roger to rise, and when he could not stand, the Samaritan half pulled, half carried him down those many steps, till they came upon the others putting on their boots at the stair-foot.

Then between them the three men who could walk carried the other out and slammed the outer door, and presently set him against a gate-post in another street, and went their wicked ways.

And after a time, a girl with furtive eyes brought brandy and hoarse, muttered kindnesses, and slid away in the shadows.

Against that gate-post the police came upon him. They took him to the address they found on him. When they came to question him he said, "Apaches," and his late variations on that theme were deemed sufficient, though not one of them touched truth or spoke of the third drug.

There has never been anything in the papers about that house. I think it is still closed, and inside it still lie in the locked room the very quiet people; and above, there is the room with the narrow couch and the scattered, cut, violet bandages, and the thing on the floor by the chair, under the lamp that burned itself out in that May dawning.

In the Dark

It may have been a form of madness. Or it may be that he really was what is called haunted. Or it may—though I don't pretend to understand how—have been the development, through intense suffering, of a sixth sense in a very nervous, highly-strung nature. Something certainly led him where They were. And to him They were all one.

He told me the first part of the story, and the last part of it I saw with my own eyes.

I.

Haldane and I were friends even in our school-days. What first brought us together was our common hatred of Visger, who came from our part of the country. His people knew our people at home, so he was put on to us when he came. He was the most intolerable person, boy and man, that I have ever known. He would not tell a lie. And that was all right. But he didn't stop at that. If he were asked whether any other chap had done any-thing—been out of bounds, or up to any sort of lark—he would always say, "I don't know, sir, but I believe so." He never did know—we took care of that. But what he believed was always right. I remember Haldane twisting his arm to say how he knew about that cherry-tree business, and he only said, "I don't know—I just feel sure. And I was right, you see." What can you do with a boy like that?

We grew up to be men. At least Haldane and I did. Visger grew up to be a prig. He was a vegetarian and a teetotaler, and an all-wooler and a Christian Scientist, and all the things that prigs are—but he wasn't a com-mon prig. He knew all sorts of things that he oughtn't to have known, that he *couldn't* have known in any ordinary decent way. It wasn't that he found things out. He just knew them. Once, when I was very unhappy, he came into my rooms—we were all in our last year at Oxford—and talked about

157

things I hardly knew myself. That was really why I went to India that winter. It was bad enough to be unhappy, without having that beast knowing all about it.

I was away over a year. Coming back, I thought a lot about how jolly it would be to see old Haldane again. If I thought about Visger at all, I wished he was dead. But I didn't think about him much.

I did want to see Haldane. He was always such a jolly chap—gay, and kindly, and simple, honourable, upright, and full of practical sympathies. I longed to see him, to see the smile in his jolly blue eyes, looking out from the net of wrinkles that laughing had made round them, to hear his jolly laugh, and feel the good grip of his big hand. I went straight from the docks to his chambers in Gray's Inn, and I found him cold, pale, anemic, with dull eyes and a limp hand, and pale lips that smiled without mirth, and uttered a welcome without gladness.

He was surrounded by a litter of disordered furniture and personal effects half packed. Some big boxes stood corded, and there were cases of books, filled and waiting for the enclosing boards to be nailed on.

"Yes, I'm moving," he said. "I can't stand these rooms. There's something rum about them—something devilish rum. I clear out to-morrow."

The autumn dusk was filling the corners with shadows. "You got the furs," I said, just for something to say, for I saw the big case that held them lying corded among the others.

"Furs?" he said. "Oh yes. Thanks awfully. Yes. I forgot about the furs." He laughed, out of politeness, I suppose, for there was no joke about the furs. They were many and fine—the best I could get for money, and I had seen them packed and sent off when my heart was very sore. He stood looking at me, and saying nothing.

"Come out and have a bit of dinner," I said as cheerfully as I could.

"Too busy," he answered, after the slightest possible pause and a glance round the room—"look here—I'm awfully glad to see you— If you'd just slip over and order in dinner—I'd go myself —only— Well, you see how it is."

I went. And when I came back, he had cleared a space near the fire, and moved his big gate-table into it. We dined there by candle light. I tried to be amusing. He, I am sure, tried to be amused. We did not succeed, either of us. And his haggard eyes watched me all the time, save in those fleeting moments when, without turning his head, he glanced back over his shoulder into the shadows that crowded round the little lighted place where we sat.

When we had dined and the man had come and taken away the dishes, I looked at Haldane very steadily, so that he stopped in a pointless anecdote, and looked interrogation at me.

"Well?" I said.

"You're not listening," he said petulantly. "What's the matter?"

"That's what you'd better tell me," I said.

He was silent, gave one of those furtive glances at the shadows, and stooped to stir the fire to—I knew it—a blaze that must light every corner of the room.

"You're all to pieces," I said cheerfully. "What have you been up to? Wine? Cards? Speculation? A woman? If you won't tell me, you'll have to tell your doctor. Why, my dear chap, you're a wreck."

"You're a comfortable friend to have about the place," he said, and smiled a mechanical smile not at all pleasant to see.

"I'm the friend you want, I think," said I. "Do you suppose I'm blind? Something's gone wrong and you've taken to something. Morphia, perhaps? And you've brooded over the thing till you've lost all sense of proportion. Out with it, old chap. I bet you a dollar it's not so bad as you think it."

"If I could tell you—or tell anyone," he said slowly, "it wouldn't be so bad as it is. If I could tell anyone, I'd tell you. And even as it is, I've told you more than I've told anyone else."

I could get nothing more out of him. But he pressed me to stay—would have given me his bed and made himself a shake-down, he said. But I had engaged my room at the Victoria, and I was expecting letters. So I left him, quite late—and he stood on the stairs, holding a candle over the bannisters to light me down.

When I went back next morning, he was gone. Men were moving his furniture into a big van with Somebody's Pantechnicon painted on it in big letters.

He had left no address with the porter, and had driven off in a hansom with two portmanteaux—to Waterloo, the porter thought.

Well, a man has a right to the monopoly of his own troubles, if he chooses to have it. And I had troubles of my own that kept me busy.

II.

It was more than a year later that I saw Haldane again. I had got rooms in the Albany by this time, and he turned up there one morning, very early indeed—before breakfast in fact. And if he looked ghastly before, he now looked almost ghostly. His face looked as though it had worn thin, like an oyster shell that has for years been cast up twice a day by the sea on a shore all pebbly. His hands were thin as bird's claws, and they trembled like caught butterflies.

I welcomed him with enthusiastic cordiality and pressed breakfast on him. This time, I decided, I would ask no questions. For I saw that none were needed. He would tell me. He intended to tell me. He had come here to tell me, and for nothing else.

I lit the spirit lamp—I made coffee and small talk for him, and I ate and drank, and waited for him to begin. And it was like this that he began:

"I am going," he said, "to kill myself—oh, don't be alarmed,"—I suppose I had said or looked something—"I shan't do it here, or now. I shall do it when I have to—when I can't bear it any longer. And I want some one to know why. I don't want to feel that I'm the only living creature who does know. And I can trust you, can't I?"

I murmured something reassuring.

"I should like you, if you don't mind, to give me your word, that you won't tell a soul what I'm going to tell you, as long as I'm alive. Afterwards . . . you can tell whom you please."

I gave him my word.

He sat silent looking at the fire. Then he shrugged his shoulders.

"It's extraordinary how difficult it is to say it," he said, and smiled. "The fact is—you know that beast, George Visger."

"Yes," I said. "I haven't seen him since I came back. Some one told me he'd gone to some island or other to preach vegetarianism to the cannibals. Anyhow, he's out of the way, bad luck to him."

"Yes," said Haldane, "he's out of the way. But he's not preaching anything. In point of fact, he's dead."

"Dead?" was all I could think of to say.

"Yes," said he; "it's not generally known, but he is."

"What did he die of?" I asked, not that I cared. The bare fact was good enough for me.

"You know what an interfering chap he always was. Always knew every-thing. Heart to heart talks—and have everything open and above board. Well, he interfered between me and some one else—told her a pack of lies."

"Lies?"

"Well, the *things* were true, but he made lies of them the way he told them—you know." I did. I nodded. "And she threw me over. And she died. And we weren't even friends. And I couldn't see her—before—I couldn't even . . . Oh, my God . . . But I went to the funeral. He was there. They'd asked *him*. And then I came back to my rooms. And I was sitting there, thinking. And he came up."

"He would do. It's just what he would do. The beast! I hope you kicked him out."

"No, I didn't. I listened to what he'd got to say. He came to say, No doubt it was all for the best. And he hadn't known the things he told her. He'd only guessed. He'd guessed right, damn him. What right had he to guess right? And he said it was all for the best, because, besides that, there was madness in my family. He'd found that out too— "

"And is there?"

"If there is, I didn't know it. And that was why it was all for the best. So then I said, 'There wasn't any madness in my family before, but there is now,' and I got hold of his throat. I am not sure whether I meant to kill him; I ought to have meant to kill him. Anyhow, I did kill him. What did you say?"

I had said nothing. It is not easy to think at once of the tactful and suit-able thing to say, when your oldest friend tells you that he is a murderer.

"When I could get my hands out of his throat,—it was as difficult as it is to drop the handles of a galvanic battery—he fell in a lump on the hearth-rug. And I saw what I'd done. How is it that murderers ever get found out?"

"They're careless, I suppose," I found myself saying, "they lose their nerve."

"I didn't," he said. "I never was calmer. I sat down in the big chair and looked at him, and thought it all out. He was just off to that Island—I knew that. He'd said good-bye to every one. He'd told me that. There was no blood to get rid of—or only just a touch at the corner of his slack mouth. He wasn't going to travel in his own name because of interviewers. Mr Somebody Something's luggage would be unclaimed and his cabin empty.

No one would guess that Mr Somebody Something was Sir George Visger, F.R.S. It was all as plain as plain. There was nothing to get rid of but the man. No weapon, no blood—and I got rid of him all right."

"How?"

He smiled cunningly.

"No, no," he said; "that's where I draw the line. It's not that I doubt your word, but if you talked in your sleep, or had a fever or anything. No, No. As long as you don't know where the body is, don't you see, I'm all right. Even if you could prove that I've said all this—which you can't—it's only the wanderings of my poor unhinged brain. See?"

I saw. And I was sorry for him. And I did not believe that he had killed Visger. He was not the sort of man who kills people. So I said:

"Yes, old chap, I see. Now look here. Let's go away together, you and I—travel a bit and see the world, and forget all about that beastly chap."

His eyes lighted up at that.

"Why," he said, "you understand. You don't hate me and shrink from me. I wish I'd told you before—you know—when you came and I was packing all my sticks. But it's too late now."

"Too late? Not a bit of it," I said. "Come, we'll pack our traps and be off to-night—out into the unknown, don't you know."

"That's where *I'm* going," he said. "You wait. When you've heard what's been happening to me, you won't be so keen to go travelling about with me."

"But you've told me what's been happening to you," I said, and the more I thought about what he had told me, the less I believed it.

"No," he said, slowly, "no—I've told you what happened to *him*. What happened to me is quite different. Did I tell you what his last words were? Just when I was coming at him. Before I'd got his throat, you know. He said, 'Look out. You'll never be able to get rid of the body— Besides, anger's sinful.' You know that way he had, like a tract on its hind legs. So afterwards I got thinking of that. But I didn't think of it for a year. Because I did get rid of his body all right. And then I was sitting in that comfortable chair, and I thought, 'Hullo, it must be about a year now, since that—' and I pulled out my pocket-book and went to the window to look at a little almanack I carry about—it was getting dusk—and sure enough it was a year, to the day. And then I remembered what he'd said. And I said to myself, 'Not much trouble about getting rid of your body, you brute.' And then I looked at the hearth-rug and— Ah!" he screamed suddenly and very loud—"I can't tell you—no, I can't."

My man opened the door—he wore a smooth face over his wriggling curiosity. "Did you call, sir?"

"Yes," I lied. "I want you to take a note to the bank, and wait for an answer."

When he was got rid of, Haldane said: "Where was I?—"

"You were just telling me what happened after you looked at the almanack. What was it?"

"Nothing much," he said, laughing softly, "oh, nothing much—only that I glanced at the hearthrug—and there *he* was—the man I'd killed a year before. Don't try to explain, or I shall lose my temper. The door was shut. The windows were shut. He hadn't been there a minute before. And he was there then. That's all."

Hallucination was one of the words I stumbled among.

"Exactly what I thought," he said triumphantly, "but—I touched it. It was quite real. Heavy, you know, and harder than live people are somehow, to the touch—more like a stone thing covered with kid the hands were, and the arms like a marble statue in a blue serge suit. Don't you hate men who wear blue serge suits?"

"There are hallucinations of touch too," I found myself saying.

"Exactly what I thought," said Haldane more triumphant than ever, "but there are limits, you know—limits. So then I thought someone had got him out—the real him—and stuck him there to frighten me—while my back was turned, and I went to the place where I'd hidden him, and he was there—ah!—just as I'd left him. Only . . . it was a year ago. There are two of him there now."

"My dear chap," I said, "this is simply comic."

"Yes," he said, "it is amusing. I find it so myself. Especially in the night when I wake up and think of it. I hope I shan't die in the dark, Winston. That's one of the reasons why I think I shall have to kill myself. I could be sure then of not dying in the dark."

"Is *that* all?" I asked, feeling sure that it must be.

"No," said Haldane at once. "That's *not* all. He's come back to me again. In a railway carriage it was. I'd been asleep. When I woke up, there he was lying on the seat opposite me. Looked just the same. I pitched him out on the line in Red Hill Tunnel. And if I see him again, I'm going out myself. I can't stand it. It's too much. I'd sooner go. Whatever the next world's like, there aren't things in it like that. We leave them here, in graves and boxes and . . . You think I'm mad. But I'm not. You can't help me—no one can help me. He *knew,* you see. He said I shouldn't be able to get rid of the body. And I can't get rid of it. I can't. I can't. He knew. He always did know things that he *couldn't* know. But I'll cut his game short. After all, I've got the ace of trumps, and I play it on his next trick. I give you my word of honour, Winston, that I'm not mad."

"My dear old man," I said, "I don't think you're mad. But I do think your nerves are very much upset. Mine are a bit, too. Do you know why I went to India? It was because of you and her. I couldn't stay and see it, though I wished for your happiness and all that; you know I did. And when I came back, she . . . and you . . . Let's see it out together," I said. "You won't keep fancying things if you've got me to talk to. And I always said you weren't half a bad old duffer."

"She liked you," he said.

"Oh, yes," I said, "she liked me."

III.

That was how we came to go abroad together. I was full of hope for him. He'd always been such a splendid chap—so sane and strong. I couldn't believe that he was gone mad, gone for ever, I mean, so that he'd never come right again. Perhaps my own trouble made it easy for me to see things not quite straight. Any way, I took him away to recover his mind's health, exactly as I should have taken him away to get strong after a fever. And the madness seemed to pass away, and in a month or two we were perfectly jolly, and I thought I had cured him. And I was very glad because of that old friendship of ours, and because she had loved him and liked me.

We never spoke of Visger. I thought he had forgotten all about him. I thought I understood how his mind, over-strained by sorrow and anger, had fixed on the man he hated, and woven a nightmare web of horror round that detestable personality. And I had got the whip hand of my own trouble. And we were as jolly as sandboys together all those months.

And we came to Bruges at last in our travels, and Bruges was very full, because of the Exhibition. We could only get one room and one bed. So we tossed for the bed, and the one who lost the toss was to make the best of the night in the arm-chair. And the bed-clothes we were to share equitably.

We spent the evening at a *café chantant* and finished at a beer hall, and it was late and sleepy when we got back to the Grande Vigne. I took our key from its nail in the concierge's room, and we went up. We talked awhile, I remember, of the town, and the belfry, and the Venetian aspect of the canals by moonlight, and then Haldane got into bed, and I made a chrysalis of myself with my share of the blankets and fitted the tight roll into the armchair. I was not at all comfortable, but I was compensatingly tired, and I was nearly asleep when Haldane roused me up to tell me about his will.

"I've left everything to you, old man," he said. "I know I can trust you to see to everything."

"Quite so," said I, "and if you don't mind, we'll talk about it in the morning."

He tried to go on about it, and about what a friend I'd been, and all that, but I shut him up and told him to go to sleep. But no. He wasn't comfortable, he said. And he'd got a thirst like a lime kiln. And he'd noticed that there was no water-bottle in the room. "And the water in the jug's like pale soup," he said.

"Oh, all right," said I. "Light your candle and go and get some water, then, in Heaven's name, and let me get to sleep."

But he said, "No—you light it. I don't want to get out of bed in the dark. I might—I might step on something, mightn't I—or walk into something that wasn't there when I got into bed."

"Rot," I said, "walk into your grandmother." But I lit the candle all the same. He sat up in bed and looked at me—very pale—with his hair all tumbled from the pillow, and his eyes blinking and shining.

"That's better," he said. And then, "I say—look here. Oh—yes—I see. It's all right. Queer how they mark the sheets here. Blest if I didn't think it was blood, just for the minute."

The sheet was marked, not at the corner, as sheets are marked at home, but right in the middle where it turns down, with big, red cross-stitching.

"Yes, I see," I said, "it is a queer place to mark it."

"It's queer letters to have on it," he said. "G. V."

"Grande Vigne," I said. "What letters do you expect them to mark things with? Hurry up."

"You come too," he said. "Yes, it does stand for Grande Vigne, of course. I wish you'd come down too, Winston."

"I'll go down," I said and turned with the candle in my hand.

He was out of bed and close to me in a flash. "No," said he, "I don't want to stay alone in the dark."

He said it just as a frightened child might have done.

"All right then, come along," I said. And we went. I tried to make some joke, I remember, about the length of his hair, and the cut of his pyjamas—but I was sick with disappointment. For it was almost quite plain to me, even then, that all my time and trouble had been thrown away, and that he wasn't cured after all. We went down as quietly as we could, and got a carafe of water from the long bare dining table in the salle-à-manger. He got hold of my arm at first, and then he got the candle away from me, and went very slowly, shading the light with his hand, and looking very carefully all about, as though he expected to see something that he wanted very desperately not to see. And of course, I knew what that something was. I didn't like the way he was going on. I can't at all express how deeply I didn't like it. And he looked over his shoulder every now and then, just as he did that first evening after I came back from India.

The thing got on my nerves so that I could hardly find the way back to our room. And when we got there, I give you my word, I more than half expected to see what he had expected to see—that, or something like that, on the hearth-rug. But of course there was nothing.

I blew out the light and tightened my blankets round me—I'd been trailing them after me in our expedition. And I was settled in my chair when Haldane spoke.

"You've got all the blankets," he said.

"No, I haven't," said I, "only what I've always had."

"I can't find mine then," he said, and I could hear his teeth chattering. "And I'm cold. I'm . . . For God's sake, light the candle. Light it. Light it. Something horrible . . ."

And I couldn't find the matches.

"Light the candle, light the candle," he said, and his voice broke, as a boy's does sometimes in chapel. "If you don't he'll come to me. It is so easy to come at any one in the dark. Oh Winston, light the candle, for the love of God! I can't die in the dark."

"I am lighting it," I said savagely, and I was feeling for the matches on the marble-topped chest of drawers, on the mantelpiece—everywhere but on the round centre table where I'd put them. "You're not going to die. Don't be a fool," I said. "It's all right. I'll get a light in a second."

He said, "It's cold. It's cold. It's cold," like that, three times. And then he screamed aloud, like a woman—like a child—like a hare when the dogs have got it. I had heard him scream like that once before.

"What is it?" I cried, hardly less loud. "For God's sake, hold your noise. What is it?"

There was an empty silence. Then, very slowly:

"It's Visger," he said. And he spoke thickly, as through some stifling veil.

"Nonsense. Where?" I asked, and my hand closed on the matches as he spoke.

"Here," he screamed sharply, as though he had torn the veil away, "here, beside me. In the bed."

I got the candle alight. I got across to him. He was crushed in a heap at the edge of the bed. Stretched on the bed beyond him was a dead man, white and very cold.

Haldane had died in the dark.

It was all so simple.

We had come to the wrong room. The man the room belonged to was there, on the bed he had engaged and paid for before he died of heart disease, earlier in the day. A French *commis-voyageur* representing soap and perfumery; his name, Felix Leblanc.

Later, in England, I made cautious enquiries. The body of a man had been found in the Red Hill tunnel—a haberdasher man named Simmons, who had drunk spirits of salts, owing to the depression of trade. The bottle was clutched in his dead hand.

For reasons that I had, I took care to have a police inspector with me when I opened the boxes that came to me by Haldane's will. One of them was the big box, metal lined, in which I had sent him the skins from India—for a wedding present, God help us all!

It was closely soldered.

Inside were the skins of beasts? No. The bodies of two men. One was identified, after some trouble, as that of a hawker of pens in city offices—subject to fits. He had died in one, it seemed. The other body was Visger's, right enough.

Explain it as you like. I offered you, if you remember, a choice of explanations before I began the story. I have not yet found the explanation that can satisfy me.

The New Samson

While he lived, no one suspected the truth. He lived in FitzJohn's Avenue, in well-upholstered bourgeois splendour. He had a motor car, a circle of well-to-do acquaintances, a large, competent, aquiline wife—a Miss Antrobus she was, I believe, one of the brewing Antrobuses. He had all the material things for which men sell their souls and wear out their bodies. He had a great reputation and an income greater still. He had also two things no one ever conceived it possible that he should have—a romance and a secret.

He was a very popular man, kindly and generous, with a pleasant if mediocre wit, and a neat little talent for after-dinner oratory. A portly, well-kept man, with a prosperous presence and a genial laugh. The best of company, people said, and there were those who considered him good-looking, handsome even. Only afterwards it was remembered that his forehead had been too narrow and those clear, grey eyes of his too small and too near together.

Architecture was his profession, and he had the reputation of extreme thoroughness. "Sees to everything himself; protects your interests, don't you know. Contractors don't get much change out of *him*," his clients would purr contentedly.

If I were to speak of him not as Maskelyne, but by the name that was his own, you would recognise it at once as the name of the man who built some of the finest of our colossal new London things; hotels, residential flats, business premises of vast new Universal Providers; and you would know his name for another, stranger reason. Anyhow, he was responsible for that palace of Sir Leo Montague Swimmonds's, on the edge of the Sussex downs. And, last and beyond all, he was responsible for the Arena.

You remember the Arena, that vast, magnificent pile, which dominated the whole of the west central district, standing head and shoulders above the highest of its brick and marble brothers? There was a complimentary

169

dinner on the night before it was opened, and Lord Goldschwein, who was on the board, proposed the health of our admirable architect.

The Arena, of all his achievements, was the one that seemed dearest to him. One would see him sometimes stand for a moment on the pavement opposite, gazing up at it with something of the frank, half-astonished pride of a child who has built a six-storied house of cards.

"Can *I* have done *that?*" he seemed to be asking himself.

His own drawing of its principal elevation hung framed in his library, the only architectural drawing on the walls of his house. He moved into offices on the ground floor of the fine block of buildings which nestled under the great wing of the Arena. But he never entered its doors or trod its beautiful staircases after the day on which the theatre was opened to the public.

"I have to build the public what it wants," he used to say; "shops, or music-halls, or hotels, but that is no reason why I should go to the music-halls, or stay at the hotels, or buy anything at the shops. I live at home, and I go to the Queen's Hall, and I do my shopping at the Stores."

He said this in his gentle, genial way more than once. To Richard Panton, his head assistant, who at his death became his successor in the great business, he once said something further. They were walking over Hampstead Heath, and London lay below them in an orange haze; he said it quite abruptly.

"It's odd how things don't change. I used to walk here with a child once. And the Heath's just the same."

Panton said nothing. Something in the other man's voice asked for that.

"My little girl," said Maskelyne; "we used to climb trees, feed the ducks. I used to run races with her. In the morning, before business."

Again Panton said nothing.

"She was my only child," said Maskelyne, hitting at the gorse bushes with his stick.

Panton had not known that Maskelyne had had a child at all.

"She was always laughing," the great architect went on, in a dull, toneless voice; "such a pretty little thing, and so loving. She used to look out for me coming home, and run out into the road before they could stop her, and jump at me, arms, and legs, clinging on like a kitten. And I lost her."

Then Panton said, "Is it long since she died, sir?" in a very respectfully sympathetic voice. And the great architect answered:

"She didn't die. She left me. Never marry, Panton. Your children eat out your heart and live on it. And when they grow up, they leave you. Empty, empty, empty. Never love anyone, Panton. It's not worth it. Did you get those details out for Worthington?" he said, and they talked business.

Now it happened that Dick Panton did love someone, an orphan girl, without a penny, of course, and he meant to marry her. So that the other man's warning fell on deaf ears. But he was sorry for the other man, too.

To his enlightenment Destiny added a further illumination. Panton was sent up from the office to fetch certain papers from the top drawer of the writing table in the library of the house in FitzJohn's Avenue. Spring cleaning had covered everything with sheets, and the carpets were up. Also a curtain, which, he had always supposed, covered a door, was taken down and a picture revealed, a beautiful young woman, sedately gowned, radiantly smiling. He looked at it while the housemaid disinterred the writing table.

"Master's daughter, that is," said the housemaid, "by the first wife. Taking face, I always think, sir."

"Yes," said Panton absently. He was curious, but he was not the kind of man who questions servants. So he said no more. The housemaid, however, read interrogation in his silence.

"Ran away with an actor chap," she said quickly, and before he could speak, added, "not married, you know."

"I don't think," he said then, "that your master would like you to tell strangers such things."

"Lor', sir," she cheerfully rejoined, "you ain't no stranger. And besides, everybody knows. She died the other day. Master and the Missus had a most awful row and . . . "

He went out and waited in the hall till the writing table was uncovered.

These were the only hints he had of Mr Maskelyne's secret. And when on Mr Maskelyne's death a sealed packet was handed to him, a packet bearing on its face a date on which it was to be opened, and the instructions contained therein carried out, he surmised that this might have to do with that part of Mr Maskelyne's life where the lost daughter had been enshrined. He put the packet away in his pocket book with a sigh for the dead man and a smile for the living woman, his own girl whom he could now afford to marry. For Mr Maskelyne, with unexpected munificence, had left him ten thousand pounds and the business. That night the date of

the marriage was fixed, and he went about his increased affairs, contentment in his heart, and in his breast pocket the dead man's letter.

He wondered a little, in those first days, what the instructions might be
which he was to carry out. But afterwards, press of the great undertakings
left to him by Mr Maskelyne, and all the joyous preparations for a life with
The Girl, drove the thing out of his mind. But when the flowery white
wedding was over, and over the rush of the train, and when he and she,
alone in their private sitting room at the Lord Warden, awaited dinner, her
touch on a bulge in the breast of his coat and her question "What's all
that?" led him to pull out the letter-case.

"Your portrait among other things, Mrs Panton," he said, and opened
the case to shew her her pictured face. With the picture came the packet left
to him by Mr Maskelyne. He stared at it stupidly. "To be opened on the
28th of April" he read, and he turned it over to look at the unbroken seal.

"Why, you haven't opened it," said the bride. "Now I shall be able to
see it! But fancy having a letter like that unopened all day!"

"Curiously enough, I had other things to think about," he said caress-
ing her hand. "I'll open it now."

"Aren't we to have even this day free from horrid business," she asked,
and added instantly, "We might as well have got married on a Friday."

"You wouldn't. You said Saturday was a lucky day."

"It doesn't seem to be! No," she said, and laughed gladly. "I didn't
mean it. Of course I'm dying of curiosity. Perhaps it's to say he's left you a
lot more money."

"Mercenary woman! I shall not gratify your curiosity," he said gaily, and
opened the letter, shielding it from her eyes with his hand. She tried to take
it from him, and for a moment he pretended to resist her. Then it seemed
unnatural not to kiss her. Then he did open the letter. A little gilt key
dropped out and fell upon the floor. He retrieved it, and she leaned against
his shoulder to read the letter with him.

Abruptly he shook her off, and said, in a voice she had never heard:
"Don't!"

"Oh! but I must," she insisted; "good husbands have no secrets from
their wives, you know."

"Don't," he said again; "I tell you this is serious."

"I'm serious too," she said persisting.

"Be quiet," he told her very sternly. "Either the man was mad or . . . No, don't look over. I'll tell you if it's necessary."

"What a nice beginning to a honeymoon," she said, bit her lip, and hummed a tune, tapping her foot on the hearth-rug.

"Oh! don't be a darling idiot," he said with impatient tenderness, and felt for her hand as he went on reading.

This was the letter.

MY DEAR PANTON,—The Sunday papers have been full of the catastrophe which I have prepared so carefully. I thought, when I prepared it, that I could leave it as an anonymous legacy. But I find I cannot. I must and will have the credit of my achievement, the achievement which is the crown of my life's labours. Other men have built; no man has built as I have built. I rely on you to send to all the best papers the following statement:

"The reason of the sudden and complete collapse of the Arena Theatre is given by its architect, the late Reginald Maskelyne, in a letter dated the day before his death. Mr Maskelyne's life had been ruined and wrecked by one of the wretched mummers we call actors, and he determined to be revenged on mummers and on the fools who flock to see them. To this end, and to no other end, he designed his masterpiece, the Arena.

"The completeness of the collapse will have been a mystery to all. It was managed very simply. You know that the great dome which covers the whole building is supported by a circular girder of double H section, with spokes radiating to the centre, on which the finial and the gilt orb rest. The least expert can see that, if this girder gives way, the roof will fall in and the walls be pressed out. This circular girder, supported on thirty-eight pillars, was constructed in four parts, and bolted together in the usual way.

"You know all this. What you do not know is now to come. At two opposite joints of the circular girder certain holes were drilled in accordance with my drawings. These holes were explained to the workmen as mistakes—unimportant, since they could not weaken the girders. But they were not mistakes; they were the heart of my design. My design was to destroy the Arena and all the people in it by one simple act. The inspector passed everything, and the holes, having been plugged with wood and painted over, were not seen.

"When the inspector had paid his last visit I went up alone one night to the narrow space between the girder and the outer casing. There I made certain preparations. For several successive nights I entered the building after the painters and decorators had left it, and by slow degrees, for it was awkward work and heavy work for one man, I did what I meant to do. I knocked the plugs out of the holes that had been called mistakes, and between the two plates forming the girder I fixed two hinged couplings capable of keeping the girder in place when I should have removed the bolts which, so far, held it. The couplings fixed, I unscrewed and removed the bolts which had hitherto held the girder together. The whole building now depended on my couplings, and each of these, owing to the leverage employed, could be knocked up and separated at one blow from a solenoid hammer fixed to the main girder. The whole of this arrangement was hidden between the girder plates, and thus safe from observation. All four solenoids I connected in parallel and joined up to a clock which I had made and fixed in the basement. The wires, running in the thickness of the wall, were also safe from remark or accident. This clock is timed to run thirteen weeks. When the large weight of this clock falls to a certain point, it closes a switch. The connection being made, the solenoids are energised and the couplings loosed, and the smash, as reported in the Sunday papers, is inevitable. The clock itself is concealed in the basement of one of those massive pillars whose solidity has earned so many compliments. The slab which covers it is only released when the bolt in the inside of the basement door is shot right home. An ingenious idea which ensures me against interruption when I am winding my clock. I wind it every three months. There is a door in the back of the cupboard in my office which leads into a cupboard in the basement of the theatre. The whole thing has been simplicity itself. The clock will run down at half-past ten on Saturday, the 27th of April, the couplings will be loosed, and my vengeance be complete. My only regret is that I shall not hear the crash of the falling masonry, not see the great cloud of dust go up from that doomed building, shall not hear the groans of the dying, and the wails for the dead. This is my vengeance on life, and I should like to taste it to the full. My desire was to perish with my building, as Samson perished with the temple of the Philistines at Gaza. But I am unfortunately cursed with unconquerable physical cowardice. I dare not face that. Yet the temple of folly will fall and Reginald Maskelyne be avenged."

That is what I want you to publish for me. People will say that I am mad, but that would not trouble me, even if I heard it. I believe that, even in my grave, I shall know of the fall of the Arena and be glad. It was only when my girl died that I learned the name of the man who betrayed her, and sent her down into hell. That man was the Manager of the Arena. He never knew that I knew. He knows now. I have neglected no precautions. The model works perfectly. I work it of a night when I cannot sleep.—Yours,

R. Maskelyne.

I enclose key of clock case; you may like to hang it on your watch chain as a memento.

The date of the letter had been altered five or six times.

Richard Panton read the letter through, and read it again. Then he held it out to his wife.

"Poor Maskelyne," he said, "he must have been quite mad, and no one suspected it."

The bride read the letter, her pique drowned in pity.

"Oh! poor Mr Maskelyne. Poor fellow," she said, "how dreadfully sad. And nobody had the slightest idea."

"You see how he mixes up the paragraph for the paper with his letter to me. Changes from the third person to the first, and the tenses . . . past, and present, and future. He must have been dreadfully unhinged. But what a devilish idea. So well worked out, too."

"Perhaps he imagined the whole thing, about the daughter and everything," she suggested hopefully.

"No," he said, "I've heard that from another source."

"Still, he must have been quite mad," she said, "because, of course, there hasn't been any accident at the Arena at all, and he says there has. So, of course—" Her voice broke off suddenly. It was like the sudden silence when a running tap is turned off. And she held the letter in hands that trembled. And her eyes met his, strangely.

"What on earth's the matter?" he cried. "What is it, dear?"

"It says the Sunday papers. To-morrow's Sunday."

"What does it matter what he says?" he said impatiently. "The poor chap was off his head. What do his ravings matter? Put it away. I don't want to think of anything but *you.*"

But she put out her hands to keep him from her. "Let me think," she said, and now it was his turn to hear a voice till then unheard by him. "Let me think; yes—yes. I see. Suppose he *wasn't* mad. Suppose he really *has* set this horrible clock going. Don't you see? He timed it to happen on a Saturday. He says the account of it will be in the Sunday papers. He meant it to happen on Saturday. Dearest, *this* is Saturday. Suppose it happens to-night!"

"It can't. He wasn't in the least that sort of man. It's all nonsense. But I'll wire, if you like, to the theatre."

"You can't wire all that."

"I'll telephone, then."

"You can't telephone the key. Oh! Dick, I believe it's all *true*. I'm certain it is. I don't believe he was mad, in that way."

Her earnestness caught at him, wakened in him a dim uneasiness.

"But the thing's not possible," he said; "you don't know how public a thing building is, how every bit of work is inspected and sniffed into by the authorities. He can't have done it. Don't be a foolish darling. Here's dinner."

The perfect waiter had indeed entered, and was drawing back the chair for her. His subordinate stood, dish-laden. But, "Send the man away," she said, quite out loud and regardless of appearances. And when the waiters had gone, open-eyed, to whisper speculation in the corridor,

"You must go back," she said earnestly. "We must go back and see. All those people, and the people who love them. Dickie, we must go. I'm certain it's all true. We must go."

"If you insist on my leaving you on our wedding night," he said ceremoniously, "of course I'll do it. If there's a train."

"Leave me?" she said. "You don't suppose I shall let you leave me? We'll both go. There must be a train."

But there was no train that would reach London in time to allow of their getting to the theatre before half-past ten.

"It's at half-past ten it was to happen," she said, when he came back with the news about the train. "Oh! Richard, I've been thinking. It's all quite clear to me. Isn't this the year that ought to be Leap Year and isn't? The Century, you know? He must have reckoned on its being Leap Year. He thought the twenty-seventh would be a Saturday. And of course it's a Friday."

"Well, then, dearest, do be calm. Don't you see that shews it's all nonsense. He said it was to happen on the twenty-seventh? If it was going to happen at all, it would have happened yesterday, wouldn't it?"

"Yes, if clocks went by the almanack. He timed his clock to go off to-day. He meant the thing to happen on the twenty-seventh. Only Saturday's the twenty-eighth. He timed it for Saturday, that's to-day. A motor would do it. Get a motor."

"Be reasonable. At least have dinner," he urged.

But she would not have dinner, and she would not be reasonable. She insisted on a motor.

So he got a motor, and, once started for London, his mood changed. He took her in his arms, calling her the dearest, cleverest, foolishest, bravest. And now it was her turn to make light of the thing, and to own, with the sweet humility so delightful in our brides, that no doubt he knew best, but still—now wasn't there just the faintest, teeniest, weeniest chance that Mr Maskelyne had really planned this awful thing? And suppose they *didn't* go, and something *did* happen, how would they feel?

Thus they comforted each other.

But as the time went on, the sense grew in them both of danger, of momentous issues hanging in the balance. It was after the puncture which delayed for ten minutes their rush through the night, that this feeling of impending disaster settled on both, spreading above them cold, black, bat-like wings that were not again lifted.

The bride grew more and more silent. The bridegroom looked at his watch more and more frequently.

"There'll be plenty of time," he said, reassuring himself, "to clear the house and examine the basement. They can say an actor is ill or something."

"Oh, yes, plenty of time," said she, with a start, and a swift, feverish cheerfulness.

But when the lights of Eltham flashed at them, they knew there was not plenty of time. And it was as they crossed London Bridge that he broke the silence in which they were holding each other's cold hands.

"Dearest, there is no time for clearing the house or anything like that. With luck, I may be just in time to stop the infernal clock. If not—well, I can't do anything else. Can I?"

"No," she said, "you can't do anything else."

You will observe that there was now no talk of Mr Maskelyne's madness, of the possibility of the whole thing's being a maniac's vain imaginings. The long, dark rush through the quiet land had given that question the chance to settle itself for both of them.

The motor was tearing along the Embankment when the bride spoke again.

"We mustn't waste time," she said. "You quite understand that I am coming with you to that cellar."

He protested—vainly.

"There will be no time to argue when we get there," she told him quietly. "I've no one but you, Dick. I'm not going to send you where I won't go myself."

"Then I shall not go," he said.

"And if you don't go, it will happen. All those people. Nothing can save them. We must go straight into your office, and through the door he speaks of. You know the door?"

"I know the cupboard. The key is labelled. It is in his desk. But I can't let you. My love, my darling, you must let me go alone."

"I am not going to be separated from you," she said strongly; "I am not going to be parted from you on our wedding night."

The motor had stopped at the theatre. She leaped out and ran along to his office door, her pale silks and laces sweeping the muddy pavement.

"Quick, quick," she whispered, and he fumbled with the latchkey.

The lamps from the street shewed the office ghostly. He switched on the electric lights, unlocked a desk.

"Go," he said, "I implore you to go. Go to Charing Cross in the motor and wait for me. I command you to go, Clara."

She laughed, took the key from his hand, opened the cupboard, and before he could stop her, she had swung the inner door open and passed through it, turned on the switch by the door, and the circular vault with its eleven pillars was flooded with light.

It was then a quarter past ten. He followed, and as he entered she swung the door to behind them, and shot home its heavy bolt.

"Now, quick," she said, "which pillar?"

There were eleven pillars, and all to the eye the same.

"Those other switches," she said, and felt at the surface of the nearest pillar with quick, fluttering finger-tips. He turned on the switches at the other side of the vault.

"Oh, go back, my darling, go back!" he cried, as the light flashed brighter.

"Try the next pillar," she urged, "feel for a hole that a key could go into."

But there was nothing. All the pillars were smooth to the touch as far as their hands could reach. Only the faint unevenness of the lines of cement between the stones. They went over each pillar, quite in vain.

"If it is true, then this is our last moment," he said suddenly; "kiss me, beloved."

He clasped her in his arms. "Let us go," he breathed quickly. "We've done all we can. We can't do anything more. It's throwing our lives away. And we can't save the others. Oh, come. It will happen now."

"Oh, hush," she said, and tore herself from him. "Be quiet, listen!"

She laid her ear to the nearest pillar; then to the next. And then she threw out her arm in a wild gesture that was, even in that awful hour, a gesture of triumph.

"I can hear it," she said; and then, "Is there *another* bolt to that door?"

He crossed to it.

"Yes," he said, and shot that other bolt home. He knew what it meant. The time had come for this devilish machine to do its work, if it was ever to do it. And the vast pile would fall, as the Temple of Gaza fell, once, on the Philistines, and of all the people in the great house he and his bride, buried beneath thousands of tons of brick and stone, would have the least chance of escape or rescue. Yet he had shot home the bolt, and her eyes loved him for it, even as the lowest stone of the pillar, against which she was leaning, swung open slowly like a door, revealing smooth polished wood and a keyhole. He had had the little gold key ready in his hand all the while. He thrust it in. Would there be time? Big Ben chimed the half hour. If the clockwork were accurate, and accuracy had been Mr Maskelyne's most inseparable attribute, they had found the keyhole just too late. He tore the door open. There was the clock. As to that, at least, Maskelyne had written truth.

The long weight had already reached the switch whose contact should establish the current and turn the enormous pile, Reginald Maskelyne's life-triumph, into the crashing engine of torment and death. He caught the weight, raising it in his hand.

Now, God be praised, the mechanism is simple. No key. To pull this, to release that. A whirring sound of chains and cogs; a breathless agony of suspense.

"I've wound it up. All right, my darling. Oh, it's all right now—it's all right, I tell you! Hold up another moment. It's safe for months now."

She was drawing long breaths of agony, leaning against the pillar, clutching the stone door of the clock cavity with tense hands.

He had to drag, almost to carry her back to the street. He pushed her and her disordered silken draperies roughly into the motor car.

"I'll be back directly," he said. "It's absolutely safe, I tell you. I *must* go and tell the manager. Tell him to have the wires cut."

She tried to hold him, to follow him, but she fell back on the cushions. In the danger's face she had been bold as a tigress. Now that the danger was past, she was weak as a new-born kitten.

When he came back to her, she was crying softly, and clutched at him as he entered the car.

"Queen's Hotel, Sydenham," he said, "we won't stay too near it. You'd dream of it all night."

"Did you tell him?" she asked, as they were whirled away.

"Oh! I told him. But the brute was half drunk. I think he thought I was. I daresay I look it. He wouldn't listen at first, and when I made him, he hiccoughed out something about mare's nests and much obliged of course don't you know. Said he'd send his electrician to look into it on Monday."

"Did you tell him *all* about it?"

"Yes, as much as he'd listen to. Oh! my love, my brave girl. How can you love me at all? I wanted you to chuck it."

"You shot the second bolt," she said, and fainted in his arms.

The Arena audience streamed out into the yellow-lighted streets, chattering, laughing, discussing the evening's entertainment, praising the actor-manager—his cleverness, his enterprise. The hansoms and taxicabs lining the street dispersed with jinglings and puffings. The great doors were closed, the lights extinguished in box-office and corridors. In the theatre the attendants were busy covering the gay richness of velvet and gilding with sad-coloured cloths and draperies. The stage-door had let out the last of the performers, the dressers had finished their work of tidying and replacement. The porter waited impatiently for the manager to come out. At last he came, walking with the stiff, conscious exactness of a man not too drunk to know that it is wise to appear sober. He only lurched a little as he thrust his fur coat between two bright swing doors on the other side of the street, and his voice was hardly huskier than usual as he demanded Angostura and soda. He dropped a couple of tabloids into the long glass, drank, and sat down on the crimson plush seat with closed eyes.

"He'll be better in a minute," the barmaid said, in a whispered titter.

The freshness of the night air as he came out into it had sent a flash of clear remembrance to his muddled brain. It died at once, but left behind it the certainty that someone had told him something, and that he must remember what it was. So he had lurched into the bar and taken the antidote.

He sat there for five minutes, a man who had been handsome, but now on his face were the lines and dents and puffings of unbridled selfishness and gross living. When his face was at rest they shewed horribly.

Suddenly he stood up; he had remembered. A man had come and told him some tale about a clock working in the basement. Nonsense, perhaps, but worth investigating. He went to the telephone box and rang up the electrician.

"Come down to the Arena at once," he said. "You'll find me in the basement." Then he went back to the Arena, to let himself in with his private key.

As he passed through the swing-doors of the bar a woman in wretched rags, with a baby in her arms, held out a box of matches, and her arm brushed against his fur coat. He pushed her roughly away. The baby cried. And the actor-manager laughed. "What you get in the way for, then?" he asked.

He found the basement as those others had left it—those two who had fought there for the lives of others, their own lives in their hands. The doors swung to behind him as he turned up the electric light and stood alone among the pillars. In one of them a door stood open—he could see the clock inside. It was still going. He remembered enough of what that man had told him to know that it was the clock which was, somehow, the engine of destruction. He stared at it.

"You stop!" he said thickly; "see?"

The clock ticked on, delicately accentuating the silence.

"You just wait," he said to the clock, and pulled out a gold cigar-case and lighted a fat cigar, and paced heavily up and down, awaiting the electrician.

But the electrician did not come. He lived at Brixton, and the trams were crowded that night. The clock ticked on.

"You be quiet," said the actor-manager. "Why didn't he stop clock? He knew. Silly cuckoo. Any fool can stop confounded clock."

He went forward, caught at the big weight, and dragged it out. But when he let it go it settled back into its place with a small, sharp clattering, and the clock ticked on. He did not like it. It was like someone laughing at him. "Tick, tick, tick, tick."

"You shut up—see?" he said, leaned forward, and dragged at the pendulum. It broke in his hand, and he lurched forward, his head struck against the pillar, and his left hand sought support and found it. He leaned all his weight on his left hand, and that left hand rested on the switch designed to make the circuit, knock out the wedge, and bring down the building.

He staggered back—and as he did so a thunderous crash overhead told him what he had done. I think he was sober then. He dashed for the door—but the door had stuck. Then he thought of a girl who had loved him, and of a beggar woman and a baby that cried. Then death came to him voiced with thunder, and clad in thousands of tons of brick and iron and solid masonry.

It was a week before the housebreakers, working day and night at what was left of the Arena, came to what was left of the actor-manager.

Thus the whole of that gigantic, heaped-up vengeance did in fact fall on one sole being—fell on the man for whom it had been primarily designed. There was a certain wild poetic justice about the thing which appealed to the world when Panton made the facts known. It possibly appealed to the actor-manager himself in that brief instant between the crash and the coming of death. To him I think that instant was not brief.

Number 17

I yawned. I could not help it. But the flat, inexorable voice went on.

"Speaking from the journalistic point of view—I may tell you, gentlemen, that I once occupied the position of advertisement editor to the *Bradford Woollen Goods Journal*—and speaking from that point of view, I hold the opinion that all the best ghost stories have been written over and over again; and if I were to leave the road and return to a literary career I should never be led away by ghosts. Realism's what's wanted nowadays, if you want to be up-to-date."

The large commercial paused for breath.

"You never can tell with the public," said the lean, elderly traveller; "it's like in the fancy business. You never know how it's going to be. Whether it's a clockwork ostrich or Sometite silk or a particular shape of shaded glass novelty or a tobacco-box got up to look like a raw chop, you never know your luck."

"That depends on who you are," said the dapper man in the corner by the fire. "If you've got the right push about you, you can make a thing go, whether it's a clockwork kitten or imitation meat, and with stories, I take it, it's just the same—realism or ghost stories. But the best ghost story would be the realest one, *I* think."

The large commercial had got his breath.

"I don't believe in ghost stories, myself," he was saying with earnest dulness; "but there was rather a queer thing happened to a second cousin of an aunt of mine by marriage—a very sensible woman with no nonsense about her. And the soul of truth and honour. I shouldn't have believed it if she had been one of your flighty, fanciful sort."

"Don't tell us the story," said the melancholy man who travelled in hardware; "you'll make us afraid to go to bed."

The well-meant effort failed. The large commercial went on, as I had known he would; his words overflowed his mouth, as his person overflowed his chair. I turned my mind to my own affairs, coming back to the commercial room in time to hear the summing up.

"The doors were all locked, and she was quite certain she saw a tall, white figure glide past her and vanish. I wouldn't have believed it if—" And so on *da capo,* from "if she hadn't been the second cousin" to the "soul of truth and honour."

I yawned again.

"Very good story," said the smart little man by the fire. He was a traveller, as the rest of us were; his presence in the room told us that much. He had been rather silent during dinner, and afterwards, while the red curtains were being drawn and the red and black cloth laid between the glasses and the decanters and the mahogany, he had quietly taken the best chair in the warmest corner. We had got our letters written and the large traveller had been boring for some time before I even noticed that there was a best chair, and that this silent, bright-eyed, dapper, fair man had secured it.

"Very good story," he said; "but it's not what I call realism. You don't tell us half enough, sir. You don't say when it happened or where, or the time of year, or what colour your aunt's second cousin's hair was. Nor yet you don't tell us what it was she saw, nor what the room was like where she saw it, nor why she saw it, nor what happened afterwards. And I shouldn't like to breathe a word against anybody's aunt by marriage's cousin, first or second, but I must say I like a story about what a man's seen *himself.*"

"So do I," the large commercial snorted, "when I hear it."

He blew his nose like a trumpet of defiance.

"But," said the rabbit-faced man, "we know nowadays, what with the advance of science and all that sort of thing, we know there aren't any such things as ghosts. They're hallucinations; that's what they are—hallucinations."

"Don't seem to matter what you call them," the dapper one urged. "If you see a thing that looks as real as you do yourself, a thing that makes your blood run cold and turns you sick and silly with fear—well, call it ghost, or call it hallucination, or call it Tommy Dodd; it isn't the *name* that matters."

The elderly commercial coughed and said, "You might call it another name. You might call it—"

"No, you mightn't," said the little man, briskly; "not when the man it happened to had been a teetotal Bond of Joy for five years and is to this day."

"Why don't you tell us the story?" I asked.

"I might be willing," he said, "if the rest of the company were agreeable. Only I warn you it's not that sort-of-a-kind-of-a-somebody-fancied-they-saw-a-sort-of-a-kind-of-a-something-sort of a story. No, sir. Everything I'm going to tell you is plain and straightforward and as clear as a time-table—clearer than some. But I don't much like telling it, especially to people who don't believe in ghosts."

Several of us said we did believe in ghosts. The heavy man snorted and looked at his watch. And the man in the best chair began.

"Turn the gas down a bit, will you? Thanks. Did any of you know Herbert Hatteras? He was on this road a good many years. No? Well, never mind. He was a good chap, I believe, with good teeth and a black whisker. But I didn't know him myself. He was before my time. Well, this that I'm going to tell you about happened at a certain commercial hotel. I'm not going to give it a name, because that sort of thing gets about, and in every other respects it's a good house and reasonable, and we all have our living to get. It was just a good ordinary old-fashioned commercial hotel, as it might be this. And I've often used it since, though they've never put me in that room again. Perhaps they shut it up after what happened.

"Well, the beginning of it was, I came across an old schoolfellow; in Boulter's Lock one Sunday it was, I remember. Jones was his name, Ted Jones. We both had canoes. We had tea at Marlow, and we got talking about this and that and old times and old mates; and do you remember Jim, and what's become of Tom, and so on. Oh, you know. And I happened to ask after his brother, Fred by name. And Ted turned pale and almost dropped his cup, and he said, 'You don't mean to say you haven't heard?' 'No,' says I, mopping up the tea he'd slopped over with my handkerchief. 'No; what?' I said.

"'It was horrible,' he said. 'They wired for me, and I saw him afterwards. Whether he'd done it himself or not, nobody knows; but they'd found him lying on the floor with his throat cut.' No cause could be assigned for the rash act, Ted told me. I asked him where it had happened, and he told me the name of this hotel—I'm not going to name it. And when I'd sympathized with him and drawn him out about old times and poor old

Fred being such a good old sort and all that, I asked him what the room was like. I always like to know what the places look like where things happen.

"No, there wasn't anything specially rum about the room, only that it had a French bed with red curtains in a sort of alcove; and a large mahogany wardrobe as big as a hearse, with a glass door; and, instead of a swing-glass, a carved, black-framed glass screwed up against the wall between the windows, and a picture of 'Belshazzar's Feast' over the mantelpiece. I beg your pardon?" He stopped, for the heavy commercial had opened his mouth and shut it again.

"I thought you were going to say something," the dapper man went on. "Well, we talked about other things and parted, and I thought no more about it till business brought me to—but I'd better not name the town either—and I found my firm had marked this very hotel—where poor Fred had met his death, you know—for me to put up in. And I had to put up there too, because of their addressing everything to me there. And, anyhow, I expect I should have gone there out of curiosity.

"No. I didn't believe in ghosts in those days. I was like you, sir." He nodded amiably to the large commercial.

"The house was very full, and we were quite a large party in the room—very pleasant company, as it might be to-night; and we got talking of ghosts—just as it might be us. And there was a chap in glasses, sitting just over there, I remember—an old hand on the road, he was; and he said, just as it might be any of you, 'I don't believe in ghosts, but I wouldn't care to sleep in Number Seventeen, for all that'; and, of course, we asked him why. 'Because,' said he, very short, 'that's why.'

"But when we'd persuaded him a bit, he told us.

"'Because that's the room where chaps cut their throats,' he said. 'There was a chap called Bert Hatteras began it. They found him weltering in his gore. And since that every man that's slept there's been found with his throat cut.'

"I asked him how many had slept there. 'Well, only two beside the first,' he said; 'they shut it up then.' 'Oh, did they?' said I. 'Well, they've opened it again. Number Seventeen's my room!'

"I tell you those chaps looked at me.

"'But you aren't going to *sleep* in it?' one of them said. And I explained that I didn't pay half a dollar for a bedroom to keep awake in.

"'I suppose it's press of business has made them open it up again,' the chap in spectacles said. 'It's a very mysterious affair. There's some secret horror about that room that we don't understand,' he said, 'and I'll tell you another queer thing. Every one of those poor chaps was a commercial gentleman. That's what I don't like about it. There was Bert Hatteras—he was the first, and a chap called Jones—Frederick Jones, and then Donald Overshaw—a Scotchman he was, and travelled in child's underclothing.'

"Well, we sat there and talked a bit, and if I hadn't been a Bond of Joy, I don't know that I mightn't have exceeded, gentlemen—yes, positively exceeded; for the more I thought about it the less I liked the thought of Number Seventeen. I hadn't noticed the room particularly, except to see that the furniture had been changed since poor Fred's time. So I just slipped out, by and by, and I went out to the little glass case under the arch where the booking-clerk sits—just like here, that hotel was—and I said:—

"'Look here, miss; haven't you another room empty except seventeen?'

"'No,' she said; 'I don't think so.'

"'Then what's that?' I said, and pointed to a key hanging on the board, the only one left.

"'Oh,' she said, 'that's sixteen.'

"'Anyone in sixteen?' I said. 'Is it a comfortable room?'

"'No,' said she. 'Yes; quite comfortable. It's next door to yours—much the same class of room.'

"'Then I'll have sixteen, if you've no objection,' I said, and went back to the others, feeling very clever.

"When I went up to bed I locked my door, and, though I didn't believe in ghosts, I wished seventeen wasn't next door to me, and I wished there wasn't a door between the two rooms, though the door was locked right enough and the key on my side. I'd only got the one candle besides the two on the dressing-table, which I hadn't lighted; and I got my collar and tie off before I noticed that the furniture in my new room was the furniture out of Number Seventeen; French bed with red curtains, mahogany wardrobe as big as a hearse, and the carved mirror over the dressing-table between the two windows, and 'Belshazzar's Feast' over the mantelpiece. So that, though I'd not got the *room* where the commercial gentlemen had cut their throats, I'd got the *furniture* out of it. And for a moment I thought that was worse than the other. When I thought of what that furniture could tell, if it could speak—

"It was a silly thing to do—but we're all friends here and I don't mind owning up—I looked under the bed and I looked inside the hearse-wardrobe and I looked in a sort of narrow cupboard there was, where a body could have stood upright—"

"A body?" I repeated.

"A man, I mean. You see, it seemed to me that either these poor chaps had been murdered by someone who hid himself in Number Seventeen to do it, or else there was something there that frightened them into cutting their throats; and upon my soul, I can't tell you which idea I liked least!"

He paused, and filled his pipe very deliberately. "Go on," someone said. And he went on.

"Now, you'll observe," he said, "that all I've told you up to the time of my going to bed that night's just hearsay. So I don't ask you to believe it—though the three coroners' inquests would be enough to stagger most chaps, I should say. Still, what I'm going to tell you now's *my* part of the story—what happened to me myself in that room."

He paused again, holding the pipe in his hand, unlighted.

There was a silence, which I broke.

"Well, what *did* happen?" I asked.

"I had a bit of a struggle with myself," he said. "I reminded myself it was not *that* room, but the next one that it had happened in. I smoked a pipe or two and read the morning paper, advertisements and all. And at last I went to bed. I left the candle burning, though, I own that."

"Did you sleep?" I asked.

"Yes. I slept. Sound as a top. I was awakened by a soft tapping on my door. I sat up. I don't think I've ever been so frightened in my life. But I made myself say, 'Who's there?' in a whisper. Heaven knows I never expected anyone to answer. The candle had gone out and it was pitch-dark. There was a quiet murmur and a shuffling sound outside. And no one answered. I tell you I hadn't expected anyone to. But I cleared my throat and cried out, 'Who's there?' in a real out-loud voice. And 'Me, sir,' said a voice. 'Shaving-water, sir; six o'clock, sir.'

"It was the chambermaid."

A movement of relief ran round our circle. "I don't think much of your story," said the large commercial.

"You haven't heard it yet," said the storyteller, dryly. "It was six o'clock on a winter's morning, and pitch-dark. My train went at seven. I got up and began to dress. My one candle wasn't much use. I lighted the two on the dressing-table to see to shave by. There wasn't any shaving-water outside my door, after all. And the passage was as black as a coal-hole. So I started to shave with cold water; one has to sometimes, you know. I'd gone over my face, and I was just going lightly round under my chin, when I saw something move in the looking-glass. I mean something that moved was reflected in the looking-glass. The big door of the wardrobe had swung open, and by a sort of double reflection I could see the French bed with the red curtains. On the edge of it sat a man in his shirt and trousers—a man with black hair and whiskers, with the most awful look of despair and fear on his face that I've ever seen or dreamt of. I stood paralyzed, watching him in the mirror. I could not have turned round to save my life. Suddenly he laughed. It was a horrid, silent laugh, and shewed all his teeth. They were very white and even. And the next moment he had cut his throat from ear to ear, there before my eyes. Did you ever see a man cut his throat? The bed was all white before."

The story-teller had laid down his pipe, and he passed his hand over his face before he went on.

"When I could look round I did. There was no one in the room. The bed was as white as ever. Well, that's all," he said, abruptly, "except that now, of course, I understood how these poor chaps had come by their deaths. They'd all seen this horror—the ghost of the first poor chap, I suppose—Bert Hatteras, you know; and with the shock their hands must have slipped and their throats got cut before they could stop themselves. Oh! by the way, when I looked at my watch it was two o'clock; there hadn't been any chamber-maid at all. I must have dreamed that. But I didn't dream the other. Oh! and one thing more. It was the same room. They hadn't changed the room, they'd only changed the number. *It was the same room!*"

"Look here," said the heavy man; "the room you've been talking about. *My* room's sixteen. And it's got that same furniture in it as what you describe, and the same picture and all."

"Oh, has it?" said the story-teller, a little uncomfortable, it seemed. "I'm sorry. But the cat's out of the bag now, and it can't be helped. Yes, it *was* this house I was speaking of. I suppose they've opened the room again. But you don't believe in ghosts; *you'll* be all right."

"Yes," said the heavy man, and presently got up and left the room.

"He's gone to see if he can get his room changed. You see if he hasn't," said the rabbit-faced man; "and I don't wonder."

The heavy man came back and settled into his chair.

"I could do with a drink," he said, reaching to the bell.

"I'll stand some punch, gentlemen, if you'll allow me," said our dapper story-teller. "I rather pride myself on my punch. I'll step out to the bar and get what I need for it."

"I thought he said he was a teetotaller," said the heavy traveller when he had gone. And then our voices buzzed like a hive of bees. When our story-teller came in again we turned on him—half-a-dozen of us at once—and spoke.

"One at a time," he said, gently. "I didn't quite catch what you said."

"We want to know," I said, "how it was—if seeing that ghost made all those chaps cut their throats by startling them when they were shaving—how was it *you* didn't cut *your* throat when you saw it?"

"I should have," he answered, gravely, "without the slightest doubt—I should have cut my throat, only," he glanced at our heavy friend, "I always shave with a safety razor. I travel in them," he added, slowly, and bisected a lemon.

"But—but," said the large man, when he could speak through our up-roar, "I've gone and given up my room."

"Yes," said the dapper man, squeezing the lemon; "I've just had my things moved into it. It's the best room in the house. I always think it worth while to take a little pains to secure it."

The Five Senses

Professor Boyd Thompson's services to the cause of science are usually spoken of as inestimable, and so indeed they probably are, since in science, as in the rest of life, one thing leads to another, and you never know where anything is going to stop. At any rate, inestimable or not, they are world-renowned, and he with them. The discoveries which he gave to his time are a matter of common knowledge among biological experts, and the sudden ending of his experimental activities caused a few days' wonder in even lay circles. Quite unintelligent people told each other that it seemed a pity, and persons on omnibuses exchanged commonplaces starred with his name.

But the real meaning and cause of that ending have been studiously hidden, as well as the events which immediately preceded it. A veil has been drawn over all the things that people would have liked to know, and it is only now that circumstances so arrange themselves as to make it possible to tell the whole story. I propose to avail myself of this possibility.

It will serve no purpose for me to explain how the necessary knowledge came into my possession; but I will say that the story was only in part pieced together by me. Another hand is responsible for much of the detail, and for a certain occasional emotionalism which is, I believe, wholly foreign to my own style. In my original statement of the following facts I dealt fully, as I am, I may say without immodesty, qualified to do, with all the scientific points of the narrative. But these details were judged, unwisely as I think, to be needless to the expert, and unintelligible to the ordinary reader, and have therefore been struck out; the merest hints been left as necessary links in the story. This appears to me to destroy most of its interest, but I admit that the elisions are perhaps justified. I have no desire to assist or encourage callow students in such experiments as those by which Professor Boyd Thompson brought his scientific career to an end.

Incredible as it may appear, Professor Boyd Thompson was once a little boy who wore white embroidered frocks and blue sashes; in that state he caught flies and pulled off their wings to find out how they flew. He did not find out, and Lucilla, his little girl-cousin, also in white frocks, cried over the dead, dismembered flies, and buried them in little paper coffins. Later, he wore a holland blouse with a belt of leather, and watched the development of tadpoles in a tin bath in the stable yard. A microscope was, on his eighth birthday, presented to him by an affluent uncle. The uncle shewed him how to surprise the secrets of a drop of pond water, which, limpid to the eye, confessed under the microscope to a whole cosmogony of strenuous and undesirable careers. At the age of ten, Arthur Boyd Thompson was sent to a private school, its Headmaster an acolyte of Science, who esteemed himself to be a high priest of Huxley and Tyndal, a devotee of Darwin. Thence to the choice of medicine as a profession was, when the choice was insisted on by the elder Boyd Thompson, a short, plain step. Inorganic chemistry failed to charm, and under the cloak of Medicine and Surgery the growing fever of scientific curiosity could be sated on bodies other than the cloak-wearer's. He became a medical student and an enthusiast for vivisection.

The bow of Apollo was not always bent. In a rest-interval, the summer vacation, to be exact, he met again the cousin—second, once removed—Lucilla, and loved her. They were betrothed. It was a long, bright summer full of sunshine, garden-parties, picnics, archery—a decaying amusement—and croquet, then coming to its own. He exulted in the distinction already crescent in his career, but some half-formed wholly-unconscious desire to shine with increased lustre in the eyes of the beloved, caused him to invite, for the holidays' ultimate week, a fellow student, one who knew and could testify to the quality of the laurels already encircling the head of the young scientist. The friend came, testified, and in a vibrating interview under the lime-trees of Lucilla's people's garden, Mr Boyd Thompson learned that Lucilla never could, never would love or marry a vivisectionist.

The moon hung low and yellow in the spacious calm of the sky; the hour was propitious, the lovers fond. Mr Boyd Thompson vowed that his scientific research should henceforth deal wholly with departments into which the emotions of the non-scientific cannot enter. He went back to London, and within the week bought four dozen frogs, twelve guinea-pigs, five cats, and a spaniel. His scientific aspirations met his love-longings, and did not fight them. You cannot fight beings of another world. He took part in a debate on "Blood Pressure," which created some little stir in medical circles, spoke eloquently, and distinction surrounded him with a halo.

He wrote to Lucilla three times a week, took his degree, and published that celebrated paper of his which set the whole scientific world by the ears, "The Action of Choline on the Nervous System," I think its name was.

Lucilla surreptitiously subscribed to a press-cutting agency for all snippets of print relating to her lover. Three weeks after the publication of that paper, which really was the beginning of Professor Boyd Thompson's fame, she wrote to him from her home in Kent.

"Arthur, you have been doing it again. You know how I love you, and I believe you love me; but you must choose between loving me and torturing dumb animals. If you don't choose right, then it's good-bye, and God forgive you.

"Your poor Lucilla, who loved you very dearly."

He read the letter, and the human heart in him winced and whined. Yet not so deeply now, nor so loudly, but that he bethought himself to seek out a friend and pupil, who would watch certain experiments, attend to the cutting of certain sections, before he started for Tenterden, where she lived. There was no station at Tenterden in those days, but a twelve-mile walk did not dismay him.

Lucilla's home was one of those houses of brave proportions and an inalienable bourgeois stateliness, which stand back a little from the noble High Street of that most beautiful of Kentish towns. He came there pleasantly exercised, his boots dusty, and his throat dry, and stood on the snowy doorstep, beneath the Jacobean lintel. He looked down the wide, beautiful street, raised eyebrows and shrugged uneasy shoulders within his professional frock-coat.

"It's all so difficult," he said to himself.

Lucilla received him in a drawing-room scented with last year's rose leaves, and fresh with chintz that had been washed a dozen times. She stood, very pale and frail; her blond hair was not teased into fluffiness, and rounded over the chignon of the period, but banded Madonna-wise, crowning her with heavy burnished plaits. Her gown was of white muslin, and round her neck black velvet passed, supporting a gold locket. He knew whose picture it held. The loose bell sleeves fell away from the slender arms with little black velvet bracelets, and she leaned one hand on a chiffonier of carved rosewood, on whose marble top stood, under a glass case, a Chinese pagoda, carved in ivory, and two Bohemian glass vases with medallions representing young women nursing pigeons. There were white curtains of darned net, in the fire-place white ravelled muslin spread a cascade brightened with threads of tinsel. A canary sang in a green cage, wainscotted with yellow tarlatan, and two red rosebuds stood in lank specimen glasses on the mantelpiece.

Every article of furniture in the room spoke eloquently of the sheltered life, the iron obstinacy of the well-brought-up.

It was a scene that invaded his mental vision many a time, in the laboratory, in the lecture-room. It symbolized many things, all dear, and all impossible.

They talked awkwardly, miserably. And always it came round to this same thing.

"But you don't mean it," he said, and at last came close to her.

"I do mean it," she said, very white, very trembling, very determined.

"But it's my life," he pleaded, "it's the life of thousands. You don't understand."

"I understand that dogs are tortured. I can't bear it."

He caught at her hand.

"Don't," she said. "When I think what that hand does!"

"Dearest," he said very earnestly, "which is the more important, a dog or a human being?"

"They're all God's creatures," she flashed, unorthodoxly orthodox. "They're all God's creatures," with much more that he heard, and pitied, and smiled at miserably in his heart.

"You don't understand," he kept saying, stemming the flood of her rhetorical pleadings. "Spencer Wells alone has found out wonderful things, just with experiments on rabbits."

"Don't tell me," she said, "I don't want to hear."

The conventions of their day forbade that he should tell her anything plainly. He took refuge in generalities. "Spencer Wells, that operation he perfected, it's restored thousands of women to their husbands—saved thousands of women for their children."

"I don't care what he's done—it's wrong if it's done in that way."

It was on that day that they parted, after more than an hour and more than two, of mutual misunderstood reiteration. He, she said, was brutal. And besides it was plain that he did not love her. To him, she seemed unreasonable, narrow, prejudiced, blind to the high ideals of the new science.

"Then it's good-bye," he said at last. "If I gave way, you'd only despise me. Because I should despise myself. It's no good. Good-bye, dear."

"Good-bye," she said. "I know I'm right. You'll know I am, some day."

"Never," he answered, more moved and in a more diffused sense than he had ever believed he could be. "I can't set my pleasure in you against the good of the whole world."

"If that's all you think of me," she said, and her silk and her muslin whirled from the room.

He walked back to Staplehurst, thrilled with the conflict. The thrill died down, went out, and left as ashes a cold resolve.

That was the end of Mr Boyd Thompson's engagement.

It was quite by accident that he made his greatest discovery. There are those who hold that all great discoveries are accident—or Providence. The terms are, in this connection, interchangeable. He plunged into work to wash away the traces of his soul's wounds, as a man plunges into water to wash off red blood. And he swam there, perhaps, a little blindly. The injection with which he treated that white rabbit was not compounded of the drugs he had intended to use. He could not lay his hand on the thing he wanted, and in that sort of frenzy of experiment, to which no scientific investigator is wholly a stranger, he cast about for a new idea. The thing that came to his hand was a drug that he had never in his normal mind intended to use—an unaccredited, wild, magic medicine obtained by a missionary from some savage South Sea tribe and brought home as an example of the ignorance of the heathen.

And it worked a miracle.

He had been fighting his way through the unbending opposition of known facts, he had been struggling in the shadows, and this discovery was like the blinding light that meets a man's eyes when his pickaxe knocks a hole in a dark cave, and he finds himself face to face with the sun. The effect was undoubted. Now it behoved him to make sure of the cause, to eliminate all those other factors to which that effect might have been due. He experimented cautiously, slowly. These things take years, and the years he did not grudge. He was never tired, never impatient; the slightest variations, the least indications, were eagerly observed, faithfully recorded.

His whole soul was in his work, Lucilla was the one beautiful memory of his life. But she was a memory. The reality was this discovery, the accident, the Providence.

Day followed day, all alike, and yet each taking, almost unperceived, one little step forward; or stumbling into sudden sloughs, those losses and lapses that take days and weeks to retrieve. He was Professor, and his hair was grey at the temples before his achievement rose before him, beautiful, inevitable, austere in its completed splendour, as before the triumphant artist rises the finished work of his art.

He had found out one of the secrets with which Nature has crammed her dark hiding-places. He had discovered the hidden possibilities of sensation. In plain English, his researches had led him thus far: he had found—by accident or by Providence—the way to intensify sensation. Vaguely, incredulously, he had perceived his discovery; the rabbits and guinea-pigs had demonstrated it plainly enough. Then there was a night when he became aware that those results must be checked by something else. He must work out in marble the form he had worked out in clay. He knew that by this drug, which had, so to speak, thrust itself upon him, he could intensify the five senses of any of the inferior animals. Could he intensify those senses in man? If so, worlds beyond the grasp of his tired mind opened themselves before him. If so, he would have achieved a discovery, made a contribution to the science he had loved so well and followed at such a cost a discovery equal to any that any man had ever made.

Ferrier, and Leo, and Horsley; those he would outshine. Galileo, Newton, Harvey; he would rank with these.

Could he find a human rabbit to submit to the test?

The soul of the man Lucilla had loved, turned and revolted. No: he had experimented on guinea-pigs and rabbits, but when it came to experimenting on men, there was only one man on whom he chose to use his new-found powers. Himself.

At least she would not have it to say that he was a coward, or unfair, when it came to the point of what a man could do and dare, could suffer and endure.

His big laboratory was silent and deserted. His assistants were gone, his private pupils dispersed. He was alone with the tools of his trade. Shelf on shelf of smooth stoppered bottles, drugs and stains, the long bench gleaming with beakers, test tubes, and the glass mansions of costly apparatus. In the shadows at the far end of the room, where the last going assistant had turned off the electric lights, strange shapes lurked, wicker-covered carboys, kinographs, galvanometers, the faintly threatening aspect of delicate complex machines all wires and coils and springs, the gaunt form of the pendulum myograph, and certain well-worn tables and copper troughs, for which the moment had no use.

He knew that this drug with others, diversely compounded and applied, produced in animals an abnormal intensification of the senses; that it increased—nay, as it were magnified a thousandfold, the hearing, the sight, the touch—and he was almost sure, the senses of taste and smell. But of the extent of the increase he could form no exact estimate.

Should he to-night put himself in the position of one able to speak on these points with authority? Or should he go to the Royal Society's meeting, and hear that ass Netherby maunder yet once again about the Secretion of Lymph?

He pulled out his notebook and laid it open on the bench. He went to the locked cupboard, unfastened it with the bright key that hung instead of seal or charm at his watch-chain. He unfolded a paper and laid it on the bench where no one coming in could fail to see it. Then he took out little bottles, three, four, five, polished a graduated glass and dropped into it slow, heavy drops. A larger bottle yielded a medium in which all mingled. He hardly hesitated at all before turning up his sleeve and slipping the tiny needle into his arm. He pressed the end of the syringe. The injection was made.

Its effect, though not immediate, was sudden. He had to close his eyes, staggered indeed and was glad of the stool near him; for the drug coursed through him as a hunt in full cry might sweep over untrodden plains. Then suddenly everything seemed to settle; he was no longer the helpless scene of incredible meetings, but Professor Boyd Thompson who had injected a mixture of certain drugs, and was experiencing their effect.

His fingers, still holding the glass syringe, sent swift messages to his brain. When he looked down at his fingers, he saw that what they grasped was the smooth, slender tube of clear glass. What he felt that they held was a tremendous cylinder, rough to the touch. He wondered, even at the moment, why, if his sense of touch were indeed magnified to this degree, everything did not appear enormous—his ring, his collar. He examined the new phenomenon with cold care. It seemed that only that was enlarged on which his attention, his mind, was fixed. He kept his hand on the glass syringe, and thought of his ring, got his mind away from the tube, back again in time to feel it small between his fingers, grow, increase, and become big once more.

"So *that's* a success," he said, and saw himself lay the thing down. It lay just in front of the rack of test tubes, to the eye just that little glass cylinder. To the touch it was like a water-pipe on a house side, and the test tubes, when he touched them, like the pipes of a great organ.

"Success," he said again, and mixed the antidote. For he had found the antidote in one of those flashes of intuition, imagination, genius, that light the ways of science as stars light the way of a ship in dark waters. The action of the antidote was enough for one night. He locked the cupboard, and, after all, was glad to listen to the maunderings of Netherby. It had been lonely there, in the atmosphere of complete success.

One by one, day by day, he tested the action of his drugs on his other senses. Without being technical, I had perhaps better explain that the compelling drug was, in each case, one and the same. Its action was directed to this set of nerves or that by means of the other drugs mixed with it. I trust this is clear?

The sense of smell was tested, and its laboratory, with its mingled odours, became abominable to him. Hardly could he stay himself from rushing forth into the outer air, to wash his nostrils in the clear coolness of Hampstead Heath. The sense of taste gave him, magnified a thousand times, the flavour of his after-dinner coffee, and other tastes, distasteful almost beyond the bearing point.

But "Success," he said, rinsing his mouth at the laboratory sink after the drinking of the antidote, "all along the line, success."

Then he tested the action of his discovery on the sense of hearing. And the sound of London came like the roar of a giant, yet when he fixed his attention on the movements of a fly, all other sounds ceased, and he heard the sound of the fly's feet on the shelf when it walked. Thus, in turn, he heard the creak of boards expanding in the heat, the movement of the glass stoppers that kept imprisoned in their proper bottles the giants of acid and alkali.

"Success!" he cried aloud, and his voice sounded in his ears like the shout of a monster overcoming primeval forces. "Success! success!"

Remained only the eyes, and here, strangely enough, the Professor hesitated, faint with a sudden heart-sickness. Following all intensification there must be reaction. What if the reaction exceeded that from which it reacted, what if the wave of tremendous sight, stemmed by the antidote ebbing, left him blind? But the spirit of the explorer in science is the spirit that explores African rivers, and sails amid white bergs to seek the undiscovered Pole.

He held the syringe with a firm hand, made the required puncture, and braced himself for the result. His eyes seemed to swell to great globes, to dwindle to microscopic globules, to swim in a flood of fire, to shrivel high and dry on a beach of hot sand. Then he saw, and the glass fell from his hand. For the whole of the stable earth seemed to be suddenly set in movement, even the air grew thick with vast overlapping shapeless shapes. He opined later that these were the microbes and bacilli that cover and fill all things, in this world that looks so clean and bright.

Concentrating his vision, he saw in the one day's little dust on the bottles myriads of creatures, crawling and writhing, alive. The proportions of the laboratory seemed but little altered. Its large lines and forms remained practically unchanged. It was the little things that were no longer little, the invisible things that were now invisible no longer. And he felt grateful, for the first time in his life, for the limits set by Nature to the powers of the human body. He had increased those powers. If he let his eyes stray idly about, as one does in the waltz for example, all was much as it used to be. But the moment he looked steadily at any one thing, it became enormous.

He closed his eyes. Success here had gone beyond his wildest dreams. Indeed he could not but feel that success, taking the bit between its teeth, had perhaps gone just the least little bit too far.

And on the next day he decided to examine the drug in all its aspects, to court the intensification of all his senses which should set him in the position of supreme power over men and things, transform him from a Professor into a demi-god.

The great question was, of course, how the five preparations of his drug would act on or against each other. Would it be intensification, or would they neutralize each other? Like all imaginative scientists, he was working with stuff perilously like the spells of magic, and certain things were not possible to be foretold. Besides, this drug came from a land of mystery and the knowledge of secrets which we call magic. He did not anticipate any increase in the danger of the experiment. Nevertheless he spent some hours in arranging and destroying papers, among others certain pages of the yellow note-book. After dinner he detained his man as, laden with the last tray, he was leaving the room.

"I may as well tell you, Parker," the Professor said, moved by some impulse he had not expected, "that you will benefit to some extent by my will. On conditions. If any accident should cut short my life, you will at once communicate with my solicitor, whose name you will now write down."

The model man, trained by fifteen years of close personal service, drew forth a note-book neat as the Professor's own, wrote in it neatly the address the Professor gave.

"Anything more, sir?" he asked, looking up, pencil in hand.

"No," said the Professor, "nothing more. Good-night, Parker."

"Good-night, sir," said the model man.

The next words the model man opened his lips to speak were breathed into the night tube of the nearest doctor.

"My master, Professor Boyd Thomson; could you come round at once, sir. I'm afraid it's very serious."

It was half past six when the nearest doctor—Jones was his unimportant name—stooped over the lifeless body of the Professor.

He shook his head as he stood up and looked round the private laboratory on whose floor the body lay.

"His researches are over," he said. "Yes, he's dead. Been dead some hours. When did you find him?"

"I went to call my master as usual," said Parker; "he rises at six, summer and winter, sir. He was not in his room, and the bed had not been slept in. So I came in here, sir. It is not unusual for my master to work all night when he has been very interested in his experiments, and then he likes his coffee at six."

"I see," said Doctor Jones. "Well, you'd better rouse the house and fetch his own doctor. It's heart failure, of course, but I daresay he'd like to sign the certificate himself."

"Can nothing be done?" said Parker, much affected.

"Nothing," said Dr Jones. "It's the common lot. You'll have to look out for another situation."

"Yes, sir," said Parker; "he told me only last night what I was to do in case of anything happening to him. I wonder if he had any idea?"

"Some premonition, perhaps," the doctor corrected.

The funeral was a very quiet one. So the late Professor Boyd Thompson had decreed in his will. He had arranged all details. The body was to be clothed in flannel, placed in an open coffin covered only with a linen sheet, and laid in the family mausoleum, a moss-grown building in the midst of a little, park which surrounded Boyd Grange, the birthplace of the Boyd Thompsons. A little property in Sussex it was. The Professor sometimes went there for week-ends. He had left this property to Lucilla, with a last love-letter, in which he begged her to give his body the hospitality of the death-house, now hers with the rest of the estate. To Parker he left an annuity of two hundred pounds, on the condition that he should visit and enter the mausoleum once in every twenty-four hours for fourteen days after the funeral.

To this end the late Professor's solicitor decided that Parker had better reside at Boyd Grange for the said fortnight, and Parker, whose nerves seemed to be shaken, petitioned for company. This made easy the arrangement which the solicitor desired to make—of a witness to the carrying out by Parker of the provisions of the dead man's will. The solicitor's clerk was quite good company, and arm-in-arm with him Parker paid his first visit to the mausoleum. The little building stands in a glade of evergreen oaks. The trees are old and thick, and the narrow door is deep in shadow even on the sunniest day. Parker went to the mausoleum, peered through its square grating, but he did not go in. Instead, he listened, and his ears were full of silence.

"He's dead, right enough," he said, with a doubtful glance at his companion.

"You ought to go in, oughtn't you?" said the solicitor's clerk.

"Go in yourself, if you like, Mr Pollack," said Parker, suddenly angry; "anyone who likes can go in, but it won't be me. If he was alive, it 'ud be different. I'd have done anything for *him*. But I ain't going in among all them dead and mouldering Thompsons. See ? If we both say I did, it'll be just the same as me doing it."

"So it will," said the solicitor's clerk; "but where do I come in?"

Parker explained to him where he came in, to their mutual content.

"Right you are," said the clerk; "on those terms I'm fly. And if we both say you did it, we needn't come to the beastly place again," he added, shivering and glancing over his shoulder at the door with the grating.

"No more we need," said Parker.

Behind the bars of the narrow door lay deeper shadows than those of the ilexes outside. And in the blackest of the shadow lay a man whose every sense was intensified as though by a magic potion. For when the Professor swallowed the five variants of his great discovery, each acted as he had expected it to act. But the union of the five vehicles conveying the drug to the nerves, which served his five senses, had paralysed every muscle. His hearing, taste, touch, scent and sight were intensified a thousandfold—as they had been in the individual experiments—but the man who felt all this exaggerated increase of sensation was powerless as a cat under kurali. He could not raise a finger, stir an eyelash. More, he could not breathe, nor did his body advise him of any need of breathing. And he had lain thus immobile and felt his body slowly grow cold, had heard in thunder the voices of Parker and the doctor; had felt the enormous hands of those who made his death-toilet, had smelt intolerably the camphor and lavender that they laid round him in the narrow, black bed; had tasted the mingled flavours of the drug and its five mediums; and, in an ecstasy of magnified sensation, had made the lonely train journey which coffins make, and known himself carried into the mausoleum and left there alone. And every sense was intensified, even his sense of time, so that it seemed to him that he had lain there for many years. And the effect of the drugs shewed no sign of any diminution or reaction. Why had he not left directions for the injection of the antidote? It was one of those slips which wreck campaigns, cause the discovery of hidden crimes. It was a slip, and he had made it. He had thought of death, but in all the results he had anticipated, death's semblance had found no place. Well, he had made his bed, and he must lie on it. This narrow bed, whose scent of clean oak and French polish was distinct among the musty, intolerable odours of the charnel house.

It was perhaps twenty hours that he had lain these, powerless, immobile, listening to the sounds of unexplained movements about him, when he felt with a joy, almost like delirium, a faint quivering in the eyelids.

They had closed his eyes, and till now, they had remained closed. Now, with an effort as of one who lifts a grave-stone, he raised his eyelids. They closed again quickly, for the roof of the vault, at which he gazed earnestly, was alive with monsters; spiders, earwigs, crawling beetles and flies, far too small to have been perceived by normal eyes, spread giant forms over him. He closed his eyes and shuddered. It felt like a shudder, but no one who had stood beside him could have noted any movement.

It was then that Parker came—and went.

Professor Boyd Thompson heard Parker's words, and lay listening to the thunder of Parker's retreating feet. He tried to move—to call out. But he could not. He lay there helpless, and somehow he thought of the dark end of the laboratory, where the assistant before leaving had turned out the electric lights.

He had nothing but his thoughts. He thought how he would lie there, and die there. The place was sequestered; no one passed that way. Parker had failed him, and the end was not hard to picture. He might recover all his faculties, might be able to get up, able to scream, to shout, to tear at the bars. The bars were strong, and Parker would not come again. Well, he would try to face with a decent bravery whatever had to be faced.

Time, measureless, spread round. It seemed as though someone had stopped all the clocks in the world, as though he were not in time but in eternity. Only by the waxing and waning light he knew of the night and the day.

His brain was weary with the effort to move, to speak, to cry out. He lay, informed with something like despair—or fortitude. And then Parker came again. And this time a key grated in the lock. The Professor noted with rapture that it sounded no louder than a key should sound, turned in a lock that was rusty. Nor was the voice other than he had been used to hear it, when he was man alive and Parker's master. And—

"You can go in, of course, if you wish it, Miss," said Parker disapprovingly; "but it's not what I should advise myself. For me it's different," he added on a sudden instinct of self-preservation; "I've got to go in. Every day for a fortnight," he added, pitying himself.

"I will go in, thank you," said a voice. "Yes, give me the candle, please. And you need not wait. I will lock the door when I come out." Thus the voice spoke. And the voice was Lucilla's.

In all his life the Professor had never feared death or its trappings. Neither its physical repulsiveness, nor the supernatural terrors which cling about it, had he either understood or tolerated. But now, in one little instant, he did understand.

He heard Lucilla come in. A light held near him shone warm and red through his closed eyelids. And he knew that he had only to unclose those eyelids to see her face bending over him. And he could unclose them. Yet he would not. He lay there, still and straight in his coffin, and life swept through him in waves of returning power. Yet he lay like death. For he said, or something in him said:

"She believes me dead. If I open my eyes it will be like a dead man looking at her. If I move it will be a dead man moving under her eyes. People have gone mad for less. Lie still, lie still," he told himself; "take any risks yourself. There must be none for her."

She had taken the candle away, set it down somewhere at a distance, and now she was kneeling beside him and her hand was under his head. He knew he could raise his arm and clasp her—and Parker would come back perhaps, when she did not return to the house, come back to find a man in grave-clothes, clasping a mad woman. He lay still. Then her kisses and tears fell on his face, and she murmured broken words of love and longing. But he lay still. At any cost he must lie still. Even at the cost of his own sanity, his own life. And the warmth of her hand under his head, her face against his, her kisses, her tears, set his blood flowing evenly and strongly. Her other arm lay on his breast, softly pressing over his heart. He would not move. He would be strong. If he were to be saved, it must be by some other way, not this.

Suddenly tears and kisses ceased; her every breath seemed to have stopped with these. She had drawn away from him. She spoke. Her voice came from above him. She was standing up.

"Arthur!" she said, "Arthur!" Then he opened his eyes, the narrowest chink. But he could not see her. Only he knew she was moving towards the door. There had been a new quality in her tone, a thrill of fear, or hope was it? or at least of uncertainty? Should he move; should he speak? He dared not. He knew too well the fear that the normal human being has of death and the grave, the fear transcending love, transcending reason. Her voice was further away now. She was by the door. She was leaving him. If he let her go, it was an end of hope for him. If he did not let her go, an end, perhaps, of reason, for her. No.

"Arthur," she said, "I don't believe . . . I believe you can hear me. I'm going to get a doctor. If you can speak, speak to me."

Her speaking ended, cut off short as a cord is cut by a knife. He did not speak. He lay in a conscious, forced rigidity.

"Speak if you can," she implored, "just one word!"

Then he said, very faintly, very distinctly, in a voice that seemed to come from a great way off, "Lucilla!"

And at the word she screamed aloud, pitifully, and leapt for the entrance; and he heard the rustle of her crape in the narrow door. Then he opened his eyes wide, and raised himself on his elbow. Very weak he was, and trembling exceedingly. To his ears her scream held the note of madness. Vainly he had refrained. Selfishly he had yielded. The cold hand of a mortal faintness clutched at his heart.

"I don't want to live now," he told himself, and fell back in the straight bed.

Her arms were round him.

"I'm going to get help," she said, her lips to his ear; "brandy and things. Only I came back. I didn't want you to think I was frightened. Oh, my dear! thank God, thank God!" He felt her kisses even through the swooning mist that swirled about him. Had she really fled in terror? He never knew. He knew that she had come back to him.

That is the real, true, and authentic narrative of the events which caused Professor Boyd Thompson to abandon a brilliant career, to promise anything that Lucilla might demand, and to devote himself entirely to a gentlemanly and unprofitable farming, and to his wife. From the point of view of the scientific world it is a sad ending to much promise, but at any rate there are two happy people hand in hand at the story's ending.

There is no doubt that for several years Professor Boyd Thompson had had enough of science, and, by a natural revulsion, flung himself into the full tide of common-place sentiment. But genius, like youth, cannot be denied. And I, for one, am doubtful whether the Professor's renunciation of research will be a lasting one. Already I have heard whispers of a laboratory which is being built on to the house, beyond the billiard-room.

But I am inclined to believe the rumours which assert that, for the future, his research will take the form of extending paths already well trodden; that he will refrain from experiments with unknown drugs, and those dreadful researches which tend to merge the chemist and biologist in the alchemist and the magician. And he certainly does not intend to experiment further on the nerves of any living thing, even his own. The Professor had already done enough work to make the reputation of half-a-dozen ordinary scientists. He may be pardoned if he rests on his laurels, entwining them, to some extent, with roses.

The bottle containing the drug from the South Seas was knocked down on the day of his death and swept up in bits by the laboratory boy. It is a curious fact that the Professor has wholly forgotten the formulae of his great discovery, the notes of which he destroyed just before experiment which so nearly was his last. This is a great satisfaction to his wife, and possibly to the Professor. But of this I cannot be sure; the scientific spirit survives much.

To the unscientific reader the strangest part of this story will perhaps be the fact that Parker is still with his old master, a wonderful example of the perfect butler. Professor Boyd Thompson was able to forgive Parker because he understood him. And he learned to understand Parker in those moments of agony, when his keen intellect and his awakened heart taught him, through his love for Lucilla, the depth of that gulf of fear which lies between the quick and the dead.

The Violet Car

Do you know the downs—the wide windy spaces, the rounded shoulders of the hills leaned against the sky, the hollows where farms and homesteads nestle sheltered, with trees round them pressed close and tight as a carnation in a button-hole? On long summer days it is good to lie on the downs, between short turf and pale, clear sky, to smell the wild thyme, and hear the tiny tinkle of the sheep-bells and the song of the skylark. But on winter evenings when the wind is waking up to its work, spitting rain in your eyes, beating the poor, naked trees and shaking the dusk across the hills like a gray pall, then it is better to be by a warm fireside, in one of the farms that lie lonely where shelter is, and oppose their windows glowing with candle light and firelight to the deepening darkness, as faith holds up its love-lamp in the night of sun and sorrow that is life.

I am unaccustomed to literary effort—and I feel that I shall not say what I have to say, or that it will convince you, unless I say it very plainly. I thought I could adorn my story with pleasant words, prettily arranged. But as I pause to think of what really happened, I see that the plainest words will be the best. I do not know how to weave a plot, nor how to embroider it. It is best not to try. These things happened. I have no skill to add to what happened; nor is any adding of mine needed.

I am a nurse—and I was sent for to go to Charlestown—a mental case. It was November—and the fog was thick in London, so that my cab went at a foot's pace, so I missed the train by which I should have gone. I sent a telegram to Charlestown, and waited in the dismal waiting room at London Bridge. The time was passed for me by a little child. Its mother, a widow, seemed too crushed to be able to respond to its quick questionings. She answered briefly, and not, as it seemed, to the child's satisfaction. The child itself presently seemed to perceive that its mother was not, so to speak, available. It leaned back on the wide, dusty seat and yawned. I caught its eye, and smiled. It would not smile, but it looked. I took out of my bag a silk purse, bright with beads and steel tassels, and turned it over and over. Presently, the child slid along the seat and said, "Let me"—after that all was easy. The mother sat with eyes closed. When I rose to go, she opened them and thanked me. The child, clinging, kissed me. Later, I saw them get into a first class carriage in my train. My ticket was a third class one.

I expected, of course, that there would be a conveyance of some sort to meet me at the station—but there was nothing. Nor was there a cab or a fly to be seen. It was by this time nearly dark, and the wind was driving the rain almost horizontally along the unfrequented road that lay beyond the door of the station. I looked out, forlorn and perplexed.

"Haven't you engaged a carriage?" It was the widow lady who spoke. I explained.

"My motor will be here directly," she said, "you'll let me drive you? Where is it you are going?"

"Charlestown," I said, and as I said it, I was aware of a very odd change in her face. A faint change, but quite unmistakable.

"Why do you look like that?" I asked her bluntly. And, of course, she said, "Like what?"

"There's nothing wrong with the house?" I said, for that, I found, was what I had taken that faint change to signify; and I was very young, and one has heard tales. "No reason why I shouldn't go there, I mean?"

"No—oh no—" she glanced out through the rain, and I knew as well as though she had told me that there was a reason why she should not wish to go there. So

"Don't trouble," I said, "it's very kind of you—but its probably out of your way and . . ."

"Oh—but I'll take you—of course I'll take you," she said, and the child said "Mother, here comes the car."

And come it did, though neither of us heard it till the child had spoken. I know nothing of motor cars, and I don't know the names of any of the parts of them. This was like a brougham—only you got in at the back, as you do in a waggonette; the seats were in the corners, and when the door

was shut there was a little seat that pulled up, and the child sat on it between us. And it moved like magic—or like a dream of a train.

We drove quickly through the dark—I could hear the wind screaming,
and the wild dashing of the rain against the windows, even through the
whirring of the machinery. One could see nothing of the country—only the
black night, and the shafts of light from the lamps in front.

After, as it seemed, a very long time, the chauffeur got down and
opened a gate. We went, through it, and after that the road was very much
rougher. We were quite silent in the car, and the child had fallen asleep.

We stopped, and the car stood pulsating, as though it were out of
breath, while the chauffeur hauled down my box. It was so dark that I
could not see the shape of the house, only the lights in the downstairs windows, and the low-walled front garden faintly revealed by their light and the
light of the motor lamps. Yet I felt that it was a fair-sized house, that it was
surrounded by big trees, and that there was a pond or river close by. In
daylight next day I found that all this was so. I have never been able to tell
how I knew it that first night, in the dark, but I did know it. Perhaps there
was something in the way the rain fell on the trees and on the water. I don't
know.

The chauffeur took my box up a stone path, whereon I got out, and
said my good-byes and thanks.

"Don't wait, please, don't," I said. "I'm all right now. Thank you a
thousand times!"

The car, however, stood pulsating till I had reached the doorstep, then
it caught its breath, as it were, throbbed more loudly, turned, and went.

And still the door had not opened. I felt for the knocker, and rapped
smartly. Inside the door I was sure I heard whispering. The car light was
fast diminishing to a little distant star, and its panting sounded now hardly
at all. When it ceased to sound at all, the place was quiet as death. The
lights glowed redly from curtained windows, but there was no other sign of
life. I wished I had not been in such a hurry to part from my escort, from
human companionship, and from the great, solid, competent presence of
the motor car.

I knocked again, and this time I followed the knock by a shout.

"Hullo!" I cried. "Let me in. I'm the nurse!"

There was a pause, such a pause as would allow time for whisperers to exchange glances on the other side of a door.

Then a bolt ground back, a key turned, and the doorway framed no longer cold, wet wood, but light and a welcoming warmth—and faces.

"Come in, oh, come in," said a voice, a woman's voice, and the voice of a man said: "We didn't know there was anyone there."

And I had shaken the very door with my knockings!

I went in, blinking at the light, and the man called a servant, and between them they carried my box upstairs.

The woman took my arm and led me into a low, square room, pleasant, homely, and comfortable, with solid mid-Victorian comfort—the kind that expressed itself in rep and mahogany. In the lamplight I turned to look at her. She was small and thin, her hair, her face, and her hands were of the same tint of greyish yellow.

"Mrs Eldridge?" I asked.

"Yes," said she, very softly. "Oh! I am so glad you've come. I hope you won't be dull here. I hope you'll stay. I hope I shall be able to make you comfortable."

She had a gentle, urgent way of speaking that was very winning.

"I'm sure I shall be very comfortable," I said; "but it's I that am to take care of you. Have you been ill long?"

"It's not me that's ill, really," she said, "it's him—"

Now, it was Mr Robert Eldridge who had written to engage me to attend on his wife, who was, he said, slightly deranged.

"I see," said I. One must never contradict them, it only aggravates their disorder.

"The reason . . ." she was beginning, when his foot sounded on the stairs, and she fluttered off to get candles and hot water.

He came in and shut the door. A fair bearded, elderly man, quite ordinary.

"You'll take care of her," he said. "I don't want her to get talking to people. She fancies things."

"What form do the illusions take?" I asked, prosaically.

"She thinks I'm mad," he said, with a short laugh.

"It's a very usual form. Is that all?"

"It's about enough. And she can't hear things that I can hear, see things that I can see, and she can't smell things. By the way, you didn't see or hear anything of a motor as you came up, did you?"

"I came up in a motor car," I said shortly. "You never sent to meet me, and a lady gave me a lift." I was going to explain about my missing the earlier train, when I found that he was not listening to me. He was watching the door. When his wife came in, with a steaming jug in one hand and a flat candlestick in the other, he went towards her, and whispered eagerly. The only words I caught were: "She came in a real motor."

Apparently, to these simple people a motor was as great a novelty as to me. My telegram, by the way, was delivered next morning.

They were very kind to me; they treated me as an honoured guest. When the rain stopped, as it did late the next day, and I was able to go out, I found that Charlestown was a farm, a large farm, but even to my inexperienced eyes it seemed neglected and unprosperous. There was absolutely nothing for me to do but to follow Mrs Eldridge, helping her where I could in her household duties, and to sit with her while she sewed in the homely parlour. When I had been in the house a few days, I began to put together the little things that I had noticed singly, and the life at the farm seemed suddenly to come into focus, as strange surroundings do after a while.

I found that I had noticed that Mr and Mrs Eldridge were very fond of each other, and that it was a fondness, and their way of shewing it was a way that told that they had known sorrow, and had borne it together. That she shewed no sign of mental derangement, save in the persistent belief of hers that he was deranged. That the morning found them fairly cheerful; that after the early dinner they seemed to grow more and more depressed; that after the "early cup of tea"—that is just as dusk was falling—they always went for a walk together. That they never asked me to join them in this walk, and that it always took the same direction—across the downs towards the sea. That they always returned from this walk pale and dejected; that she sometimes cried afterwards alone in their bedroom, while he was shut up in the little room they called the office, where he did his accounts, and paid his men's wages, and where his hunting-crops and guns were kept. After supper, which was early, they always made an effort to be cheerful. I knew that this effort was for my sake, and I knew that each of them thought it was good for the other to make it.

Just as I had known before they shewed it to me that Charlestown was surrounded by big trees and had a great pond beside it, so I knew, and in as inexplicable a way, that with these two fear lived. It looked at me out of their eyes. And I knew, too, that this fear was not her fear. I had not been two days in the place before I found that I was beginning to be fond of them both. They were so kind, so gentle, so ordinary, so homely—the kind of people who ought not to have known the name of fear—the kind of people to whom all honest, simple joys should have come by right, and no sorrows but such as come to us all, the death of old friends, and the slow changes of advancing years.

They seemed to belong to the land—to the downs, and the copses, and the old pastures, and the lessening corn-fields. I found myself wishing that I, too, belonged to these, that I had been born a farmer's daughter. All the stress and struggle of cram and exam., of school, and college, and hospital, seemed so loud and futile, compared with these open secrets of the down life. And I felt this the more, as more and more I felt that I must leave it all—that there was, honestly, no work for me here such as for good or ill I had been trained to do.

"I ought not to stay," I said to her one afternoon, as we stood at the open door. It was February now, and the snowdrops were thick in tufts beside the flagged path. "You are quite well."

"*I* am," she said.

"You are quite well, both of you," I said. "I oughtn't to be taking your money and doing nothing for it."

"You're doing everything," she said; "you don't know how much you're doing.

"We had a daughter of our own once," she added vaguely, and then, after a very long pause, she said very quietly and distinctly:

"He has never been the same since."

"How not the same?" I asked, turning my face up to the thin February sunshine.

She tapped her wrinkled, yellow-grey forehead, as country people do.

"Not right here," she said.

"How?" I asked. "Dear Mrs Eldridge, tell me; perhaps I could help somehow."

Her voice was so sane, so sweet. It had come to this with me, that I did not know which of those two was the one who needed my help.

"He sees things that no one else sees, and hears things no one else hears, and smells things that you can't smell if you're standing there beside him."

I remembered with a sudden smile his words to me on the evening of my arrival:

"She can't see, or hear, or smell."

And once more I wondered to which of the two I owed my service.

"Have you any idea why?" I asked. She caught at my arm.

"It was after our Bessie died," she said—"the very day she was buried. The motor that killed her—they said it was an accident—it was on the Brighton Road. It was a violet colour. They go into mourning for Queens with violet, don't they?" she added; "and my Bessie, she was a Queen. So the motor was violet. That was all right, wasn't it?"

I told myself now that I saw that the woman was not normal, and I saw why. It was grief that had turned her brain. There must have been some change in my look, though I ought to have known better, for she said suddenly, "No. I'll not tell you any more."

And then he came out. He never left me alone with her for very long. Nor did she ever leave him for very long alone with me.

I did not intend to spy upon them, though I am not sure that my position as nurse to one mentally afflicted would not have justified such spying. But I did not spy. It was chance. I had been to the village to get some blue sewing silk for a blouse I was making, and there was a royal sunset which tempted me to prolong my walk. That was how I found myself on the high downs where they slope to the broken edge of England—the sheer, white cliffs against which the English Channel beats for ever. The furze was in flower, and the skylarks were singing, and my thoughts were with my own life, my own hopes and dreams. So I found that I had struck a road, without knowing when I had struck it. I followed it towards the sea, and quite soon it ceased to be a road, and merged in the pathless turf as a stream sometimes disappears in sand. There was nothing but turf and furze bushes, the song of the skylarks, and beyond the slope that ended at the cliff's edge, the booming of the sea. I turned back, following the road, which defined itself again a few yards back, and presently sank to a lane, deep-banked and bordered with brown hedge stuff. It was there that I came upon them in the dusk. And I heard their voices before I saw them, and before it was possible for them to see me. It was her voice that I heard first.

"No, no, no, no, no," it said.

"I tell you yes," that was his voice; "there—can't you hear it, that panting sound—right away—away? It must be at the very edge of the cliff."

"There's nothing, dearie," she said, "indeed there's nothing."

"You're deaf—and blind—stand back I tell you, it's close upon us."

I came round the corner of the lane then, and as I came, I saw him catch her arm and throw her against the hedge—violently, as though the danger he feared were indeed close upon them I stopped behind the turn of the hedge and stepped back. They had not seen me. Her eyes were on his face, and they held a world of pity, love, agony—his face was set in a mask of terror, and his eyes moved quickly as though they followed down the lane the swift passage of Something—something that neither she nor I could see. Next moment he was cowering, pressing his body into the hedge—his face hidden in his hands, and his whole body trembling so that I could see it, even from where I was a dozen yards away, through the light screen of the over-grown hedge.

"And the smell of it!"—he said, "do you mean to tell me you can't smell it?"

She had her arms round him.

"Come home, dearie," she said. "Come home! It's all your fancy—come home with your old wife that loves you."

They went home.

Next day I asked her to come to my room to look at the new blue blouse. When I had shewn it to her I told her, what I had seen and heard yesterday in the lane.

"And now I know," I said, "which of you it is that wants care."

To my amazement she said very eagerly, "Which?"

"Why, he—of course"—I told her, "there was nothing there."

She sat down in the chintz covered armchair by the window, and broke into wild weeping. I stood by her and soothed her as well as I could.

"It's a comfort to know," she said at last. "I haven't known what to believe. Many a time, lately, I've wondered whether after all it could be me that was mad, like he said. And there was nothing there? There always *was* nothing there—and it's on him the judgment, not on me. On him. Well, that's something to be thankful for."

So her tears, I told myself, had been more of relief at her own escape. I looked at her with distaste, and forgot that I had been fond of her. So that her next words cut me like little knives.

"It's bad enough for him as it is," she said—"but it's nothing to what it would be for him, if I was really to go off my head and him left to think he'd brought it on me. You see, now I can look after him the same as I've always done. It's only once in the day it comes over him. He couldn't bear it, if it was all the time—like it'll be for me now. It's much better it should be him—I'm better able to bear it than he is."

I kissed her then and put my arms round her, and said, "Tell me what it is that frightens him so—and it's every day, you say?"

"Yes—ever since. I'll tell you. It's a sort of comfort to speak out. It was a violet coloured car that killed our Bessie. You know our girl that I've told you about. And it's a violet coloured car that he thinks he sees—every day up there in the lane. And he says he hears it, and that he smells the smell of the machinery—the stuff they put in it—you know."

"Petrol?"

"Yes, and you can *see* he hears it, and you can *see* he sees it. It haunts him, as if it was a ghost. You see, it was he that picked her up after the violet car went over her. It was that that turned him. I only saw her as he carried her in, in his arms—and then he'd covered her face. But he saw her just as they'd left her, lying in the dust . . . you could see the place on the road where it happened for days and days."

"Didn't they come back?"

"Oh yes . . . they came back. But Bessie didn't come back. But there was a judgment on them. The very night of the funeral, that violet car went over the cliff—dashed to pieces—every soul in it. That was the man's widow that drove you home the first night."

"I wonder she uses a car after that," I said—I wanted something common-place to say.

"Oh," said Mrs Eldridge, "it's all what you're used to. We don't stop walking because our girl was killed on the road. Motoring comes as natural to them as walking to us. There's my old man calling—poor old dear. He wants me to go out with him."

She went, all in a hurry, and in her hurry slipped on the stairs and twisted her ankle. It all happened in a minute and it was a bad sprain.

When I had bound it up, and she was on the sofa, she looked at him, standing as if he were undecided, staring out of the window with his cap in his hand. And she looked at me.

"Mr Eldridge mustn't miss his walk," she said. "You go with him, my dear. A breath of air will do you good."

So I went, understanding as well as though he had told me, that he did not want me with him, and that he was afraid to go alone, and that he yet had to go.

We went up the lane in silence. At that corner he stopped suddenly, caught my arm, and dragged me back. His eyes followed something that I could not see. Then he exhaled a held breath, and said, "I thought I heard a motor coming." He had found it hard to control his terror, and I saw beads of sweat on his forehead and temples. Then we went back to the house.

The sprain was a bad one. Mrs Eldridge had to rest, and again next day it was I who went with him to the corner of the lane.

This time he could not, or did not try to, conceal what he felt. "There—listen!" he said. "Surely you can hear it?"

I heard nothing.

"Stand back," he cried shrilly, suddenly, and we stood back close against the hedge.

Again the eyes followed something invisible to me, and again the held breath exhaled.

"It will kill me one of these days," he said, "and I don't know that I care how soon—if it wasn't for her."

"Tell me," I said, full of that importance, that conscious competence, that one feels in the presence of other people's troubles. He looked at me.

"I will tell you, by God," he said. "I couldn't tell *her.* Young lady, I've gone so far as wishing myself a Roman, for the sake of a priest to tell it to. But I can tell *you,* without losing my soul more than it's lost already. Did you ever hear tell of a violet car that got smashed up—went over the cliff?"

"Yes," I said. "Yes."

"The man that killed my girl was new to the place. And he hadn't any eyes—or ears—or he'd have known me, seeing we'd been face to face at the inquest. And you'd have thought he'd have stayed at home that one day, with the blinds drawn down. But not he. He was swirling and swivelling all about the country in his cursed violet car, the very time we were burying her. And at dusk—there was a mist coming up—he comes up behind me in this very lane, and I stood back, and he pulls up, and he calls out, with his damned lights full in my face:

"'Can you tell me the way to Hexham, my man?' says he.

"I'd have liked to shew him the way to hell. And that was the way for me, not him. I don't know how I came to do it. I didn't mean to do it. I didn't think I was going to—and before I knew anything, I'd said it. 'Straight ahead,' I said; 'keep straight ahead.' Then the motor-thing panted, chuckled, and he was off. I ran after him to try to stop him—but what's the use of running after these motor-devils? And he kept straight on. And every day since then, every dear day, the car comes by, the violet car that nobody can see but me—and it keeps straight on."

"You ought to go away," I said, speaking as I had been trained to speak. "You fancy these things. You probably fancied the whole thing. I don't suppose you ever *did* tell the violet car to go straight ahead. I expect it was all imagination, and the shock of your poor daughter's death. You ought to go right away."

"I can't," he said earnestly. "If I did, some one else would see the car. You see, somebody *has* to see it every day as long as I live. If it wasn't me, it would be someone else. And I'm the only person who *deserves* to see it. I wouldn't like any one else to see it—it's too horrible. *It's* much more horrible than you think," he added slowly.

I asked him, walking beside him down the quiet lane, what it was that was so horrible about the violet car. I think I quite expected him to say that it was splashed with his daughter's blood. . . . What he did say was, "It's too horrible to tell you," and he shuddered.

I was young then, and youth always thinks it can move mountains. I persuaded myself that I could cure him of his delusion by attacking—not the main fort—that is always, to begin with, impregnable, but one, so to speak, of the outworks. I set myself to persuade him not to go to that corner in the lane, at that hour in the afternoon.

"But if I don't, someone else will see it."

"There'll be nobody there to see it," I said briskly.

"Someone will be there. Mark my words, someone will be there—and then they'll know."

"Then I'll be the someone," I said. "Come—you stay at home with your wife, and *I'll* go—and if I see it I'll promise to tell you, and if I don't—well, then I will be able to go away with a clear conscience."

"A clear conscience," he repeated.

I argued with him in every moment when it was possible to catch him alone. I put all my will and all my energy into my persuasions. Suddenly, like a door that you've been trying to open, and that has resisted every key till the last one, he gave way. Yes—I should go to the lane. And he would not go.

I went.

Being, as I said before, a novice in the writing of stories, I perhaps haven't made you understand that it was quite hard for me to go—that I felt myself at once a coward and a heroine. This business of an imaginary motor that only one poor old farmer could see, probably appears to you quite commonplace and ordinary. It was not so with me. You see, the idea of this thing had dominated my life for weeks and months, had dominated it even before I knew the nature of the domination. It was this that was the fear that I had known to walk with these two people, the fear that shared their bed and board, that lay down and rose up with them. The old man's fear of this and his fear of his fear. And the old man was terribly convincing. When one talked with him, it was quite difficult to believe that he was mad, and that there wasn't, and couldn't be, a mysteriously horrible motor that was visible to him, and invisible to other people. And when he said that, if he were not in the lane, someone else would see it—it was easy to say "Nonsense," but to think "Nonsense" was not so easy, and to *feel* "Nonsense" quite oddly difficult.

I walked up and down the lane in the dusk, wishing not to wonder what might be the hidden horror in the violet car. I would not let blood into my thoughts. I was not going to be fooled by thought transference, or any of those transcendental follies. I was not going to be hypnotised into seeing things.

I walked up the lane—I had promised him to stand near that corner for five minutes, and I stood there in the deepening dusk, looking up towards the downs and the sea. There were pale stars. Everything was very still. Five minutes is a long time. I held my watch in my hand. Four—four and a half—four and a quarter. Five. I turned instantly. And then I saw that *he* had followed me—he was standing a dozen yards away—and his face was turned from me. It was turned towards a motor car that shot up the lane— It came very swiftly, and before it came to where he was, I knew that it was very horrible. I crushed myself back into the crackling bare hedge, as I should have done to leave room for the passage of a real car—though I knew that this one was not real. It looked real—but I knew it was not.

As it neared him, he started back, then suddenly he cried out. I heard him. "No, no, no, no—no more, no more," was what he cried, with that he flung himself down on the road in front of the car, and its great tires passed over him. Then the car shot past me and I saw what the full horror of it was. There was no blood—that was not the horror. The colour of it was, as she had said, violet.

I got to him and got his head up. He was dead. I was quite calm and collected now, and felt that to be so was extremely creditable to me. I went to a cottage where a labourer was having tea—he got some men and a hurdle.

When I had told his wife, the first intelligible thing she said was: "It's better for him. Whatever he did he's paid for now—" So it looks as though she had known—or guessed—more than he thought.

I stayed with her till her death. She did not live long.

You think perhaps that the old man was knocked down and killed by a real motor, which happened to come that way of all ways, at that hour of all hours, and happened to be, of all colours, violet. Well, a real motor leaves its mark on you where it kills you, doesn't it. But when I lifted up that old man's head from the road, there was no mark on him, no blood—no broken bones—his hair was not disordered, nor his dress. I tell you there was not even a speck of mud on him, except where he had touched the road in falling. There were no tyre-marks in the mud.

The motor car that killed him came and went like a shadow. As he threw himself down, it swerved a little so that both its wheels should go over him.

He died, the doctor said, of heart-failure. I am the only person to know that he was killed by a violet car, which, having killed him, went noiselessly away towards the sea. And that car was empty—there was no one in it. It was just a violet car that moved along the lanes swiftly and silently, and was empty.

The Haunted House

It was by the merest accident that Desmond ever went to the Haunted House. He had been away from England for six years, and the nine months' leave taught him how easily one drops out of one's place.

He had taken rooms at the Greyhound before he found that there was no reason why he should stay in Elmstead rather than in any other of London's dismal outposts. He wrote to all the friends whose addresses he could remember, and settled himself to await their answers.

He wanted someone to talk to, and there was no one. Meantime he lounged on the horsehair sofa with the advertisements, and his pleasant grey eyes followed line after line with intolerable boredom. Then, suddenly, "Halloa!" he said, and sat up. This is what he read:—

A HAUNTED HOUSE.—Advertiser is anxious to have phenomena investigated. Any properly-accredited investigator will be given full facilities. Address, by letter only, Wildon Prior, 237, Museum Street, London.

"That's rum!" he said. Wildon Prior had been the best wicket-keeper in his club. It wasn't a common name. Anyway, it was worth trying, so he sent off a telegram.

"Wildon Prior, 237, Museum Street, London. May I come to you for a day or two and see the ghost?—WILLIAM DESMOND."

On returning next day from a stroll there was an orange envelope on the wide Pembroke table in his parlour.

"Delighted—expect you to-day. Book to Crittenden from Charing Cross. Wire train.—WILDON PRIOR, Ormehurst Rectory, Kent."

"So that's all right," said Desmond, and went off to pack his bar, and ask in the bar for a time-table. "Good old Wildon; it will be ripping, seeing him again."

A curious little omnibus, rather like a bathing-machine, was waiting outside Crittenden Station, and its driver, a swarthy, blunt-faced little man, with liquid eyes, said, "You a friend of Mr Prior, sir?" shut him up in the bathing-machine, and banged the door on him. It was a very long drive, and less pleasant than it would have been in an open carriage.

The last part of the journey was through a wood; then came a church-yard and a church, and the bathing-machine turned in at a gate under heavy trees and drew up in front of a white house with bare, gaunt windows.

"Cheerful place, upon my soul!" Desmond told himself, as he tumbled out of the back of the bathing-machine.

The driver set his bag on the discoloured doorstep and drove off. Desmond pulled a rusty chain, and a big-throated bell jangled above his head.

Nobody came to the door, and he rang again. Still nobody came, but he heard a window thrown open above the porch. He stepped back on to the gravel and looked up.

A young man with rough hair and pale eyes was looking out. Not Wil-don, nothing like Wildon. He did not speak, but he seemed to be making signs; and the signs seemed to mean, "Go away!"

"I came to see Mr Prior," said Desmond. Instantly and softly the win-dow closed.

"Is it a lunatic asylum I've come to by chance?" Desmond asked him-self, and pulled again at the rusty chain.

Steps sounded inside the house, the sound of boots on stone. Bolts were shot back, the door opened, and Desmond, rather hot and a little an-noyed, found himself looking into a pair of very dark, friendly eyes, and a very pleasant voice said:—

"Mr Desmond, I presume? Do come in and let me apologize."

The speaker shook him warmly by the hand, and he found himself fol-lowing down a flagged passage a man of more than mature age, well-dressed, handsome, with an air of competence and alertness which we as-sociate with what is called "a man of the world." He opened a door and led the way into a shabby, bookish, leathery room.

"Do sit down, Mr Desmond."

"This must be the uncle, I suppose," Desmond thought, as he fitted himself into the shabby, perfect curves of the arm-chair.

"How's Wildon?" he asked, aloud. "All right, I hope?"

The other looked at him. "I beg your pardon," he said, doubtfully.

"I was asking how Wildon is?"

"I am quite well, I thank you," said the other man, with some formality.

"I beg your pardon"—it was now Desmond's turn to say it—"I did not realize that your name might be Wildon, too. I meant Wildon Prior."

"I am Wildon Prior," said the other, "and you, I presume, are the expert from the Psychical Society?"

"Good Lord, no!" said Desmond. "I'm Wildon Prior's friend, and, of course, there must be two Wildon Priors."

"You sent the telegram? You are Mr Desmond? The Psychical Society were to send an expert, and I thought—"

"I see," said Desmond; "and I thought you were Wildon Prior, an old friend of mine—a young man," he said, and half rose.

"Now, don't," said Wildon Prior. "No doubt it is my nephew who is your friend. Did he know you were coming? But of course he didn't. I am wandering. But I'm exceedingly glad to see you. You will stay, will you not? If you can endure to be the guest of an old man. And I will write Will tonight and ask him to join us."

"That's most awfully good of you," Desmond assured him. "I shall be glad to stay. I was awfully pleased when I saw Wildon's name in the paper, because—" And out came the tale of Elmstead, its loneliness and disappointment.

Mr Prior listened with the kindest interest.

"And you have not found your friends? How sad! But they will write to you. Of course, you left your address?"

"I didn't, by Jove!" said Desmond. "But I can write. Can I catch the post?"

"Easily," the elder man assured him. "Write your letters now. My man shall take them to the post, and then we will have dinner, and I will tell you about the ghost."

Desmond wrote his letters quickly, Mr Prior just then reappearing.

"Now I'll take you to your room," he said, gathering the letters in long, white hands. "You'll like a rest. Dinner at eight."

The bed-chamber, like the parlour, had a pleasant air of worn luxury and accustomed comfort.

"I hope you will be comfortable," the host said, with courteous solicitude. And Desmond was quite sure that he would.

Three covers were laid, the swarthy man who had driven Desmond from the station stood behind the host's chair, and a figure came towards Desmond and his host from the shadows beyond the yellow circles of the silver-sticked candles.

"My assistant, Mr Verney," said the host, and Desmond surrendered his hand to the limp, damp touch of the man who had seemed to say to him, from the window above the porch, "Go away!" Was Mr Prior perhaps a doctor who received "paying guests," persons who were, in Desmond's phrase, "a bit balmy"? But he had said "assistant."

"I thought," said Desmond, hastily, "you would be a clergyman. The Rectory, you know—I thought Wildon, my friend Wildon, was staying with an uncle who was a clergyman."

"Oh, no," said Mr Prior. "I rent the Rectory. The rector thinks it is damp. The church is disused, too. It is not considered safe, and they can't afford to restore it. Claret to Mr Desmond, Lopez." And the swarthy, blunt-faced man filled his glass.

"I find this place very convenient for my experiments. I dabble a little in chemistry, Mr Desmond, and Verney here assists me."

Verney murmured something that sounded like "only too proud," and subsided.

"We all have our hobbies, and chemistry is mine," Mr Prior went on. "Fortunately, I have a little income which enables me to indulge it. Wildon, my nephew, you know, laughs at me, and calls it the science of smells. But it's absorbing, very absorbing."

After dinner Verney faded away, and Desmond and his host stretched their feet to what Mr Prior called a "handful of fire," for the evening had grown chill.

"And now," Desmond said, "won't you tell me the ghost story?"

The other glanced round the room.

"There isn't really a ghost story at all. It's only that—well, it's never happened to me personally, but it happened to Verney, poor lad, and he's never been quite his own self since."

Desmond flattered himself on his insight.

"Is mine the haunted room?" he asked.

"It doesn't come to any particular room," said the other, slowly, "nor to any particular person."

"Anyone may happen to see it?"

"No one sees it. It isn't the kind of ghost that's seen or heard."

"I'm afraid I'm rather stupid, but I don't understand," said Desmond, roundly. "How can it be a ghost, if you neither hear it nor see it?"

"I did not say it was a ghost," Mr Prior corrected. "I only say that there is something about this house which is not ordinary. Several of my assistants have had to leave; the thing got on their nerves."

"What became of the assistants?" asked Desmond.

"Oh, they left, you know; they left," Prior answered, vaguely. "One couldn't expect them to sacrifice their health. I sometimes think—village gossip is a deadly thing, Mr Desmond—that perhaps they were prepared to be frightened; that they fancy things. I hope the Psychical Society's expert won't be a neurotic. But even without being a neurotic one might—but you don't believe in ghosts, Mr Desmond. Your Anglo-Saxon common sense forbids it."

"I'm afraid I'm not exactly Anglo-Saxon," said Desmond. "On my father's side I'm pure Celt; though I know I don't do credit to the race."

"And on your mother's side?" Mr Prior asked, with extraordinary eagerness; an eagerness so sudden and disproportioned to the question that Desmond stared. A faint touch of resentment as suddenly stirred in him, the first spark of antagonism to his host.

"Oh," he said, lightly, "I think I must have Chinese blood, I get on so well with the natives in Shanghai, and they tell me I owe my nose to a Red Indian great grandmother."

"No negro blood, I suppose?" the host asked, with almost discourteous insistence.

"Oh, I wouldn't say that," Desmond answered. He meant to say it laughing, but he didn't. "My hair, you know—it's a very stiff curl it's got, and my mother's people were in the West Indies a few generations ago. You're interested in distinctions of race, I take it?"

"Not at all, not at all," Mr Prior surprisingly assured him; "but, of course, any details of your family are necessarily interesting to me. I feel," he added, with another of his winning smiles, "that you and I are already friends."

Desmond could not have reasoningly defended the faint quality of dislike that had begun to tinge his first pleasant sense of being welcomed and wished for as a guest.

"You're very kind," he said; "it's jolly of you to take in a stranger like this."

Mr Prior smiled, handed the cigar-box, mixed whisky and soda, and began to talk about the history of the house.

"The foundations are almost certainly thirteenth century. It was a priory, you know. There's a curious tale, by the way, about the man Henry gave it to when he smashed up the monasteries. There was a curse; there seems always to have been a curse—"

The gentle, pleasant, high-bred voice went on. Desmond thought he was listening, but presently he roused himself and dragged his attention back to the words that were being spoken.

"—that made the fifth death. . . . There is one every hundred years, and always in the same mysterious way."

Then he found himself on his feet, incredibly sleepy, and heard himself say:—

"These old stories are tremendously interesting. Thank you very much. I hope you won't think me very uncivil, but I think I'd rather like to turn in; I feel a bit tired, somehow."

"But of course, my dear chap."

Mr Prior saw Desmond to his room.

"Got everything you want? Right. Lock the door if you should feel nervous. Of course, a lock can't keep ghosts out, but I always feel as if it could," and with another of those pleasant, friendly laughs he was gone.

William Desmond went to bed a strong young man, sleepy indeed beyond his experience of sleepiness, but well and comfortable. He awoke faint and trembling, lying deep in the billows of the feather bed; and lukewarm waves of exhaustion swept through him. Where was he? What had happened? His brain, dizzy and weak at first, refused him any answer. When he remembered, the abrupt spasm of repulsion which he had felt so suddenly and unreasonably the night before came back to him in a hot, breathless flush. He had been drugged, he had been poisoned!

"I must get out of this," he told himself, and blundered out of bed towards the silken bell-pull that he had noticed the night before hanging near the door.

As he pulled it, the bed and the wardrobe and the room rose up round him and fell on him, and he fainted.

When he next knew anything someone was putting brandy to his lips. He saw Prior, the kindest concern in his face. The assistant, pale and watery-eyed. The swarthy manservant, stolid, silent, and expressionless. He heard Verney say to Prior:—

"You see it was too much—I told you—"

"Hush," said Prior, "he's coming to."

Four days later Desmond, lying on a wicker chair on the lawn, was a little disinclined for exertion, but no longer ill. Nourishing foods and drinks, beef-tea, stimulants, and constant care—these had brought him back to something like his normal state. He wondered at the vague suspicions vaguely remembered, of that first night; they had all been proved absurd by the unwavering care and kindness of everyone in the Haunted House.

"But what caused it?" he asked his host, for the fiftieth time. "What made me make such a fool of myself?" And this time Mr Prior did not put him off, as he had always done before by begging him to wait till he was stronger.

"I am afraid, you know," he said, "that the ghost really did come to you. I am inclined to revise my opinion of the ghost."

"But why didn't it come again?"

"I have been with you every night, you know," his host reminded him. And, indeed, the sufferer had never been left alone since the ringing of his bell on that terrible first morning.

"And now," Mr Prior went on, "if you will not think me inhospitable, I think you will be better away from here. You ought to go to the seaside."

"There haven't been any letters for me, I suppose?" Desmond said, a little wistfully.

"Not one. I suppose you gave the right address? Ormehurst Rectory, Crittenden, Kent?"

"I don't think I put Crittenden," said Desmond. "I copied the address from your telegram." He pulled the pink paper from his pocket.

"Ah, that would account," said the other.

"You've been most awfully kind all through," said Desmond, abruptly.

"Nonsense, my boy," said the elder man, benevolently. "I only wish Willie had been able to come. He's never written, the rascal! Nothing but the telegram to say he could not come and was writing."

"I suppose he's having a jolly time somewhere," said Desmond, enviously; "but look here—do tell me about the ghost, if there's anything to tell. I'm almost quite well now, and I should like to know what it was that made a fool of me like that."

"Well"—Mr Prior looked round him at the gold and red of dahlias and sunflowers, gay in the September sunshine—"here, and now, I don't know that it could do any harm. You remember that story of the man who got this place from Henry VIII. and the curse? That man's wife is buried in a vault under the church. Well, there were legends, and I confess I was curious to see her tomb. There are iron gates to the vault. Locked, they were. I opened them with an old key—and I couldn't get them to shut again."

"Yes?" Desmond said.

"You think I might have sent for a locksmith; but the fact is there is a small crypt to the church, and I have used that crypt as a supplementary laboratory. If I had called anyone in to see to the lock they would have gossiped. I should have been turned out of my laboratory—perhaps out of my house."

"I see."

"Now, the curious thing is," Mr Prior went on, lowering his voice, "that it is only since that grating was opened that this house has been what they call 'haunted.' It is since then that all the things have happened."

"What things?"

"People staying here, suddenly ill—just as you were. And the attacks always seem to indicate loss of blood. And—" He hesitated a moment. "That wound in your throat. I told you you had hurt yourself falling when you rang the bell. But that was not true. What is true is that you had on your throat just the same little white wound that all the others have had. I wish"—he frowned—"that I could get that vault gate shut again. The key won't turn."

"I wonder if I could do anything?" Desmond asked, secretly convinced that he had hurt his throat in falling, and that his host's story was, as he put it, "all moonshine." Still, to put a lock right was but a slight return for all the care and kindness. "I'm an engineer, you know," he added, awkwardly, and rose. "Probably a little oil. Let's have at this same lock."

He followed Mr Prior through the house to the church. A bright, smooth old key turned readily; and they passed into the building, musty and damp, where ivy crawled through the broken windows, and the blue sky seemed to be laid close against the holes in the roof. Another key clicked in the lock of a low door beside what had once been the Lady Chapel, a thick oak door grated back, and Mr Prior stopped a moment to light a candle that waited in its rough iron candlestick on a ledge of the stonework. Then down narrow stairs, chipped a little at the edges and soft with dust. The crypt was Norman, very simply beautiful. At the end of it was a recess, masked with a grating of rusty ironwork.

"They used to think," said Mr Prior, "that iron kept off witchcraft. This is the lock," he went on, holding the candle against the gate, which was ajar.

They went through the gate, because the lock was on the other side. Desmond worked a minute or two with the oil and feather that he had brought. Then with a little wrench the key turned and re-turned.

"I think that's all right," he said, looking up, kneeling on one knee, with the key still in the lock and his hand on it.

"May I try it?"

Mr Prior took Desmond's place, turned the key, pulled it out, and stood up. Then the key and the candlestick fell rattling on the stone floor, and the old man sprang upon Desmond.

"Now I've got you," he growled, in the darkness, and Desmond says that his spring and his clutch and his voice were like the spring and the clutch and the growl of a strong savage beast.

Desmond's little strength snapped like a twig at his first bracing of it to resistance. The old man held him as a vice holds. He had got a rope from somewhere. He was tying Desmond's arms.

Desmond hates to know that there in the dark he screamed like a caught hare. Then he remembered that he was a man, and shouted "Help! Here! Help!"

But a hand was on his mouth, and now a handkerchief was being knotted at the back of his head. He was on the floor, leaning against something. Prior's hands had left him.

"Now," said Prior's voice, a little breathless, and the match he struck shewed Desmond the stone shelves with long things on them—coffins he supposed. "Now, I'm sorry I had to do it, but science before friendship, my dear Desmond," he went on, quite courteous and friendly. "I will explain to you, and you will see that a man of honour could not act otherwise. Of course, you having no friends who know where you are is most convenient. I saw that from the first. Now I'll explain. I didn't expect you to understand by instinct. But no matter. I am, I say it without vanity, the greatest discoverer since Newton. I know how to modify men's natures. I can make men what I choose. It's all done by transfusion of blood. Lopez—you know, my man Lopez—I've pumped the blood of dogs into his veins, and he's my slave—like a dog. Verney, he's my slave, too—part dog's blood and partly the blood of people who've come from time to time to investigate the ghost, and partly my own, because I wanted him to be clever enough to help me. And there's a bigger thing behind all this. You'll understand me when I say"—here he became very technical indeed, and used many words that meant nothing to Desmond, whose thoughts dwelt more and more on his small chance of escape.

To die like a rat in a hole, a rat in a hole! If he could only loosen the handkerchief and shout again!

"Attend, can't you?" said Prior, savagely, and kicked him. "I beg your pardon, my dear chap," he went on, suavely, "but this is important. So you see the elixir of life is really the blood. The blood is the life, you know, and my great discovery is that to make a man immortal, and restore his youth, one only needs blood from the veins of a man who unites in himself blood of the four great races—the four colours, black, white, red, and yellow. Your blood unites these four. I took as much as I dared from you that night. I was the vampire, you know." He laughed pleasantly. "But your blood didn't act. The drug I had to give you to induce sleep probably destroyed the vital germs. And, besides, there wasn't enough of it. Now there is going to be enough!"

Desmond had been working his head against the thing behind him, easing the knot of the handkerchief down till it slipped from head to neck. Now he got his mouth free, and said, quickly:—

"That was not true what I said about the Chinamen and that. I was joking. My mother's people were all Devon."

"I don't blame you in the least," said Prior, quietly. "I should lie myself in your place."

And he put back the handkerchief. The candle was now burning clearly from the place where it stood—on a stone coffin. Desmond could see that the long things on the shelves were coffins, not all of stone. He wondered what this madman would do with his body when everything was over. The little wound in his throat had broken out again. He could feel the slow trickle of warmth on his neck. He wondered whether he would faint. It felt like it.

"I wish I'd brought you here the first day—it was Verney's doing, my tinkering about with pints and half-pints. Sheer waste—sheer wanton waste!"

Prior stopped and stood looking at him.

Desmond, despairingly conscious of growing physical weakness, caught himself in a real wonder as to whether this might not be a dream—a horrible, insane dream—and he could not wholly dismiss the wonder, because incredible things seemed to be adding themselves to the real horrors of the situation, just as they do in dreams. There seemed to be something stirring in the place—something that wasn't Prior. No—nor Prior's shadow, either. That was black and sprawled big across the arched roof. This was white, and very small and thin. But it stirred, it grew—now it was no longer just a line of white, but a long, narrow, white wedge—and it shewed between the coffin on the shelf opposite him and that coffin's lid.

And still Prior stood very still looking down on his prey. All emotion but a dull wonder was now dead in Desmond's weakened senses. In dreams—if one called out, one awoke—but he could not call out. Perhaps if one moved— But before he could bring his enfeebled will to the decision of movement—something else moved. The black lid of the coffin opposite rose slowly—and then suddenly fell, clattering and echoing, and from the coffin rose a form, horribly white and shrouded, and fell on Prior and rolled with him on the floor of the vault in a silent, whirling struggle. The last thing Desmond heard before he fainted in good earnest was the scream Prior uttered as he turned at the crash and saw the white-shrouded body leaping towards him.

❀

"It's all right," he heard next. And Verney was bending over him with brandy. "You're quite safe. He's tied up and locked in the laboratory. No. That's all right, too." For Desmond's eyes had turned towards the lidless coffin. "That was only me. It was the only way I could think of, to save you. Can you walk now? Let me help you, so. I've opened the grating. Come."

Desmond blinked in the sunlight he had never thought to see again. Here he was, back in his wicker chair. He looked at the sundial on the house. The whole thing had taken less than fifty minutes.

"Tell me," said he. And Verney told him in short sentences with pauses between.

"I tried to warn you," he said, "you remember, in the window. I really believed in his experiments at first—and—he'd found out something about me—and not told. It was when I was very young. God knows I've paid for it. And when you came I'd only just found out what really had happened to the other chaps. That beast Lopez let it out when he was drunk. Inhuman brute! And I had a row with Prior that first night, and he promised me he wouldn't touch you. And then he did."

"You might have told me."

"You were in a nice state to be told anything, weren't you? He promised me he'd send you off as soon as you were well enough. And he had been good to me. But when I heard him begin about the grating and the key I knew—so I just got a sheet and—"

"But why didn't you come out before?"

"I didn't dare. He could have tackled me easily if he had known what he was tackling. He kept moving about. It had to be done suddenly. I counted on just that moment of weakness when he really thought a dead body had come to life to defend you. Now I'm going to harness the horse and drive you to the police-station at Crittenden. And they'll send and lock him up. Everyone knew he was as mad as a hatter, but somebody had to be nearly killed before anyone would lock him up. The law's like that, you know."

"But you—the police—won't they—"

"It's quite safe," said Verney, dully. "Nobody knows but the old man, and now nobody will believe anything he says. No, he never posted your letters, of course, and he never wrote to your friend, and he put off the

Psychical man. No, I can't find Lopez; he must know that something's up. He's bolted."

But he had not. They found him, stubbornly dumb, but moaning a little, crouched against the locked grating of the vault when they came, a prudent half-dozen of them, to take the old man away from the Haunted House. The master was dumb as the man. He would not speak. He has never spoken since.

The Pavilion

There was never a moment's doubt in her own mind. So she said afterwards. And everyone agreed that she had concealed her feelings with true womanly discretion. Her friend and confidante, Amelia Davenant, was at any rate completely deceived. Amelia was one of those featureless blondes who seem born to be overlooked. She adored her beautiful friend, and never, from first to last, could see any fault in her, except, perhaps, on the evening when the real things of the story happened. And even in this matter she owned at the time that it was only that her darling Ernestine did not understand.

Ernestine was a prettyish girl with the airs, so irresistible and misleading, of a beauty; most people said that she was beautiful, and she certainly managed, with extraordinary success, to produce the illusion of beauty. Quite a number of plainish girls achieve that effect nowadays. The freedom of modern dress and coiffure and the increasing confidence in herself which the modern girl experiences aid her in fostering the illusion; but in the 'sixties, when everyone wore much the same sort of bonnet, when your choice in coiffure was limited to bandeaux or ringlets, and the crinoline was your only wear, something very like genius was needed to deceive the world in the matter of your personal charms. Ernestine had that genius; hers was the smiling, ringletted, dark-haired, dark-eyed, sparkling type.

Amelia had the blond bandeau and the kind appealing blue eyes, rather too small and rather too dull; her hands and ears were beautiful, and she kept them out of sight as much as possible. In our times the blonde hair would have been puffed out to make a frame for the forehead, a little too high; a certain shade of blue and a certain shade of boldness would have made her eyes effective. And the beautiful hands would have learned that flowerlike droop of the wrist so justly and so universally admired. But as it was, Amelia was very nearly plain, and in her secret emotional self-

235

communings she told herself that she was ugly. It was she who, at the age of fourteen, composed the remarkable poem beginning:—

> I know that I am ugly: did I make
> The face that is the laugh and jest of all?

and went on, after disclaiming any personal responsibility for the face, to entreat the kind earth to "cover it away from mocking eyes," and to "let the daisies blossom where it lies."

Amelia did not want to die, and her face was not the laugh and jest, or indeed the special interest, of anyone. All that was poetic licence. Amelia had read perhaps a little too much poetry of the type of *"Quand je suis morte, mes amies, plantez un saule au cimetière"*: but really life was a very good thing to Amelia, especially when she had a new dress and someone paid her a compliment. But she went on writing verses extolling the advantages of The Tomb, and grovelling metrically at the feet of One who was Another's, until that summer when she was nineteen and went to stay with Ernestine at Doricourt. Then her muse took flight, scared, perhaps, by the possibility, suddenly and threateningly presented, of being asked to inspire verse about the real things of life.

At any rate, Amelia ceased to write poetry about the time when she and Ernestine and Ernestine's aunt went on a visit to Doricourt, where Frederick Powell lived with his aunt. It was not one of those hurried motor-fed excursions which we have now and call week ends, but a long, leisurely visit, when all the friends of the static aunt called on the dynamic aunt, who returned the calls with much ceremony, a big barouche, and a pair of fat horses. There were croquet parties and archery parties and little dances, all pleasant informal little gaieties arranged without ceremony among people who lived within driving distance of each other and knew each other's tastes and incomes and family history as well as they knew their own. The habit of importing huge droves of strangers from distant countries for brief harrying raids did not then obtain. There was instead a wide and constant circle of pleasant people with an unflagging stream of gaiety, mild indeed, but delightful to unjaded palates.

And at Doricourt life was delightful even on the days when there was no party. It was perhaps more delightful to Ernestine than to her friend, but even so, the one least pleased was Ernestine's aunt.

"I do think," she said to the other aunt whose name was Julia—"I dare say it is not so to you, being accustomed to Mr W. Frederick, of course from his childhood, but I always find gentlemen in the house so unsettling, especially young gentlemen, and when there are young ladies also. One is always on the *qui vive* for excitement."

"Of course," said Aunt Julia, with the air of a woman of the world; "living as you and dear Ernestine do, with only females in the house—"

"We hang up an old coat and hat of my brother's on the hat stand in the hall," Aunt Emmeline protested.

"—the presence of gentlemen in the house must be a little unsettling. For myself, I am inured to it. Frederick has so many friends. Mr Thesiger perhaps the greatest. I believe him to be a most worthy young man, but peculiar." She leaned forward across her bright-tinted Berlin woolwork and spoke impressively, the needle with its trailing red poised in air. "You know, I hope you will not think it indelicate of me to mention such a thing—but dear Frederick—your dear Ernestine would have been in every way so suitable."

"Would have been?" Aunt Emmeline's tortoise-shell shuttle ceased its swift movement among the white loops and knots of her tatting.

"Well, my dear," said the other aunt, a little shortly, "you surely must have noticed—"

"You don't mean to suggest that Amelia— I thought Mr Thesiger and Amelia—"

"Amelia! I really must say! No, I was alluding to Mr Thesiger's attentions to dear Ernestine. Most marked. In dear Frederick's place I should have found some excuse for shortening Mr Thesiger's visit. But of course I cannot interfere. Gentlemen must manage these things for themselves. I only hope that there will be none of that trifling with the most holy affections of others which—"

The less voluble aunt cut in hotly with "Ernestine's incapable of anything so unladylike."

"Just what I was saying," the other rejoined blandly, got up, and drew the blind a little lower, for the afternoon sun was glowing on the rosy wreaths of the drawing-room carpet.

Outside in the sunshine Frederick was doing his best to arrange his own affairs. He had managed to place himself beside Miss Ernestine Meutys on the stone steps of the pavilion, but then, Mr Thesiger lay along the lower step at her feet, a very good position for looking up into her eyes. Amelia was beside him, but then it never seemed to matter whom Amelia sat beside.

They were talking about the pavilion on whose steps they sat, and Amelia, who often asked uninteresting questions, had wondered how old it was. It was Frederick's pavilion after all, and he felt this when his friend took the words out of his mouth and used them on his own account, even though he did give the answer the form of an appeal.

"The foundations are Tudor, aren't they?" he said. "Wasn't it an observatory or laboratory or something of that sort in Fat Henry's time?"

"Yes," said Frederick; "there was some story about a wizard or an alchemist or something, and it was burned down, and then they rebuilt it in its present style."

"The Italian style, isn't it?" said Thesiger; "but you can hardly see what it is now, for the creeper."

"Virginia creeper, isn't it?" Amelia asked, and Frederick said, "Yes, Virginia creeper." Thesiger said it looked more like a South American plant, and Ernestine said Virginia was in South America, and that was why. "I know, because of the war," she said modestly, and nobody smiled or answered. There were manners in those days.

"There's a ghost story about it, surely?" Thesiger began again, looking up at the dark closed doors of the pavilion.

"Not that I ever heard of," said the pavilion's owner. "I think the country people invented the tale because there have always been so many rabbits and weasels and things found dead near it. And once a dog, my uncle's favourite spaniel. But, of course, that's simply because they get entangled in the Virginia creeper—you see how fine and big it is—and can't get out, and die as they do in traps. But the villagers prefer to think it's ghosts."

"I thought there was a real ghost story," Thesiger persisted.

Ernestine said, "A ghost story. How delicious! Do tell it, Mr Doricourt. This is just the place for a ghost story. Out of doors and the sun shining, so that we can't *really* be frightened."

Doricourt protested again that he knew no story.

"That's because you never read, dear boy," said Eugene Thesiger. "That library of yours—there's a delightful book—did you never notice it?—brown tree-calf with your arms on it; the head of the house writes the history of the house as far as he knows it. There's a lot in that book. It began in Tudor times—1515, to be exact."

"Queen Elizabeth's time." Ernestine thought that made it so much more interesting. "And was the ghost story in that?"

"It isn't exactly a ghost story," said Thesiger. "It's only that the pavilion seems to be an unlucky place to sleep in."

"Haunted?" Frederick asked, and added that he must look up that book.

"Not haunted exactly. Only several people who have slept the night there went on sleeping."

"Dead, he means," said Ernestine, and it was left for Amelia to ask:—

"Does the book tell anything particular about how the people died, what killed them, or anything?"

"There are suggestions," said Thesiger; "but there, it *is* a gloomy subject. I don't know why I started it. Should we have time for a game of croquet before tea, Doricourt?"

"I *wish you'd* read the book and tell me the stories," Ernestine said to Frederick, apart, over the croquet balls.

"I will," he answered fervently; "you've only to tell me what you want."

"Or perhaps Mr Thesiger will tell us another time—in the twilight. Since people like twilight for ghosts. Will you, Mr Thesiger?" She spoke over her blue muslin shoulder.

Frederick certainly meant to look up the book, but he delayed till after supper; the half-hour before bed when he and Thesiger put on their braided smoking-jackets and their braided smoking-caps with the long yellow tassels, and smoked the cigars which were, in those days still, more of a luxury than a necessity. Ordinarily, of course, these were smoked out of doors, or in the smoking-room, a stuffy little den littered with boots and guns and yellow-backed railway novels. But tonight Frederick left his friend in that dingy hutch and went alone to the library, found the book and took it to the circle of light made by the colza lamp.

"I can skim through it in half an hour," he said, and wound up the lamp and lighted his second cigar. Then he opened the shutters and windows, so that the room should not smell of smoke in the morning. Those were the days of consideration for the ladies who had not yet learned that a cigarette is not exclusively a male accessory like a beard or a bass voice.

But when, his preparations completed, he opened the book, he was compelled to say "Pshaw!" Nothing short of this could relieve his feelings. (You know the expressions I mean, though of course it isn't pronounced as it's spelt, any more than Featherstonehaugh or St Maur are.)

"Pshaw!" said Frederick, fluttering the pages. His remark was justified. The earlier part of the book was written in the beautiful script of the early sixteenth century, that looks so plain and is so impossible to read, and the later pages, though the handwriting was clear and Italian enough, left Frederick helpless, for the language was Latin, and Frederick's Latin was limited to the particular passages he had "been through" at his private school. He recognized a word here and there—*mors,* for instance, and *pallidus* and *pavor* and *arcanum,* just as you or I might; but to read the complicated stuff and make sense of it! Frederick said something just a shade stronger than "Pshaw!"—"Botheration!" I think it was; replaced the book on the shelf, closed the shutters, and turned out the lamp. He thought he would ask Thesiger to translate the thing, but then again he thought he wouldn't. So he went to bed wishing that he had happened to remember more of the Latin so painfully beaten into the best years of his boyhood.

And the story of the pavilion was, after all, told by Thesiger.

There was a little dance at Doricourt next evening, a carpet dance they called it. The furniture was pushed back against the walls, and the tightly-stretched Axminster carpet was not so bad to dance on as you might suppose. That, you see, was before the days of polished floors and large rugs with loose edges that you can catch your feet in. A carpet was a carpet in those days, well and truly laid, conscientiously exact to the last recess and fitting the floor like a skin. And on this quiet tolerable surface the young people danced very happily, some ten or twelve couples. The old people did not dance in those days, except sometimes a quadrille of state to "open the ball". They played cards in a room provided for the purpose, and in the dancing-room three or four kindly middle-aged ladies were considered to provide ample chaperonage. You were not even expected to report yourself to your chaperone at the conclusion of a dance. It was not like a real ball. And even in those far-off days there were conservatories.

It was on the steps of the conservatory, not the steps leading from the dancing-room, but the steps leading to the garden, that the story was told. The four young people were sitting together, the girls' crinolined flounces spreading round them like huge pale roses, the young men correct in their high-shouldered coats and white cravats. Ernestine had been very kind to both the men, a little too kind perhaps—who can tell? At any rate, there was in their eyes exactly that light which you may imagine in the eyes of rival stags in the mating season. It was Ernestine who asked Frederick for the story, and Thesiger who, at Amelia's suggestion, told it.

"It's quite a number of stories," he said, "and yet it's really all the same story. The first man to sleep in the pavilion slept there ten years after it was built. He was a friend of the alchemist or astrologer who built it. He was found dead in the morning. There seemed to have been a struggle. His arms bore the marks of cords. No; they never found any cords. He died from loss of blood. There were curious wounds. That was all the rude leeches of the day could report to the bereaved survivors of the deceased."

"How funny you are, Mr Thesiger!" said Ernestine, with that celebrated soft, low laugh of hers. When Ernestine was elderly, many people thought her stupid. When she was young, no-one seems to have been of this opinion.

"And the next?" asked Amelia.

"The next was sixty years later. It was a visitor that time, too. And he was found dead, just the same marks, and the doctors said the same thing. And so it went on. There have been eight deaths altogether—unexplained deaths. Nobody has slept in it now for over a hundred years. People seem to have a prejudice against the place as a sleeping apartment. I can't think why."

"Isn't he simply killing?" Ernestine asked Amelia, who said:—

"And doesn't anyone know how it happened?"

No one answered till Ernestine repeated the question in the form of "I suppose it was just accident?"

"It was a curiously recurrent accident," said Thesiger, and Frederick, who throughout the conversation had said the right things at the right moment, remarked that it did not do to believe all these old legends. Most old families had them, he believed. Frederick had inherited Doricourt from an unknown great uncle of whom in life he had not so much as heard, but he was very strong on the family tradition. "I don't attach any importance to these tales myself."

"Of course not. All the same," said Thesiger, deliberately, "you wouldn't care to pass a night in that pavilion."

"No more would you," was all Frederick found on his lips.

"I admit that I shouldn't enjoy it," said Eugene; "but I'll bet you a hundred you don't *do* it."

"Done," said Frederick.

"Oh, Mr Doricourt!" breathed Ernestine, a little shocked at betting "before ladies."

"Don't!" said Amelia, to whom, of course, no one paid any attention; "don't do it!"

You know how, in the midst of flower and leafage, a snake sometimes will suddenly, surprisingly rear a head that threatens? So, amid friendly talk and laughter, a sudden fierce antagonism sometimes looks out and vanishes again, surprising most of all the antagonists. This antagonism spoke in the tones of both men, and after Amelia had said "Don't!" there was a curiously breathless little silence. Ernestine broke it. "Oh," she said, "I do wonder which of you will win! I should like them both to win, wouldn't you, Amelia? Only I suppose that's not always possible, is it?"

Both gentlemen assured her that in the case of bets it was very rarely possible.

"Then I wish you wouldn't," said Ernestine. "You could *both* pass the night there, couldn't you, and be company for each other? I don't think betting for such large sums is quite the thing, do you, Amelia?"

Amelia said no, she didn't, but Eugene had already begun to say:—

"Let the bet be off, then, if Miss Meutys doesn't like it. That suggestion was invaluable. But the thing itself needn't be off. Look here, Doricourt.

I'll stay in the pavilion from one to three and you from three to five. Then honour will be satisfied. How will that do?"

The snake had disappeared.

"Agreed," said Frederick, "and we can compare impressions afterwards. That will be quite interesting."

Then someone came and asked where they had all got to, and they went in and danced some more dances. Ernestine danced twice with Frederick and drank iced sherry and water, and they said good night and lighted their bedroom candles at the table in the hall.

"I do hope they won't," Amelia said, as the girls sat brushing their hair at the two large white muslin-frilled dressing-tables in the room they shared.

"Won't what?" said Ernestine, vigorous with the brush.

"Sleep in that hateful pavilion. I wish you'd ask them not to, Ernestine. They'd mind, if *you* asked them."

"Of course I will if you like, dear," said Ernestine, cordially. She was always the soul of good-nature. "But I don't think you ought to believe in ghost stories, not really."

"Why not?"

"Oh, because of the Bible and going to church and all that," said Ernestine. "Do you really think Rowland's Macassar has made any difference to my hair?"

"It is just as beautiful as it always was," said Amelia, twisting up her own little ashen-blonde handful.

"What was that?" said Amelia.

That was a sound coming from the little dressing-room. There was no light in that room. Amelia went into the little room, though Ernestine said, "Oh, don't! How can you? It might he a ghost or a rat or something," and as she went she whispered, "Hush!"

The window of the little room was open and she leaned out of it. The stone sill was cold to her elbows through her print dressing jacket.

Ernestine went on brushing her hair. Amelia heard a movement below the window and listened. "To-night will do," someone said.

"It's too late," said someone else.

"If you're afraid it will always be too late or too early," said someone. And it was Thesiger.

"You know I'm not afraid," the other one, who was Doricourt, answered hotly.

"An hour for each of us will satisfy honour," said Thesiger, carelessly. "The girls will expect it. I couldn't sleep. Let's do it now and get it over. Let's see. Oh, damn it!"

A faint click had sounded.

"Dropped my watch. I forgot the chain was loose. It's all right, though; glass not broken even. Well, are you game?"

"Oh, yes, if you insist. Shall I go first, or you?"

"I will," said Thesiger. "That's only fair, because I suggested it. I'll stay till half-past one or a quarter to two, and then you come on. See?"

"Oh, all right. I think it's silly, though," said Frederick.

Then the voices ceased. Amelia went back to the other girl.

"They're going to do it to-night."

"Are they, dear?" Ernestine was as placid as ever. "Do what?"

"Sleep in that horrible pavilion."

"How do you know?"

Amelia explained how she knew.

"Whatever can we do?" she added.

"Well, dear, suppose we go to bed?" suggested Ernestine, helpfully. "We shall hear all about it in the morning."

"But suppose anything happens?"

"What could happen?"

"Oh, *anything!*" said Amelia. "Oh, I do wish they wouldn't! I shall go down and ask them not to."

"*Amelia!*" The other girl was at last aroused. "You *couldn't!* I shouldn't *let* you dream of doing anything so unladylike. What would the gentlemen think of you?"

The question silenced Amelia, but she began to put on her so lately discarded bodice.

"I won't go if you think I oughtn't," she said.

"Forward and fast, auntie would call it," said the other. "I am almost sure she would."

"But I'll keep dressed. I sha'n't disturb you. I'll sit in the dressing-room. I *can't* go to sleep while he's running into this awful danger."

"Which he?" Ernestine's voice was very sharp. "And there isn't any danger."

"Yes, there is," said Amelia, sullenly, "and I mean *them*. Both of them."

Ernestine said her prayers and got into bed. She had put her hair in curl-papers, which became her like a wreath of white roses.

"I don't think auntie will be pleased," she said, "when she hears that you sat up all night watching young gentlemen. Good night, dear!"

"Good night, darling," said Amelia. "I know you don't understand. It's all right."

She sat in the dark by the dressing-room window. There was no moon, but the starlight lay on the dew of the park, and the trees massed themselves in bunches of darker grey, deepning to black at the roots of them. There was no sound to break the stillness, except the little cracklings of twigs and rustlings of leaves as birds or little night-wandering beasts moved in the shadows of the garden, and the sudden creakings that furniture makes if you sit alone with it and listen in the night's silence.

Amelia sat on and listened, listened. The pavilion shewed in broken streaks of pale grey against the wood, that seemed to be clinging to it in dark patches. But that, she reminded herself, was only the creeper. She sat there for a very long time, not knowing how long a time it was. For anxiety is a poor chronometer, and the first ten minutes had seemed an hour. She had no watch. Ernestine had—and slept with it under her pillow. The stable clock was out of order; the man had been sent for to see to it. There was nothing to measure time's flight by, and she sat there rigid, straining her ears for a foot-fall on the grass, straining her eyes to see a figure come out of the dark pavilion and cross the dew-grey grass towards the house. And she heard nothing, saw nothing.

Slowly, imperceptibly, the grey of the sleeping trees took on faint dreams of colour. The sky turned faint above the trees, the moon perhaps was coming out. The pavilion grew more clearly visible. It seemed to Amelia that something moved along the leaves that surrounded it, and she looked to see him come out. But he did not come.

"I wish the moon would really shine," she told herself. And suddenly she knew that the sky was clear and that this growing light was not the moon's cold silver, but the growing light of dawn.

She went quickly into the other room, put her hand under the pillow of Ernestine, and drew out the little watch with the diamond "E" on it.

"A quarter to three," she said, aloud. Ernestine moved and grunted.

There was no hesitation about Amelia now. Without another thought for the ladylike and the really suitable, she lighted her candle and went quickly down the stairs, paused a moment in the hall, and so out through the front door. She passed along the terrace. The feet of Frederick protruded from the open French window of the smoking-room. She set down her candle on the terrace— it burned clearly enough in that clear air—went up to Frederick as he slept, his head between his shoulders and his hands loosely hanging, and shook him.

"Wake up!" she said. "Wake up! Something's happened! It's a quarter to three and he's not come back."

"Who's not what?" Frederick asked, sleepily.

"Mr Thesiger. The pavilion."

"Thesiger?—the— *You,* Miss Davenant? I beg your pardon. I must have dropped off."

He got up unsteadily, gazing dully at this white apparition still in evening dress with pale hair now no longer wreathed.

"What is it?" he said. "Is anybody ill?"

Briefly and very urgently Amelia told him what it was, implored him to go at once and see what had happened. If he had been fully awake, her voice and her eyes would have told him many things.

"He said he'd come back," he said. "Hadn't I better wait? You go back to bed, Miss Davenant. If he doesn't come in half an hour—"

"If you don't go this minute," said Amelia, tensely, "I shall."

"Oh, well, if you insist," Frederick said. "He has simply fallen asleep as I did. Dear Miss Davenant, return to your room, I beg. In the morning, when we are all laughing at this false alarm, you will be glad to remember that Mr Thesiger does not know of your anxiety."

"I hate you," said Amelia, gently; "and I am going to see what has happened. Come or not, as you like."

She caught up the silver candlestick, and he followed its wavering gleam down the terrace steps and across the grey dewy grass.

Half-way she paused, lifted the hand that had been hidden among her muslin flounces, and held it out to him with a big Indian dagger in it.

"I got it out of the hall," she said. "If there's any *real* danger—anything living, I mean. I thought—but I know I couldn't use it. Will you take it?"

He took it, laughing kindly.

"How romantic you are!" he said, admiringly, and looked at her standing there in the mingled gold and grey of dawn and candle-light. It was as though he had never seen her before.

They reached the steps of the pavilion and stumbled up them. The door was closed, but not locked. And Amelia noticed that the trails of creeper had not been disturbed; they grew across the doorway as thick as a man's finger, some of them.

"He must have got in by one of the windows," Frederick said. "Your dagger comes in handy, Miss Davenant."

He slashed at the wet, sticky green stuff and put his shoulder to the door. It yielded at a touch and they went in.

The one candle lighted the pavilion hardly at all, and the dusky light that oozed in through the door and windows helped very little. And the silence was thick and heavy.

"Thesiger!" said Frederick, clearing his throat. "Thesiger! Hullo! Where are you?"

Thesiger did not say where he was. And then they saw.

There were low stone seats to the windows, and between the windows low stone benches ran. On one of these something dark, something dark and in places white, confused the outline of the carved stone.

"Thesiger!" said Frederick again, in the tone a man uses to a room that he is almost sure is empty. "Thesiger!"

But Amelia was bending over the bench. She was holding the candle crookedly, so that it flared and guttered.

"Is he there?" Frederick asked, following her; "is that him? Is he asleep?"

"Take the candle," said Amelia, and he took it obediently. Amelia was touching what lay on the bench. Suddenly she screamed. Just one scream, not very loud. But Frederick remembers just how it sounded. Sometimes he hears it in dreams and wakes moaning, though he is an old man now, and his old wife says, "What is it, dear?" and he says, "Nothing, my Ernestine, nothing."

Directly she had screamed she said, "He's dead," and fell on her knees by the bench. Frederick saw that she held something in her arms.

"Perhaps he isn't," she said. "Fetch someone from the house—brandy—send for a doctor. Oh, go, go, go!"

"I can't leave you here," said Frederick with thoughtful propriety; "suppose he revives?"

"He will not revive," said Amelia, dully; "go, go, go! Do as I tell you. Go! If you don't go," she added, suddenly and amazingly, "I believe I shall kill you. It's all your doing."

The astounding sharp injustice of this stung Frederick into action.

"I believe he's only fainted or something," he said. "When I've roused the house and everyone has witnessed your emotion you will regret—"

She sprang to her feet and caught the knife from him and raised it, awkwardly, clumsily, but with keen threatening, not to be mistaken or disregarded. Frederick went.

When Frederick came back with the groom and the gardener—he hadn't thought it well to disturb the ladies—the pavilion was filled full of white revealing daylight. On the bench lay a dead man, and kneeling by him a living woman on whose warm breast his cold and heavy head lay pillowed. The dead man's hands were full of the green crushed leaves, and thick twining tendrils were about his wrists and throat. A wave of green seemed to have swept from the open window to the bench where he lay.

The groom and the gardener and the dead man's friend looked and looked.

"Looks like as if he'd got himself entangled in the creeper and lost 'is 'ead," said the groom, scratching his own.

"How'd the creeper get in, though? That's what I says." It was the gardener who said it.

"Through the window," said Doricourt, moistening his lips with his tongue.

"The window was shut, though, when I come by at five last night," said the gardener, stubbornly. "'Ow did it get all that way since five?"

They looked at each other voicing, silently, impossible things.

The woman never spoke. She sat there in the white ring of her crinolined dress like a broken white rose. But her arms were round Thesiger, and she would not move them.

When the doctor came he sent for Ernestine, who came flushed and sleepy-eyed and very frightened and shocked.

"You're upset, dear," she said to her friend, "and no wonder. How brave of you to come out with Mr Doricourt to see what happened! But you can't do anything now, dear. Come in and I'll tell them to get you some tea."

Amelia laughed, looked down at the face on her shoulder, laid the head back on the bench among the drooping green of the creeper, stooped over it, kissed it, and said to it quite quietly and gently, "Good-bye, dear; good-bye!" took Ernestine's arm, and went away with her.

The doctor made an examination and gave a death-certificate. "Heart-failure" was his original and brilliant diagnosis. The certificate said nothing, and Frederick said nothing of the creeper that was wound about the dead man's neck, nor of the little white wounds, like little bloodless lips half-open, that they found about the dead man's neck.

"An imaginative or uneducated person," said the doctor, "might suppose that the creeper had something to do with his death. But we mustn't encourage superstition. I will assist my man to prepare the body for its last sleep. Then we need not have any chattering women."

"Can you read Latin?" Frederick asked. The doctor could. And, later, did.

It was the Latin of that brown book with the Doricourt arms on it that Frederick wanted read. And when he and the doctor had been together with the book between them for three hours, they closed it and looked at each other with shy and doubtful eyes.

"It can't be true," said Frederick.

"If it is," said the more cautious doctor, "you don't want it talked about. I should destroy that book if I were you. And I should root up that creeper and burn it. It is quite evident, from what you tell me, that your friend believed that this creeper was a man-eater; that it fed, just before its flowering time, as the book tells us, at dawn; and that he fully meant that the thing, when it crawled into the pavilion seeking its prey, should find *you* and not him. It would have been so, I understand, if his watch had not stopped at one o'clock."

"He dropped it, you know," said Doricourt, like a man in a dream.

"All the cases in this book are the same," said the doctor; "the strangling, the white wounds. I have heard of such plants; I never believed." He shuddered. "Had your friend any spite against you? Any reason for wanting to get you out of the way?"

Frederick thought of Ernestine, of Thesiger's eyes on Ernestine, of her smile at him over her blue muslin shoulder.

"No," he said, "none. None whatever. It must have been accident. I am sure he did not know. He could not read Latin." He lied, being, after all, a gentleman; and Ernestine's name being sacred.

"The creeper seems to have been brought here and planted in Henry the Eighth's time. And then the thing began. It seems to have been at its flowering season that it needed the—that, in short, it was dangerous. The little animals and birds found dead near the pavilion. But to move itself all that way, across the floor! The thing must have been almost conscient," he said, with a sincere shudder. "One would think," he corrected himself at once, "that it knew what it was doing, if such a thing were not plainly contrary to the laws of Nature."

"Yes," said Frederick, "one would. I think if I can't do anything more I'll go and rest. Somehow all this has given me a turn. Poor Thesiger!"

His last thought before he went to sleep was one of pity.

"Poor Thesiger," he said; "how violent and wicked! And what an escape for me! I must never tell Ernestine. And all the time there was Amelia. Ernestine would never have done *that* for *me!*" And on a little pang of regret for the impossible he fell asleep.

Amelia went on living. She was not the sort that dies even of such a thing as happened to her on that night, when for the first and last time she held her love in her arms and knew him for the murderer he was. It was only the other day that she died, a very old woman. Ernestine, who, beloved and surrounded by children and grandchildren, survived her, spoke her epitaph. "Poor Amelia," she said; "nobody ever looked the same side of the road where she was. There was an indiscretion when she was young. Oh, nothing disgraceful, of course. She was a lady. But people talked. It was the sort of thing that stamps a girl, you know."

Appendix:
From *My School-Days*

Part IV: In the Dark

How can I write of it, sitting here in the shifting shade of the lime-trees, with the sunny daisied grass stretching away to the border where the hollyhocks and lilies and columbines are, my ears filled with the soft swish-swish of the gardener's scythe at the other end of the lawn, and the merry little voices of the children away in the meadow?

Only by shutting my eyes and ears to the sweet sounds and sights of summer and the sun can I recall at all for you the dead silences, the frozen terrors of the long, dark nights when I was little, and lonely, and very very much afraid.

The first thing I remember that frightened me was running into my father's dressing-room and finding him playing at wild beasts with my brothers. He wore his great fur travelling coat inside out, and his roars were completely convincing. I was borne away screaming, and dreamed of wild beasts for many a long night afterwards.

Then came some nursery charades. I was the high-born orphan, whom gipsies were to steal, and my part was to lie in a cradle, and, at the proper moment to be carried away shrieking. I understood my part perfectly—I was about three, I suppose—and had rehearsed it more than once. Being carried off in the arms of the gipsy (my favourite sister) was nothing to scream at, I thought, but she told me to scream, and I did it. Unfortunately, however, there had been no dress rehearsals, and when, on the night of the performance the high-born orphan found itself close to a big black bonnet and a hideous mask, it did scream to some purpose, and presently screaming itself into some sort of fit or swoon, was put to bed, and stayed there for many days which passed dreamlike. But that old woman haunted my dreams for years—haunts them still indeed. I tell you I come across her in my dreams to this day. She bends over me and puts her face close to mine, and I wake with a spasm of agonised terror; only now it is not horrible to me to waken "in the dark." I draw a few long breaths and as soon as my heart beats a little less wildly I fall asleep again. But a child who wakes from an ugly dream does not fall asleep so quickly. For to a child who is frightened, the darkness and the silence of its lonely room are only a shade less terrible than the wild horrors of dreamland. One used to lie awake in the silence, listening, listening to the pad-pad of one's heart, straining one's

253

ears to make sure that it was not the pad-pad of something else, something unspeakable creeping towards one out of the horrible dense dark. One used to lie quite, quite still, I remember, listening, listening. And when my nurse came to bed and tucked me up, she used to find my pillow wet, and say to the under-nurse—

"Weakness, you know. The precious poppet doesn't seem to get any stronger."

But my pillow was not wet with tears of weakness. These were the dews of agony and terror.

My nurse—ah, how good she was to me—never went downstairs to supper after she found out my terrors which she very quickly did. She used to sit in the day nursery with the door open "a tiny crack," and that light was company, because I knew I had only to call out, and someone who loved me would come and banish fear. But a light without human companionship was worse than darkness, especially a little light. Night-lights, deepening the shadows with their horrid possibilities are a mere refinement of cruelty, and some friends who thought to do me a kindness by leaving the gas burning low gave me one of the most awful nights I ever had.

It was a strange house in Sutherland Gardens—a house with large rooms and heavy hangings—with massive wardrobes and deep ottoman boxes. The immense four-post beds stood out about a yard from the wall, for some "convenience of sweeping" reason, I believe. Consider the horror of having behind you, as you lay trembling in the chill linen of a strange bed, a dark space, no comforting solid wall that you could put your hand up to and touch, but a dark space, from which, even now, in the black silence something might be stealthily creeping—something which would presently lean over you, in the dark—whose touch you would feel, not knowing whether it were the old woman in the mask or some new terror.

That was the torture of the first night. The next I begged that the gas might be left "full on." It was, and I fell asleep in comparative security. But while I slept, came some thrifty soul, and finding the gas "burning to waste" turned it down. Not out—down.

I awoke in a faint light, and presently sat up in bed to see where it came from, and this is what I saw. A corpse laid out under white draperies, and at its foot a skeleton with luminous skull and outstretched bony arm.

I knew, somewhere far away and deep down, my reason knew that the dead body was a white dress laid on a long ottoman, that the skull was the opal globe of the gas and the arm the pipe of the gas-bracket, but that was not reason's hour. Imagination held sway, and her poor little victim, who was ten years old then, and ought to have known better, sat up in bed, hour after hour, with the shadowy void behind her. The dark curtains on each side, and in front that horror.

Next day I went home, which was perhaps a good thing for my brain.

When my father was alive we lived in a big house in Kennington Lane, where he taught young men agriculture and chemistry. My father had a big meadow and garden, and had a sort of small farm there. Fancy a farm in Kennington!

Among the increase that blessed his shed was a two-headed calf. The head and shoulders of this were stuffed, and inspired me with a terror which my brothers increased by pursuing me with the terrible object. But one of my father's pupils to whom I owe that and many other kindnesses, one day seized me under one arm and the two-headed horror under the other, and thus equipped we pursued my brothers. They fled shrieking, and I never feared it again.

In a dark stone-flagged room where the boots were blacked, and the more unwieldy chemicals housed, there was nailed on the wall the black skin of an emu. That skin, with its wiry black feathers that fluttered dismally in the draught, was no mere bird's skin to me. It hated me, it wished me ill. It was always lurking for me in the dark, ready to rush at me. It was waiting for me at the top of the flight, while the old woman with the mask stretched skinny hands out to grasp my little legs as I went up the nursery stairs. I never passed the skin without covering my eyes with my hands. From this terror that walked by night I was delivered by Mr Kearns, now public analyst for Sheffield. He took me on his shoulder, where I felt quite safe, reluctant but not resisting, to within a couple of yards of the emu.

"Now," he said, "will you do what I tell you?"

"Not any nearer," I said evasively.

"Now you know I won't let it hurt you."

"Yes."

"Then will you stroke it, if I do first?"

I didn't want to.

"To please me."

That argument was conclusive, for I loved him.

Then we approached the black feathers, I clinging desperately to his neck, and sobbing convulsively.

"No-no-no-not any nearer!"

But he was kind and wise, and insisted. His big hand smoothed down the feathers.

"Now, Daisy. You know you promised. Give me your hand."

I shut my eyes tight, and let him draw my hand down the dusty feathers. Then I opened my eyes a little bit.

"Now you stroke it. Stroke the poor emu."

I did so.

"Are you afraid now?"

Curiously enough I wasn't. Poor Mr Kearns paid dearly for his kindness. For several weeks I gave him no peace, but insisted on being taken, at all hours of the day and night to "stroke the poor emu." So proud is one of a new courage.

After we left Kennington, I seem to have had a period of more ordinary terrors—of dreams from which to awaken was mere relief; not a horror scarcely less than that of the dream itself. I dreamed of cows and dogs, of falling houses, and crumbling precipices. It was not till that night at Rouen that the old horror of the dark came back, deepened by superstitious dread.

But all this time I have not told you about the mummies at Bordeaux. And now there is no room for them here. They must go into the next chapter.

Part V: The Mummies at Bordeaux

It was because I was tired of churches and picture-galleries, of fairs and markets, of the strange babble of foreign tongues and the thin English of the guide-book, that I begged so hard to be taken to see the mummies. To me the name of a mummy was as a friend's name. As one Englishman travelling across a desert seeks to find another of whom he has heard in that far land, so I sought to meet these mummies who had cousins at home, in the British Museum, in dear, dear England.

My fancy did not paint mummies for me apart from plate-glass cases, camphor, boarded galleries, and kindly curators, and I longed to see them as I longed to hear my own tongue spoken about me.

I was consumed by a fever of impatience for the three days which had to go by before the coming of the day on which the treasures might be visited. My sisters who were to lead me to these delights, believed too that the mummies would be chiefly interesting on account of their association with Bloomsbury.

Well, we went—I in my best blue silk frock, which I insisted on wearing to honour the occasion, holding the hand of my sister and positively skipping with delicious anticipation. There was some delay about keys, during which my excitement was scarcely to be restrained. Then we went through an arched doorway and along a flagged passage, the old man who guided us explaining volubly in French as we went.

"What does he say?"

"He says they are natural mummies."

"What does that mean?"

"They are not embalmed by man, like the Egyptian ones, but simply by the peculiar earth of the churchyard where they were buried."

The words did not touch my conception of the glass cases and their good-natured guardian.

The passage began to slope downward. A chill air breathed on our faces, bringing with it a damp earthy smell. Then we came to some narrow stone steps. Our guide spoke again.

"What does he say?"

"We are to be careful, the steps are slippery and mouldy."

I think even then my expectation still was of a long clean gallery, filled with the white light of a London noon, shed through high skylights on Egyptian treasures. But the stairs were dark, and I held my sister's hand tightly. Down we went, down, down!

"What does he say?"

"We are under the church now; these are the vaults."

We went along another passage, the damp mouldy smell increasing, and my clasp of my sister's hand grew closer and closer.

We stopped in front of a heavy door barred with iron, and our guide turned a big reluctant key in a lock that grated.

"*Les voilà,*" he said, throwing open the door and drawing back dramatically.

We were in the room before my sisters had time to see cause for regretting that they had brought me.

The vision of dry boards and white light and glass cases vanished, and in its stead I saw this:

A small vault, as my memory serves me, about fifteen feet square, with an arched roof, from the centre of which hung a lamp that burned with a faint blue light, and made the guide's candle look red and lurid. The floor was flagged like the passages, and was as damp and chill. Round three sides of the room ran a railing, and behind it—standing against the wall, with a ghastly look of life in death—were about two hundred skeletons. Not white clean skeletons, hung on wires, like the one you see at the doctor's, but skeletons with the flesh hardened on their bones, with their long dry hair hanging on each side of their brown faces, where the skin in drying had drawn itself back from their gleaming teeth and empty eye-sockets. Skeletons draped in mouldering shreds of shrouds and grave-clothes, their lean fingers still clothed with dry skin, seemed to reach out towards me. There they stood, men, women, and children, knee-deep in loose bones collected from the other vaults of the church, and heaped round them. On the wall near the door I saw the dried body of a little child hung up by its hair.

I don't think I screamed or cried, or even said a word. I think I was paralysed with horror, but I remember presently going back up those stairs, holding tightly to that kindly hand, and not daring to turn my head lest one of those charnel-house faces should peep out at me from some niche in the damp wall.

It must have been late afternoon, and in the hurry of dressing for the *table d'hote* my stupor of fright must have passed unnoticed, for the next thing I remember is being alone in a large room, waiting as usual for my supper to be sent up. For my mother did not approve of late dinners for little people, and I was accustomed to have bread-and-milk alone while she and my sisters dined.

It was a large room, and very imperfectly lighted by the two wax candles in silver candlesticks. There were two windows and a curtained alcove, where the beds were. Suddenly my blood ran cold. What was behind that curtain? Beds. "Yes," whispered something that was I, and yet not I; "but suppose there are no beds there now. Only mummies, mummies, mummies!"

A sudden noise; I screamed with terror. It was only the door opening to let the waiter in. He was a young waiter, hardly more than a boy, and had always smiled kindly at me when we met, though hitherto our intercourse had not gone farther. Now I rushed to him and flung my arms round him, to his immense amazement and the near ruin of my bread and milk. He spoke no English and I no French, but somehow he managed to understand that I was afraid, and afraid of that curtained alcove.

He set down the bread and milk, and be took me in his arms and together we fetched more candles, and then he drew back the awful curtain, and shewed me the beds lying white and quiet. If 1 could have spoken French I should have said:

"Yes; but how do I know it was all like that just now, before you drew the curtain back?"

As it was I said nothing, only clung to his neck.

I hope he did not get into any trouble that night for neglected duties, for he did not attempt to leave me till my mother came back. He sat down with me on his knee and petted me and sang to me under his breath, and fed me with the bread and milk, when by-and-by I grew calm enough to take it. All good things be with him wherever he is! I like best to think of him in a little hotel of his own, a quiet little country inn standing back from a straight road bordered with apple trees and poplars. There are wooden benches outside the door, and within a whitewashed kitchen, where a plump rosy-faced woman is busy with many cares—never busy enough, however, to pass the master of the house without a loving word or a loving look. I like to believe that now he has little children of his own, who hold out their arms when he opens the door, and who climb upon his knees clamouring for those same songs which he sang, out of the kindness of his boyish heart, to the little frightened English child, such a long, long time ago.

The mummies of Bordeaux were the crowning horror of my childish life; it is to them, I think, more than to any other thing, that I owe nights and nights of anguish and horror, long years of bitterest fear and dread. All the other fears could have been effaced but the shock of that sight branded it on my brain, and I never forgot it. For many years I could not bring myself to go about any house in the dark, and long after I was a grown woman I was tortured, in the dark watches, by imagination and memory, who rose strong and united, overpowering my will and my reason as utterly as in my baby days.

It was not till I had two little children of my own that I was able to conquer this mortal terror of darkness, and teach imagination her place, under the foot of reason and the will.

My children, I resolved, should never know such fear. And to guard them from it I must banish it from my own soul. It was not easy, but it was done. It is banished now, and my babies, thank God, never have known it. It was a dark cloud that overshadowed my childhood, and I don't believe my mother ever knew how dark it was, for I could not tell anyone the full horror of it while it was over me; and when it had passed I came from under it, as one who has lived long years in an enchanter's castle, where the sun is darkened always, might come forth into the splendour of noontide. Such an one breathes God's sweet air and beholds the free heavens with joyous leaps of heart; but he does not speak soon nor lightly of what befell in the dark, in the evil days, in the Castle of the Enchanter.

Bibliography

I. Short Story Collections

Grim Tales. London: Innes, 1893. [Contents: "The Ebony Frame"; "John Charrington's Wedding"; "Uncle Abraham's Romance"; "The Mystery of the Semi-Detached"; "From the Dead"; "Man-Size in Marble"; "The Mass for the Dead."]

Fear. London: Stanley Paul, 1910. [Contents: "The Five Senses"; "The Head"; "In the Dark"; "The Ebony Frame"; "Hurst of Hurstcote"; "Uncle Abraham's Romance"; "From the Dead"; "Man-Size in Marble"; "John Charrington's Wedding"; "The New Samson"; "The Violet Car"; "The Shadow"; "The Followers"; "The Three Drugs."]

II. Publications of Individual Stories

"John Charrington's Wedding." *Temple Bar* (September 1891). In *Grim Tales* (q.v.). In *Fear* (q.v.).

"The Ebony Frame." *Longman's* (October 1891). In *Grim Tales* (q.v.). In *Fear* (q.v.).

"The Mass for the Dead." *Argosy* (April 1892). In *Grim Tales* (q.v.).

"From the Dead." *Illustrated London News* (3 September 1880). In *Grim Tales* (q.v.). In *Fear* (q.v.).

"Uncle Abraham's Romance." In *Grim Tales* (q.v.). In *Fear* (q.v.).

"The Mystery of the Semi-Detached." In *Grim Tales* (q.v.).

"Man-Size in Marble." In *Grim Tales* (q.v.). In *Fear* (q.v.).

"Hurst of Hurstcote." *Temple Bar* (June 1893). In *Something Wrong* (London: Innes, 1893). In *Fear* (q.v.).

"The Power of Darkness." *Strand Magazine* (April 1905). In *Man and Maid* (London: T. Fisher Unwin, 1906).

"The Shadow." *Black and White* (23 December 1905) (as "The Portent of the Shadow"). In *Fear* (q.v.).

"The Head." *Strand Magazine* (May 1907). In *Fear* (q.v.).

"The Three Drugs." *Strand Magazine* (February 1908) (as "The Third Drug"). In *Fear* (q.v.).

"In the Dark." In *Fear* (q.v.).

"The New Samson." *Strand Magazine* (December 1909). In *Fear* (q.v.).

"Number 17." *Strand Magazine* (June 1910).

"The Five Senses." In *Fear* (q.v.).

"The Violet Car." In *Fear* (q.v.).

"The Haunted House." *Strand Magazine* (December 1913).

"The Pavilion." *Strand Magazine* (November 1915). In *To the Adventurous* (London: Hutchinson, 1923).

About S. T. Joshi

S. T. JOSHI is the author of *The Weird Tale* (1990), *H. P. Lovecraft: The Decline of the West* (1990), and *Unutterable Horror: A History of Supernatural Fiction* (2012). He has prepared corrected editions of H. P. Lovecraft's work for Arkham House and annotated editions of Lovecraft's stories for Penguin Classics. He has also prepared editions of Lovecraft's collected essays and poetry. His exhaustive biography, *H. P. Lovecraft: A Life* (1996), was expanded as *I Am Providence: The Life and Times of H. P. Lovecraft* (2010). He is the editor of the anthologies *American Supernatural Tales* (Penguin, 2007), Black Wings I-II-III (PS Publishing, 2010, 2012, 2013), *A Mountain Walked: Great Tales of the Cthulhu Mythos* (Centipede Press, 2014), *The Madness of Cthulhu* (Titan Books, 2014-15), and *Searchers After Horror: New Tales of the Weird and Fantastic* (Fedogan & Bremer, 2014). He is the editor of the *Lovecraft Annual* (Hippocampus Press), the *Weird Fiction Review* (Centipede Press), and the *American Rationalist* (Center for Inquiry). His Lovecraftian novel *The Assaults of Chaos* appeared in 2013.

www.ingramcontent.com/pod-product-compliance
Lightning Source LLC
Chambersburg PA
CBHW070500030726
47503CB00004B/1115